EARTHFL

A POTABLE STUDY OF LOVE AND COLLUSION

EARTH
FLOWN

FRANCES WREN

ILLUSTRATED BY
LITARNES

First published in the United States in 2024 by Studio Shoga, an imprint of Litarnes, Florida.

▲▼C
Edited by Jacqueline Lee + M.E. Hughes
Coverart + Interior Illustrations by Mia Lapine, t/a *Litarnes*
Designed by Frances Wren

Published by Studio Shoga

ISBN 979-8-9897562-0-9 • ebook
ISBN 979-8-9897562-1-6 • illustrated paperback *(this edition)*
Library of Congress Control Number: 2024905632

First edition, April 2024
STUDIOSHOGA.COM

Where there's love, there will be vice;
Where there's greed, there is a price.
Sow them desperate and afraid,
You'll find there's profit to be made.

Thank you for considering *Earthflown* as your next read!

Please continue with discretion, as the story handles sensitive subjects such as mental illness, externalised and internalised bigotry / prejudice of many flavours. It deals candidly with eugenics, abuse, violence, and other such issues. While exploring the aforementioned, *Earthflown* is not intended as a parable: the events reflect the author's pessimism, rather than endorsement.

There's likely too much romance for the conventional scifi / crime reader, and too much cartel shenanigans for the conventional romance reader. *Earthflown* is a true (read: unmarketable) genre soup, and the lingering questions are intentional.

Although there is no graphic sexual content, there are some descriptions of medical procedures, violence, and gaslighting. Detailed content warnings are available at **earthflown.com**.

This novel is written in UK English.

for Mies
(and Shoga)

— and the chronically exhausted:
it only takes one to operate a guillotine.

TERMINOLOGY

aptee   colloquial reference to an individual with aptitude.

aptitude   umbrella term for certain genetic abilities to manipulate energy. Subcategories include firestarters, watercallers, ghosts, and telekinetics. Despite fundamental differences, the term also now encompasses empaths and healers.

CM15   shorthand for a series of proprietary compounds by Arden Pharmaceuticals which ensures water potability.

dampener   a mid-range, usually non-directional device designed to minimise the effects of certain aptitudes. Often mandated on transport and other high-risk facilities.

edited   colloquial references to human germline gene editing.

fusive   new energy storage method, with mobile and industrial applications – including in the water sector as an CM-15 alternative (chemical-based water treatment).

glass   therapeutic and recreational drug that requires large quantities of CM15 to manufacture.

Level   vertical-zoning designation, usually associated with an established district, eg. Level 4, Lower Barbican. The smaller the number, the closer to sea-level. Due to the gradual nature of flood-zoning and stratification, a Level designation does not necessarily represent the same distance from sea-level in each district.

localisation the act of restricting the effect of one's aptitude to a certain radius, or the application of that aptitude in a very targeted manner.

suppressor short-range device (cf. dampener) designed to be worn by an aptee to decrease their aptitude's effects.

VMs   shorthand for vital-sign monitoring devices worn by healers in clinical care.

Xu's Scale international standard for quantifying the destructive potential of firestarters and telekinetics.

ORGANISATIONS

Arden Foundation
private foundation whose philanthropic reach encompasses medical research and the performing arts. Established and continues to fund the 'Medical and Aptitude Research Institute, England' (MARIE).

Arden Pharmaceuticals
British multinational, headquartered in London. Co-founded by Beatrice Arden (Javier Arden's paternal grandmother).

Ascenda Corporation
British construction and property development firm, responsible for much of London's stratified infrastructure and public works. Majority-controlled by the Mansfields.

Langley Logistics
logistics firm providing cold-chain and specialist transport / handling services.

Sainte-Ophie Biotech
French multinational with roots in bio-med and genetic engineering. Co-founded by Marion Sainte-Ophie (mother of Marie Sainte-Ophie).

St Ophie's Hospital
public teaching hospital (and tier-1 trauma centre) in lower central London. Its relocation to Level 9 was partly funded by Sainte-Ophie Biotech.

Sentinel, The
news media organisation, headquartered in London.

Sixty-Fourthers
decentralised water-rights' movement advocating for fusive-powered water infrastructure.

Special Investigations Agency
government agency targeting organised crime – including glass trafficking. Houses the national aptee-forensics unit.

Zhang Futuristics
R&D tech firm based in Kaohsiung, Taiwan. Pioneer in fusive-cell applications, including for water treatment.

ZERO

Corinna had been looking forward to this murder for weeks – she wasn't there for the last one. Even without her brother, adrenaline surely tasted better in person. She adjusted the surveillance feed in her visor.

Beside her sat a ghost.

"Our thief is early, for once," said Peter, languid with a plan well-oiled. "If he *is* one of Robert Langley's runners, we're doing Robert a favour by weeding this idiot out."

The Langleys and the Ardens enjoyed a symbiosis that came naturally to parasites sharing a common host – the public purse. Robert Langley ran a logistics outfit, including cold-chain and specialised transport for Arden Pharmaceuticals. Handling volatile compounds like CM15 was a delicate business. A dangerous one too, when the compound in question (a) monopolised clean drinking water, and (b) underpinned the addictive glass trade. The two went hand-in-hand, which may explain Robert's other hobby: running Europe's largest glass cartel.

Corinna's lip curled. "If he's Bobby's thief, then you're more incompetent than I thought."

"And if you weren't Beatrice Arden's granddaughter, that nickname alone could get you a world of trouble."

Peter checked his handgun with deft passes of an invisible hand. A film of heat brushed Corinna's arm as Peter uncurled his fingers, bringing them into view one by one. It took meticulous fine control to localise like this.

"Robert's turning 150 next April," her ghost continued. "You'd think someone would have managed to poison him by now."

"And? You want me to send flowers?"

"I want you to be careful. Men like Robert don't grow this old without pruning risk. You're not untouchable."

Corinna laughed. "Everyone lives past a hundred these days. Bobby's earned a fortune thanks to me."

"Your grandmother might disagree."

"Which one?"

"Beatrice. Without her, Robert wouldn't have been so inclined to spare my life—"

"*I* saved your life," snapped Corinna.

Her maternal and paternal grandparents did not get along. By all accounts, Marion Sainte-Ophie had been apoplectic when her only daughter, Marie, ran off with Thomas Arden – the son of a business competitor who was neither French nor Catholic.

"I still think we should have tipped off the police and not involved Robert at all," Peter said. "I've been watching these kids for months. We know all their routes, their stash houses."

"You're really fucking chatty today," said Corinna. "We need to make an example out of these parasites. Can't rely on law enforcement to generate the right kind of media coverage."

On the surveillance, a figure in Arden Pharma uniform swiped through two sets of security doors.

The building housed a CM15 distribution centre, fresh vials having arrived for the week from the manufacturing plants.

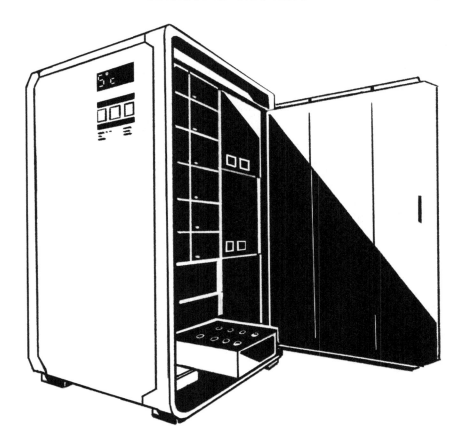

Like most stratified cities, London's irregular climb forcibly decentralised water treatment facilities, flood-zone by reluctant flood-zone. The gradual failure of conventional water filtration spurred an arms race between pollutants, chemical purification, and side effects. 'CM15' wasn't even the latest iteration of Arden Pharma's ubiquitous water purifying compound – the name had simply stuck.

This messy transition resulted in critical infrastructure that bore the scars of private funding: entrenched reliance on Arden Pharma.

Their thief paused for the biometrics, which was Peter and Corinna's cue to leave the cab.

Here on Level 9, the rain dripped, molasses slow, thick with the cumulative weight of shadows cast by the Levels above. This close to midnight, the very air sagged with relentless damp.

With a wave of her hand, the nearest streetlight stuttered – just enough for them to cross the narrow street. They stepped between two buildings wedged like crooked nicotine teeth, buried beneath the hooded lip of a motorway.

Corinna strode through the warehouse, careless. It wasn't a break-in when you owned the place. Peter slipped out of focus, like heat above chrome rails. There were ghosts in every city, but technology had long since rendered this aptitude cinematic only. Useful in a fight if no one wore heat-mapping eyewear.

On camera, their thief examined one of the transport cases.

Corinna flicked her visor up to crown her hair, slicked back and white-blonde against the lead of her pantsuit.

She nodded, once.

Peter kicked open the door, bursting into the room as a shift of air. An answering clatter: their thief cursed. Peter ducked left and Corinna went straight. Ozone frayed between palm and glove.

A lady did not rush.

"Hello, Tim."

The man froze. Behind him, sealing off the other exit, was a refracted silhouette. *Peter.*

Timothy Hersch didn't seem to notice, eyes fixed on Corinna, dry with surprise and contempt. "Miss Arden," he said, straightening. "Gave me a fright there. Sorry."

Corinna tilted her head. Was there any fear? It was hard to tell, without her twin here to act as the world's most accurate emotional barometer. But Javier would have insisted on leaving things to the police. Corinna rarely involved him in any fun these days.

"So you do know who I am," she said.

"Yes, ma'am," said Tim, knuckles white on his tablet.

Corinna took another step forwards, relishing the way Tim flinched back when she lifted a hand. She stroked the edge of a padded case. "Then let's get to the point. You've been very naughty."

Tim's gaze darted over Corinna's shoulder, to the exit. "I'm running the standard spot checks ahead of dispatch."

"A dispatch for Level 4? Did you think no one would notice a few missing — *ah-ah!*"

Tim had turned to make a run for it – only for an invisible force to swing him around by the shoulders. He shrieked as Peter materialised, a shit-eating grin reappearing first as the ghost let his invisibility drop like water.

Localising was taxing, but Peter always knew how to entertain her. Corinna shot him a promising look beneath her lashes.

"Jesus Christ!" Tim shouted, wild with a hindbrain fear of things that go *bump* in the dark. "You've got ghosts on payroll now?"

"Boo," said Peter, flat tone at odds with the amusement in his eyes. He wrenched Tim's arms high between the man's shoulder blades.

"I wasn't finished," said Corinna.

"There's been a misunderstanding," Tim blurted.

Corinna yawned. "I'm not here for a confession. We already know everything. You were hired because of your activism, not despite it."

"I don't know what y—"

Tim's voice cut off in a gurgle, courtesy of Peter's elbow.

"Manners," said Peter. "The lady's talking."

A digital read-out set into the shelves glowed 23:45 in chemical green. In her periphery, every cobot was frozen as planned. Plenty of time.

"We've known about you skimming the stock for a while." Corinna reached into her jacket and pulled out a slim, flat case. She set it on the nearest surface, unhurried. "You should have stuck to holding placards like the rest of your Sixty-Fourther friends."

Tim's jaw worked, no doubt swallowing a few choice words.

Corinna flicked the case open, lifting a loaded syringe free from its protective foam.

"People are expecting me," said Tim. "Someone's gonna notice if I don't turn up."

"We're counting on it," said Peter.

In the face of their composure, Tim rapidly lost his own, panic lending vigour to his struggling. "Call the police then. Go on!"

"Oh, they'll find you eventually." Corinna tapped the syringe.

Tim's eyes tracked the movement with undisguised horror.

Corinna stepped closer so she could see the needle reflected in the wet of his eyes. Tim's breath was tepid with sugar, coming fast and shallow. She held her free hand close to his face and ignited a kernel of fire, rolling it like a coin above her gloved knuckles.

Tim's pupils stuttered as she grew the flame, floating it close enough to singe his eyelashes. "Shit, shit, no, please!"

Corinna exhaled. It just wasn't the same, without her other half. Tim sounded scared, but it *felt* flat. She snapped her fingers, fire vanishing into her closed fist. *Three minutes.* "Okay, I'm bored."

Peter clamped a gloved hand around Tim's left wrist and offered the arm to Corinna.

"No, wait! *Wait*, I don't want—!"

Corinna slid the needle home, depressing the syringe, eyes never leaving Tim's face. It was a rictus of dread.

"Say thank you," Peter hummed. "You know how much high-quality glass commands, these days? There are worse ways to go."

"Fuck you...t-that's too much—" The drug was kicking in fast, slurring Tim's words.

Corinna slapped the syringe back into its case, slotting it in Peter's jacket pocket. She palmed his lapel. "Let's go."

Tim clawed at Peter's arm. "...What're y-you gonna do to me?"

"Us? Nothing." Peter hauled Tim towards the exit. "You, on the other hand, had an accident main-lining glass."

Tim slumped, gaze skittering. "I've never done glass, I don't want—"

"Exactly, a newbie mistake," said Peter. "Glass is tricky to dose, but you wanted the great dreams. Happens to the best of us."

The squeal of Tim's sneakers on the tiled floor was starting to crawl on her nerves. Corinna flipped her visor back down, checking the surveillance. *All clear.* She opened the door for Peter. "Are you going to read him a bedtime story as well?"

"If it'll shut him up," Peter grunted.

She tapped her earpiece. It rang twice.

"Evening." A pinch of an accent and a punch of tobacco.

Corinna curled her lip. Here in the rain and rot, she didn't have to hide her disdain. "This is a courtesy call. Our friend's going home soon. No one touches what's in the car."

"The lads know," said Robert Langley. "I trust your dog can keep everything else clean."

Corinna looked at Peter's back. "Thanks for the ride. I'll bring snacks when I come by next."

"Good girl," said Robert, words like whisky poured over ice with a shaky hand. "It's been a while since we've caught up in person. You're all that my boy talks about these days, and I'm not getting any younger. Should I expect some good news?"

Corinna swallowed her disgust. *Marry Charlie? He wouldn't survive me.* "Is it traditional for the lady to ask?" she demurred.

"Tradition," laughed Robert, sandpaper rough. "Well. Send my regards to Beatrice."

"I will," Corinna lied, and hung up before she was forced to thank him twice.

Across the street, the cab sat where they had left it. Through the mist of rain, she watched Peter shoving Tim into the front seat.

A flicker of movement in her periphery.

Corinna frowned up at the blank office building behind their cab, cataloguing its facade. A few floors were in her line of sight, the rest blocked by an overpass and the Level above.

The skin between her shoulders itched with paranoia.

The rain wasn't helping. She pushed her senses outwards, shaking off the heavy thrum of electromagnetic rails above them. Stepping out of the alley, she tore off a glove to better feel the lattice of energy through her palm.

Then something hit her hard between the ribs.

The pain slammed into Corinna's chest at the same time as the ground. She bit back a scream, head cracking against concrete as the impact took her clean off her feet.

She'd been shot.

Someone fucking *shot her.*

"Rina!" Peter shouted.

Corinna threw out her hand in the direction of the sniper, adrenaline blowing her senses wide open. In that moment, she could feel the heat of two living bodies, the echo of a generator tank through cracked insulation...Everything dripped with vivid colour, vision sharpening before blanking into *pain, pain, pain*—

Most people believed firestarters were immune to fire – to firearms, heat, anything that sparked. Centuries of popular myth and cinema had painted a flattering picture: firestarters walking through burning houses, forests ablaze, starting wars with upraised palms.

But in truth, firestarters had flesh that burned like any other. They simply controlled the flames before turning to ash. It was mostly instinctive, reflexive.

People did not think about the sheer fallibility of human reflex. Or the fact that the bullet was discrete from the combustion. Firestarters weren't bullet-proof, especially against something she didn't feel coming.

The second bullet though: that she did anticipate.

Corinna felt the tell-tale flare of combustion and *yanked*. An answering burst of amber in the pupil of one window: a heart-stuttering *crack* followed by a resounding *bang*. A rifle, imploding mid-shot.

Satisfied, Corinna let her hand drop. She tried to breathe through the pain wiping her vision white. Rain soaked into her scalp, her visor cracked, water filming her lashes. She coughed. *Funny*, she thought. *Can't taste any blood.*

She couldn't taste anything.

"Fuck." A hand ripping at her shirt, slapping her cheek. "Rina! Stay awake!"

An alarm began wailing.

"Sniper." Corinna spat blood. "M-my gloves—"

"I'm calling the hospital. St Ophie's is minutes away." Peter's hand was a lead weight against the goddamn hole in her chest.

Breathing felt like sinking into razor wire. "N-not one of ours. Mum's gonna kill me. Mémé Marion — they'll ask ques—" She heaved, or tried to. "Get Jav."

"You're not going to make it," snapped Peter. "Yes, I need an ambulance. 29-year-old female aptee, gunshot wound, left chest. Firestarter. We're outside Bright's on Heygate, Level 9."

Peter yanked off her visor, her remaining glove. Each motion was happening to someone else. She could finally taste blood, filmy with the grit of rain. The ground was freezing against her cheek.

"Did I get them? Peter—"

"I'm a ghost, not a fucking healer! Do you know what your brother will do to me if I let you bleed out? He'll liquify my brains—"

With the last of her adrenaline, Corinna grabbed Peter's wrist. He hissed with pain, nose flaring at the smell of burned skin and leather.

"You owe me," she coughed.

Peter stared at her, uncharacteristically frozen. Then he slapped a first-aid film over her chest wound, clasping her hands over the top as if readying her for an open casket. "Keep pressure on this."

Corinna jerked, heels scraping against the concrete. "*Jav.*" God, it hurt. She should have brought her twin. Jav could turn off the pain, and then she'd be able to talk properly.

"Ambulance is coming. Stay awake." Peter straightened, face obscured by rain and chalky resignation. "I'll call Javier."

Corinna started to count.

She didn't remember stopping.

ONE

St Ophie's Hospital, Lower Lambeth, Level 9.
Sunday, 3 October —— midnight.

Ethan's bare hands had been marinating in blood for almost three hours. There were two ways to spot a healer in surgery: lack of gloves and the vitals' monitor glowing on their temple. Green for go, yellow for yawn, red you're dead. Judging by the erratic trip of his heart, Ethan guessed he was at five yawns.

Right on cue, a nurse said, "Dr Faulkner, your VM's at amber seven."

"M'fine," said Ethan, barely moving his lips. Every distraction came with a hot-cold rush akin to fainting; a flashing hyperawareness of *a torn nail on the patient's left fourth finger, a cluster of bruises at the base of—*

"Graft's in place," said Ivy Caröe. The paediatric surgeon did not look up from her scoped display.

"Ready for tissue advancement," said Ethan, voice strained with the effort of localising. Ten hours into his shift and his surgical glasses were pinching a migraine. "Incision's pulling on me."

"Blood pressure?"

"MAP at sixty-eight."

"Scarpa's trying to close," said Ethan. "Can't hold on for much longer."

"Shouldn't have to. We've gone fast, given the complications. On my count, let's seal. Three..." Caröe was one of the few telekinetics who employed their aptitude while operating. Robotic hands were advanced enough to handle most delicate cases but sometimes nothing beat a skilled telekinetic. Watching her operate without motion mimicry was always impressive, hands stone still as a minuscule blade floated above the open heart. "...two, one."

Ethan *pulled*.

People often asked what healing was like but Ethan never had a satisfactory response. How could one articulate the sensation of a wound knitting together? The itch and the pain were merely symptoms of the process. It was like describing respiration: instinctive, necessary, controllable to a point.

Under the magnification, tissue visibly moved, threading over the edge of the graft in timelapse and fusing to the mesh.

"Steady," said Caröe. "Keep it to the scaffolding, you're at the anterior edge."

If healing was instinctual, then his medical training was all about fine-tuning and controlling that instinct. The crux of secondary or transference healing lay in the 'where' rather than the 'how': a still-unfathomable ability to remind cells of what they were meant to be, forgotten in the womb.

"VM's at amber eight," a nurse said. "Dr Faulkner?"

Without training, a patient might awaken with no scars, mis-fused bones, and a dead healer on the floor. Because, contrary to popular imagination, the human body didn't have an 'undo' button. Localised regeneration was harder than it looked, especially when it came to delicate thoracic aortic surgery.

"Dr Faulkner?"

Like breathing, you could pause for a while – but at some point, you lost control and the body took over. Someone pushed Ethan firmly away from the operating table. The detachment mid-healing was a jolt to the base of his neck, and Ethan stumbled as the world rushed into focus.

"Let's sit you down," the nurse said.

"No, I can still—"

"Patient's stable," said Caröe. "We'll finish up here."

Their surgical resident leaned in at Caröe's direction, sparing Ethan a cool glance over one shoulder. Thanks to the way healers were fast-tracked through the hospital hierarchy, Ethan wasn't close to any of his fellow graduates. He had no real friends, besides Vegas, for the same reason that he was immune to hospital politics: special treatment and exhaustion.

His eyes refocused haltingly in the absence of surgical lenses. It took another minute for Ethan's heartbeat to match the wheeze of the bypass machine.

Ethan's pager went off as he dumped his gown. *Emergency department.* He shoved an earpiece in and uncapped his drink bottle. "Allo," he said, and promptly inhaled water, dissolving into a coughing fit.

"Please tell me you're not dying too."

"Sadly alive." Ethan sneezed. "I was about to clock off though."

"We need you in trauma bay twelve. How's your VM?"

Ethan smacked the bottle against closed eyes for a cold, blissful second. "Amber." Exhaustion clung to his throat with every swallow. There was a reason that healers had lower capped hours. He sidestepped an oncoming gurney. "I should be fine to stabilise whatever this is though. Bay twelve, you said? What kind of aptee do we have?"

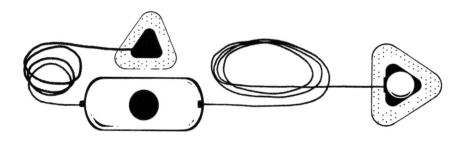

"Firestarter. 29-year-old female. Old-fashioned gunshot wound, left chest, so maybe walk a little faster."

"Arrived when?"

"Minutes ago. I know you've just come from an op, but Louise isn't on-call right now, and Dr Kelsey—"

"No, you're right to page me." Ethan shouldered the swinging doors into a wall of noise. "See you...right now, hi." At the nurses' station, Abbey leapt to meet him halfway. "Gunshot wound? Singular?"

"Yep!"

They both flattened themselves against the wall as two paramedics sprinted by. St Ophie's was the largest level-one trauma centre in Lower London, with a breakneck pace to match.

"Healer incoming!" Abbey announced into her earpiece. To Ethan, she said, "I think Lasya almost fainted when she realised it was just her and Dr Kelsey tonight."

Ethan snorted. Vegas give-me-coffee Kelsey hated night shifts. "Is Lasya our new emergency reg? Don't think I've met her."

"I wish. She's FY-1. Graduated, like, yesterday."

Unlike most operating rooms, the aptee units lacked windows. A screen streamed a high-angle view of the interior. Vegas stood out by her red hair, while their patient was barely visible as the EMTs pulled the ambulance bed out of the way.

Ethan donned a new mask and stepped into a low-ceilinged claustrophobia of voices and choreographed chaos.

"—systolic's at fifty, Dr Kelsey," someone called.

"Oh-two sat's barely in the eighties," said Vegas. "Is that second IV going?"

"On it. What do you want?"

"Second unit of PRBCs. Are we keeping track?"

"Yep, type and screen?"

"Thanks," said Vegas. "Let Lasya do that IV. Hang a litre of NS, rapid infusion. Where the hell is...*Ethan*, there you are. We've got a gunshot wound, left chest, BP in the 50s. Been pushing fluids." She paused, stethoscope bell on the patient's chest. She switched to the other side. "Sounds bilateral. Lasya, have you ever intubated?"

The trainee – identifiable by huge nervous eyes – said, "No, doctor."

"Forget the IV, you're on the ET tube." Vegas took the 'teaching' part of 'teaching hospital' seriously.

Lasya handed the sixteen-gage to the lead nurse, yanking open a nearby drawer. She visibly hesitated at the array of ET tubes.

"Try a seven," Ethan prompted, when Vegas let the pause sink, gaseous to the ground. His flatmate shot him a stink eye as Lasya hurried to thread her stylet, casting Ethan a grateful look.

A paramedic rattled off the rest of the stats. "BP was seventy over palpable. Scene was too loud to hear breath sounds, but we put an ARS in for any tension pneumo—"

"Dr Kelsey, dressing's not holding."

The patient lurched, coughing wetly, blood splashing into the clear tube. Lasya flinched and almost yanked the tube right out of their patient's throat. A nurse pushed her aside to suction the patient's mouth.

"Someone hook up that oxygen please," said Vegas. "Lasya, do you need to leave the room?"

The trainee steeled herself. "No, doctor."

"Good. Put pressure on that dressing."

Ethan jammed the ultrasound probe under the patient's xiphoid, eyes trained on the screen. He turned one wrist carefully for a proper subxiphoid view, skin cold from the excess gel.

"We're dumping fluids, but her BP isn't coming up." Vegas peered at the ultrasound. "She might be..."

Several things happened at once: a warning beep shrieked through the room, drowning out Ethan's yelp. Something seized in his own chest. Vegas grabbed the probe with one hand and shoved Ethan back protectively with the other. He dry-retched.

"Here we go," a nurse muttered.

On the screen, an ominous swathe of ink outlined the heart. Ethan and Vegas shared a brief look.

"There's hemopericardium," said Vegas, all previous lassitude gone. "Let's open those IV's up!"

"They're at two-twenty." The nurse squeezed both sides of the IV bag, forcing the liquid down.

Ethan grabbed the ultrasound screen, heart still ratcheting from the shock from patient skin contact. *Snap out of it, you have a job to do.*

"Pulses are gone," said Lasya, voice high.

"Let's start compressions and a milligram of epi," said Vegas. "We need a thoracotomy. Kit please, someone! Ethan?"

"Other views are clear. If she's a firestarter, I don't want to move her without suppressors."

"Should I activate them now?" asked a nurse. "They'll throw off the scanners, but I don't want to be burned to a crisp either…"

"Don't turn them on until I say so." Vegas squeezed past Lasya to pour iodine across their patient's chest. The empty bottle met the ground. "I'll lead re-suss and get the chest tube. Ethan, slow the haemorrhage. Thoracotomy." She began a chest-tube incision along the patient's fifth rib.

"Got it." Ethan picked up a scalpel. A hand whipped out: it was one of the nurses, unceremoniously wedging a visor over his mask. "Oh, thanks," he said sheepishly. Bracing himself, he palmed the patient's chest. Haemorrhage pressed against every nerve ending in Ethan's hands, muscles twitching in sympathy.

Ethan made the first cut and blood spurted scarlet across his visor. Gritting his teeth, he continued to cut until — "Rib spreaders," he gasped, "where're they?"

Every wound frayed the edge of Ethan's concentration like fingernails peeling sinew. He closed his eyes. *Arteries. From the rib fragments and bullet shrapnel, intercostal and mammary…*His own blood sloshed, slick-wet inside their veins.

His VM's haptic sensor delivered a warning jolt to his temple – designed to snap him out of a haze. *Red.* Ethan ignored it.

"Chest-tube's in." Vegas sounded far away. "Another mill of Epi!"

Ethan's left hand was pressing hard enough into their patient's skin that he was leaving bruises as fast as he healed them. The pad of his right index finger slipped on bone. Dizziness refracted his vision.

"Hilum," Ethan bit out, "I need a clamp." When no one moved, he risked a glance up. The team stared back. "Somebody clamp this, please. If I keep going, I'll have nothing left for the heart." A clamp dutifully appeared. "We're at pericardium."

Knuckles buried between ribs, Ethan could feel the split in the pericardial sac around the heart, like water bursting through a balloon. He waited another second, then shook his head. "Cardiac activity's shit. Just fibrillating. I'm taking over compressions."

Vegas fed the remaining chest tube. "Has someone called trauma surgery?"

"Yes, it's Mr Lim."

"This is gonna hurt, so I'll cross over," said Ethan. "Can't slip then."

"Wait!" Vegas grabbed Ethan by the chin, heedless of her bloody hand. "Your VM's red."

Ethan shook her off, climbing onto the gurney to straddle their patient. The woman's hair pooled white on the blue plastic, no colour in her cheeks. She looked like the cadaver she would soon become if they didn't hurry.

"Go brief Lim." Ethan locked his knees, closing his hand around the patient's heart. It filled his palm and weighed only as a life could. He held his breath: a physical trick to stave off transference healing's inexorable pull.

"Fine." Vegas left without another word.

Ethan squeezed his hand around the heart, gently. Seventy beats per minute. Steady does it. *One. Two. Three. Four.* He tried to sync his heartbeat to the one in his hand. It shrivelled, seizing in adrenaline. *Steady does it.*

Localised healing was hard enough without shrapnel embedded in the organs. The ribs, the skin...a large bump at the back of her head, deep scrapes across her left cheekbone and jaw. No abrasion on her hands; she didn't break her fall.

He kept squeezing, gasping in tandem behind his visor and mask. *Twenty, twenty-one, twenty-two.* Ethan's heart lurched like air bubbles trapped under water. Through a fog, he heard the thud of double doors, voices, felt the gurney shudder as the nurses rushed them into the hallway.

"Systolic at fifty!"

Good. Distracted, the thoracotomy incision immediately suctioned close around his wrist, mirrored by a viscous pull of the gunshot wound knitting shut. *Shit! Too soon.* Ethan choked, wrenching his lucidity taut.

*Fifty, fifty-one...*The lights shifted. The bang of doors. A nurse bearing a scalpel.

Ethan made an unintelligible noise as someone cut his wrist free from the patient's newly healed flesh. "Sixty-four," he recited, "sixty-five..."

"Careful," said a nurse, helping Ethan off the gurney.

Two other nurses transferred the patient to the surgical table, where she disappeared behind sheets and blue gloves. Ethan's hand dripped red; fingers stiff from repetition.

He caught Lim wincing at Ethan's bare hands.

"Dr Faulkner," a nurse held out a gown. "Size eight?"

"Yeah, gimme a minute." Ethan yanked off his face-shield. He wiped the sweat from his hairline, stumbling out of the room to scrub in. Glasses, visor, skull cap. A new mask, scalding water, sandpaper sponge beneath his nails, scrubbing to his elbows.

Someone helped Ethan into his gown.

Lim, the lead trauma surgeon with greying hair and ageless hands, turned to Ethan as they stepped up to the operating table. "You're red. For how long?"

"Barely a minute. Elevated heart rate throws off my VM. It should go down to amber soon." At Lim's raised eyebrows, Ethan added, "If I don't take care of her lung, she's going to suffer that for the rest of her life."

Lim snorted. "Just don't faint in my OR."

IT HAD BEEN A WHILE since Ethan assisted Lim. Five years in the system as a healer and Ethan held a consultant title while his fellow graduates were still junior registrars. Being a genetic anomaly didn't bestow him with more experience, but healers always had the luxury of extra theatre hours, first pick of specialities, their choice of rotations. It wasn't exactly a recipe for making friends. But all those theatre hours, coupled with being one of only three healers in a nine-hundred-bed hospital, built good stamina. Judging by the cold sweat and wooziness, Ethan knew he was rapidly approaching the end of his.

"How's the apical lobe progressing, Dr Faulkner?"

"Almost regenerated. I won't be able to handle the ribs though."

A soft click of metal against plastic.

"No need. Be on stand-by until we resettle the heart," said Lim. "Emily, imaging check please."

The registrar expanded the holographic scan across the operating site. It pooled around Ethan's wrists like water rippling around stone. The proximity of the scanner was a burst of static on his nerve-endings. He could barely ignore the screaming pull of fragmented ribs and the midline sternotomy. The phantom ache forced Ethan into shallow, rapid breaths, wishing fervently for an empath to turn off the pain.

As Lim began reinflating the lung, Ethan felt tentatively for any remaining thoracic haemorrhage. *Nope.* Healed by virtue of prolonged contact and his thread-bare control.

"Let's take off the cross-clamp," said Lim. "That okay, Dr Faulkner?"

"Your VM's at amber nine," warned the nurse.

"It'll be fine, let's get it over with," said Ethan.

The rush of blood, when it came, dragged a high noise from the back of Ethan's throat. His aptitude flared in response to the trigger, overwhelmed in the face of the open incision sites, still-sluggish head wound, broken skin. It might have been fine if Ethan hadn't come from a three-hour op and back-to-back thoracotomy.

He gagged, elbows locked stiff.

Lim's gaze shot up in alarm. "Someone move him — not *you*, Em!"

The room darkened like a photo negative. Gravity listed to one side and suddenly Ethan was staring at blurry masked faces, haloed by surgical lights. He didn't remember falling.

The floor was freezing. The abrupt temperature change made his eyes roll back in their sockets. Someone palmed his cheek, shining a pin-light in Ethan's eyes.

"Pulse?" Lim was saying, still poised at the surgical table. "Is he breathing?"

"...'m okay," slurred Ethan.

"Get him out of my OR. Em, let's not keep her on bypass any longer."

The room spun as Ethan struggled to his feet. *Whatever you do, don't throw up.* "The heart—"

"You're no good to me like this," said Lim. "Christ, Faulkner, I'm not having a healer die mid-op. Do you want my head on a spike? Get out!"

"Come on." The nurse none-too-gently herded Ethan towards the exit.

He slipped, feet numb, and she carried him through the stride without pause. As soon as they were out of the operating room, she sat him in the nearest chair.

"Follow my finger."

"I'm fine," Ethan protested. The words rattled inside his skull.

The nurse tutted. "I'm amazed Mr Lim let you assist. There's a traffic light system for a reason. When you collapsed! Poor Emily, I think this was her first time with a healer."

Ethan stared at his nails, filed down to the quick; a crescent of blood and failure congealed at his fingertips. Walking to the sink, he elbowed the water timer, restarting the pressurised jet. It was one of the few places where full-water taps were permitted.

Ethan was grateful for his mask when someone else approached.

"The patient's brother is asking — oh, Dr Faulkner! Are we finished?"

"No, I just stepped out," Ethan said, before the trauma nurse could say anything.

The trauma nurse passed her tablet to her colleague. "Can you brief ICU? One of the aptee wards is free. I should stay with Mr Lim."

"Sure. Dr Faulkner, would you mind speaking to the brother?"

"That's not the healer's problem," the trauma nurse admonished. "Mr Lim will handle it."

"Lim's busy," said Ethan, desperate to leave. "I'm happy to chat on my way out."

The nurses exchanged a dubious look. Sighing, Ethan wiped his hands on his scrubs and escaped before they could protest further.

· · ·

THIS SIDE OF MIDNIGHT, the waiting room was at its most liminal. Anxiety, resignation, and stress pooled like shadows huddling at their owners' feet. Exhaustion exerted such gravity that it threatened to cleave Ethan's soul clean from his bones.

He scanned the room, gaze landing on a man arguing with a nurse. From here, all Ethan could see were broad shoulders and a head of white-blonde hair. The nurse's eyes creased with relief when she spotted Ethan approaching.

"—absolutely ridiculous," the man was saying. "I demand to talk to her consultant."

Oh, thought Ethan, *you're one of* those *relatives.*

The man wore a heavy wool coat over haphazard but expensive clothes: bright silk shirt, pressed slacks, leather shoes. No socks.

"Sir," the nurse interjected, "this is Dr Faulkner."

Ethan took off his surgical mask unhurriedly, followed by his cap.

Mr Trustfund hadn't paused for breath. "—transferring her out of this dump so she can get—" Ethan removed his visor and glasses, then folded them with exaggerated care. "—some actual competent medical..."

When he glanced up, Trustfund was staring at him, seemingly concussed. Ethan's brain had clearly surrendered all higher functions because his first observation was *huh, nice cheekbones.* The admiration faded as his hand cramped with the phantom sensation of a heart between his fingers.

Ethan raised both eyebrows. "You were saying something about my incompetence?"

"I..." Trustfund cleared his throat. He had a white-knuckled grip on his own wrist, eyes red-rimmed, face flushed from crying.

Ethan's irritation wavered. He blamed the post-operation crash for his sudden onslaught of pity. He nodded at the nurse. "Thanks, I can take it from here."

Trustfund gestured at the VM on Ethan's temple. "You're a healer?"

"Yes." Ethan held out his hand. "I was part of the team looking after your sister."

Trustfund hesitated before shaking Ethan's hand. It wasn't common etiquette for healers to offer skin contact, but in that moment, Ethan wanted to demonstrate his control.

"Javier," said Trustfund. "Apologies for speaking out of turn. No one has told me anything for hours, and I'm rather frantic."

Ethan steered them away from foot traffic. Javier followed, straight-backed and reminiscent of military doctors, steps neat and economical.

"Your sister should be out of surgery soon. She came in with a bullet wound through the lung. It was touch and go for a bit. She's a firestarter, yes?"

Javier nodded.

"Right," said Ethan. "As you probably know, conventional stimulants and anaesthetics often interact with aptitudes unpredictably, depending on the aptee and where they fall on Xu's Scale. We don't have an empath on call, so it was important to stabilise her quickly. She'll need to wear suppressors while she's recovering. She might be more comfortable with her own if they're graded six or higher?"

Javier stepped forwards, a tad too close for comfort. He kept fidgeting with his open cuffs, eyes darting towards the door. His old-fashioned watch bore fingerprint smudges on its face, like rosaries after prayer. "I've made arrangements elsewhere," he said.

"She's just had surgery, it's best to keep her stable here. This is a level one trauma centre, the ICUs are kitted for aptees." Ethan could sense an underlying current of worry, visceral at the back of his mouth. It dulled the blade of his irritation. *How odd.* Exhaustion usually made him more apathetic, not less.

"Let me see her," said Javier. "That's why you came out to get me, right?"

"I came to set that poor nurse free. Someone will let you know as soon as she's settled." Ethan turned to leave.

Javier grabbed him by the wrist – and something snapped taut around Ethan's breastbone. He blinked, eyes inexplicably wet. *What the fuck?* Ethan pulled his arm back.

Javier hung on. "No. Take me to her now."

Ethan stared pointedly between his hand and Javier's arresting gaze. They held each other at metaphorical gunpoint for a moment longer, before Javier let go.

"I understand you're upset," said Ethan slowly, "but she's still in theatre—"

"Why aren't *you* with her?" Javier demanded. Something must have broken through Ethan's deadpan because Javier switched tack so fast that it gave Ethan whiplash. "I don't trust the security here. My sister was *shot*. I need to see her. Please."

Up close, their resemblance was clear: the same severe features, same nose, same arching brow. Ethan wondered if Javier was a firestarter as well. Maybe he would explode something if Ethan didn't oblige.

"You're not a firestarter too, are you?" Ethan searched for the symbol on Javier's visitor sticker. Hospitals were one of the places where certain aptitudes must be disclosed.

"I'm not. But you can't stop me from seeing her, either way."

"Fancy a demonstration?"

Javier opened and closed his mouth. "Sorry. It's been a long night. *Please* let me see her?"

"This isn't about asking nicely," said Ethan, exasperated. "Look, you can wait in the ICU lobby. I'll ask Trauma how long she might be."

"Thank you," said Javier, audible relief bookending a shaky exhale.

Ethan turned towards the lifts, tapping his pager. Javier followed, long stride clipped short so they walked shoulder-to-shoulder.

ICU picked up on the second ring.

"This is Dr Faulkner. I wanted to check on Mr Lim's firestarter."
Ethan glanced at Javier. "Right. Thanks. See you soon."

Desperate family members spanned the spectrum, but Javier
oscillated so wildly between tearful worry and shrewd solicitousness that
he must be a breath away from dissolving into the floor tiles. As they
waited for the lift, a nurse passed, ushering a woman into a nearby room.

Apropos of nothing, Javier flinched violently, elbow hitting the wall.
Ethan stared. "You okay?"

Out of sight, a sudden sobbing wail, barely muffled. Javier stared at
the wall, gaze unfocused, knuckles white around his left wrist. Ethan
looked towards the wall too, concern unfurling in his stomach.

There was nothing there.

Before he could ask again, the lift chimed open and the new people
seemed to snap Javier out of his daze.

"Sorry." Javier flashed Ethan an unconvincing smile as they stepped
into the lift. "Hospitals stress me out."

Ethan pressed the button for the ICU floor. "Understandable."
When they arrived, he led them down a walkway framed by windows
fogged by condensation and the ever-present glow of artificial lights.
Stopping by the first empty chair, Ethan sat Javier down and pulled out
his stethoscope.

"Uh," said Javier.

"Inhale for me, please."

Javier obeyed. Ethan pressed two fingers to Javier's throat under the
guise of counting his pulse. He avoided Javier's gaze, a luminous hazel.
Elevated pulse, shallow breathing. Not unusual.

"I thought we were heading to the ICU," said Javier.

Deep bruises circled his left knee, around the hip, torn blisters on
the feet and the tender fray of a calf muscle. No injection sites. A
migraine pulsed warningly behind Ethan's left eye. He pulled out a
penlight. "Are you taking any medications?"

"Just painkillers for my migraine. Why?"

"What kind of painkillers? Any other substances?"

"I received a call that my sister was in hospital and flew here as fast as
I could. No time to ingest any illegal substances."

"I didn't say illegal."

"Look, we can do a blood test later. May I *please* see Rina?"

"I don't need to run any tests to know." Not quite true, but most people overestimated healers. Ethan tapped his VM light.

"Do you also know that you have blood..." Javier gestured at his chin.

Ethan clapped a hand to his face. His fingers came away with rust. *Oh great, I've been wandering around the waiting room covered in blood.* "Occupational hazard," he muttered, striding towards the ICU with Javier not far behind.

A nurse sporting a dark ponytail met them halfway down the corridor. He grinned as they drew level.

"Hey Paul," said Ethan, "I was in OR-5 with Lim. Firestarter?"

"Dr Faulkner." Paul smacked his tablet against Ethan's elbow. "I'm meant to put you in a cab home if I see you."

"How is she?" asked Ethan, eyeing Javier whose posture was drawn tight, as if ready to bolt any minute.

Paul had the cheerful energy of someone who recently shot several mils of caffeine straight into a vein. "We just got her settled. Standard suppressors and local. Do you need me?"

"No, cheers." Ethan knocked, perfunctory, before scanning his pass and opening the door. Like the containment bays downstairs, the aptee wards in the ICU had no windows.

Javier took one look at the prone figure on the bed and made a sound like he too had been shot through the lung. "Rina!" he cried, barrelling past Ethan, stopping unsteadily at the side of the bed. His hands shook, hovering above his sister.

Ethan took stock of the various IV lines, the neck brace, ventilator mask, and the suppressor bands around her bicep, next to her blood-pressure cuff. "She's had her ribs reset, and several incisions," he said gently. "You can hold her hand."

Ignoring the chair, Javier sank to his knees, clutching his sister's right hand in both of his own. He pressed his mouth to the back of her knuckles, head bowed, eyes squeezed shut. "Rina, *Rina*," he said, reverent. "Thank God you're...I thought maybe..."

Inexplicably, Javier fumbled with his watch. He made a noise of frustration and ripped it off, dropping it with a wince-worthy clack.

Without the watch, Javier unravelled from the spine, anchored only by his sister's hand. He cried, noiseless, lips white from swallowing back the sound, hair in his eyes. Side by side, the two were photographs of the other, taken worlds apart.

"I'm going to kill him," Javier murmured. "Useless. Had one job."

Ethan realised, belatedly, that his own eyes were wet. He tried to focus on the holographic display at the end of the bed.

"Don't leave me." Javier sagged against the unyielding bedframe. "I don't know what I'd..."

Sympathy weighed heavier than usual. Ethan's knees popped as he crouched down. He retrieved the watch, slipping it into Javier's coat pocket.

Javier looked up, startled. "Oh. Thank you." He sniffled. "When will she wake up?"

"Probably not for another few hours. I regenerated part of her lung and her ribs are still fractured. She needs time to recover."

"Why didn't you heal her the rest of the way?" Javier asked, still on his knees, a man at prayer.

"I've been in back-to-back surgeries all night." Ethan tilted his head so Javier could see the red light of his VM. "I'll pass out."

"Call someone else."

"I'm the only healer that's—"

"Then bring another in." Javier's voice rose with his anxiety. "Why should she suffer when you could easily—"

"Listen," Ethan began.

"You cannot be the only healer on call! I'm having her moved."

And we're back at square one. "She's not going anywhere. Moving will only jeopardise her condition."

"You said she was stable!"

"Yes, if she *remains* in a stable environment."

"Then we need a healer who can do their job," snapped Javier.

Ethan pinched the bridge of his nose. He pulled up his pager, maintaining Javier's gaze which turned guilty. "Paul? I need to speak to you about future care plans."

Javier stood, hand tethered to his sister. "She's not safe here."

"You're not endangering my patient. Not after I regenerated half a lung. I kept her heart beating in my hand while she haemorrhaged from six places. And now you want to move her because you don't trust my medical opinion? No." Lim's voice rang in Ethan's ears: *you're no good to me like this.*

There was a rap at the door. "Everything alright?" asked Paul.

"This gentleman has concerns with security, my competency as a healer, and wants to transfer his sister out." Ethan spoke quickly to hide the tremor in his voice. "I advise against it. Lim can make the call on bringing in an external consultant; I'm not her admitting physician. If she doesn't wake up in the next two or three hours, redo the neuro and check her scans."

"Yes, doc," said Paul.

Javier opened his mouth. "I didn't mean—"

"No." Ethan was desperate to leave. "I apologise for my outburst. I understand you want the best for your sister. I can't do more right now, but what's best for Rina is to stay here."

"That's not..." Javier ran his fingers through his hair. "Of course I'm grateful—"

"I don't do this for gratitude," snapped Ethan. Because what was he doing, really? Reallocating minutes for hours, hours for days, moving dust from grave to grave. *What if he had passed out on that gurney? She would have died before they reached the OR.* His fingers curled around an empty weight. "I should step out."

"Wait, please—"

"Get some rest," said Ethan. He hesitated, hand on the door. "And maybe ease off your...painkillers."

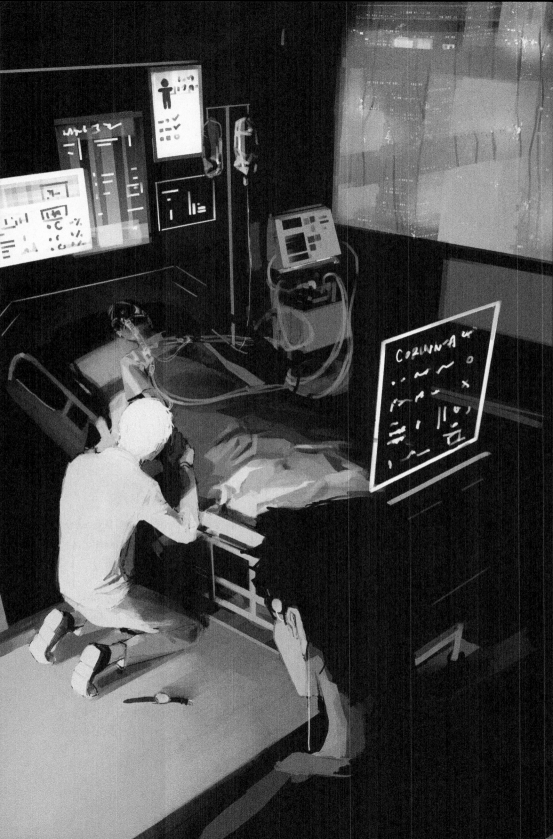

TWO

Lower Walworth, Level 4. Monday, 4 October.

As far as tips went, this one read like a nosy pedestrian. But with a geo-pin ten minutes down the block, it was too convenient for Ollie to ignore. It read:

Bloke in parked auto-cab all night just staring at nothing. Backseat piled with bags. Last week police came to our building on a glass raid. Don't think they got everyone.

Above him, light-rail criss-crossed the airspace as if someone had taken a blunt pencil and methodically shaded out the sun. Last night's rain added a fresh coat of grey to every sole. Ollie activated a dot-mic under his collar as he walked, snapping a stabiliser to his phone one-handed and wedging his earbud firmly in place.

No matter the Level, London at 5.30 am was always miserable. If it wasn't the gale stripping skin from bone, it was the damp coiling fog. Not worth waking up for, but years chasing the relentless news cycle had bestowed Ollie with chronic insomnia. He lived and died by his phone; alerts on max volume for emergencies.

His girlfriend disagreed with Ollie's definition of 'emergency': "When my pager rings, someone is literally dying. When your phone rings, someone's already dead and it can wait until morning."

At least this person waited until we broke up before texting this early. Without his better half, Ollie was prone to self-narration.

He started recording as he approached the cab. Condensation lay, undisturbed, over its metal chassis. The tipster was right: the vehicle must have been parked for a few hours. A dark silhouette was slumped against the window.

"Hey." Ollie rapped the hood. The sound bounced off metal and gravel, hungry and hollow. He glanced up and down the deserted street. A traffic camera winked at him across the road. "Y'alright in there?"

No movement. The man's chin rested on his chest, face turned away.

Uneasy, Ollie wiped the condensation from a window, phone tilted to avoid reflections. At first, the figure appeared asleep: eyes closed, face slack. Then he noticed a dark line trailing from nose to mouth.

"Oh shit. Oi!" Ollie yanked on the door handle – and stumbled as the door flew open, unlocked.

The man fell bodily onto the street.

Ollie leapt backwards. "Bloody hell!"

He slapped the still-recording phone onto the roof of the car, dropping to his heels. The man's joints were locked in a sitting position. Ollie pulled his right glove off with his teeth and pressed two fingers to the guy's throat. His heart sank.

Ollie speed-dialled an old friend.

Nick picked up after eight rings. "It's five-fucking-forty."

"Morning buttercup. I have a present for—"

"No."

"You don't even know what it is."

"Not interested," said Nick.

"Well, too bad. I found a dead body and it won't stay fresh for long. See you soon!"

Ollie had about twenty minutes before Nick, or some random, arrived. He stuck a disposable button-cam on a nearby lamppost and wondered when corpses had become so blasé. Reporting on glass trafficking must inoculate one against such things.

Ollie stared at the body. Early twenties, blunt chin, short hair. Arden Pharmaceuticals' logo clearly visible against corporate blue. A lanyard. He used a pen to flip the plastic ID: *Timothy Hersch,* it read below a terrible headshot.

Sunlight struggled against the gloom as the morning edged towards six. Ollie passed the time by systematically documenting everything within sight, including the duffle bags. He hoped they weren't explosives, and that if they were, no one he hated would take over his scoop (or obituary).

Something reflective caught his eye. Ollie crouched down. A syringe lay beneath the dashboard. The man's left arm was half extended, palm up. And near the crook of that elbow, a tell-tale mark. *Not another one...*

Ollie took a few close-ups of the injection site. Had this guy decided to mainline on the way home? Why risk doing it in a cab and being caught on the security camera?

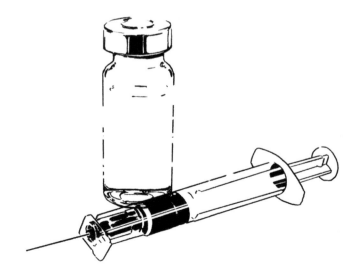

If only Ollie was a telekinetic – then he could open the duffles without contaminating the crime scene more than he already had. The zippers appeared too thin to be insulated against telekinesis.

As if spurred by Ollie's diminishing inhibition, a car peeled off the elevated motorway. *Bugger.* He texted Violet, one of the newsroom interns.

> 05:58 · OLIVER — Do we know a Timothy Hersch? Sent you his pic, can you run it for me? Thanks!

Much of Lower London was never retrofitted for airborne vehicles, with many roads below Level 5 being too narrow to accommodate newer, larger public transport. But most emergency vehicles were land-and-air ready, and the cruiser pulled up on solid wheels.

Ollie checked the dot mics and readied his best shit-eating grin. "Morning." He saluted. "Ayyy, Nick!"

He received two identical looks of baleful, decaffeinated resentment.

"Save it, Roskopf." Claudia donned her gloves. Straight to business. "Step away from the crime scene, thanks."

Ollie held up one palm, the other still holding his phone.

"Put that away," sighed Nick. His collar was popped against the morning chill, a beanie flattening his dark-blonde hair.

Ollie pouted. "But I've got ten punches on our friendship loyalty card..."

Claudia checked over their deceased subject with quick, practised motions to the throat, wrist, and eyes. "He's long gone. Possible overdose, going by the syringe there. When did you find him?"

"When I called Nick," said Ollie. "So, twenty minutes ago."

"What were you doing out here so early?"

"Investigating a tip. This guy didn't respond when I knocked, so I tried the door and he fell out. Called Nick when I couldn't find a pulse."

"Instead of triple-nine?" Nick donned gloves. After perfunctory checks, he opened the back passenger doors and gestured at the bags. "Did you touch these?"

"That's my statement, by the way," said Ollie, "so there's no need for—"

"Nice try, you're coming back to the precinct with me. Answer the question."

Ollie blew out his cheeks. "No, I didn't touch them. I'm very well behaved. Also thought it might have been a bomb or something."

"Bomb?" asked Claudia sharply. "What makes you say that?"

"Paranoia," Nick snorted. "I'll run a reading." He strode back to the cruiser, returning with a tar-black scanner. After a moment, he announced, "Clear."

Ollie side-stepped to get an unobstructed shot of the duffle bags and was met with an elbow to the chest.

"Don't think so, buddy," said Claudia.

"If I'm going to be blown to pieces, I want to get a good photo first." Ollie held his phone above his head. "Hurry up."

"Be quiet."

They all held their breath as Nick carefully unteethed the zipper. He turned down the fabric, revealing the corner of a matte-black container, stamped with the Arden Pharma logo. Each container possessed double latched lids, the security light glinting a curious green. *Unlocked.*

Ollie looked from the box to the dead body on the ground.

"Please tell me that's *not* what I think it is," groaned Claudia.

Nick popped the lid on the closest container. "Fucking hell."

There, in neat tessellating rows, were about thirty vials of CM15.

The water purifying compound was in retail-ready form, vials fitted with mouth pieces for residential purifiers. Blood pounded in Ollie's ears, staticky with the kind of adrenaline that only came from a good scoop.

CM15 – disgusting amounts of it – was required to produce 'glass': a therapeutic and recreational drug. Finicky to dose and volatile to transport, glass was one of London's best-enjoyed exports. The British cartel dominated the Continent, having access to the cheapest glass in Europe, courtesy of tax-payer subsidised CM15.

Claudia slapped Ollie's phone down. "Turn that off. I'm serious."

Beside her, Nick was speaking rapidly into his earpiece. "...to secure the scene, before people start milling about. The lab will need to confirm, yeah. Deceased is wearing Arden Pharma uniform. Wait, *what?*"

Ollie stuffed the phone into his pocket, holding his hands up in faux acquiescence. When Claudia turned away, he winked at his camera on the lamppost.

"Do you think our friend couldn't wait to sample the goods and decided to celebrate en route to wherever this stash was going?" asked Ollie. "There was a raid around here just last week, right?"

Claudia slid the syringe into a clear evidence bag. "No comment."

"And *was* there a break in?" Nick said into his earpiece, eyes on the corpse. "Right. The traffic cameras might tell us, while we wait for the cab log." He nodded to Claudia. "They'll head down soon. Still on Level 9."

"Yellowstone?" said Claudia. "I thought the fire was contained. Is everyone okay?"

"Yeah, fine. They just found some shit outside." Nick looked meaningfully across at Ollie, who had been doing his best to blend into the pavement. "Ian wants the CM15 back at the precinct. I'll get the evidence bags."

"You take the goods and the journalist," said Claudia. "I'd rather babysit the corpse."

"Oi. Rude." Ollie watched them seal each CM15 case in clear plastic.

"We'll need to examine the tip you received," Nick added.

"It's anonymised," said Ollie, stalling. The problem with dot mics and cams: once the phone went out of range, it would stop uploading footage. Ollie had maybe five hundred metres at most before it cut out. "How about I give you a nice, tidy, written statement back at the studio?"

Claudia and Nick loaded the last of the cases into the cruiser, strapping them down.

"Get in the car," said Nick.

"I haven't had breakfast," Ollie tried. "The most important meal — *oww*!" Nick shoved him into the cruiser, slamming the door closed. "Blimey."

The dashboard read 06:25. Nick threw himself into the driver's seat, and there was a chorusing *thluck* as all the doors locked. They peeled away from the kerb: Ollie, Nick, and the overpowering scent of artificial mint freshener.

"Put on your seat belt," said Nick.

"Can we stop at a drive-through?" No response. "Ian *always* lets us stop off at the drive through."

"Are you going to be like this the entire ride up to Level 10?" Nick asked through gritted teeth.

"Yup," said Ollie, popping the consonant like gum.

Angling his phone away from his friend, Ollie opened a map and typed 'Yellowstone Level 9' into the search bar. It lagged as they passed through an intra-building tunnel, the image loading once they emerged. He zoomed in on the square labelled 'Yellowstone Office Complex and Retail Centre'.

"You know you can't publish any of this. The body. The CM15."

"Uh huh," said Ollie. They found some shit outside, Nick had said. And there, opposite the Yellowstone office building, were a few unlabelled squares surrounding a box labelled 'Bright's Chemists'.

"This is now an active investigation," Nick continued.

Ollie waved a hand. "Keep talking, I love this part of our routine." A hunch shrieked, sustained, between his ears. He searched 'bright's chemists arden pharma own' and grinned at the results.

Nick's eyes narrowed. "What are you so smug about?"

"Oh, nothing," Ollie sing-songed. "Did you confirm if there was a break-in at Bright's Chemists?"

"No idea what you're on about," said Nick.

The cruiser jolted as they re-entered the main grid, shooting forwards like a pill capsule through an oesophagus. They must have passed Level 7.

"The pharmacy opposite the Yellowstone offices." Ollie thumbed his phone to check it was still recording. "They found something outside, yeah? I'm assuming Hersch stole all those vials from the Arden storage facility attached to Bright's. How did he set off a fire alarm in a totally different building across the street?"

Nick's mouth worked silently. That was confirmation enough.

"C'mon." Ollie leaned forwards. "Hersch was in Arden Pharma uniform. Bright's is owned by Arden Pharma. We've got retail CM15 in the backseat, and *you* said there was a break-in last night—"

"Never said anything of the sort. Be quiet."

"Let's stop at Bright's on Level 9. You're out of dental floss, so you can go shopping. And I'll ask if they're missing, oh, several cases of CM15."

Nick stared resolutely ahead.

"Or nah?" asked Ollie.

"Very much *nah*."

"Are you grumpy because you haven't had breakfast either? Look, we're almost at the turn-off for this Level!"

"We aren't stopping. We're going straight to the precinct: you, me, and the evidence."

"Can you at least confirm if someone stole CM15 from Bright's or adjacent Arden storage facilities, sometime in the past three hours?"

"No comment."

"Five hours?"

"..."

"Five and a half—?"

"I swear to god, Ollie."

Nick's love language was tolerance – a virtue that Ollie lacked. It probably explained their decades-plus friendship; when resignation met persistence.

"Who were you talking to on the phone anyway?" asked Ollie. "Daddy Garner?"

Nick made a strangled noise. "Ian's my *boss*."

"He likes me more than you, since I'm not the one shagging his son." Ollie grinned at Nick's constipated expression. "How long has it been, now? Two years? Two and a half? Surprised you still have a job."

"Clearly I've passed the test."

"It's a catch-22. If you break up with Ethan, your career's over. And Ethan might never die. I can't imagine a worse punishment."

"I've got gaffer's tape in the glovebox, you know."

Before he could annoy Nick until he cracked and let something slip, Ollie's phone buzzed.

06:44 · VIOLET — Bossman! Tim Hersch came up twice. 64er articles in the past year. Also Queen's College London student union blog posts and the recent parliament sit-in. Links below.

06:45 · OLIVER — Thanks! Assume you are talking about March protests. Send me anything else you find. And if there's anything on a fire at Yellowstone. Level 9. Maybe 6 hours ago?

06:45 · VIOLET — Where are you? Can I come? Get me out of the office.

Ollie snorted.

06:46 · OLIVER — No can do, Florence will kill me for not sharing.

06:47 · VIOLET — I helped her and George set up those emergency alert things, I'll ask about the fire.

06:47 · OLIVER — If I send fire emoji, tell legal I'm at the L10 precinct.

06:51 · VIOLET — Have u been arrested?!

"Who are you talking to?" Nick asked suspiciously.

"No comment," said Ollie.

He clicked through the links from Violet, mind blurring as fast as the cityscape. *If the CM15 had been en route to a stash house, was that a charitable or glass-cartel flavoured stash?* Sixty-Fourther activists weren't shy about stockpiling the expensive water purification drug, usually for altruism. Sixty-Fourthers being glass traffickers was mostly a conservative fever dream – though it wouldn't be the first time someone was caught with fingers in both pies.

The water rights' movement was a generation old, but only in the past few years had the Sixty-Fourthers emerged from the political fringe. Some genius decided to reference the 64th United Nations resolution on the right to safe drinking water, and the name stuck, despite being a mouthful.

London's Levels were rooted in crisis. The older the Level, the more entrenched its CM15-infrastructure, since non-chemical purification relied on more energy than the Lower grids could handle. Fusive cells could meet the energy demand but that tech was still in its infancy. It also repelled politicians in several ways: eye-watering upfront cost, benefits that would not yield within one's average political term in office, and opposition from Arden Pharmaceuticals.

It didn't help that CM15 was a British invention, having carried Whitehall on a new wave of imperial fervour. Like the foundations of London, that pride had been eroded by high water bills and new health risks every other year. The Sixty-Fourther's anti-CM15 and anti-Arden rhetoric was amassing popularity, triggering political self-preservation as they barrelled into an election year. When people became discontented, they asked questions. Or, God forbid, turned out to the polls.

Behind Ollie and Nick, the vials of CM15 sat, silent and unyielding.

Where CM15 went, so did the glass trade. The two appeared hand in hand: across the headlines, in sting operations, and in the morgue. Ollie doubted this story would be much different.

Special Investigations Agency, Central London Precinct, Level 10.

IT WAS ALMOST 7.30 am by the time Ollie finished giving his statement.

The interview room was low-ceilinged, the carpet stained from years of listening. They were in an older wing of the building that served as an inter-Level precinct, housing the Special Investigations Agency plus local police operations.

Nick pressed his face against his mug as if he could absorb the caffeine through his eyelids. "A man is dead. Your source could be involved at worst, a witness at best."

"You want my phone? Do the paperwork."

"You rustled up a case theory rather quickly in the car. Why's that."

"I'm good at my job? Because you have loud phone conversations right next to me? Because our friend had the Arden Pharma logo on his shirt, the same Arden Pharma where all the CM15 comes from?" Ollie paused. "I can keep going."

A knock interrupted them – a man poked his head around the door. "Holt. Garner wants to talk to you. They ID'd the vials you brought in—"

Nick made a cutting motion across his throat, looking pointedly at Ollie

"I was there," said Ollie.

The guy waved. "Seriously, Garner's not happy."

"Fine." Nick drained his mug and smacked Ollie on the shoulder as he passed. "Don't move. I'll be right back."

Ollie swung his feet onto Nick's vacated chair. "Uh huh." He had two missed calls. Ollie thumbed the icon as soon as the door swung shut.

Florence González – Sentinels' best political correspondent and Ollie's by-line buddy – answered on the third ring.

"I'm at the SIA," Ollie said by way of greeting.

"Morning to you too. Violet said you're after a fire."

"I was hoping you and your infamous spreadsheet can help me out."

Florence huffed. "My civil-unrest spreadsheet, my construction kick-backs' spreadsheet, or my—"

"If you know about the Yellowstone fire already, then it must have triggered one of your alert thingies. Was it the Sixty-Fourther one?"

"Nice try, this is my scoop."

Ollie had to trade some intel. "I found a dead body this morning," he offered. "And a whole lotta CM15."

Silence.

"And I care about this because...?"

"The fact that a Sixty-Fourther is dead after stealing CM15 is mighty incendiary, don't you think? Especially with the CM15 manufacturing subsidy getting slashed next week?"

Florence snorted. "The Sixty-Fourthers have been petitioning to lower the subsidy, but no one thinks it'll get slashed. Still. With the numbers we're working with, any decrease would be seismic for Arden Pharma – and our utility bills in the short run." A pause. "I suppose you've got a good hook. I'll help you if I come first on the by-line."

"But the dead body's obviously gonna lead."

"Yeah? Mine or yours?"

Ollie almost dropped his phone. "You also found a—?!"

"Not exactly. We don't know yet. Let's hash it — yes, I know you booked the room Julian, keep your knickers on. Christ, I gotta go."

Ollie waved his hands at nobody. "Do not say anything to that scab. Remember, you owe me! From Feb!"

"Calm down. Something exploded at Yellowstone. We've been keeping tabs of Ascenda's major projects and assets since they're the favoured bid for the Earthflown tender. Yellowstone is one of theirs. And after the Sixty-Fourthers tried to occupy an Arden depot, I also set alerts for the major CM15 facilities in London. Yellowstone tripped both, being so close to an Arden distribution centre."

Thus far, non-CM15-based water purification required more energy than the typical decentralised infrastructure of a tiered city could handle. No one had quite figured out how to make the process more energy efficient, or a method to store enough energy without triggering every firestarter in a mile radius. That is, until the new generation fusive-cells came along.

After snoozing on fusive tech for a decade or two, public malcontent had finally galvanised the great bureaucracy. The government issued a tender: an election-year wish-list to retrofit Lower Levels (read: key constituents), spruce up public services, and wean the water infrastructure off CM15 dependency for something fusive-powered instead. The tender had a vague name to go with equally vague goalposts: Project Earthflown.

Being a keystone firm that built half of London, Ascenda's logo was embedded in the cityscape. *And in twenty years, we'd no doubt be reporting on some corruption inquiry over the whole tender.*

"Can I get in on those notifications?" Ollie asked hopefully.

"You may grovel," said Florence. "George lives on Level 9, so he managed to grab photos. Fire services, police, ambulance – someone was dying I think."

"Dying? From the fire? Did George see—"

"No, he can't teleport, jeez. So if you can find anything at the precinct..."

Ollie drummed his fingers on the table, eyeing the door. Nick might return at any moment. "Did George catch which side of the street the ambulance was on?"

"Lemme check the photos. Hang on...across the road from Yellowstone."

Outside Bright's Chemists, then. Or more specifically, the Bright's attached to Arden Pharma's depot, where all the CM15 lived. Excitement charred Ollie's lungs. Did Hersch run into someone between Level 9 and Level 4? Waylaid by security? Who got hurt?

"I'll call you right back." Ollie hung up, almost knocking his chair over as he scrambled for the door.

If he was lucky, Nick would still be talking to Garner.

Ollie rounded the end of the hallway, following someone who was swiping through the double doors. He held the door open for the lady behind him.

"Thanks," she said, distracted.

"No problem," chirped Ollie.

Usually all it took was a long stride and a high chin. Confidence glossed over any doubt, and Ollie knew the floorplan from years of visiting. Past the door, the immediate area was open plan, the perimeter lined with smaller rooms and offices. The bullpen was half-sunk into the floor, with three sets of double doors around the hexagonal room.

Ollie recognised Claudia's voice and he ducked behind some fake shrubbery, scanning the room for Nick.

"...searched the entire cab," Claudia was saying. "No gun or any other kind of weapon. Could have tossed it, I guess."

Ollie's ears perked up at the word 'cab'. Florence hadn't said anything about firearms.

Inconveniently, Ian's office was on the other side of the desks. Ollie puffed out his cheeks. If he remained here for much longer, someone was going to question why there was a man behind a pot plant.

"The two things could be totally unconnected," Claudia's colleague was saying.

"Two things?" said someone else. "I think you meant three. The fire, the shooting, and now Mr Overdose."

"She's a firestarter and there was a fire. I'm counting that as one thing."

Ollie frowned. Who was this firestarter? The victim outside Bright's, or the arsonist at Yellowstone?

Ian Garner's familiar baritone cut through the chatter. "Why are we standing around gossiping? Did someone chase that 999 call?"

"I'll fetch Ollie," said Nick.

Uh oh. Maybe he could shout 'surprise!' and make a run for it.

"We've got a close match, just after the fire, sir," Claudia said. "The GSW was automatically logged at the scene, but St Ophie's hasn't had a chance to submit the full report."

"Sounds about right," said Ian. "Do we have an ID on the caller?"

"Working on it."

"Good. What about St Ophie's?"

"A&E said the patient was transferred to Highgate Private Hospital around 2.30 am."

"What?" Ian cursed. "I was told she was bleeding to death."

"Highgate's tight-lipped. I can go in person and—"

A commotion interrupted her.

Then Nick's voice: "Can't find Ollie. Reception didn't see him leave."

A pause.

"Oliver," said Ian, in the same tone of voice he used when Ollie took the last bread roll at family dinner. "Roskopf, you have three seconds."

There was nothing for it. Ollie stepped out from behind his pot plant. "Fancy seeing you here."

"I cannot believe—" Nick threw up both hands. "I told you to stay put."

"Come with me," Ian snapped. "Both of you."

Nick frog-marched Ollie out of the bullpen. "Are you shitting me right now?" he hissed. "How did you even get in here?"

"Tailgated." Ollie batted his eyelashes. "I have a trustworthy face."

Nick shoved him into an interview room after Ian. "Sit."

Ollie remained standing. "The paper knows I'm here, y'know."

"Silence," barked Ian.

Ollie looked from Nick to Ian. He sat.

"Now, son," Ian started. "We both have jobs to do."

"And you're always the starring protagonist in my articles, sir."

Ian's eyebrows weren't amused. "This is an active investigation."

"A guy is found with a syringe. A backseat's worth of CM15. And you don't think he overdosed on glass?" said Ollie.

"No assumptions until tox comes back."

"Right," drawled Ollie. "Because you think he shot someone outside Yellowstone. That's why Clauds was searching for a gun, right?"

"For heaven's sake," Nick muttered.

Ian gestured between the three of them. "This isn't a press interview. Things are volatile right now and no, that's not a comment on the case at hand. More speculation is the last thing we need."

"Because Hersch is a Sixty-Fourther?" Ollie leaned forwards. "Did you get the cab's logs already? Was he coming from Level 9? Did he leave before or after the shooting? Or the fire?"

"For the record, I didn't tell him anything," said Nick.

Ollie was undeterred. "Who was shot outside Bright's? An Arden employee as well? That area's mostly offices; dead quiet at that hour, so probs not a passer-by..."

"Oliver," sighed Ian.

"I'm assuming Tim got that stash from the Arden facility behind Bright's. They don't keep those vials sitting with the chips and milk."

"Do you want me to charge you for tampering with evidence?"

"Think of the optics," Ollie wheedled. "Can't you give me a statement? We're practically family. One teensy weensy—"

Ian pointed at the door. "Get out."

Ollie bolted.

OUTSIDE THE PRECINCT, the morning blared and coughed with commuters. Ollie caught a whiff of strong coffee as someone strode past. His stomach gurgled.

During rush hour, braving the steep pedestrian stairs down a Level was faster than taking the inter-Level lifts. Plus, the firestarter and telekinetic dampeners, installed on all public transport tended to wreak havoc on phone reception.

Ollie jogged, recounting the facts that he had scrounged thus far.

Judging by Florence's tipoff and his own eavesdropping, three events had occurred in proximity: a fire at Yellowstone and a shooting, both on Level 9, and an Arden Pharma employee found dead on Level 4 with a heap of stolen CM15. Overdosed on glass, probably.

Not to forget the firestarter and a gunshot victim. Given the late hour, the firestarter and / or the gunshot victim were likely working at Yellowstone or Bright's.

A quick search for 'firestarter Yellowstone brights arden pharma* london' merely crowded the top results with Corinna Arden. *Dammit.* Ollie scrolled past all the glossy photos. Too many unknown variables.

"C'mon, c'mon. Think."

Firestarters weren't exactly dime a dozen, but they were common enough that most people knew of one. Since the UK had no mandatory aptee registry, any proper search would take longer than it took the police to reach St Ophie's Hospital. And nothing sutured lips tighter than the appearance of law enforcement.

Ollie sprinted towards the mouth of pedestrian stairs, feet clanging on metal. Rushing traffic howled upwards in a gale of dust, coating the throat and nose. He grabbed the handrail, using his momentum to round the corner of the landing and leap five steps down at once.

There was a good chance his girlfriend's shift schedule hadn't changed, meaning that she (a) was working at the hospital last night, and (b) would be furious to be woken at 8 am. Ollie tapped call on his watch before his nerves failed him.

A sleep-hoarse voice answered after five rings. "...Ollie? What the fuck."

"Baby, don't hang up, it's urgent."

"My sleep is urgent." Pause. "Are you okay?"

"Yes—"

"Bye."

"Wait, Vegas! Sorry for waking you." No response. "Baby?"

"What."

Three more flights to go. "Were you on night shift earlier?" Vegas grunted in affirmation. *Better get to the point.* "Did anyone come into A&E with a gunshot wound?"

"None of your business," said Vegas.

"Don't hang up, this is really impor—!"

"Oh please, you think all your stories are important. Plot twist: they're not. I can't believe you'd dare ring me for work. After everything I said!" Vegas made a noise in between a scoff and a yawn.

Ollie could see her now: hair doubled in volume, the dip of her frown, the crushed grey light smudging the freckles on the slope of her neck. He realised he had started to smile and shook his head to clear it. "Hear me out. Was there a GSW victim last night? A female firestarter, maybe?"

Another pause.

"How on earth do you know about that?"

Ollie made a silent fist pump, and almost broke his neck as he slipped on a step. "Been chatting to the police, can you give me a name?"

"No," said Vegas flatly.

"Baby—"

"Stop calling me that. We broke up. And I'm hanging up—"

"Did you speak to their family? Emergency contact?"

"Ughh!"

Reaching street level on Level 9, Ollie glanced at his watch. Almost fifteen minutes had passed since he left the station. Shit.

St Ophie's Hospital was a formidable structure, unmistakable thanks to the carve-outs for helicopters and other EMS fliers. It left a gap-tooth airspace against its neighbouring residential and retail buildings, allowing the sun past the spiral motorway.

Through his earphones, Ollie heard a roller door, followed by a yelp.

"—than, Ethan," Vegas was saying. "Ethan, wake up."

"Wh's going on?" came another familiar voice.

"Ollie wants to ask you about the firestarter from last night."

"Hi," said Ollie. A large sign loomed above him: St Ophie's Hospital, Accidents and Emergency.

"Why're you still taking his calls?" Ethan asked.

Vegas made an indecent noise, muffled. "Your new silicon pillow is awesome. Can I borrow?"

"No, leave it alone. And don't change the subject, I thought we decided to block Ollie for real."

Ollie dodged a cyclist. "I can hear you, y'know."

"Piss off," said Ethan.

"Wait—!" But the dial tone was already droning in Ollie's ear. He immediately redialled, but it cut off after one ring. That little shit. Ollie switched to his work number and called again.

"You have reached the Kelsey-Faulkner household," Ethan answered. "No one here likes you. Sod off after the tone—"

"I just need to know the name of the firestarter who came into A&E about six, eight hours ago. Or whoever it was that came in for a gunshot wound. I know someone did."

"Patient confidentiality. Bye."

"Vegas said it was a female firestarter!"

"I said nothing," came Vegas' voice. Ollie must be on speaker. "I gotta go pee. Charge my phone once you're done, Ethan."

"I'm already done, charge it yourself."

"Apparently she was shot outside a Bright's," said Ollie. "I was chatting to your dad and Nick just now."

"Patient confidentiality," Ethan repeated, tone as dead as his soul.

In for a penny, in for a pound. "Must've been pretty bad, to get a healer involved. Were there complications you couldn't handle?"

"I know you're not deaf, ergo, you must be dumb. Patient con-fi-den—"

"I'm asking because your patient, whoever it was, got flown to Highgate around three this morning."

There was a deafening pause.

"What?" Ethan shouted. "I'm gonna kill him!"

"Kill who?" asked Ollie hopefully.

Ethan hung up.

Ollie shrugged and pocketed his phone, striding through the double doors into St Ophie's A&E. It had been worth a try.

Time to do this the hard way.

THREE

7 Kensington Palace Gardens, Upper Kensington, Level 16.
Tuesday, 5 October.

The adrenaline spike woke Jav first. "Rina," he croaked, projecting a reflexive calm as her expression pinched awake. He palmed her pulse. "Shh, you're okay. I'm here. We're at mum and dad's."

Rina's breathing was shallow with disorientation, "...Jav?"

The force of relief almost collapsed his lungs. "I'm so angry at you right now." His twin sank back into her pillows, tension draining into Jav's hand. Smiling never felt this painful.

"Liar," said Rina, hoarse. She wrapped cold fingers around Jav's bare wrist. "You're happy to see me."

Jav couldn't feel his legs. He must have drifted off at some point, tethered to his other half.

"Water?" asked Rina.

"Right, sorry."

The water carafe gurgled in the late afternoon sun. Rina and Jav stayed over at their parents' house often enough to leave clothes in the wardrobe, *eau du parfum* on the vanity, life littering the shelves. She took the proffered glass and threw it back as if chugging liquor.

"Slow down, you'll choke," Jav warned without conviction. Rina tipped her drink higher so he preemptively passed her a tissue for the coughing. He wasn't disappointed. "Congrats," sighed Jav. "Let's not test your new lungs for leaks yet, please."

Rina slapped the empty glass into his hand, sneezing violently. She had lost the pallor of hospital lights, but her eyes were still ringed with shadow. Jav couldn't shake the scent of disinfectant, the claustrophobic misery. But now that Rina was awake, her chrome-clean presence slowly overpowered that memory.

Rina sat up fully, movements stiff from sleep rather than pain. Good old-fashioned healing. "I assume Peter did as he was told then, seeing as I'm home."

"Ah. About that." Jav took a deep breath. "The ambulance took you to St Ophie's."

"...I'm going to skin Peter with my nail clippers."

"It was the closest hospital. You were *dying*." Jav grimaced as Rina's irritation filled his mouth with loose enamel. "Stop being so loud. I got you to Highgate before the police arrived."

Rina threw herself back onto her pillows. "So? An alarm probably went off the moment you walked through the door!"

Jav crossed his arms. "As if you wouldn't have been recognised—"

"Bet Marc's caught wind of this already. Now I have to make up a fucking alibi before mémé Marion finds out."

Marc Sainte-Ophie was Jav's least favourite cousin on mum's side of the family. Alas, Marc also visited London the most often – ostensibly on Sainte-Ophie Biotech business. Jav always tried to abscond before overhearing too much and was now paying for his wilful ignorance.

"It's only been some-fifteen hours," said Jav. "Why would Marc be keeping such close tabs on you?"

"He thinks I'm up to no good."

"And he'd be right, wouldn't he? Is it about the subsidy vote next week?"

The Sainte-Ophies had helped rebuild St Ophie's Hospital in London and retained a financial and governance interest ever since. The two shared a namesake in Sainte Elise Ophie, one of the more famous healers in Catholic canon. Grandma Beatrice said Sainte-Ophie Biotech just wanted to stick a finger in Arden Pharma's pie.

"Maybe I was mugged." Rina sniffed.

"I'm not here to workshop your alibi." The words scored Jav's throat like bile. "Even with healers, you almost died. I could only sit and wait for some doctor to come out and t-tell me that you'd—! That you had—!"

"Hey." Rina yanked him closer by the wrist. "*Hey*. I'm fine." When Jav resisted, she clasped a hand to his nape, her inexorable calm making him shudder.

He relented into the hug, lying down on the bed next to her. "But your ribs..."

"Doesn't hurt, c'mon," Rina murmured. She pulled the covers over the two of them, as if they were eight years old again.

Jav tucked his cheek against her shoulder, her chin digging into his hairline, eyes squeezed shut against the pressure of her collarbone. He tried to suffocate his sobs by holding his breath until lightheaded.

Neither spoke for a long while.

"Sorry for scaring you," said Rina. Jav made a wet noise, unconvinced. "I feel awful."

"Yeah, because *I* feel awful," Jav muttered.

"Meh." A huff. "I'm sorry for getting shot."

"...And?"

"And what? If I hadn't got shot, you wouldn't be upset. Ergo, I'm sorry someone shot me."

Jav was too tired to push. "Close enough."

"You think I planned to almost die? Where's Peter."

"Don't know. Dead in a ditch, hopefully." Jav covered his face with both hands, Rina's amusement too scalding in the aftermath of fear.

"Oi." Rina tugged at his arms. When Jav refused to budge, she pushed his hands together, squishing his cheeks like a goldfish. "Let's go home," she started, but froze when a door slammed somewhere downstairs.

Jav stood, wordlessly stepping into the doorway to throw his senses wide. He relaxed as soon as he recognised the thrum of irritation drawing rapidly closer. "Giulia," he announced. Rina wrinkled her nose. "I'll head her off."

He intercepted their older sister at the end of the hall. Jav tried projecting a mild happiness but it bounced back like sunlight on ice. "Hey—"

"Is she awake?" Giulia demanded. She was wearing a paler shade of lipstick than normal, a sure sign of her foul mood. She had taken it out on Jav that morning, after enduring the brunt of their father's telling-off.

Jav blocked the doorway. "The healers said there'd be residual pain, disorientation—"

"Cut the crap." Giulia shouldered past.

On the bed, Rina lay with her eyes closed, hair strewn artfully over the pillows. Giulia dropped her handbag in the nearest chair and stalked across the room. She leaned over her younger sister, hands on hips.

There might have been a lurch of uncomfortable relief but Giulia's baseline static of anxiety made her difficult to read. Surreptitiously, Jav pulled his suppressor watch from his pocket.

"I know you're awake," said Giulia. Rina didn't react. "We've been talking to investigators all morning. I haven't slept since Jav called me at two-bloody-am, so I've had it up to *here*."

"C'mon, Giulia," said Jav, "she's had surgery."

"Be quiet or get out."

"Normal people would be more upset when their baby sisters get shot," said Rina, eyes still closed. "I could be in a coma."

"As if," said Giulia. "Jav would be hysterical."

"See, this is why everyone thinks you're a robot. And a bitch."

"If you're well enough to insult me, you're well enough to deal with the mess you've made. Did Jav show you the news articles yet?"

Rina turned to him. "Was she even a tiny bit sad?"

Jav looked from one sister to another: Rina's apathy was at odds with Giulia's thundercloud of stress. "She's been worried sick."

It was the wrong thing to say: Giulia's anger slapped him hard in the face.

"Do *not* try that on me," snapped Giulia. "I can feel you projecting. Get out. Rina and I need to have words."

"Don't tell him what to do." Rina shot back. She paused. "Though I *could* kill for a smoothie."

Jav wanted to bang his head against the wall. He settled for an eyeroll. "Fine. Don't set anything on fire while I'm gone."

The kitchen was colder than the rest of the house. The staff kept the fridges stocked, even though their parents were still in New York, and their youngest sister, Maddy, hadn't yet returned from her semester abroad.

It felt good to do something with his hands: moving rinsed away the aftertaste of Giulia's unease. Growing up, she had never been comfortable with Jav's empathy. Whether it was the years between them or a distrust of all empaths, they never managed to bridge that gap.

A thump, upstairs, followed by shouting.

Glancing at the ceiling, Jav pointedly switched on the blender. It screamed to life, drowning out the raised voices. By the time the fruit was liquefied, the coffee was ready. He fetched a glass straw, poured the smoothie, and popped a strawberry into his mouth.

Jav re-entered the bedroom just in time to hear Rina say, "Well, I wanted to make the Monday news cycle!"

He froze.

Rina continued, "Instead of last-minute hit jobs on fusive versus CM15, they'll be too busy talking about Sixty-Fourthers stealing CM15 for glass – and not 'the greater good'. You wanted noise. I made some noise. *You're welcome.*"

"You said that you'd tip the police off about a stash house or two," Giulia snapped. "Not get shot and end up in the news! What do you think will happen when your name gets out?"

Jav stared at Giulia. "You knew about all this? Beforehand?!"

Reclined on a mountain of pillows, Rina dragged one index finger down the screen of Giulia's tablet. "There's no pleasing some people."

"You could have died," spat Giulia. "Dad raged at me for an hour."

"Ha! Imagine how much trouble you'd be in if I had actually died."

Jav frowned. "That's not funny."

"It's a little bit funny. Daddy loves me the most." Rina side-eyed Giulia. "More than you, anyway."

Giulia thumped the nearest shelf with a fist. "Parliament might still cave and decrease CM15 subsidies next week, what with the election coming up and Sixty-Fourthers camped outside, screaming about their water bills! You were meant to generate scandal about those activists, not create an excuse for us to get audited. The SIA has always been obsessed with missing stock and now it looks like Arden Pharma allows CM15 to walk out the back door every week."

"Okay, it hasn't been *every* week," said Rina, who enjoyed Giulia's blood pressure as a spectator sport.

Wordlessly, Jav held out the coffee.

Giulia blinked, a flash of guilt. "Oh. Thanks."

"You're welcome." Jav offered Rina her smoothie.

"Who's that straw for?"

"People recovering from surgery." Jav glared at Giulia. "People who should be *resting*."

"I want a ham and cheese croissant," said Rina.

Giulia snorted. "See? There's nothing wrong with her."

The sun would combust before Rina and Giulia stopped sniping. Jav wanted a nap. "Will one of you please tell me what happened last night?"

"I got shot in the chest, not the stomach," Rina sulked. "I could eat."

"No croissants until you explain yourself," said Giulia.

Rina held her gaze and sucked noisily on her straw. "Don't you want plausible deniability, sister dear?"

Giulia snatched her tablet back. "*Arden employee found dead in suspected glass overdose*," she read aloud from a Sentinel article she had sent Jav earlier, "*...once again raising questions as to Arden Pharma's supply chain, and its role in London's glass epidemic.* They're massaging the pity angle, listen: *Mr Hersch was in his final year at Queen's College London and a vocal supporter of CM15 alternatives such as fusive-powered water purification. He volunteered with 'Sixty-Fourth Blues', an inter-collegiate organisation behind the recent viral 'One Drop' campaign* *pressuring vulnerable MPs to phase-out CM15 manufacturing subsidies under the* Water Act. *As the most generous subsidy of its kind in Europe, if Parliament votes to decrease the subsidy next Thursday, it would be the first time it has done so since the subsidy was first established five decades ago. As its sole beneficiary, Arden Pharma—"*

"Why aren't they talking about his glass addiction? I thought people loved a good hypocrisy narrative. That'll teach me to rely on a 'respected' news outlet." Rina made grabby motions at Jav's phone. "How did our tabloid's do?"

Jav passed it over, breathing as shallowly as possible to avoid inhaling Giulia's stress cloud.

"Oh yeah, this is much better," said Rina. *"Exposed! The real reason 64ers want to ban CM15."*

"Was getting shot part of the plan too?" asked Giulia.

"Sure, if the shooter was a Sixty-Fourther," said Rina. "You can't buy that kind of public sympathy. Glass half full, Giulia."

It took a moment for Jav's brain to catch up. "Wait, it's public knowledge that *you* were shot?"

"Not by name, small mercies," said Giulia. "The article mentions that *someone* was shot outside Bright's. They're speculating that Hersch was involved."

"I made a pun," whined Rina. *"Glass* half — no, Jav! Gimme, I'm not done reading."

Jav scrolled back to Giulia's original message. "How on earth do they already know the victim was a 'female firestarter'?"

"The investigators came calling this morning, they know it's Rina," said Giulia, steely. "Do you know who else called me? Marc."

Rina groaned into her glass, annoyance spiking right through Jav's temples.

"You think *Marc* went to the press?" Jav asked.

Giulia shook her head. "If he believed going public would tank the vote, he would leak Rina by name. Marc wouldn't risk the sympathy that might net us. The subsidy is all that's preventing Sainte-Ophie Biotech from crossing the English Channel. The minute they can compete, they'll make a move. Hell, mémé Marion might take a hit to the margin just to spite grandma Bea."

"What's the point of all the horrible brunches we've been hosting then?" asked Jav, feeling out-of-the-loop. "I thought Marc had come around on pricing."

"He has. A race to the bottom would hurt Sainte-Ophies as well, and Marc doesn't have mémé Marion's...prejudices." Giulia turned to Rina. "But that was before *you* decided to gift them leverage, idiot. Marc's not going to keep quiet for free."

Rina's aura concaved with displeasure. "Maybe we should get my name out early. Before Marc *or* the SIA. Set the narrative."

Giulia collapsed into a chair. "We need a watertight reason for what you were doing on Level 9 in the dead of night—"

"Heh. Watertight." Rina yawned. "Let's leak my name, make clear that the shooting coincided with Tim stealing CM15. People will join the dots."

How can the solution be more *media attention?* "Slow down," Jav pleaded. "Picketers camp outside HQ every other week. This doesn't sound safe."

Rina *tsk*'d. "I have nepotism to thank for my job title. No one holds me personally responsible for the water crisis. Plus, I'm beautiful – it'll keep the news cycle focused on the 'violent 64ers' narrative a bit longer. An excuse for Westminster to distance themselves. Play the law-and-order card."

"Don't do anything until I give the all-clear." Giulia's mouth flattened with severity. "I need to talk with mum and dad."

Rina wrapped her lips around her straw. Her smoothie was almost gone, making for an obnoxious wet rattle as she sucked. "Your phone's buzzing."

Giulia stood. "If you can keep Rina out of trouble for more than eight consecutive hours, that'd be fucking great. And, for heaven's sake, don't let her talk to the press. Or Marc."

"Yes, because everyone listens to me in this family," said Jav.

Giulia swept out of the bedroom, leaving behind only a lipstick stain on her coffee cup.

"Wow. What a waste of time," Rina drawled.

"*I heard that!*"

Jav clawed a hand down his face.

1 Madeleine Avenue, Upper Chelsea, Level 22.
Thirty minutes later.

RINA INSISTED ON TAKING their mother's favourite car, instead of
the two-seater Jav had flown the night before. "You have no survival
instincts," she scoffed, bundled up in Jav's wool coat and a pair of
oversized sunglasses. "Someone might have tampered with it. Boom, no
more Jav."

"If only," Jav said testily.

Each passing vehicle shaved another millimetre of enamel from his
teeth.

Below, to their left, Kensington Gardens and Hyde Park were jade
shards set in tarnished metal. The city towered above old Buckingham
Palace, left to rot. As one moved inland, the flood-zones abated – and so
did the Levels. Here, London's skeleton staggered into the soft earth,
like some great beast brought to its knees. Most of Mayfair and
Kensington stopped at Level 16. They still hosted London's most
expensive residential addresses, overlooking the rarest of commodities:
unobstructed sky.

As they drew closer to home, the car's stabiliser fins retracted into
the chassis in preparation for landing.

Their penthouse sat two floors above the next tenant: one to house
Rina's collection of sports cars and solo fliers, the other serving as a wine
cellar and general buffer. The car parked itself neatly beside the glass
lobby, lights brightening to greet them.

After Peter's call last night, Rina's absence had been an anvil on Jav's
chest the whole way down to Level 9. She sat next to him now but
breathing still hurt. Rina laced their fingers together, her calm an
unyielding mirror.

"It'll take more than this to get rid of me," she murmured.

Jav exhaled. "I was scared."

"I know."

What's the point of picking a fight now? "You do feel shit," Jav
observed.

"Yeah, 'cause I'm starving."

The car door lifted with a soft hiss, retracting into the sloped roof as they stepped out. Security scanners passed over them with a pleasant chime, lobby doors *whooshing* back. The lift was all stone and bronze mirrors that framed a plush moss wall. Jav preferred the AI assistant to be muted: he hated conversing with anything that lacked an emotional presence.

Rina kicked off her shoes as soon as the lift doors opened. "Finally!" she exclaimed, striding through the living room towards the stairs. "Can you make me an espresso martini?"

"Absolutely not," Jav called.

The blinds were still down from last night. Jav tapped the controls on the wall and sunlight streamed across the floor, dappled from the trees in the conservatory and refracting off the aquarium. The place was a time capsule. His tablet was still lying on the couch where he had left it, next to an abandoned carafe of water, Puccini cued on the speakers.

His twin reappeared, voice first. She was on the phone. "...obviously. Get over here, we need to talk."

Jav raised an enquiring eyebrow.

"Peter," mouthed Rina. Jav scowled and made for the kitchen. Rina followed. "*Yes,* now. *Hurry up. I want to take a bath and sleep for days.*"

Jav opened the fridge, locating a container of leftover salmon. He shoved it into the microwave. Rina poked him urgently, gesturing between the dish and herself.

"This is mine," he said. "Find something else."

Rina narrowed her eyes. "And pick up some ham and cheese croissants on the way here. At least five, I'm starving, and Jav's being a little bitch."

"There's other food in the fridge. Why do you always want what I'm eating?"

The microwave dinged. Retrieving the salmon, Jav promptly burned his tongue on his first inhale.

"Did the sniper take your balls too?" Rina was saying. "*Non, c'est une boulangerie.* Call yourself a professional? I want my croissants!" She hung up and began picking at Jav's salmon.

Jav let her eat, resigned. "Is Peter really bringing croissants?"

"If he wants to live."

"Good. I want some too."

"You can have *one*."

"One? I've been worried sick: I want half the bag."

"Fine..." Rina scraped the fork clean between her teeth. "Only because I love you."

Jav huffed. "What's his ETA?"

Rina grinned; cheek squirrelled full. "Enough time for you to shower and make that martini."

WHEN PETER FINALLY ARRIVED, Rina was lying with her head in Jav's lap, eating olives from the jar with a pair of chopsticks.

In exchange for serving as a pillow, Rina had made Jav a mug of tea – baby oolong with a dash of milk and sugar. The warmth only accelerated his drowsiness, but Jav got dressed to confront Peter with dignity.

The ghost arrived in a cloud of fresh pastry and impatience. Stress vignetted his presence, jaw unshaven.

"Shoes," said Jav automatically.

Rina sat up, olive jar in hand.

Peter's relief punched straight through Jav's chest, shoulders slumping (though that might have been the ten kilograms of French bread).

"Shoes," Rina echoed.

Peter obeyed. "You look better," he said quietly.

"No thanks to you," snapped Jav. He stood up. "You have one job – to protect Rina – and you *left her.*"

"I had a sniper and dead bodies to deal with." Peter shook back one sleeve to reveal a raw, wet burn mark in the shape of Rina's grip.

She snorted. "Still can't believe you called triple-nine."

A second-hand violence lurched beneath Jav's ribs.

"You were dying," said Peter, flatly.

"*You* should have taken her straight to St Ophie's," said Jav.

Peter turned to Rina. "Does Barbie have to be here for this?"

"Watch it."

Rina slid off the couch, crossing the room to stand in front of Peter. He was a full head taller. She leaned up on her toes to kiss him.

Peter's spine bowed like a plant deprived of light. He held her by the shoulders, palms reverent, eyes darting like a blind man's touch.

Jav looked away.

"I'm sorry," said Peter, barely audible. "I had no choice."

"You chickened out," Rina huffed. She kissed him again though, half amused, half forgiving.

Peter adored Corinna. It was impossible to fake relief like that, or the steadiness through the years. Jav knew what real love and fondness felt like, first and second hand. This was something very close. Devotion, maybe.

Yet Peter had left Rina to bleed to death, simply because she had asked. Jav always thought they had an understanding: that his sister's wellbeing came first. Perhaps love and loyalty were not the same thing after all – not when Jav had trusted Peter to act in Rina's best interest, and Peter had obeyed her with such little remorse.

Rina swiped the bakery bag from Peter's hand, breaking the tension. She pulled out a wrapped croissant, paper translucent with butter. Peter settled into an armchair.

"So. The sniper," said Rina, mouth full. "Who was it?"

Peter glanced at Jav, who glared right back. Rina waved a regal hand for Peter to continue.

"I'm still looking into it," said Peter, grudgingly. "He accessed Yellowstone using a janitor's swipe. You blew half his face off, which doesn't make things easier."

"Is that what the fire was about?" asked Jav.

Peter barked out a laugh, and Jav fought a familiar urge to leave the room. If anything, last night proved the dangers of not being across Rina's extra-curriculars.

"Self-defence." Rina conjured a flame and extinguished it with a kiss blown in Jav's direction. "Your tea's getting cold."

"Impressive as it was, I wish you hadn't killed him," said Peter. "Now we can't ask any questions."

Rina shrugged. "If you use firearms against a firestarter..."

"For someone with the intel to ambush us, a strange oversight. Presuming it *was* an oversight."

Jav snorted. "How reassuring. A discount hitman."

"How dare you," said Rina. "I'm expensive."

"I'm concerned that Langley has a hand in this," said Peter.

"Which Langley?" asked Jav.

"Robert, obviously. His nephew's an idiot."

"And in love with me," said Rina, leaning back in her chair.

"Trust me, it's not love," Jav muttered. "Charlie is a rude, chauvinistic—"

Rina kicked Peter with her bare foot. "What makes you think it was Bobby?"

"He lent us the cab. He's the only other person who knew what we were planning, unless you think Giulia found out."

Shaking her head, Rina's butter-fuelled delight gave way to something pensive. "Why would Bobby want me dead?"

"The goal might have been to scare you. Combustible weapons to kill a firestarter? Robert's not that stupid."

Rina's emotions flipped like a coin. "Do I look scared to you? Do I *feel* scared?" She turned to Jav, irritation cold enough to freeze his tea. "Show Peter how angry I am."

"Router-Jav is down for maintenance." Jav sipped his drink as slowly as possible. Alas, there were no right things to say when discussing your sister's would-be assassin. "Surely Mr Langley wouldn't risk upsetting grandma Bea?"

"*Giulia* is grandma's favourite." Rina pulled a face. "If I die, Mummy can just make another one. Gran's never in London these days, so Bobby's clearly getting ideas."

Affection that long-lived rarely ran cold, but Jav was too tired to argue.

"You don't have to be dead for Robert to make a point," said Peter. "I'm sure he's worried about the anti-CM15 sentiment ahead of the vote next week. Wants to muddy the waters. Redirect the narrative."

Rina narrowed her eyes. "We were doing that already, by framing Hersch."

"*Yes*, of which Robert was well aware. He probably didn't think we went far enough. And you must admit, Sixty-Fourthers trafficking glass is not a new story. Sixty-Fourthers shooting Corinna Arden *is*."

Impatience and spite did not mix well, coating Jav's migraine like cheap absinthe. He tried to wash it away with the last of his tea, eyelids suddenly heavy. "Could it have been angry activists?"

"Hersch had no unusual connections," said Peter. "Give me some credit."

"No! You left my sister in a gutter—"

"Bobby wouldn't risk it," said Rina. "No Ardens; no CM15. No CM15; no glass."

Peter sighed. "Your cousins are right across the Channel—"

"And Sainte-Ophie's compound is more expensive, less efficient, and more regulated. Bobby only has such a tight grip on the Continent because he can undercut them, thanks to *our* cheap supply. I also have Charlie eating out of the palm of my hand. They won't defect to Sainte-Ophies."

"*Yet*," said Peter. "Once the subsidy goes, there's little stopping Robert from switching CM15 suppliers. Unless Marc's finally ready to commit?"

"He's a work in progress," said Rina, sour.

"Marc did seem more amenable," Jav agreed. "Audrey is expecting any day now. Babies make people happy." Audrey was Marc's wife, infinitely more pleasant than her husband – and eight-months pregnant. "As Giulia said..."

"No one wants a race to the bottom," Rina finished.

Peter's eyebrows disappeared into his hairline. "Do you think Robert is unaware? You've promised him something you can't guarantee – and have no intention of keeping."

"What more does he expect us to do?" snapped Rina. "Personally remove every spine in Whitehall? We've scared most of them into line: no one wants to put their name next to anything that might raise the water bill ahead of the election. And for those who aren't sure: voilà, media cover."

"*For now.* And when the subsidy resurfaces for another vote in two years?" Peter's mouth worked silently before settling into a grimace. "Your parents aren't so short sighted. And neither is Robert."

Rina ran her hand absently up and down Jav's arm, aura spitting with static as she stewed. Jav realised he had sunk into the sofa, drowsiness blurring the room. He hoped the exhaustion would keep Rina's temper low.

"You think Robert suspects that Marc is more open to cooperation?" she asked.

Peter shrugged. "He must suspect something. Maybe he thinks Beatrice wouldn't allow it. The Arden–Sainte-Ophie family feud isn't exactly a secret."

"How fortunate the geriatrics aren't at the negotiating table." Rina snapped her fingers. "Who else wants me dead? Ideas? Jav?"

Jav buried his face in her shoulder. "The Sixty-Fourthers probably hate us the most," he mumbled.

"I'll make enquiries," said Peter. "In the meantime, we can safely assume the police will come to that same conclusion."

"I can't see how the optics of me dying at the hands of Sixty-Fourthers would help Marc, so he's probably out – though we have *so* many cousins. All fucking idiots." Rina tilted her head. "Giulia is always pissy about anything I do, so I'm sure she'd love me dead."

"That's not funny," Jav protested. The pressure of Rina's bony shoulder against his forehead was helping with the migraine, somewhat.

"Nath's forever lecturing me about ruining Ascenda's Earthflown bid, but he has no balls," Rina continued. "Who am I forgetting?"

"You've nominated your sister, extended family, and your godbrother – that's plenty for me to work on," said Peter.

Rina's fingers carded through Jav's hair. It took a moment for him to realise she was calling his name. His head felt too big for his neck; heavy.

Jav rubbed his eyes. "Sorry?"

"I said, any loose ends at the hospital that we should know about? Would hate for Marc to find any extra ammunition."

"We need a list of everyone you spoke to," Peter agreed. "Her consultant, whoever admitted her, et cetera."

Loose ends. Unbidden, Jav thought of Dr Faulkner, serene as he retrieved Jav's watch and composure from Rina's bedside. Walking into his presence had been a blinding balm, dampening the hair-raising thrum of fear and misery. It was like being suddenly submerged in water. God knows what Peter did to such loose ends.

No doubt sending his anxiety, Rina's insistent apathy scraped Jav's soul clean from his bones. "We need to make sure nobody says anything unexpected. It's just a precaution. Let's start with the emergency department."

"You had a healer. Um." Jav frowned, vowels like marbles between his teeth. "Faulkner. He saved your life."

"Okay, play nice. Take them out to dinner. Make them feel appreciated. Keep tabs."

"Marc no doubt knows this information already," said Peter.

"Jav's more persuasive," said Rina. "Who else?"

Jav nodded. The room had grown dark; a warm press against his cheek. He didn't remember closing his eyes. *Huh.*

Peter's voice floated, as if from the next room. "Dammit, how long will he be out? We need those names."

"At least six hours. Oops, I figured we needed to chat alone."

Gravity listed gently starboard. The remnants of Jav's migraine receded to a dull throb. A hand combed his hair back from his forehead, soothing, metronomic, over and over.

Then, nothing.

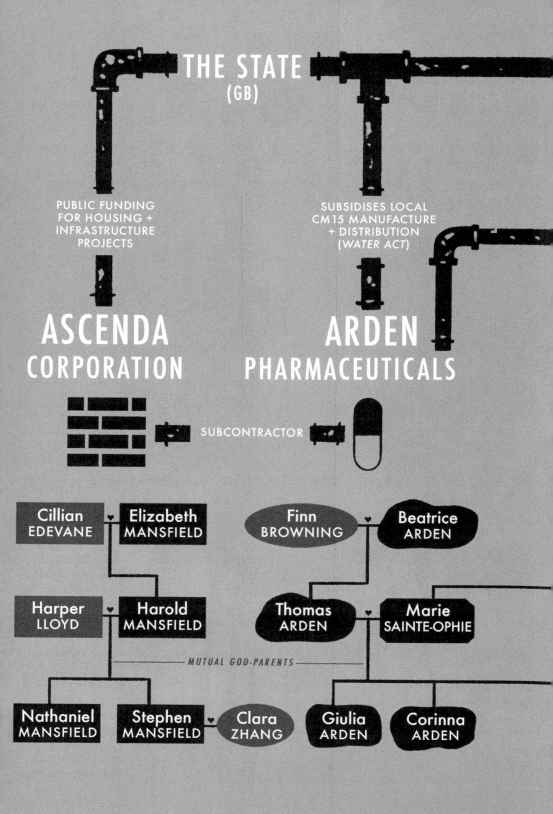

THE STATE
(GB)

PUBLIC FUNDING
FOR HOUSING +
INFRASTRUCTURE
PROJECTS

SUBSIDISES LOCAL
CM15 MANUFACTURE
+ DISTRIBUTION
(WATER ACT)

ASCENDA
CORPORATION

ARDEN
PHARMACEUTICALS

SUBCONTRACTOR

Cillian EDEVANE ♥ Elizabeth MANSFIELD

Finn BROWNING ♥ Beatrice ARDEN

Harper LLOYD ♥ Harold MANSFIELD

Thomas ARDEN ♥ Marie SAINTE-OPHIE

MUTUAL GOD-PARENTS

Nathaniel MANSFIELD

Stephen MANSFIELD ♥ Clara ZHANG

Giulia ARDEN

Corinna ARDEN

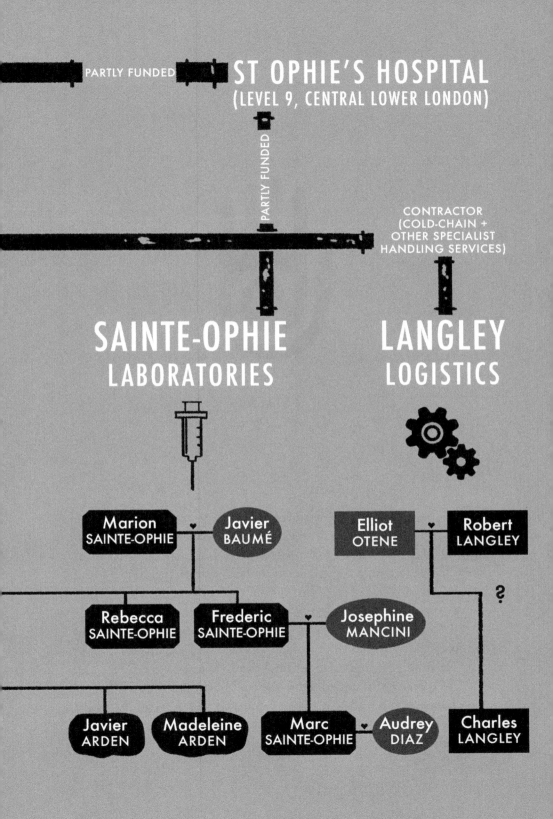

FOUR

Monday, 4 October.

Ethan was having a terrible week, and it was only Monday. He
endured a police interview (*"No, I did* not *sign off on her
transfer. I don't know why she was taken off Mr Lim's list."*)
only to be accosted by his own father in the corridor. Hospital
administration seemed extra antsy about their missing firestarter, and by
dinner time, everyone was in a black mood.

"If only you had blocked Ollie like you *said* you had," Ethan
complained.

"We didn't even know about Highgate," snapped Vegas.

"Well, somebody tattled. How else could Ollie have known?"

"Because he is a sneaky piece of shit who will do anything to get a
story!" Vegas burst into tears. "I miss him so much…"

"Why? You argue all the time."

"He gets me. That's why he's so good at pissing me off! I've never seen you and Nick fight. Ever."

Talk less, fight less, thought Ethan. Nick had always been quiet, especially out of the bedroom. And lately, it felt like he had forgotten Ethan existed. The eternal dilemma of Vegas-and-Ollie was that Vegas cared deeply about every word that Ollie said. And Ollie talked non-stop.

Vegas sniffled. "He's gonna run off with Florence. They have so many by-lines together, 'González and Roskopf'. And she always wears those sexy pantsuits. See — Ethan, you're not looking. *Ethan.*"

"Lord," he sighed, and got up to fetch the wine. Perhaps Tuesday would be better.

St Ophie's Hospital, Lower Lambeth, Level 9. The next day.

TUESDAY WAS NOT BETTER.

Opposite Ethan sat four suits, three ties, no personalities. He only recognised the trauma department head, Nejiam, and her severe jawline. Admin, HR, and legal were stock photographs against the world's beigest wall.

Ethan wished vehemently for the OR: behind a mask and visor, expressions were optional. "The patient suffered extensive damage to her left apical segment. If I hadn't intervened, we would've had to consign that part of the lung entirely. She might have been predisposed to ARDS, lifelong pulmonary fibrosis, and so on."

"You fainted and almost went into iaomic myoclonus," said Nejiam.

"Momentary lapse when we took off the clamps, but I had finished regenerating her lung at that point."

"You placed your colleagues in an unacceptable position by not taking Mr Lim's concerns more seriously."

"We're concerned for your well-being," said HR, with lipstick-drawn sincerity. "It's especially critical for someone with your skillset."

Ethan swallowed a dozen retorts and focused on appearing apologetic. Eyes wide but not too much, lest it be mistaken for attitude.

"I'll be more cautious going forwards. This has never happened before."

"To this extent," said Admin. "The incident has raised serious safety issues."

Ethan bristled. "Vital monitors aren't an exact science. I made a call—"

"You were not her consultant," said Nejiam.

"She was a firestarter in bad shape. We didn't want to risk traditional anaesthesia, and every minute—"

"No one is suggesting that Dr Kelsey erred in consulting you. However, the fact you stayed even *after* you had fainted. We're still reviewing the events leading up to the Highgate transfer."

"I never signed off on that."

"Do you know the patient in a personal capacity?"

Ethan blinked. "As I told the officers yesterday: no." *Everyone knew* of *the Ardens.*

"How about the patient's family?"

Yes. I know the whole family except this one sibling. For her, I have miraculous amnesia. "No."

A long pause.

"Exhaustion is no laughing matter for healers," said HR.

"I'm not laughing," said Ethan. "Mum set a good example."

"And we'd prefer to keep this as an internal disciplinary matter."

"But you're punishing me because she was transferred under someone else's watch? I specifically told the ICU staff that she wasn't stable—"

"You are conflating two issues," said Nejiam. "We will take your comments regarding Highgate under advisement. However, about your VM: I don't think you grasp the seriousness. You could have killed a patient."

"I had already *healed* the — if I hadn't been there—"

"No doubt Lim would have been perfectly competent," said Nejiam.

"We have an obligation to your health and safety, doctor," said HR. "Protocols exist for a reason. We were absolutely devastated when your mother passed away."

Elise Faulkner died in the back of an ambulance, having attended a rare call-out to Level 6. Healers did not, as a rule, get dispatched. There had been a structural-failure above a primary school building. The children survived, while St Ophie's lost a healer. The whole debacle must have been quite expensive for the hospital.

Ethan was seven.

HR leaned forwards. "We think it best that you take some time. Two weeks, starting tomorrow."

"Tomorrow? I have scheduled operations—"

"We've handled it. When you return, you'll be taken off night shifts, and instead of consulting for emergency—"

"For how long?"

"Three months."

"Three *months*?"

"You'll also undertake refresher safety training—"

"I lapse once, post-op, with no repercussions for the patient, and I'm banned from the ER for three months?"

"You habitually operate on high amber," said Nejiam.

"How will Lou and Niharika cover the shifts? The risks—"

"Flouting safety procedure is a risk, doctor," said Admin. "You are not the only healer in this hospital."

"I am thirty per cent of them."

"Dr Faulkner," said HR. "We'd prefer not to escalate this matter to the Healer's Guild or the General Medical Council. Work with us here."

Ethan tilted his chin. "Maybe you should look into the resourcing issues."

"Our priority is always the safety of our patients and staff," said Nejiam.

"You should never feel pressured to work over your shift," HR continued. "We'll revise how your pager is screened."

"Right," said Ethan.

"Some rest and reflection will do you good," said Nejiam.

Ethan glanced at Admin's fancy mechanical watch, the impatient drum of his fingers, soft from counting money. "Right. If that's all, I need to scrub in."

"Thanks for your time, doctor," said HR.

Ethan smiled, as bland as the walls.

HE DIDN'T MAKE it far before being waylaid.

St Ophie's Hospital was structurally wrapped around two foundational pillars. It began on Level 9, its top floors rising above street-level on Level 10. This accommodated two sets of ambulance bays, with oversized lifts taking Level 10 entrants to the Level 9 emergency department. The adjacent goods lift always stank of sweat and half-hearted disinfectant, which Ethan banked on to keep his coast clear.

"Dr Faulkner! I'm *so* glad I caught you." Brooke leaned over the counter and hollered, "Soph! He's here." She turned to Ethan. "We would've given them to Vegas if we couldn't find you."

"Given what to Vegas?"

A door slammed nearby.

"This came for you, earlier," said Sophie, face and torso hidden behind the largest bouquet of flowers that Ethan had ever seen in his life.

"Oh." Ethan stepped back. "Oh, no."

Sophie heaved the bouquet onto the counter, pastel-blues nestled in a tasteful explosion of grey and gold paper. Ethan was no floral expert, but everyone knew how much water they took to grow. Live flowers made for an excessive gesture. He scored a petal with his thumbnail. Yep, alive.

Brooke was studying her phone. "Blue orchids. Amaranthus. Baby's breath, oh la la."

"For the department...?"

"They're addressed to *you*." Sophie handed him a palm-sized envelope.

Ethan accepted gingerly.

The textured paper bore *Dr Ethan*

Faulkner in neat cursive.

"Must be some VIP patient," said Brooke. "Or a secret admirer."

"I don't have admirers," said Ethan.

"Girlfriend?" Sophie suggested.

"Don't have one of those either."

"Can't be from anyone here," said Sophie, sounding inexplicably pleased. "No doctor has handwriting that neat."

Brooke batted her eyelashes. "Nurse, maybe?"

"Ha! On what salary?"

Conscious of eager eyes, Ethan angled the note away from his audience:

> *Dear Ethan,*
>
> *In my distress, I'm afraid I said some terrible things. It's been driving me mad with regret. You saved my sister's life, and I'm forever in your debt. I know you don't accept gratitude as currency – perhaps you'll let me apologise over dinner? Please call.*
>
> *—— Javier*

It was generally considered bad taste to single out one physician, though well-meaning patients often directed thank-yous to the healer. *Mad with regret indeed*. Next to the signature were twelve neat digits.

Ethan snorted. "As if."

"Someone's having a good day," came a familiar voice.

Ethan spun around – and there, to his horror, stood Lim.

The trauma surgeon looked pointedly between the flowers and Ethan. "Happy patient?"

"They're not for me." Ethan shoved the card into his pocket. How could healers seal specific arteries but had no control over blushing? "Thanks Soph. I'll pass these on to Vegas."

Brooke was having none of it. "Why?"

Ethan legged it.

Bergenia Residences, Lower Lambeth, Level 9. Later that evening.

VEGAS WAS OUTRAGED for all the wrong reasons. "What do you mean you *lost* the note?"

"It means I don't know where it is. And that I can't be bothered looking." Ethan dumped ramen noodles into a colander.

Vegas and Ethan's shifts had finally synched up. Whenever this happened, they tried to cook and eat in. Boiling pre-portioned ingredients still counted.

"I found out via group chat," Vegas griped, retrieving two eggs. "You'd think to give several Ks worth of flowers to big sister Vegas, but *no.*"

"I had to dispose of the evidence."

"Did he really say 'mad with regret'?"

Ethan licked the broth spoon. "Yep."

"I hope *I* drive Ollie mad with regret."

"Doesn't he write you poetry and essays?"

"Via three thousand text messages. Was Javier hot?"

Ethan snorted. "Not hot enough to be saying things like 'mad with regret'."

"O-*ho!*" Vegas waggled her eyebrows. "I wonder what he's up to."

"What do you mean?"

"C'mon. The Ardens? Arden Pharma? And remember how Ollie said on the phone that he talked to your dad and Nick already, which means that his sister's GSW—"

"It's No-llie season: this is a conspiracy-free zone. Between him and dad, everyone's shady as hell. I'm not going to speculate."

Vegas squinted. "That hot, huh."

Ethan rolled his eyes. "Look, the real tragedy is the five hundred training modules I have to do. Cardiovasc monopolises Lou. That leaves Niharika, if I'm off: 1.5 healers for a level-one trauma centre. What could go wrong?"

"Ethan, I love you, but stop complaining about your punishment vacation."

"It's not a *vacation*." Ethan reached for spring onions. Vegas rapped him across the knuckles with her chopsticks. "Ow!"

"You got off easy. Two weeks paid leave, then zero on-calls? Boo hoo. Peel the eggs."

Their flat was small but comfortable for central London. They had partitioned the living room into a second bedroom, with just enough space left for a couch and TV. The rain blurred the squat windows with condensation and daubs of light.

Vegas sighed. "I should have stopped you when your VM went red."

"She wouldn't have made it to the OR," said Ethan, frustrated. "You're all acting like I recklessly—"

"It *was* reckless. If someone decides to operate while drunk..."

"That's not the same. I was merely—"

"Not in a state to safely do your job? You might as well be inebriated if your VM's red."

"I'm sorry for whinging." Ethan took out his guilt on the sesame-seed grinder.

"Are you sorry for not stopping when I told you to?"

"I'm not sorry for saving her life."

"*We* saved her life."

"You know what I mean. We. Team effort." Ethan dropped the peeled tea-egg into her bowl. "I'm taking credit for her lung though."

"I'm sure it was the most beautiful lung ever regenerated."

Ethan inhaled a spoonful of soup. Neither he nor Vegas had had time to go buy any new protein, but the miracles of artificial flavouring enabled a tonkotsu broth that had never met a pig – lab cultured or otherwise.

"You'd think Lim would at least acknowledge a job well done," Ethan groused.

"Lim saw his career flashing before his eyes."

"I *fell over*. There aren't enough healers on the roster, banning me makes no economic sense."

"They're economically scared you'll die on the job."

"This was my first offence—"

"Only takes one time! They kept asking me why I didn't stand you down once red. You're not the only one who got blow-back."

Guilt returned in full force. "Wait, you're not in trouble, are you?"

"Not as such." Vegas sighed explosively. "Just don't complain where others can hear you."

"Yes. Okay. I'm sorry."

They devoured the rest of their dinner in companionable silence, then stood in sync to clear the bowls and cutlery.

"When are you off on leave?" asked Vegas.

"Friday's my last day." Ethan fetched the sorbet and two spoons. "Was meant to be Wednesday, actually, but it's been crazy ever since Ari left us early. Her new place paid out her penalties and loans and everything."

Numerous state-funded incentives sought to funnel healers into the healthcare system, and almost every incentive was conditional on those healers working in public hospitals afterwards.

"By the time you're back, everyone will've forgotten why you went on leave in the first place," said Vegas.

"The flowers didn't help. You should have seen Lim's face."

"Oh, boo-hoo. I'm sure nobody'll even remember."

The next morning.

VEGAS COULD NOT HAVE BEEN MORE WRONG. "A love letter?" she cackled.

Ethan lunged for the envelope. "Give me that!"

Vegas shoved the roses, bloom-first, into his face. "*Dear Ethan,*" she narrated in a plummy accent. "First-name terms already? So forward."

"People are staring," Ethan hissed.

"*Perhaps orchids were a little impersonal,*" Vegas continued, ducking out of reach. "*I truly am sorry. You met me at my worst, and I can't stop thinking about* — Lord save us, I can't." She wheezed like a faulty bypass machine. "*Please give me a chance to apologise, or at least be put out of my misery. Sincerely, Javier.*"

Brooke seemed riveted. "He sounds—"

"Like a twat?" said Ethan.

"—so romantic!"

"Oooh, a phone number," said Vegas from the safety of two tables away.

Ethan almost broke a tooth scrambling to stop her. "Vegas, *no*."

"Vegas, yes," said Vegas, phone aloft.

"Are you mad, don't *text* him—"

Paul appeared in the mailroom entrance. "Whoa, are those real?"

Sophie followed behind, laden with coffee.

"Dr Faulkner has an admirer," sang Brooke. "His name's Javier."

"What?" exclaimed Sophie, visibly crestfallen. "The same one who sent the flowers yesterday?"

"Come talk to me in person, you coward," Vegas read as she typed. "Also, it's rude to single one person out. God save the nurses...five exclamation marks."

"Amen," chorused Brooke, Sophie, and Paul.

Ethan threw up his hands. "Why."

"I want to see if he'll keep sending flowers," said Vegas.

"So you want to bankrupt him."

"Please. As if that lot can't afford it."

"Weren't you dating a cop?" Paul laughed at Ethan's scowl. "Wait. Javier's that ponce that airlifted his sister out two days ago."

"Was he good looking?" Sophie demanded.

Paul shrugged. "Blonde."

Paul's a good chap, thought Ethan, *but so very straight*. He thumbed one of the powder-soft petals. Unfathomable: pouring money into the things destined to wilt.

Vegas tucked the card into Ethan's shirt pocket and pinched his cheek before he could duck. "Aww, you're all red," she cooed.

"At least block him."

Right on cue, Vegas's phone began vibrating. Her personal number. *Incoming call*, it said in cheerful sans-serif. Ethan grabbed the phone and slapped the decline button.

"I was trying to score you free dinner," Vegas protested.

Ethan deleted the text thread for good measure. "Listening to a snob is not free."

"Snobs are the worst," agreed Sophie, examining the bouquet

critically.

"Party-poopers. Right, I've gotta find my trainee." Vegas gave Ethan the two-fingered 'I'm watching you' gesture. "Be gone before six, you."

"Piss off," Ethan said, and collapsed into the nearest chair.

A MINOR KERFUFFLE occurred as Ethan scrubbed into his last surgery. The technician held up her phone in lieu of an explanation. It took a minute for Ethan to recognise the mail room in the photo: the whole place was overflowing with roses. It looked as if someone had detonated a paper-and-ribbon bomb.

"They were addressed to emergency, and trauma. Must have cost a fortune," she said.

"Must have."

"Abbey told me that Paul heard that Brooke said you're dating a florist."

"Oh, bugger," said Ethan.

HE SHOULD HAVE KNOWN that Javier was the type of idiot to take Vegas literally. Ethan might have devised an escape route if he hadn't been distracted with a VIP coronary revascularisation.

Besanko, the head of cardiovascular surgery, was ancient but had hands like a bomb technician. "Young man. You come highly recommended. Ivy likes you. A chip off the old block, she says."

Ethan smiled. "That's—"

"I also hear you fainted in Lim's OR."

Hospital gossip moved fast. Besanko made a show of peering at Ethan's VM. Ethan stared ahead, feeling like a racehorse having its teeth examined.

Besanko grunted. "Our patient has the vascular type of Ehlers-Danlos syndrome. So I need you for obvious reasons."

"I thought EDS had been on the mandatory prenatal editing list for decades now. Or was it just the recommended list?"

"Mandatory. But Mr Pemberton was born in the United States."

"Ah."

"Indeed. Now, unfortunately for me, Niharika is off dealing with some ED referral, so I'll walk you through this one."

"I've assisted with delicate cases before."

Besanko raised both bushy white eyebrows. His bald head reflected the white surgical lights like a hard-boiled egg. "I shall. Walk you. Through it."

"...Of course, sir."

Besanko clearly trusted Ethan about as far as he could throw him.

Even in elective surgeries, healers usually regenerated only the critically necessary. There simply weren't enough healers to go around. If their stamina was exhausted for non-life-threatening issues, mid-shift, someone else might pay with their life. Two exceptions existed: complicated cases and generous financial donations. With their current patient, it was both.

"Watch what you're doing," Besanko barked, when Ethan closed his eyes to concentrate. "Don't get cocky, lad."

Ethan kept his eyes shut, feeling the artery knit beneath his hands, a phantom itch crawling across his chest. In the span of three breaths, it was over. He broke skin contact before the incision could close. Detachment felt like waking, mid fall.

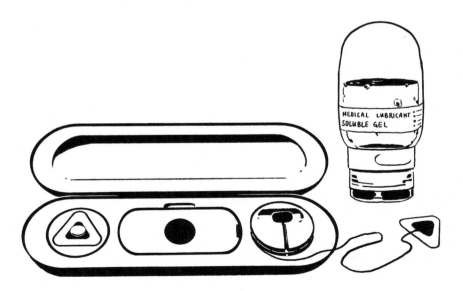

IT WAS CLOSE to seven by the time Ethan left the OR. Retrieving his moisturiser, Ethan swabbed around the VM tab on his temple, digging a fingernail beneath the plastic to peel it off. He repeated the process with the monitors on his chest and neck. Tossing the disposable adhesives, he slotted the VMs back in their charging case to wash at home.

The A&E lobby on Level 9 served as a general thoroughfare onto the street. Staff moved through the rows of chairs, triaging. Ethan made a beeline for the exit, head down.

"Dr Faulkner!" It was Brooke, manning a desk.

"Ah. I'm off," said Ethan. "Did someone need me?"

Brooke didn't answer, waving frantically over Ethan's shoulder. He turned – and sighed. It was Javier, making his way towards them on mile-long strides, shoes agleam, overdressed in a dark grey three-piece, pea coat folded neatly over one elbow.

Ethan wanted to disappear into the floor. "You're kidding."

"He's been waiting for an hour," Brooke whispered. "So polite. A gentleman."

"Uh huh. Because he bribed you with that champagne behind the printer."

Brooke sniffed. "You're *welcome.*"

"Hold on, how did he even know when I'd—"

"Dr Faulkner! I'm so glad I caught you."

Ethan pinched the bridge of his nose. *Whatever you do, don't blush. Have some bloody self-respect.* Maybe Javier would go away if Ethan feigned obliviousness for long enough.

"Doctor?"

Or not. Sighing, Ethan turned. "Yes?"

Up close, Javier was a far cry from the harried, tearful wreck that Ethan had met three days ago. His eyes were no longer red-rimmed, his hair was coiffed. Not a crease in sight.

"You called me a coward for not coming in person. So here I am." Javier carried himself with a carelessness that reeked of wealth – but his smile was uncertain.

He's nervous. Good. "I was just leaving." Ethan pushed away from the reception without another glance.

Javier followed. "Won't you let me apologise? For the other night?"

Ethan breezed past the double doors. The cold air hit him full in the face. He pulled his coat up to his chin, risking a glance sideways.

Javier was staring at Ethan with a barefaced earnestness rarely seen beyond trainees. "The flowers were meant to be sincere. I figured it would be uncouth to ambush you in person."

"You thought *flowers* were the low-key option," said Ethan flatly.

"Well, I didn't exactly count on death by faux pas." Javier huffed. "Should have dropped by earlier."

"About that: it was my friend who texted you. Not me."

Javier's expression fell. Ethan bit back a smile.

"Ah. That's awkward." Javier rocked back on his heels. "You, um, she told me you'd be clocking off at six." He held up his phone.

> 07:20 · EF — Ask for me at reception. L9A&E
> side. Do NOT be late!

Ethan snorted. "Yeah, that's her. You needn't have come in."

"No. I wanted to apologise in person." An ambulance flew past, sirens blaring. Javier's gaze darted all over Ethan's expression. "I can't imagine what you must think of me."

Ethan crossed his arms. "I thought you were on drugs. Or otherwise mentally impaired."

"I only had painkillers."

"Then perhaps we should re-evaluate your prescription." Ethan blamed his defensiveness on Javier's jawline. "What else possessed you to ignore expert medical opinion and transfer my patient barely half an hour post-surgery? You risked her safety, I hope you know that."

Javier wrung his hands. "I do know, and I'm so sorry. Rina has strict instructions for—"

"Dying in transit?" Maybe Vegas was right. Maybe *Ollie* was right, good Lord, and something dodgy transpired. Ethan mentally shook his head. Life was too exhausting to judge books by their contents. Covers must suffice.

"There was a healer on board," said Javier. "They assured me—"

"Oh, I suppose if a *healer* said so."

Javier slapped a hand over his eyes. "I'm so—"

"Sorry? Yes, I got that much."

To Javier's credit, he had yet to run away. His pitiful expression finally punctured the balloon of Ethan's righteous annoyance: it took healthy vertebrae to grovel with such panache.

"Will you at least put your coat on," said Ethan. "I'm cold just looking at you."

Javier obediently donned his peacoat. "I really am sorry."

"Well. It's done now. I've heard worse, anyway. It's difficult for family, so I don't take anything personally."

"It wasn't a lack of confidence in your skills, or prejudice against m—"

"You're *fine*." Ethan thought of Nejiam's severe disapproval, of Lim's face. But he had saved her, and that's what mattered. "No point self-flagellating about counterfactuals. Next time...well. Let's hope there's no next time."

"Right."

The light from the hospital bleached Javier's hair white. He seemed at a loss, as if he hadn't expected Ethan to forgive him in so few words. Forgiving strangers was easy – to care was to pay by the word.

Ethan cleared his throat. "How's your sister? Any chest pains or shortness of breath?"

"She's well. The doctors at Highgate said we were lucky to have such a skilled healer when it mattered the most."

"It was a team effort. I'm glad to hear that she's okay."

"Me too."

What remained of the tension bled out until there was barely any left to ink the shadows about their shoes.

Javier shifted his weight from one foot to the other. "I hope your friend liked the flowers. I sent a few different types; hedged my bets."

"Cheers for that. Now everyone thinks I'm dating a florist."

"And are you?" asked Javier, without missing a beat. "Dating a florist?"

Ethan narrowed his eyes. "I don't have time to date."

"But you have time for dinner."

You've already apologised ten times, so what's this? Judging by the flowers: a dinner and a romp. It was rarely more than a dinner and a romp. "I suppose my schedule's clear, since they fired me."

Fatal dismay swept across Javier's face. "They *what*?" Two passers-by quickened their footsteps at his shout; a security guard glanced over. Ethan struggled to keep a straight face. "I can fix this. There's always a shortage—"

"Listen—"

"Hold on, I'm calling my sister."

Ethan started to laugh. "Sorry," he wheezed, "I — your *face*, I didn't think you'd...please, no more faces. Look away, look away."

Javier went pink but stared heavenwards. Once Ethan stopped laughing, Javier said, reproachfully, "You gave me a heart attack."

"As if they'd fire me. I've been put on mandatory leave for a fortnight. And banned from emergency until Jan."

"They came after you? When I..." Javier trailed off at Ethan's raised eyebrow. "Nothing."

"You're a piss poor liar."

"People usually believe me."

"Charming. Well, I'm freezing, so." Ethan turned to leave.

Javier made a show of checking his watch. "Have you eaten?"

"Nice try."

The parking lot entrance arched from the asphalt like the ribs of some half-excavated fossil, where vehicles were rotated down into storage. The only street-level parking was reserved for disability-coded rides and emergency vehicles. Like water, there was never enough.

"Perhaps dinner, later this week," Javier suggested.

"I don't need an apology dinner," said Ethan.

"How about a no-adjective dinner?"

Ethan thought of Nick: *easy, no strings?* He side-eyed Javier's broad shoulders and the sharp tuck of his waist. The overcoat did nothing to hide the flattering silhouette. Ethan was perpetually tired, but he wasn't *blind*.

The prospect of the two weeks ahead loomed, suddenly empty. Vegas would be busy and tired. And with break-up season in full swing, Ollie wasn't around to play VR with. He hadn't seen Nick for ages. And what was the absence of strings if not the hedging of bets; to be at arms' length while pressed hand to heart, pulse to pulse? Two weeks was a long time to be alone with one's thoughts.

"Alright," said Ethan. "I'm free on Friday."

Javier lit up like a lightbulb, dimples accompanied by a distinct jolt between Ethan's ribs – sugar straight to the veins. *Better head home before I say anything else.*

"Fantastic! Where—"

"I don't mind."

The pedestrian light turned green.

"May I come pick you up from work?" asked Javier.

Ethan maintained his deadpan. "You may."

"When suits best?"

"Before midnight, or I'll turn into a pumpkin."

Javier laughed, surprise creasing his brow.

"And no more flowers," Ethan added.

"As you wish."

"The car park entrance was back there, by the way."

"It looks like it might rain." Javier hovered like an imploring shadow.

Ethan didn't break his stride. "Don't follow me home, please, we've only just met."

"Oh. I'm sorry — wait!" Javier called, heedless of the shoals of pedestrians parting around them. "May I have your number?"

"No need," Ethan tossed over his shoulder, "Vegas has yours."

"*Who?*"

It took only ten minutes to get back to his flat, and Ethan grinned like a lunatic the whole way home.

FIVE

Arden Pharmaceuticals (corporate), Upper Mayfair, Level 14.
Friday, 8 October.

Rina clicked her lipsticks together like poker chips. "Nude Guava or Sand?" In consultation with their mother, Giulia had decreed that Jav and Rina walking into the SIA precinct would be tabloid bait. Plain-clothed investigators were coming to Arden HQ instead. "I want optimum trauma, not too polished. So they'd feel uncomfortable pushing me too hard."

Arthur, their lawyer, stood sentinel by the door. "Please don't say things like 'optimum trauma' within earshot of the investigators."

Rina admired her reflection in a paua shell hand-mirror. She had applied pallor and matching eyebags, carefully messing her hair. She bopped Jav on the nose with a lipstick. "Well?"

"Guava." Jav passed her a tissue. "Blot it."

"I think this is as ugly as I'm gonna get."

"Our friends have arrived," said Arthur. "Miss Arden?"

"Who did they send?"

"Ian Garner and Nick Holt."

"Dammit. Garner has it out for us." Rina wrinkled her nose. "Have we dealt with Holt before?"

Arthur offered his phone. "You haven't met him personally, but he's been in Garner's department for a few years. Transferred from a private firm."

"Hmm, I can't tell if he's straight or not." Rina swiped through the photos. "Jav, take off your jacket."

Arthur snorted.

"That is not how bisexuality works," said Jav.

Rina snapped her fingers. "Lose the tie."

Ignoring Arthur's thrum of amusement, Jav shrugged off his suit jacket and his dignity. He draped them both over the back of the nearest chair, pulling his tie off. Rina batted his hands away impatiently, unbuttoning his collar.

Jav raised his eyebrows. "Happy?"

Rina's skin was warm and dry as she laced their fingers together, apathy fitting like a glove. She looked to Arthur. "You're wearing dampeners?"

Arthur nodded. "As always. But neither Garner nor Holt are registered aptees, let alone empaths. Such non-disclosures would jeopardise admissibility."

"Can't be too careful," said Rina. "We need you to keep a cool head in there."

ARDEN PHARMA HQ overlooked Hyde Park to the west and
Green Park to the south-east: two swathes of chartreuse in a sea of grey,
thanks to grandfathered zoning.

Pascal Hansen – Giulia's 'assistant' of eight years – was waiting for
them. Pascal didn't stink of sustained cortisol, in contrast to Giulia who
projected stress like a homing beacon.

Jav suspected there was a correlation between Pascal's unflappable
demeanour and his boring taste in suits. Pascal also had an unsettling
habit of appearing like an astral projection wherever Giulia felt like
micromanaging. It reminded Jav a little too much of Peter.

Pascal cast a brief, judgemental eye over Jav's attire. "What took you
so long?"

"Powdering my nose."

To Arthur, Pascal afforded a polite nod. "Precautions are in place. If
you need interference, I'm just outside."

"Cheers," said Arthur. "I'll keep a tight leash on our friends. Giulia's
expecting a debrief afterwards."

"Very good." Pascal opened the door and stepped back.

It was one of the smaller, informal meeting rooms; armchairs set
around a low coffee table. The London sun struggled valiantly against
the clouds, grey with fatigue.

Both investigators turned in unison.

Ian Garner looked vaguely late fifties, while Nick Holt appeared
around the same age as Jav and Rina. Unfortunately, Ian was no stranger
to Jav: Rina and Jav's best friend, Stephen, regularly ran into law
enforcement while out joyflying. They would take turns having Jav in
the passenger seat, 'for extra oomph,' as Rina liked to say. Terror was
exhilarating, and endorphins by any other name...

Judging by Ian's rumble of contempt, those incidents were fresh in
his mind too. Nick felt less hostile, though his attention ran taut as
piano wire.

"Mr Garner," said Rina, "thanks for trekking upstairs."

"No trouble." Ian gestured to Nick. "This is my colleague, Mr
Holt."

Rina turned to Arthur. "You don't have to sit through this," she said
with faux uncertainty. "I assume it'll just be a recount, right?"

"Nowhere else I'd rather be," said Arthur.

"We would prefer to speak to Mr Arden separately," said Ian.

"I'm her emotional support sibling." Jav flashed his best toothpaste-commercial smile.

To his relief, Nick smiled back – if barely. Projecting calm usually unspooled any apprehension, but Jav had to go slowly, like thumbing soft fraying thread.

After a pause, Ian acquiesced.

Jav poured Rina and Arthur each a glass of water. He nodded at Nick and Ian's half-empty coffees. "May I offer either of you a top-up?"

"I'm good, thanks," Nick said, while Ian just grunted.

They all took their seats.

Rina latched onto Jav's hand, eyes on Ian. "I could have given a written statement."

"Things get lost on the page. You look well, Miss Arden."

The dissonance between Ian's warm expression and steely focus gave Jav goosebumps.

"Thanks to the healers," said Rina.

Ian's gaze flickered. A flash of something heavy in the chest.

Jav leaned forwards. "She's meant to be recovering in bed."

"Of course," said Ian. "Let's get started then. Miss Arden, please tell me what you were doing late Sunday evening, before the incident."

"Sure," said Rina. "New CM15 stock typically comes in Sunday nights, and I try to drop in. Check on things. Someone shot me as I left the building."

"Do you often visit during these hours?"

"It's a family business. I don't work nine to five."

"When did you arrive that evening?"

"Around half-past ten?"

They had rehearsed these details back home: Rina, Peter, and Jav around the kitchen island. Then they choreographed the talking points with Arthur, down to the punctuation. None of that stemmed the nausea of anxiety rising in Jav's throat.

"They'd likely have footage,' Peter had said, "at least of us turning off the Level. Thirty minutes after we switched cars."

"So you were inside the building for just under an hour before you came out," said Ian. "And that's when you were shot?"

"I suppose."

"Did you sense the combustion at all? I understand you're a firestarter."

Jav raised both eyebrows, projecting doubt so that Rina could remain demure.

"I can't remember clearly," said Rina. "Just pain."

"Then what happened?"

"I heard a second bang, but not sure if that was the gun or me hitting my head."

Something hound-like flicked upwards in Ian's face, and Jav immediately palmed it down.

"What happened after that?" asked Ian, anticipation crackling like a fine film of sugar.

The man suspected something. Jav projected a chest-crushing pressure at his sister, an echo of his own fear. Her gaze didn't change, but she squeezed his hand in warning. Jav didn't relent: *you're meant to be confused and upset.* Beside him, Rina tensed, eyes growing wet. She shook her head, pressed a fist to her mouth.

"Take your time," said Ian, voice round with paternal warmth that ran up against a bedrock of scepticism.

Rina nodded.

"Did you see or hear or sense anyone?" Ian asked.

"Um. Not sure."

Jav passed her his pocket square. She sniffled and Jav bled a sympathetic echo over the room, hoping it was subtle enough to ease Ian's intense focus.

It wasn't.

"We have a recording," said Ian. "Someone called an ambulance for you."

Across the room, Arthur's attention went neon sharp.

"Are you certain you don't recall anyone else in the vicinity?" Ian persisted.

"Peter called me. How will we explain Peter's presence?" Jav had asked.

"We're not going to explain anything," Peter had replied, "I was never there."

"I don't remember," said Rina shakily. "I didn't see anyone."

"We'd be grateful if you could have a listen, see if you recognise the voice," Nick chimed in. "Whoever called the ambulance may have also seen the shooter."

"You haven't found them yet?" Jav asked with exaggerated indignance.

"We're looking at all possible avenues. Identifying the caller would be of great help."

"Could you trace the call?" suggested Jav, reciting his lines.

"We are working in parallel," said Nick.

Jav tamped down on Rina's spark of irritation. He hoped she was maintaining an appropriately upset expression.

"Could it have been an employee who came out, after hearing the gunshot?" Ian suggested.

Rina's frown was pitch perfect. "I guess we should give it a listen."

The recording was clear, marred only by the wail of a fire alarm and the static of rain. Thanks to the modulator, Peter didn't sound like himself – but there was no disguising the frantic thread beneath the calm: "*Yes, I need an ambulance, 29-year-old female aptee, gunshot wound, left chest. Firestarter. We're outside Bright's on Heygate, Level 9*".

In the background, staccato gasps. The sound of someone struggling to breathe, choking and wet.

Jav felt sick. It didn't matter if someone was genuinely experiencing a particular emotion. The act of emoting was performative: body language, rhythm of breathing, pulse, and gaze – and of course, words. And where Rina's performance fell short, Jav's empathy made up for it.

He pulled Rina into a hug, which was her cue for an anxiety attack. His collar would be ruined, but at least his tie was spared: silk and water did not mix.

"Maybe we should take a break," suggested Arthur.

"Just a few more questions," said Ian.

Rina milked the moment for a beat longer, then pulled back. She ran her fingers through her hair. "Sorry. It's been a lot."

"Of course," said Nick. "These things are difficult to relive. As Ian said, we only have a few more questions and we'll be out of your hair."

"Do you recognise the voice on that call?" asked Ian.

"I'm not sure."

"They appear to know a lot about you. Your age, your aptitude. An employee, perhaps?"

"Don't know," said Rina. "Sorry."

"Miss Arden is something of a public figure," said Arthur dismissively. "Entirely probable that a random passer-by recognised her."

"Perhaps," said Ian. "But the cameras didn't catch anyone approaching on either end of that street. No passer-by. No footage of Miss Arden getting shot either."

Rina blinked. "Like they were broken?"

"Like they were tampered with," said Ian.

"So whoever shot my sister...fudged the cameras so they could make a clean getaway?"

Ian spared Jav a glance. "Certainly, something is amiss."

"You bet something's *amiss*," snapped Jav. "Someone shot my sister." Ian didn't react, so he tried naiveté instead. "How did they even get a gun? Isn't that illegal?"

A burst of derision from Nick, beneath his poker face.

Arthur turned a patronising stare on Ian. "We've established that Miss Arden – like many of us, I'm sure – cannot identify someone from a short recording. Is there anything else you need from her today?"

"Yes." Ian nodded at his colleague. Nick spun his tablet around, displaying a photo of Timothy Hersch. "Do you recognise this man?"

Rina leaned in, hair fanning across her cheek. "From the news?"

"Giulia updated us," said Jav.

"I see," said Ian. "Did you happen to see Mr Hersch that evening?"

"Don't think so?" said Rina.

"You didn't see him, or don't remember seeing him?" asked Ian.

"I'm not sure if I remember who I saw."

"You said you were there for stock. Mr Hersch worked in the warehouse. With the stock."

"Big warehouse." Rina tucked a strand of hair behind one ear.

Nick spun his stylus around his fingers. "From where did you leave the building?"

"Side exit because it was covered. I didn't have an umbrella with me."

"The side exit being the loading-bay exit?"

"Yes."

"It had been raining all evening," Nick said. "You didn't think to take an umbrella with you?"

"Guess I forgot."

Jav nudged her with an elbow. "You left your phone at home too. Typical."

"Forget my own head next," said Rina.

"And where were you that evening, Mr Arden?" asked Ian.

"Had dinner with a friend," said Jav. "Went home after."

"At what time—"

Arthur cleared his throat. "Pardon. What's the relevance here?"

Ian didn't look away from Jav. "When did you arrive at St Ophie's Hospital?"

"I don't recall precisely. May have broken a few speed limits."

A vein twitched above Ian's eye. "Understandable. Miss Arden was admitted as a Jane Doe. How did you hear about the incident?"

"Mr Garner, we're twins." Rina pressed a hand to Jav's cheek. "I always know if Jav is in trouble. One time, when we were seven—"

Arthur cleared his throat again.

"So, telepathy?" asked Ian in the world's most polite deadpan. "I wasn't aware that you're an aptee, Mr Arden."

It was clear sarcasm – there were no such things as telepaths – but the proximity to the truth sent a jolt of panic down Jav's spine. "I got a call," he blurted. "From the hospital."

Ian stilled. "Who did you speak with?"

Jav looked desperately at Arthur, whose eyes promised a thorough scalding afterwards. *Bollocks.* "Not sure. But I don't want anyone getting into trouble. We're very grateful to the St Ophie's staff..."

"Indeed," said Ian, unconvinced.

Nick's expression was affixed in bland concern. When he noticed Jav's attention, his gaze sharpened. They were very green.

Jav looked away.

"Well," said Arthur, slapping a hand to his knee. "We should let you two get back to your busy schedules. Unless there's something critical we haven't discussed?"

Ian reeked of distaste, calloused as his hands. Nick was harder to read – disinterest didn't usually taste this strongly of contempt. After a moment, they both stood.

"I look forward to the write-up," said Arthur.

"Of course." Ian nodded to Rina. "Get well soon."

"Thank you," said Rina. "Oh bother, I left my—"

"Bag in the other room," Jav finished, pushing open the door.

Rina turned to Arthur, Ian, and Nick, "I'll be just a second, then I can walk you all out."

"That's not necessary, Miss," said Nick.

"I'll show our friends out," Arthur said. "You get some rest."

Rina blew Arthur a kiss. "Thank you. Safe trip downstairs, gentlemen."

"We'll be in touch," said Ian.

Rina tugged Jav through the door, reanimating Pascal who likely hadn't moved an inch the whole interview. As soon as they were out of sight, Rina's expression wiped blank.

"Look, I'm sorry," Jav began. He stopped short at her glare.

They returned to the briefing room.

Rina went straight for the locked drawer and fished out her phone. "*We have to plant a call at St Ophie's. Yes, I know what we had* planned, *I'm telling you the new plan.*" She stared at Jav the whole time she spoke, irritation thrumming. "*Do you think Marc would be that thorough? Pin it on someone unimportant, then. Intern, nurse, whatever. Fine. Talk soon.*"

"Rina," Jav tried again, "I had to give him something plausible. Ian felt really sceptical."

"You should have kept your mouth shut when Arthur gave you an out."

"But Ian was on edge," Jav protested. Rina's displeasure felt like ice against his teeth. "Like he knew something. If there's an easily explained quest—"

"What's done is done. Peter will take care of it." Rina circled his wrists with her thumb and forefinger, in lieu of suppressors. He blinked rapidly at the touch; nerves blown wide open with anxiety. "What else did Ian feel like?" she asked.

"Suspicious. He was waiting for us to slip up, I think."

"He bought your line about the cameras, at least." His twin let go, rolling her eyes. "Stop with the guilt, I feel crap already."

Jav rubbed his wrists, self-conscious. "Sorry, I can turn my suppressors on. Have the police asked for surveillance records? Were you even in the building when you said you—"

"Not your problem."

"I'm *worried* about you."

"Yes." Rina slid on a pair of dark sunglasses. "I can bloody feel it."

They left the room together, arms linked. As they emerged into the voluminous lobby, Jav sensed pinpricks of attention on the back of his neck.

"Miss Arden," said the receptionist, standing as they approached. "So glad to see you up and about. I can't believe you're in the office already."

To Jav's shock, Rina acknowledged her existence.

"Not yet." She peered over her sunnies. "The police just wanted to chat about what happened. Paperwork."

The receptionist nodded, vibrating with curiosity. "We were all so shocked when we heard." She cleared her throat, glancing at Jav. "Good afternoon to you too, Mr Arden."

Jav smiled back. "Afternoon, Yvonne. I best shuffle Rina home. Doctor's orders."

"Yes, of course. Feel better!"

As they walked away, Jav raised an eyebrow at his twin. "You want to tell me what that was all about?"

Rina raised an eyebrow. "Didn't you see the email? Went round corporate this morning."

They stepped into the lift. The existing occupant took one look and legged it, briefcase in hand, head down. Rina grinned.

"What email?" Jav turned on his phone to find four missed calls and twenty-seven texts. They were all from Stephen. Jav switched to his work account – and froze. "We told the entire office?" Rina shoved him out of the lift, through the lobby and towards the waiting car. "Lord, *please* say you ran this past Giulia—"

A flare of indignation. "I don't need her *permission.*" Rina slid into the passenger seat, slamming the door shut. "For your information, it was mum's idea. And it's company policy."

"Policy. You wanted to follow *policy.*" Jav punched the home icon on the dashboard. The car hummed to life, wheels swivelling forty-five degrees and sliding them horizontally out of the parking space.

"What do you think is gonna get more coverage? Some boring audit, or..." Rina leaned in for a dramatic whisper, "an assassination attempt?"

"You're not important enough to be upgraded from 'murder'."

"Excuse you."

"Seatbelt, please."

Rina held Jav's gaze, reclining her seat until she lay fully horizontal. "No."

Exasperated, Jav reached over to strap her in, receiving twenty individual finger jabs to the stomach for his trouble.

"Let's stop for food on the way home," said Rina. "Being pathetic was exhausting, I don't know how you keep it up."

Jav desperately wanted a nap.

RINA DEMOLISHED an entire bento in five minutes and spent the rest of the ride licking soy sauce and wasabi off her chopsticks.

"You could have shared." Jav ducked as Rina attempted to grab his nose with her lipstick-stained chopsticks.

"You're off to a sushi feast in three hours. Without me."

"Oh, I'm *sorry,* did you want to come too?"

"I dunno, is Ethan straight?"

Jav shot her a stink-eye. His phone flashed insistently as they pulled into the garage. Stephen, again.

"He could be bi." Rina kicked off her heels, catching them deftly by the straps. "Hedge our bets. Plus, I'm still hungry."

Jav's phone kept ringing. He swiped the screen. "For heaven's sake, *what?*"

His best friend's voice blasted through the speakers. "Ayy! You've been avoiding me," Stephen whined. "Clara says hi, by the way."

"Hi Clara," said Jav.

Rina shoved her face close. "Hiii Clara." And promptly disappeared into the living room.

"Oh my god, Rina!" said Stephen. "Are you okay?"

"She's gone already, but yeah, she's fine," said Jav. "Isn't it late over there?"

"Yeah, but I was up talking to mum and dad. They're freaked out by everything. Even Nath is worried. He 'sends his well wishes', by the way."

Jav pulled a face. Nathaniel was Stephen's older brother. Their parents – Harold and Harper Mansfield – were godparents to all the Arden children, and vice versa with Jav's parents and the Mansfield brothers. Nath shared Giulia's birthday because their mums wanted all their kids to pair off as best friends, and timed things accordingly. They needn't have bothered with Nath, who was standoffish and shared nothing with Giulia except eldest-sibling solidarity.

"How are the in-laws?" Jav asked, taking the stairs two at a time. He pushed open his bedroom door.

"Almost-in-laws," laughed Stephen. "Clara's āmā still hates me. Keeps calling me 'white ghost' in Taiwanese. She doesn't know that I understand her now."

Jav snorted. "Oh, I think she knows. Did Nath end up flying over?"

"Unfortunately. He's such a micromanager, but eh. There's a lot on, with the new-gen fusive prototypes and RFIs for Project Earthflown."

Both Stephen and Nath worked for Ascenda, the Mansfield family firm which dealt in construction, property, and infrastructure – including water infrastructure. Stephen never took his nepotism as seriously as his brother...at least, until three years ago. Because three years ago, Jav introduced Stephen to Clara Zhang – the same Zhangs that brought fusive cells from theory to practice. Overnight, Stephen gained an unforeseen interest in telekinetic engineering and batteries.

It was a match made in both business and heaven. Frankly, Jav never got enough credit. Nor had Stephen put in half as much effort in finding Jav *his* soulmate.

"The food though. Baos for days." Stephen's voice turned away for a moment. "*Hun? I gotta help Jav with a crisis—*"

Jav frowned at his phone. "What crisis?"

"*—want me to get...okay.* Turn on the 'gram, I haven't seen you in forever."

"It's been a week."

"Holo-gram! Holo-gram!"

"Lord, fine," said Jav, before the chanting could begin in earnest. "Gimme a sec." He set his phone down, swiping the holo-streaming function and shrugging off his suit jacket.

The camera threw up a three-dimensional projection of Stephen, whose face was split in a familiar grin. "*Oi.* Come back."

"This is linen, it'll crease if I don't hang it up." Setting his jacket aside, Jav returned his empathic suppressors to their homes, recessed lights glowing as he pulled out the locked drawer.

"Sooo," drawled Stephen. "You excited for your date?"

Second-hand emotions couldn't be felt remotely, of course, but they had known each other since diapers. Jav's brain long associated Stephen with bursts of genuine happiness, such that mere pixels now triggered endorphins.

"Not a date," said Jav.

"Not with that attitude."

Jav flopped backwards onto his bed. "I have a migraine."

"Oh no...painkillers not helping?" Stephen flomped over in sympathy. They stared at each other across the gulf that was the carpet at the end of Jav's bed.

"They wore off already. Gotta wait another hour."

"You can't date successfully with a migraine."

Jav rolled over, face down in his duvet. "It's not a date," he muttered.

"What was that?" Stephen cupped a hand to his ear. "I can't hear bullshit very well, in my old age."

Jav moaned into the fabric. "I think it's a 'thank you' dinner."

"We've been over this. You said Ethan didn't want a 'thank you' dinner."

"He said *a* dinner."

"There's no such thing as 'a' dinner with someone who saved your sister's life. It's either a thank-you dinner or a sexy dinner. If the other doctors aren't coming, then it's a sexy dinner. Are you taking him somewhere sexy?"

"Ito-an. His friend told me to pick born seafood."

"Ito's is classy. And good that his friends are in on it."

"No, she just gave me a list of...demands."

Stephen leaned towards the camera. "Text Ethan directly then."

"I still don't have his bloody number."

"Oh. Fail. Did you accept my mark-ups? Your note was way too stuffy."

"I did everything you said, and it was *awful*."

"Did you keep sending flowers?"

"No. Ethan asked me not to."

"You gotta put your money where your mouth is. Clara loves flowers even though she says they're a waste of water."

"Well, it's too late now." Jav chewed his lip. "He thinks I'm an idiot."

"That's fine: Clara thinks I'm an idiot and we're getting married!"

Jav gave Stephen a baleful stare. "You *are* an idiot."

Stephen worked the m-word into any and every conversation these days. Jav couldn't even blame him. Clara had a rock-solid aura and was one of the few people who Rina actively liked (as opposed to passively disliked).

"I insulted the hospital where he worked and implied that he was incompetent. *After* he saved Rina's life." Jav slapped a pillow over his own face. "He thought I was on drugs."

"Okay. Not the best start. But you said he took the apology well."

Jav freed one eye to squint. "I made him laugh..."

"That's good."

"*At* me, not with me."

"Choosing beggars, mate." Stephen wiggled his eyebrows. "If he wasn't interested, he wouldn't have said yes to dinner. Dinner is what you do before getting *done*."

"How profound."

Stephen fancied himself a relationship counsellor. But it was hard to begrudge him when he and Clara hummed with affection whenever they were in sight of each other. Jav aspired to have someone look at him with the same fierce exasperation.

A horrible thought occurred to him. "What if it's a pity date?"

Stephen made a noise of ominous hesitation. "You're admitting it's a date."

"What are we even going to talk about? I should have asked him out to coffee instead. Or brunch."

"Anything before five is for cowards. This is why you should see more people! You'd be less nervous if you practised."

"...You know why I don't," said Jav quietly.

Stephen sighed. "Look. There are plenty reasons *other* than empathic projection that people might want to date you. Money. Sex. Money. *Money.*"

"How reassuring." Jav rubbed his eyes. "I thought omakase was smart. Someone interrupts you every few minutes with food, so even the longest awkward silence wouldn't be that long. Right?"

"Ugh."

"*Right?*"

"Don't overthink it." Stephen waved. "Just look hot and pay attention. You have a good listening face. Take a bath before you leave."

Jav glanced at the timestamp at the edge of the hologram. He had about two hours. "Good call, I look like death. Wait, tell me which suit to wear."

Leaping off the bed, Jav made for his walk-in which began life as a guest bedroom but now served as his wardrobe. Floor-to-ceiling windows bracketed wooden shelving, framing the Chelsea sunset.

He returned with two outfits, holding them up for the camera. "I'm thinking casual, since Ethan's coming from work. Navy or slate? I don't want to send the wrong message."

Stephen yawned. "What message?"

"That I'm straight."

"Ha!"

"So? Which one?"

"Can't tell. Chuck them on."

Jav undressed. Years of costumes, greenrooms, and frantic backstage swaps made even the fiddliest of buttons a matter of muscle memory. He was pulling on the second outfit when a new figure came into view.

It was Clara, wearing a silky negligee, stylus tucked behind one ear. "Are we playing dress up?"

Stephen's head whipped around.

Jav had about two seconds before he lost Stephen completely. He snapped his fingers. "Oi, focus—"

"*Baobei*!" Stephen cried.

Clara traded kisses with Stephen over the back of the couch. "This has been a very long 'crisis'. I'm feeling neglected."

Jav cleared his throat.

Stephen didn't look up from where his nose was buried in Clara's neck. "Mate, I gotta go."

"Tell me if you'd wear the navy or the grey one."

"Navy."

"Okay, grey it is."

"This for the date?" Clara flashed Jav a thumbs up as Stephen worked kisses down her throat. "You look *fine*. Stop stressing."

"...Thanks."

"It's almost one." Clara pushed Stephen away with a palm to the face. The camera shifted briefly out of focus as she walked towards it. "Debrief us later, yeah?"

"Good luck!" called Stephen.

The call disconnected with a cheerful chirrup. Silence rushed in to fill the space where the hologram had been.

Jav caught sight of his forlorn expression in the mirror. "Look hot and listen well," he muttered. Taking a deep breath, he smoothed his lapel. "Well. At least you've already made the worst impression possible."

SIX

Six-thirty loomed fast like an unexpected shadow. It surveyed Jav with the gaze of a cat: dispassionate in the face of dry food, luminous yellow on the dashboard. He had muted all his contacts after several rounds of hope-then-disappointment every time his phone lit up.

"Stop it," Jav muttered into the silence. "Patients can't wait; you can."

He checked his hair in the rear-view mirror again, pinching the collar of his shirt with a critical eye. His watch and cufflinks were polished to a shine, doubling as empathic suppressors. He fiddled with the on-off mechanisms, settling on 'off' with a guilty pang. Given their rocky introduction, the thought of traversing dinner with five senses instead of six left Jav queasy.

6.45 pm.

It wasn't the *lack* of experience wining and dining: between ballet sponsors and business cocktails, projecting happiness was easy. Ignoring the headache was the real challenge.

Contrary to popular belief, empathic projection required much more effort than empathic reception – if the empath could project at all. Most empaths spent their lives overwhelmed by others' emotions. This mostly-one-way street didn't stop the pervasive anxiety of empaths as omniscient mind readers.

There was limited literature, and Jav only had a sample size of one. His mum always explained the headaches away as a strength of his aptitude, her pride warm enough to lend comfort. Still, he rarely left the house without suppressors on. That brought its own debilitating migraines, come evening, but at least he could take sleeping pills and knock himself out.

Maybe music would settle his nerves. Jav gestured for the volume... and promptly had a heart attack when a text notification pinged through the car's speakers.

> 18:55 · UNKNOWN — Running late. Out in 5, are we still on?
>
> 18:55 · UNKNOWN — This is Ethan by the way.

"Yes!" Jav exclaimed to nobody. He allowed himself three seconds of excited vibrating, then composed himself.

> 18:56 · JAVIER — No rush. I'm out front :)

Disproportionate relief fizzed with anticipation. Saving Ethan's number, Jav checked his hair one last time and got out of the car. The damp night clung to skin and clothes with an aspiration of snow. People hurried past, anxiety clouding their features. Jav stuffed both hands into his pockets, trying not to fidget with his suppressors.

Minutes later, a pleasant flare of recognition hit Jav in the side of the neck. He spun around.

"Sorry I'm late," said Ethan. "Hope you haven't been out here for long?"

Jav's stomach made a bid for his rib cage. "Not at all. Perfect timing."

"Were you running late too?"

"Oh. Um." Jav cleared his throat. "I was waiting in the car."

Ethan's smile creased his eyes. They were grey, pale as the glass behind him. "A while, then. Sorry, my handover got delayed."

"No doubt you're in high demand."

"Eh, admin waits for no-one." Ethan wore a shirt and blazer over dark jeans plus a shapeless coat – one arm in and one arm out. His ankle boots disappeared into the long silhouette of his legs. "You look nice."

Jav's eyes darted back to Ethan's face. "Thanks. You look—"

"Casual?"

"—lovely."

Ethan was tired about the eyes, but no less cute for it. His smile did not sit generously on his mouth, but was offset by the charcoal sweep of his eyelashes and a gaze as dry as Giulia's favourite vermouth. Ethan's unruffled presence outlined every feature in flattering shadow, making the slope of his neck all the more attractive.

Jav wondered if all doctors were so anchor-steady by training, or whether it was just healers. He felt two parts overdressed and ten parts smitten. Jolting to life, he realised the silence had stretched a tad long. "Let's get you out of the cold."

"Where're we off to?" Ethan fell into step beside Jav.

"Ito-an." The car door unlocked at Jav's touch. "Edo style sushi. I hope that's alright."

A bright splash of surprise made him pause.

Ethan was staring, bug-eyed at the vehicle. "Is this a vintage engine or just the shell?"

"Uh...I think it's the original guts too?" Jav had prepared for many conversation topics, but car talk had not made the agenda. In fact, he picked *this* car because (a) it was less flashy than any of Rina's, (b) it complemented his suit, and (c) a convertible would have been too forward.

Jav lifted the passenger door for Ethan, who ogled the car's matte exterior for a beat longer before ducking in. Jav took the driver's side, not that it mattered in driverless mode. Given the claustrophobic veins of London's Metropolitan Grid, Stephen's joyflying was the only time their cars went on manual. Right now, Jav deeply regretted tuning out of Stephen's car-talk.

"I've only ever seen photos of this model," Ethan gushed, giddy like popped champagne. "Oh my god, the original joysticks!"

The car hummed to life.

Ethan pulled at the double seatbelts. "You kept the racing harness. I love that this is kitted out for dives and flips. Have you ever flown off-grid?"

There was clearly a right and a wrong answer.

"Sometimes?" said Jav.

Ethan strapped himself in, propping his elbow on the armrest between them, curiosity hitting the back of Jav's tongue. Ethan's attention was palpable.

Oh, thought Jav dizzily, *you're one of* those *people.*

"You don't get motion sick, do you?" asked Ethan.

"Not exactly," said Jav, unwilling to admit it took him an hour to recover after Stephen's loop-de-loops.

"Have you got the boring new software, or the good stuff?"

Ethan seemed much more enthused by the car than Jav's company, but the night was young. There was still hope if Jav could recall any car trivia.

"The good stuff?"

Ethan's expression turned sly, eyes glinting like coins in a magician's hand. "You know, all that Eighties code. Before the new safety regs came in. I can see the wings and stabilisers: this baby was built for free falls."

"Free falls?"

"Is there an echo in here?"

"Sorry." Jav laughed – louder than was attractive. "I'm not sure about the specs. It was a birthday present from my godparents."

"Damn." Ethan drew out the vowel. The car took the express flightpath up three Levels, the coloured lights casting Ethan's profile in neon. "I've never gone diving in a Bugatti before..."

"You could take her flying next time. Once we know it's safe."

Ethan raised an eyebrow. "Next time, huh? Wait, you'd let me fly?"

"...Yes?"

"I don't have a licence."

"Do you know how?"

"Nope." Ethan's bemusement was like a gulp of whisky. "Naughty. I could get us both killed."

"There are fail-safes, right? Plus, you're a healer."

"Healers aren't necromancers, no matter what the movies will tell you. Especially where brain injuries are involved."

"Well, I don't know how to free dive either, so I'd have to enlist a friend."

"They're good, are they?"

"He's...fine." A rapid montage of Stephen tearing between skyscrapers played behind Jav's eyelids. Stephen's adrenaline-endorphin rush was always visceral – and once amplified by Jav's empathic feedback loop, euphoric. Rina loved it. Stephen loved it. Jav endured the police-station visits for their happiness.

"He single?" asked Ethan. He laughed at Jav's scowl.

"Engaged, actually."

"Congrats?"

"And straight," Jav added.

"Oh," said Ethan. "My condolences."

ITO-AN WAS TUCKED down a laneway in Upper Soho: an island of slatted bamboo amidst a sea of glass and brick facades. People were out enjoying their Friday evening, the streets overspilling with music and the clink of cutlery. The sepia contrasted the grey-blue of Lower London.

Someone wolf whistled as the Bugatti glided to a stop. Ethan stumbled onto the kerb.

"Careful," said Jav, rounding the bonnet.

"I thought the ground was closer. Where to?"

"Just up here." Jav chanced a hand to the small of Ethan's back.

Behind them, the car pulled itself back onto the road, disappearing through an intersection. Ethan turned to watch it go.

"I'll call it back once we're done," Jav said.

"You aren't worried about it getting keyed?"

"It's not going to a *public* parking facility."

A long L-shaped counter dominated the restaurant interior; fifteen seats facing three chefs. Ito was a balding man in his seventies, slightly bent over but energetic. As they took Jav and Rina's usual seats, Ito looked pointedly from Ethan to Jav.

"A friend," Jav supplied.

"I see." Ito's hands flitted: knife, ingredients, white cloth, rice. Two decades in London had sanded his accent. "Anything you don't like, tell me."

Ethan nodded, curiosity burning in lovely kerosene. He was taking in the restaurant, examining the jade chopstick holder. All of Ethan's fingernails were filed down to the quick, palms smooth and unblemished. "You come here often?"

"Of course. I couldn't take you somewhere I hadn't vetted," said Jav.

"How did you know I liked sushi?"

"Vegas told me."

"Oh."

"She was very insistent that I took you somewhere born not grown." Ethan rolled his eyes. "No one can tell the difference, right?"

"Depends on the texture, I think. Especially with seafood."

"Quite right." Ito presented two pieces of glossy tuna. "*O-toro.*"

Taking a bite, Ethan's pop of happiness smoothed out his brow. "Shit, this is good," he groaned.

Jav almost missed his own mouth with his food.

"*Chu-toro,*" said Ito, placing two more pieces as soon as they were done chewing. The chef radiated airy satisfaction as he prepared the next roll, pressing the rice down onto nori and swiftly shaping the sashimi.

"I take back what I just said about grown seafood," said Ethan.

"Saké?" Jav offered.

"Why not."

After the rolls came ikura, followed by a steady procession of translucent fish, eel glazed with a lacquer of miso-soy, aburi scallops, and squid sliced so thin it draped like melting sugar. They ate in companionable silence, the soft chatter of the other diners fogged by a recording of water burbling on stone.

Ito's restaurant was always soothing.

It was difficult to feel hard-done-by while eating delicious food.

"So." Ethan picked at the palate cleanser. "What do you do, then?"

Ah. Back on script. "I work with the Arden Foundation."

"Sounds...charitable." Ethan's previous bright interest dimmed.

"Yes," said Jav automatically. "I've only been there for about a year, so it's still new. We're involved with a lot of research grants. Not on par with what you do, of course."

Ethan blinked. "Well. I imagine the money goes a long way compared to one person in the emergency department."

"But you save lives every day," said Jav. Ethan's dry expression threw him off kilter. "You're doing God's work."

"God's the one sending them to the hospital in the first place. And it's not like I had a choice."

"You didn't want to pursue medicine?"

"When you're a healer, it's a waste not to, right? Mum was a doctor too. Dad said I went through a pilot phase when I was little." Ethan shrugged. "Did you always want to be a charity person?"

"Public relations. Not something people dream of."

"What were you doing before that?"

"Sorry?"

"You said you started this gig a year ago. What were you doing before?"

Jav hesitated, wondering if Ethan was about to write him off. "I was with the Royal Ballet."

A flare of interest. "As a dancer?"

Jav perked up. "Yes, I was a principal for about three years. I still teach part-time, and I get to branch out from classical."

Ethan gave him an obvious once-over and Jav resisted the urge to preen. "Huh. How long have you been dancing?"

"Since I was six. We lived in Paris for a little bit with mum's parents—"

"We?"

"Rina and I. You met her, sort of."

"Right. You don't have an accent."

Jav laughed. "I moved back to London when I was twelve. Dad's British, see. I joined the Royal Ballet after graduation. Been here ever since."

Ito cleared his throat, glaring at the gunkan sushi, uneaten on their respective plates. "Quickly, please. I want to hear the nori crunch."

"Apologies, Ito-san," said Jav.

Ethan picked off one piece of glistening roe with his chopsticks.

"No, all in one bite," Ito commanded with grandfatherly authority.

"Yessir." Ethan gave Javier an amused look before shoving the sushi in his mouth. He gave Ito a thumbs up. "Yum."

"The flavour changes if you wait. This is uni: sea urchin."

"If you haven't tried it before, you're in for a treat," said Jav.

Ito made a shushing motion, pinching his index and thumb together like a duckbill. Ethan and Jav ate the next few dishes in silence, sneaking grins like children. Jewel-slices of fish were interrupted by grilled tiger prawns, followed by a set of miniature temaki overspilling with salmon roe.

"I have something special. Flown in." Ito slapped his board with a flourish. "Abalone."

"Ohhh," said Ethan. "Wow, it's trying to escape.'"

"You haven't had abalone for months," said Jav. "New supplier?"

"You never book," sniffed Ito. "No notice, no abalone."

"*Tsk-tsk*, Javier." Ethan nodded at Ito. "I'll make sure he books ahead."

"You will?" Jav asked hopefully.

Ethan held his gaze and threw back his saké in one, long swallow. Jav reached hastily for his own drink.

"Six months in advance," said Ito. "Waitlist."

Ethan tapped his shoe against Jav's ankle. "See you in six months."

"Months," Jav protested.

"No patience," Ito tutted, blanching the abalone. "Spoiled."

Ethan's cheeks were flushed with sake, shoulders relaxed. The hiss of the old-fashioned gas burner smelled of salt and stone. Jav couldn't stop smiling, despite Ito's knowing stare.

"Didn't peg you for a dancer," said Ethan after a moment.

Jav tilted his head. "What did you think I was?"

"A model. Or finance bro."

Jav choked on his drink, offended. "A *banker*?"

"You wore so many layers, who can tell? What did you think I was?"

"...A doctor?"

"Oh. Duh." Ethan ran a hand through his hair. "Hospital."

"I didn't realise you're such an expert on cars though."

"Nah. My ex is a mechanic."

"Right, right." Jav tried not to look too concerned. He needed Stephen back in London ASAP for a crash course on flying.

Ito came to his rescue, fanning out precise yellow rectangles. "Tamago."

Ethan picked up his chopsticks, fingers loose as if cradling a paintbrush. He had lovely pianist hands, steady and uncalloused. Absently, Jav wondered if healers could even develop calluses.

"Yum. I can die happy now," said Ethan, demolishing his egg.

Jav set his chopsticks down.

Ito raised an eyebrow.

"May we have some of this to go?" asked Jav.

"Ta ma-no-go," said Ito, deadpan.

"You let Rina take food away." Jav turned to Ethan. "Rina's everyone's favourite. I suppose we can get dessert elsewhere."

Ito's fondness paired better than any wine. "Kei?" One of the younger chefs turned immediately. "Extra tamago."

Within minutes, a little cloth-wrapped container appeared. Ito adjusted the knot at the top of the package before proffering it to Ethan with both hands. "Make sure Mr Arden books next time."

Ethan grinned. "A deal I can't refuse."

Jav stood, nodding at Ito. "Thank you. Delicious as usual."

Ito bowed, prompting a server to appear with their things. Jav held Ethan's coat out and received a promising look in return. It took Ethan three goes to thread his arms through the sleeves.

Ethan turned as they left. "We didn't pay?"

"I have a card on tab."

"Of course you have." Ethan's contentment settled over them both.

Jav loved it when words matched sentiment. He had never felt someone be so satisfied from *eggs*.

They stepped out into the brisk night air; the static of strangers immediately crowding Jav's periphery. He wanted to hold Ethan's hand – anybody's hand – to muffle the noise. They returned the way they came, shoulder to shoulder. The wind tore at their sleeves, but the Bugatti was there, waiting for them by the kerb.

Ethan stopped. "When did you call the car?"

"During dessert." Jav held the car door open. "Tamago's always last."

"Are we in a rush?"

Jav was mortified. "*No,* of course not. It's cold out and might rain. I didn't want you to be standing, waiting—"

"Javier," Ethan slid into his seat. "Relax." Someone catcalled across the street. A honk of a car horn. "And get in already."

He got in. The rest of the world went quiet with the slam of the door. Jav busied himself with his seat belt. "Fancy more dessert? Drinks?"

"Usually I'd say yes, but I'm stuffed."

"Same. I think Ito went full out today." Jav held the steering wheel, then took his hands off again.

Ethan yawned. "I can feel a food coma coming. I'm extra boring when I'm tired, sorry."

"I'm sure you won't be. Shall we drop you home?"

"Could we?" said Ethan, cheek on the headrest. "It'll be out of your way though. Back on Level 9."

"No problem, the car flies itself."

Ethan tapped his address into the dashboard navigation, and Jav tried to appear unaffected with the newfound information.

"Thanks for dinner," Ethan said. "You've got good taste."

Jav prayed that his voice remained in its normal octave. "I'm glad you enjoyed it." *Oh lord, how robotic.* "To be honest, I was a bit worried."

"About?"

"When Vegas told me you wanted to go to a sushi restaurant, I did wonder if it was a setup. That you actually hated seafood." Jav rubbed the back of his neck. "After the flower faux pas, and all that."

"You apologise too much but your gut instinct's right. Vegas *is* a troll."

"I think she and Rina would get along."

"Sending flowers to the entire A&E was a good move. She was impressed." Ethan held up a finger. "That's not an invitation to send any more."

Jav nodded. "No flowers. Got it."

"It's not a lifetime ban. But I'd hate to cross paths like that again."

A lead weight of disappointment sank fast into the pit of Jav's stomach. "Oh," he managed.

Ethan squinted. "As in the hospital. Because you only go to a hospital when you're injured or sick."

"Oh!"

Ethan rolled his eyes, but Jav couldn't feel much beyond his own phosphorescent relief.

The car dropped ever-so-slightly as they left the grid, stabilisers extending either side of the chassis.

Ethan patted the car. "Now, that's smooth."

Teals and oranges flickered through the window, rendering Ethan in cinematic stop-motion. He was the picture of drowsiness, head tilted back, hands curved around the tamago box in his lap. Jav couldn't remember the last time he'd felt so impulsively smitten and awkward. He tapped the dashboard, indecisive. Background music?

"That's a lot of classical." Ethan nodded at Jav's playlists.

"Ballet stuff," said Jav, swiping to the search bar. "What genre do you prefer?"

"Anything. Not long 'til I'm home anyway."

"Oh. Right."

"I don't know much about ballet. Only that you point your feet and go..." Ethan made a flourish that would have made Balanchine proud.

"Something like that," said Jav, pleased that Ethan had brought up the topic of dancing twice now. Usually, people tried to segue back to pharmaceuticals as quickly as possible.

Ethan eyed him thoughtfully. "Did you lift people over your head?

"Yes?"

"Have you ever dropped someone?"

"Only in practice. And it's usually a fast slip, not a drop. Thonk."

"Thonk indeed. Do you practise with sacks of flour or something?"

Jav huffed out a laugh. "No, no, we use the real thing. Human beings."

"Risky."

"We start with easier lifts. Years of rehearsal. I'd imagine med school is similar, but a lot more intellectually difficult."

Ethan snorted. "Not sure if I'd describe it as intellectual. Gotta think on your feet, I suppose. Memorising. Demo once, do it yourself."

"That's very modest. I'd be terrified. Are you trained by healers?"

"For the healing aspect, yes. Ish. You can only practise so much on organoids. The trouble is, if you make a mistake while regenerating, it can't be 're-done' easily. It's not a manual suture, which is the point."

"That sounds very stressful."

"Yeah, it can get intense. The OR is usually the most peaceful place in the hospital. Unless someone picks shitty music."

"I thought surgeons only rocked out on *Healer's Anatomy*." Jav tried to imagine solemn-faced Ethan bopping about whilst wielding a scalpel.

Ethan laughed. "Ortho's the place to go if you want to 'rock out'. Elective surgeries aren't usually too bad. But if you need a healer in a hurry, things aren't great. We're tools—" Jav frowned "—of last resort. Until we truly understand secondary healing, anyway."

It took a moment for Jav to place the aftertaste: apathy, there and gone. "That's certainly a utilitarian way of looking at it."

Ethan pulled a face. "Vegas says I don't have a filter. I shouldn't complain."

You don't sound happy, but you don't feel sad. "I wouldn't call that complaining." Jav bit his lip, hoping his sympathy rang clear. "Maybe you'll have a better soundtrack on your next operation."

The car wheels lowered as they rode the off-ramp to Level 9.

"I've been put on punishment vacation for two weeks, so I can blast whatever I want at home. Speaking of..."

The car stopped under the shadows of a blocky residential tower, windows chequered yellow and grey with life and absence.

"Ah," said Jav. "This is you."

"This is me," Ethan agreed. He thumped his chest, depressing the catch on the harness. Under the low ceiling, the pause grew intimate. "Thanks for dinner. I had a good time."

"Me too," said Jav.

Ethan considered him, a cat evaluating a stranger's hopeful hand. Jav wished he wouldn't tilt his chin like that, throat bared in sweeping cursive. Ethan turned away, palm on the door.

"Would you like to do this again, sometime?" Jav blurted out.

Ethan turned back. "Dinner?"

"Doesn't have to be dinner."

"I don't need thank-yous. It's my job."

Jav thumbed the unlocking mechanism on his watch-suppressor, a nervous habit. "That's not...I had a lovely evening. And would very much like to see you again."

"Oh." Ethan's emotions were fogged by Jav's own anticipation. "You know, I'm boring when I'm tired. And I'm always tired."

Jav wondered what Ethan wanted to hear – and whether anyone ever gave him the answer he was looking for, as opposed to the answer he expected. "You'd be surprised how many energetically boring people I know. Plus, you're tired right now and I find you perfectly charming."

Finally, Ethan smiled. "Let's do Sunday then."

Bingo. "A Sunday or this Sunday?"

"Latter. Unless you're busy?"

"No! No, I'm free."

"I'm gonna sleep for twenty-four hours straight. I'll be starving by the time I wake up. You can swing by around ten."

Jav bit the inside of his mouth, so buoyed he might have hit the ceiling if not for his seat belt. "Perfect. Shall we figure out a place later?"

"You can pick." Ethan pushed the door outwards and up. He swung one leg over the ledge...and promptly fell face-first out of the car. There wasn't even time for a customary flare of alarm – he simply vanished.

"Ethan!"

A disembodied voice: "Ow..."

"Are you alright?" Jav clambered into the empty seat as Ethan got to his feet.

"Thought the ground was closer." Ethan had grime on one cheek, his bottom lip swelling from a cut.

Jav fumbled for the first-aid kit in the glovebox.

"Is that a *plaster*?" Ethan wiped a hand across his mouth, smudging blood across his mouth. He wobbled and slapped a hand onto the roof of the Bugatti for balance. "Water bottle, quick."

Jav obliged, watching Ethan splash water on his face and scrub roughly with one hand. In one moment to the next, the abrasions faded, cuts smoothing back into unblemished skin.

"Thanks. Having this grit healed under skin is foul." Ethan handed Jav his water bottle back. "I may have had too much saké."

"But we ba— you don't sound drunk?"

"It's my legs. I'm perfectly sober above the waist."

"I think you hit your head," said Jav, still derailed by Ethan's sudden exit. "Let me walk you to your flat?"

"And have Vegas pay me out for the rest of eternity? No. You saw nothing."

"But—"

Ethan snatched the plaster from Jav's limp hand, ripped the packet open and slapped it across Jav's forehead. "There," he said. "For the wrinkles you're going to have if you don't *relax*."

They stared at each other, nose to nose, breath misting in the chill. Ethan's gaze flicked down. He thumbed the corner of Jav's lip, where Jav had nicked himself shaving that morning.

Then Ethan stepped back, nonchalant. "See you Sunday?"

"...See you Sunday," Jav echoed.

He waited until Ethan disappeared safely into the building before exhaling in a rush. Jav touched the plaster on his forehead, then the corner of his mouth. He smiled, unsurprised. The cut had vanished without a trace.

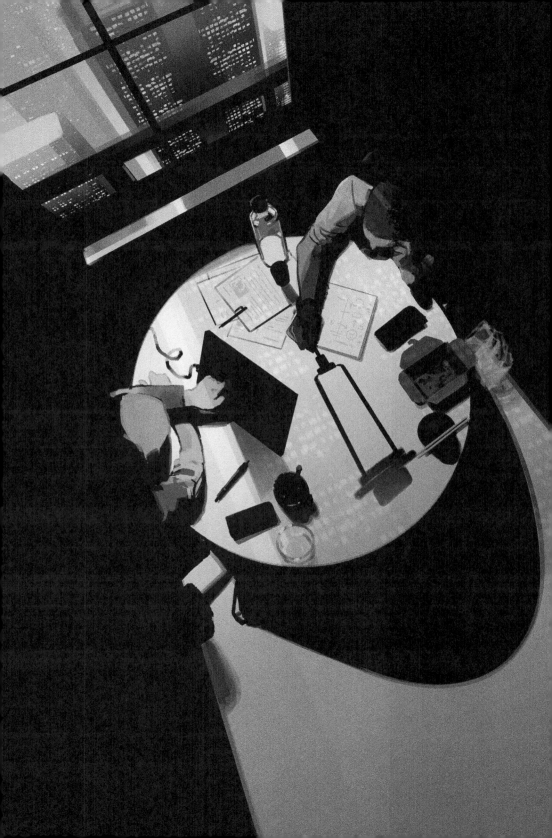

SEVEN

The Sentinel Studios, Upper Bloomsbury, Level 13.
Monday, 11 October.

Someone leaked the Arden HQ email to The Daily Herald.

"And the New Postal," said Florence.

Ollie slapped a folder against his face. "*I* broke that story," he fumed. "Corinna Arden even came up when I searched for possible firestarter employees! I cannot *believe* this."

Florence took a dead-eyed sip from her coffee mug, her third since their interview with a few Sixty-Fourthers several hours ago. Ollie just finished hammering out a write-up, but it felt overshadowed by the gleefully dramatic headlines: *Warning shots on the eve of the water vote!*

It was now 11 pm and they were surrounded by take-away boxes and charging electronics. With Corinna Arden in the picture, the stakes just got higher.

"We'd have been barred by patient privacy anyway," said Florence.

"Looks like the Ardens didn't care, seeing as they sent a mass office email five days later."

"At least your theory seems popular: that Hersch had something to do with Corinna Arden getting shot." Florence swiped her tablet. "'... *Arden Pharma has since released a statement confirming that Corinna Arden was the victim of the shooting last Sunday*'," she read. "*The leaked email also reveals that the 'incident occurred' as Miss Arden was leaving work late that evening...'*

'Neither the statement nor email mentions Timothy Hersch, an employee working at the same Level 9 facility the night of the shooting. Hersch was found dead in an auto-cab a few hours later...'"

"No one has claimed credit for the shooting yet," said Ollie. "But lone-wolf or not, we're now subjecting all Sixty-Fourthers to a moral litmus test, instead of talking about fusive versus CM15."

"So, you think the shooter was a water rights activist?"

"You *don't* think it was an activist?"

Florence yawned. "I don't think we have enough information. You said Hersch didn't have a gun on him."

"The police didn't find one, but he could have tossed it. Or Hersch had a friend waiting outside, and *they* shot Corinna Arden. Not sure how that explains the Yellowstone fire though." Ollie scratched his chin. "Does anyone know where Corinna Arden sits on Xu's Scale?"

The Xu's Scale measured the destructive risk of firestarters and telekinetics. It was often misapplied to other aptitudes and referenced in safety standards. Ollie pulled up the photos on his tablet, zooming in on the shattered window, pouring smoke.

"It's possible Arden tripped something combustible after getting shot," said Florence. "But those things are usually insulated against firestarters."

"I talked to the clean-up crew and building management at Yellowstone," Ollie admitted. "No burst pipes or shoddy batteries, that they know of."

"When the hell did you do that?"

"You told me Ascenda built the place. Figured they might also be managing the building, like with ours." Ollie grinned. "I may have also pretended to be a subcontractor."

Florence rolled her eyes. "One of these days, you're gonna get arrested. Has Nick got anything fun to share?"

Ollie groaned. "No, he's pissed about our article, even though I was *so* considerate about everything I heard at the precinct."

"The timing alone is suspicious. And I'm not talking about Hersch and Arden getting shot. There's no way those are unconnected."

"So you do think the shooter was a Sixty-Fourther."

"I didn't say that. But we're three days away from the CM15 subsidy vote. If they start phasing that out now, it'd put some real teeth behind the campaign promises for fusive water infrastructure. Demonstrate that Project Earthflown is more than a flash in the election pan." Florence drew five boxes with her stylus and labelled, in neat capitals: Hersch, 64er, Arden Pharma, CM15 Subsidy, and Project Earthflown. "We've got vulnerable MPs up for re-election in a few months, impatient water rights activists, a pharmaceutical monopoly...and a pot of public money."

She ruled a line between *CM15 Subsidy* and *Project Earthflown*, then an arrow down to *Arden Pharma*. "Ever since we broke the story about Hersch, it's all been about Sixty-Fourthers trafficking glass or stashing CM15 to turn a profit on the black market. It's hard to own the moral argument when people think 'both sides' are in it for the money."

"The focus on glass trafficking can't be good for Arden Pharma either. They're getting CM15 from somewhere, and the Ardens are the only game in town." Ollie rubbed his eyes. "Aren't Sixty-Fourthers blaming cheap CM15 for our glass epidemic?"

Over the years, Ollie and Florence's beats overlapped. Where CM15 went, corruption and glass followed – though neither the Ardens nor Langleys had ever been successfully prosecuted. Ian might have been driven to an early grave by now, had he not a healer for a son.

"I think this is all smoke," said Florence. "Noise."

After decades of anti-Arden sentiment, fusive-powered purification was finally gaining traction. Historically, the upfront cost of fusive-cells and retrofitting CM15-based water infrastructure had always been a political non-starter. The party in power never wanted to risk upsetting a major donor and committing to an expensive project, the fruits of which might be enjoyed by the opposition.

Project Earthflown's mere existence spoke to changing political tides, one that could no longer ignore the public resentment of their water bills.

"The Ardens must see the writing on the wall," said Ollie.

"Newer developments are fusive-ready, for those who can afford it," said Florence. "The demand for CM15 *will* go down, it's a question of what that transition looks like. How much Arden Pharma stands to lose, and how quickly."

"And how quickly is *my* water bill going down?"

Florence snorted. "We're in for a long wait. If the subsidies get cut faster than the retrofitting progress, we're the poor sods padding Arden Pharma's margin. That's if your neighbourhood gets retrofitted at all. I wouldn't count on it."

"Or here's a novel idea: we could let other pharmaceuticals compete on price."

"Given there's five ex-Arden execs and board members on the Earthflown developmental committee, I doubt they'll be blindsided by anything." Florence was still circling 'Arden Pharma' on her flow chart. "Corinna Arden getting shot is a great distraction though."

"You reckon it was a set up?"

"No. But the Ardens sent that office-wide email knowing it would leak. Might have been a Sixty-Fourther, like you said."

Ollie slumped in his seat, disappointed. "Right."

"Then Hersch overdosed on a post-heist high."

"Probably."

Florence squinted at him. "This was your theory. Why are you sulking."

"It's not adding up. If Hersch was skimming stock and delivering the goods, why did no one check in with the delivery guy when he failed to show? The shooting happened around midnight. We were tipped off five hours later." Ollie tilted his chair back on two legs. "It doesn't take five hours to go down five Levels."

"Maybe they got spooked. I agree there's a few too many coincidences. *I* could chat to Nick if he's mad at you."

"You were on the by-line too," Ollie muttered.

"Can't we bait him with Ethan?"

That wasn't a half bad idea. Nick never left Ethan on 'read', but Ethan went out of his way to be unhelpful whenever Ollie needed something. They'd have to route it through Vegas.

Yawning, Florence began packing her things. Ollie followed suit, the office lights flickering on as they walked towards the lifts. He elbowed the 'down' button to take them to the Level 13 street exit.

"Have you been enjoying my spreadsheet?" asked Florence. "Spotted anything that George and I've missed?"

After Ollie's encounter at the precinct, Florence had magnanimously granted Ollie access to her key-word alerts. They tracked Ascenda and other smaller bidders for the Earthflown tender, alongside meticulous annotations. Ollie had spent the ensuing week trawling the data. Neither Ollie nor Florence managed to find any red flags about the Yellowstone building.

He shook his head. "Not yet. There are heaps of false positives when I search – since Ascenda subcontracts to Arden Pharma for water fit-outs."

They watched the floor numbers tick down. "It's all very incestuous. Corporate incest. Harold Mansfield still has a controlling stake in Ascenda." At Ollie's blank look, Florence held up one hand, crossing her index and third fingers. "Harold Mansfield and Thomas Arden went to Oxford together. Pretty sure Mansfield is Corinna Arden's godfather."

"That's the least surprising thing you've said all night."

"I got excited, initially – but Ascenda's footprint in London means it was more likely than not that Yellowstone was one of theirs." Florence shrugged. "Still. A potential hook if nothing else."

"Better watch our backs if we want to follow the money."

The lift chimed to a stop. They crossed the deserted lobby, footsteps echoing.

"You headed to Level 9?" asked Florence.

"Nah, Level 4."

"Vegas still mad at you?"

Ollie pulled his beanie down over his ears. "Good-fucking-bye—"

"Don't slip and die," laughed Florence and gave Ollie a hug.

They split at the kerb, rain clinging to their faces. Ollie trudged towards the nearest light-rail station. He paused at the traffic light, feet drenched green from its reflection in a puddle. It reminded him of the vials of CM15, stacked neat and quiet behind a corpse.

The light turned red.

Ollie felt very much alone.

THERE WERE GENERALLY two kinds of stories: the ones you chased and the ones that chased you. As it turned out, Hersch was the latter.

After a few days loitering fruitlessly around Yellowstone and trying to get Ian on the phone, the story came knocking. Ollie received a call to his work number, the screen flashing on his desk.

"You've got a call," said Julian, the very embodiment of redundancy.

"Have you been demoted to my secretary or something?" said Ollie.

"It's distracting. You should pick up."

"*You* should mind your business."

The phone kept flashing. Ollie clicked accept. "'Ello, it's Roskopf."

A pause. Then a voice, scratchy, too close to the microphone. "The journalist?"

"Yes." Ollie drew out the vowel. "With whom am I speaking?"

"Tim didn't kill anybody."

Ollie slid his feet off his desk with a *thump*. "Right. And you are...?"

"Martin Hersch. You wrote those articles about my son."

Martin did not sound like a fan.

"I was a co-author—"

"Tim didn't do drugs. You've got it all wrong. The police...look, I need your help."

"I'm more than happy to talk—"

"Not over the phone. In person."

Ollie glanced at his calendar. Martin probably didn't like the way his son was implicated in an attempted homicide. The swirl of press and social media attention had not been kind, and this was unlikely to be a friendly chat. On the other hand, Tim Hersch's university classmates were being thoroughly unhelpful.

"Please," said Martin. "The cops won't believe me."

Ollie undocked his tablet one-handed and shoved his earpiece in. "Alright, sir. Where would you like to meet?"

OLLIE TEXTED FLORENCE in case Martin decided to murder him for implying that Tim had been a glass runner, an accomplice to an almost-murder, or both.

> 14:06 · OLIVER — If I don't text back tonight, come to this address to pick up my dead body. Send it to my dad, it'll make his day.

He was across London on Level 5 by the time Florence texted back.

> 14:45 · FLORENCE — Will I get any insurance money if you die? :)

Martin Hersch lived in one of the many brutalist towers that shouldered Lower London. The shadows were heavy here, dragging viscous against every shaft of light.

Ollie stepped up to the intercom and punched in Martin's flat number. "It's Oliver Roskopf. From The Sentinel."

"Fourth floor," came the same, gruff voice.

The lobby door clacked open. Checking the recorder on his lapel, Ollie stepped into a narrow lift which rattled the entire journey up. It deposited him into a beige hallway that smelled of damp carpet and unopened windows. In the middle of the workday, the building was drowsy with absence.

Ollie jumped at the loud *thluck* of a lock turning.

A door peeled ajar to reveal a threadbare man with red rimmed eyes. He waved Ollie closer, stepping back wordlessly into his flat. Swallowing his hesitation, Ollie paused on the threshold, eyes darting to the man's bare feet.

"Shoes are fine," said Martin.

"Thanks for reaching out," said Ollie. "I'm sorry about what happened to your son."

"Are you now," said Martin, expression static.

"Yes. I want to help if I can."

Martin was clean shaven, cheeks hollowed by grief. They stood beside a small kitchenette that crowded the doorway. Beyond, a couch and small table with two chairs, one bearing a jacket, one without. Curtains half drawn.

Ollie cleared his throat. "You wanted to chat?"

"Tim never did drugs," said Martin abruptly. "He had good grades. Went to some protests and things, but caused no trouble."

"And how would you like me to help, Mr Hersch?"

"I want you to right the bloody record." Martin shed inertia to anger. "My son was murdered and everyone's talking about it like it was his fault! Like he had something to do w-with that shooting. Somebody *killed my son.*"

Ollie held up his palms, placating.

Martin jabbed a finger at him. "You made it sound like he was part of some cartel. *You* fix it. If you tell the truth, then maybe the coppers will finally do their jobs and figure out who killed my boy. Do you know how many articles I've read that say...like it was some kind of...Tim's never so much as shoplifted—!" As suddenly as it came, the fury drained from the man's expression, skin raw with exhaustion.

There was a long, tense silence.

"Would you like a cuppa?" asked Martin.

Ollie blinked. "Ah. I'm alright. Thanks."

Martin opened a cupboard, retrieving two mugs as if Ollie hadn't spoken. There were a few dirty plates; a half-empty bottle of vodka on the counter. A Queen's College Debating Society magnet stuck to the fridge.

"One sugar?" asked Martin.

"Yeah, thanks," said Ollie, off balance.

"Sorry. My temper's not...it's been difficult."

"I totally understand, please don't apologise." Ollie accepted the tea. "I *am* sorry about Tim."

"Someone killed him." Martin held Ollie's gaze in a frenetic grip.

Ollie didn't flinch. "Do you have any idea who? I assume you've told the police everything that you're about to tell me."

"Course I did. And who knows? Thieves trying to steal CM15, and Tim just got in the way? Traffickers working for Langley? Hell, Arden Pharma? They're all crooked." Martin took a shaky sip of tea. "Tim was working a late shift. Wanted the extra overtime to save up for a trip."

"Can you think of anyone specifically who might have a grudge? Did Tim mention any hate online, threats...stuff like that?

"Tim got a few nasty messages after the 'One Drop' ad went viral. But I'm an ad man – I was proud of him! It was a great campaign. I didn't want to be overbearing, you know? He gets passionate about his causes." Martin kneaded his temple. "I should have told him to keep his head down. For heaven's sake, he still lives at home. Do you think I wouldn't notice if Tim was using glass? It wasn't an accident; it wasn't his fault."

Martin's oscillating tenses made Ollie's stomach knot with sympathy. "I'm sure you knew him best," he said, quietly. "So Tim wasn't behaving differently, staying out late...anything like that?"

"He was stressed about classes, I suppose. It's his last year at uni."

"Do you think his friends might have got him involved with... things?"

Martin shot him a flat look. "If by 'things' you mean water rights protests, then yes. Can't speak to much else."

"Maybe a friend asked Tim for a favour. To take advantage of his job at the CM15 depot."

"The cops told me that the toxicology report was pretty conclusive. But I know it wasn't an accident. I *know*, in my gut." Martin's words were rough like rosary beads between the hands of an agnostic. "You don't believe me."

"I want to believe you," said Ollie. "But the police and the investigators have access to evidence that we don't."

"I told them that Tim's never done glass before. They said overdoses are common for first time users."

"And now you want to go to the press to tell your side of the story?"

"No one's gonna believe me like that. The police won't do anything unless they're embarrassed into it." He veered between emotional and clinical. "I work in advertising. Messaging is important."

"Ah."

"I looked you up, before I called. You've been writing about glass for years. Water rights. Sixty-Fourthers."

Ollie straightened. "You mentioned Langley, before."

"Been reading your old articles, haven't I? That scandal a few years back about CM15 non-for-profit repositories having their stock skimmed for glass, the investigation into funny numbers. Wasn't there a Royal Commission?"

"Yes, there was," said Ollie, impressed. "But why would Tim get on Langley's radar?"

"Tim was shelving purifiers in the dead of night." Martin's voice rose in volume. "Maybe he saw something he shouldn't have. Wrong place; wrong time. For all I know, Langley and the Ardens are in on it. And if a big corporation is in on it, you can bet that the cops are in on it too."

Ollie could see the tinge of paranoia on Martin's skin now. Whatever the police had told him, it had clearly been too vague, too evasive. And to a grieving parent, that resembled a coverup rather than professional negligence. "Sounds like you've got a theory you're sure of," he said carefully.

"Someone's getting away with murder," said Martin, mouth trembling, pressed thin. "I'm going to find out who it is, if that's the last thing I fucking do."

Ollie felt like a fraud, to be so detached in front of a man coming apart at the seams. He had no frame of reference for this kind of loss, and perhaps should have been more guilty for feeling so invigorated by a good hook.

If it bleeds, it leads.

The last fortnight was a blur of insomnia, photos etched into Ollie's retinas. He missed Vegas something fierce. "I'm not sure what you'd like me to do. You don't want an interview—"

"Not yet, not until we find out who killed Tim."

"And you think *I'll* be able to do that?"

"You're an investigative reporter, aren't you? So, investigate. The police won't." Martin leaned forwards. "Please, I don't know what else to do. I can't afford a lawyer."

"Mr Hersch." Ollie rubbed his nose. "Martin. I promise I'll do my best. But police do have access to a lot of evidence that we don't. So they're either still investigating or there's not enough evidence to move forwards."

"You—"

"I'd hate to disappoint you, that's all. I can't imagine what you're going through, and I don't want to promise something I can't deliver."

"But you believe me?"

With a sinking feeling, Ollie saw the hope reflected in Martin's eyes. "I believe that things aren't as neat as the cops think. And I want to find out why."

Martin deflated. He ran a hand through his hair, thinning at the front and greying on the sides. "Okay," he murmured, "okay. Thank you." He stood, almost knocking over his mug. "I have the toxicology report. The autopsy. Will that help? You can take a copy." Without waiting for an answer, he disappeared into one of the bedrooms, returning a second later with a tablet. "They sent this yesterday. Anything seem off to you?"

Ollie chewed the inside of his lip. "I know a few doctors who could take a look."

"Right. Thank you." Martin glanced over his shoulder, into the room from which he had just emerged. Ollie could make out a blue duvet, drawers, and the side of a large desk. "Tim's room. The police had a look already, in case there was anything."

Ollie wondered how long Martin had sat in his son's room, toxicology in hand, waiting.

The flat was cramped: most London flats were, especially in the lower Levels before engineers figured out how to space things out without collapsing. An illustrated poster of Old London hung behind a computer monitor. Tim's desk was a time capsule: VR visor, styluses scattered near the keyboard, a gaming mouse on the left.

Martin followed his gaze. "Tim kept complaining about his laggy headset. Told him I'd get him a new one for Christmas..." He broke himself off.

Ollie stared at the mouse, heart racing. He pulled out his phone, navigating quickly to the photo album: Timothy Hersch, body stiff in death, face blank and eyes closed. Angling his screen away from Martin, Ollie swiped rapidly until he found the close-up shots.

Adrenaline punched him in the throat like a buzz of electricity.

"Martin, was Tim left-handed?"

"Yes. Why?"

"Glass is administered intravenously. Can be hit and miss, even if someone is well-practised."

"But Tim—"

"So if you're *not* experienced, why would you self-inject with your non-dominant hand?"

Martin's features went slack with shock. "Are you saying...?"

"That someone else mainlined your son? Possibly." Ollie held up the tablet. "I'm going to email this toxicology report to myself, that alright?" Martin nodded. "Here's my number. Give me a call if you think of anything else that might help, or if the police get in touch again – anything at all. I can't publish if they hit me with an injunction."

"Is this enough to prove...?"

"No, but it's a start. I need to talk to a few people. See if we can find you a lawyer, pro bono." Ollie held out a hand.

Martin's grip had a dead man's grip, bruising and cold. "Thank you," he said, consonants numb. "Thank you."

"Let's keep in touch. Good news or bad news, yeah?"

It took only three steps back to the dining table, and five to the door. It wasn't until he was out on the street, back amongst the living, did Ollie dare to breathe normally again.

EIGHT

Special Investigations Agency, Central London Precinct, Level 10. Thursday, 14 October.

What started as an olive branch became, like most enduring things, routine. Depending on his shift, Ethan would bring his dad lunch or dinner at the precinct. There would be fortnightly droughts if things got busy. But anything was better than the five-years they spent not speaking to each other.

Ethan had blurry memories of sitting in dad's office while mum was at St Ophie's. Like the institution it housed, the precinct clung to precedent and all its wear and tear.

The receptionist waved. "Ethan! Back so soon?"

"Have the week off. Is dad in?"

"Sure is, poppet. I've beeped him, so you can go right in."

He had about forty minutes to spare. After security, Ethan made his way on autopilot through the bullpen until he stood outside dad's office.

Before he could knock, a gruff voice called, "Come in."

Ethan opened the door – and stopped short. Sitting directly across from him was Oliver.

"—so if no one approached the car on Level 4, and the cameras on that Level 9 street corner *happened* to be malfunctioning, someone must have jabbed Hersch before he got into the goddamn cab!"

'Sitting' ascribed unwarranted structural integrity. Ollie was poured into the seat like a cat in a bowl, one ankle propped across the opposite knee as if he owned the place.

"Ugh," said Ethan, flat. "It's you."

Ollie grinned, teeth blinding against his dark skin, the picture of ease. "Nice to see you too."

"Ethan." Ian Garner stood, rounding the desk. "You're early."

"Hey, dad."

For an awkward pause, they just looked at each other. Then Ian pulled Ethan into a tight hug, smelling of recycled air and the same laundry detergent that Ethan still bought. At least one hug per visit. Stilted or not, those were the rules.

Cheek pressed against dad's collar, Ethan felt a torn nail, a mild burn on the palm. He leaned into the hug for a beat longer, just until they healed.

"How's your week off?" Ian asked.

"Fine. Here: wonton soup noodles, extra greens. Don't wait, it'll go cold."

"You know you can visit without bringing anything."

"The food around here is crap." Ethan pulled out two mandarin oranges and a pot of yoghurt. "Dessert."

Ollie leaned in. "Did those come with the noodles?"

"From the supermarket, dumbass." Ethan blocked Ollie's questing hand with an elbow. "Piss off. What are you doing here anyway?"

"My job," said Ollie.

"Being a nuisance," said Ian simultaneously.

Ollie pouted. "I came bearing new evidence—"

"I'm glad you've got time off," Ian interrupted, smiling at Ethan. "They work you too hard. When's your contract up again?"

"Next August, but I don't wanna transfer unless Vegas does."

When Ethan and his dad started speaking to each other again, Ian was hesitant to broach any hospital-related topic. They had moved past that now, but that meant regular fretting about Ethan's life-style choices. The hugs were worth it.

"Does Vegas have time off too?"

"No."

Ian frowned. "That's not fair."

"We don't have the same exact job, dad. She did want to do family dinner on Saturday if you're free."

Ian met Vegas when she and Ethan started at St Ophie's. Ian promptly adopted her; no doubt grateful that *anyone* was willing to befriend Ethan in med school. Vegas now orchestrated their family events, and Ian was clearly far more excited to see her than Ethan. *What was the point of being an only child if you weren't even the favourite child?*

"Sorry kiddo, work is gnarly. How about next Saturday: we can go out for Ollie's birthday, my shout. I assume Vegas has something else planned on Ollie's actual birthday."

Ethan smirked. "Nope, she dumped Ollie weeks ago."

"Is that right," said Ian. "Get out of my office, Roskopf."

Ollie threw up both hands. "Come on!"

"Soup's getting cold," said Ethan innocently.

Proper bone broth was expensive, but left to his own devices, Ian would be living on microwave pies. Coronary disease in a box.

Ian fished out a wonton. "I love this restaurant. You want one?"

"Nah, I'm meeting a friend for dinner."

"You don't have any friends." Ollie eyed Ethan's blazer. "Wait. Is that mine?"

"No. And stop manspreading."

Ollie plonked his feet onto the carpet. "While you're here: would you say it's common for someone to mainline with their non-dominant hand?"

"Quiet," Ian said sharply.

"I just want a professional opinion," Ollie batted his eyelashes. "Someone else must have dosed Hersch, he was left-handed—"

"Roskopf!"

"*Fine*. There are plenty of other doctors in London."

"Yes, ask one of those and leave Ethan alone. Don't involve Vegas either. I'll know, if you cite some 'anonymous source'."

Ollie's left knee jiggled as he visibly buffered for more bad ideas.

"O-*kay*," said Ethan. "I'll leave you two to it."

Ian's expression softened. "Get some sleep. And you don't need to trek me dinner on your week off. I can get delivery."

"But you never do." Ethan leaned in for a one-armed squeeze goodbye. "Gotta run. Love you?" He stumbled over the last two words – then stumbled for real when he smacked his elbow against the door frame.

Ollie sniggered. Clearly journalists survived on instant coffee and schadenfreude.

"Love you too," said Ian. "Try have an early night, okay?"

"Okay," lied Ethan, and closed the door behind him.

En route to the lobby, someone pinched Ethan on the arse. He slapped at the hand – and missed. "*Nick*, you piece of—!"

Nick laughed. "Ten–nil to me?"

"More like five–five."

Nick followed him into the hallway, smirking up a storm. He'd cut his hair since Ethan saw him last, darker blonde than the London winter deserved. Nick wore his grin like the sky wore the sun – that is to say, very well.

"Doesn't count if dad's not around to see," said Ethan.

"I'd rather torture him with his own imagination," said Nick.

Ian disapproved of workplace PDA. Naturally, Ethan and Nick kept a tally of who could elicit the most dramatic frown. It didn't matter that they weren't dating, per se. The mere implication was enough to trigger Ian's fatherly angst.

"Are you aware that Ollie's in there, being a pest?" asked Ethan.

"Must have slipped his leash," said Nick.

"I told you: don't let Ollie in near dinner time. He gives dad indigestion."

They came to a stop beside the main exit. Gale whistled past glass and concrete, created by the wind tunnels between the buildings, roads, and sheer drops. It wasn't as bad as central Upper London, but the howl was enough to raise hair from skin.

Nick leaned against the wall, crossing his arms. His shirt pulled tight over his shoulders; sleeves rolled untidily to the elbows. "It's been a while. You doing okay?"

"Yeah, just tired." *Like the last hundred times.* Ethan chewed the inside of his mouth. "Sorry I didn't text back."

"All good." Nick's smile was easy; all almond eyes and cuspids. "Night shifts?"

"Mhm."

"That's rough."

"Got to sleep a bit more this week. Can't complain."

"I'll be clocking off around seven tonight." Nick cocked his head. "You wanna...?"

Ethan blinked. If he hadn't run into Nick at all, would Nick still have asked? *I suppose it's called an arrangement of convenience for a reason.* "Can't, sorry. I have a thing." He waited, unsure if he wanted Nick to interrogate or let it go. He didn't know which was worse. "Maybe next week?"

Nick pushed away from the wall. "Sure. Text me."

Ethan swallowed. "Okay."

Nick considered him for a beat longer, expression inscrutable despite the smile. Then he gave Ethan a lazy salute and turned back the way they came. He was gone by the time Ethan unstuck his tongue.

It's not as if you'll be seeing much of Javier, soon. The impulsiveness of it all made time difficult to measure: Ethan couldn't say no to a third, fourth, fifth meetup. Javier's unequivocal interest was tangible, though he hadn't so much as tried to hold Ethan's hand. Even if it *were* to turn into something...judging by Nick's nonchalance, perhaps Ethan's permanent absence wouldn't be too different to what they had now.

Ethan glanced at the time, looked out at the grey rain, and called a cab.

THE JOURNEY TO COVENT GARDEN took an extra half-hour thanks to protesters on the main thoroughfares. According to Ethan's newsfeed, Sixty-Fourthers had detonated a homemade jammer, severing a key intersection from the city mainframe.

It was almost seven when Ethan arrived outside The Little Snail. By the time Ethan got inside, he was drenched.

The maître-d looked him up and down. "Evening, sir. May I help you?"

"I'm late." Ethan shook off his overcoat. "Booking's under Javier. With a J, not an X."

The maître-d examined what Ethan could only presume to be a definitive list of who was naughty and who was nice. Soft piano music floated through the low ceiling.

"And your name, sir?"

"Ethan."

The maître-d's expression cleared. "Dr Faulkner. Right this way."

A spiral staircase opened abruptly into an airy room, a wall of windows overlooking the opera house next door. Lamps hung from the double-storeyed ceiling; white linen tables crowded with silver. A grand piano greeted newcomers with polished teeth.

Javier stood as they approached. "Ethan," he said, a veritable vision in dimples and a three-piece suit.

It was like walking in front of a heater. Ethan blinked rapidly. "Hey. Sorry I'm late. Do we still have time?"

"Of course. Everything alright?"

"Just traffic." Ethan glanced around at the tuxedos and floor-length dresses. He realised that Javier was waiting for him to sit first. He sat, eyeing the menu. There were no prices. "Um. What would you recommend?"

He had been late for two dates out of five. While Javier didn't seem upset, Ethan could hear Tom's voice, sighing, 'It's fine, let's just postpone', and 'A break would work'. Nick took it a step further by meeting Ethan only at work or at home. At least Ethan's punishment vacation lasted only two weeks: not enough time for anyone to be disappointed.

Perhaps sensing his guilt, Javier said, "Pre-theatre is always a rush. That's why there's a set menu."

"You don't have to make excuses for me. I'm often late."

"Well, you have a very important job."

Ethan squinted. "It's my week off. I woke up late and dropped dad's dinner off – got stuck in traffic."

A rush of pleasant helium in his chest.

"You bring dinner for your dad?" Javier's eyes shone. "That's so sweet."

"He'd live off instant meals, otherwise. It's a medical precaution."

Javier treated Ethan with the same attentiveness of a trainee doctor. At least he was slightly less polished now, after four meals together in the span of a week. The only person Ethan saw this often was Vegas, and they lived together.

"I like junk food," Javier said, hushed as if confessing some unholy vice.

Ethan eyed Javier's waistcoat, dubious. "I thought dancers had athletes' diets. Nothing but chicken and sunflower seeds."

"It's not that strict. And I'm not performing anymore, so." Javier's expression fell for a split second, and Ethan felt a sympathetic squeeze in his stomach. "The real shame is my baby sister, Maddy. She has the perfect build for a ballerina. Straight lines. Great turn out."

"Turn what."

"The way one angles their feet." Javier held his hands out, wrists touching, thumbs angled away. "You can train your posture when you're young and bendy. But it comes down to the hips you're given, you know?"

Ethan lowered his gaze deliberately to Javier's hips and back up again. "I *don't* know. Maybe you can give me a demonstration later."

Javier ducked his head. For someone so well put together, he blushed easy.

The universe interrupted in the form of entrees. "The mains will be out shortly," said the waiter, bowing forty degrees.

To Ethan's immense satisfaction, Javier barely reacted, eyes glued to Ethan's face. "Thanks."

Five pieces of ravioli, stuffed with shellfish, were arranged on painterly strokes of sauce and microscopic dots of cream. Ethan's stomach made a disapproving noise.

Javier laughed. "We can get something more filling later."

"After? You said *Giselle* was two hours."

"We could go back to mine for dumplings."

"You're inviting me over, after dinner and a show. For dumplings?"

"Or whatever you fancy," said Javier.

Aha! thought Ethan. *We're finally getting somewhere.*

"We made paella over the weekend so that's still pretty fresh."

...Or not.

The Royal Opera House, Covent Garden, Level 9.

ETHAN REMEMBERED Christmas Nutcracker with mum, dad, and gran. The memories were too fuzzy for the wave of nostalgia that hit as soon as they stepped inside. Javier strode forwards with the confidence of someone who knew every alcove and fire-exit.

Ethan craned his neck back to admire the soaring frescoes.

"Those were reclaimed from the flooded original." Javier led them along a curving balcony. "The layout pays homage to the old design – even the obstructed box seats."

They stopped in front of the two remaining empty seats in the middle of the balcony. From their vantage point, Ethan could see the tops of the orchestra, warming up. The audience below was awash with stars, chandelier light catching jewellery and teeth.

Javier proffered a glossy programme. "Keepsake. You said it's been a while since you last visited."

"Yeah, I was six." Their last Christmas with mum. "I've never seen *Giselle* though. Want to speed-run the plot? No spoilers."

Javier beamed, eyes creasing. "Yes! Okay, okay, so. It's a love story." This close, Ethan could smell his cologne, woodsy with citrus. "Giselle is a beautiful peasant girl who falls in love with a duke who is pretending to be a peasant, so they can be together."

"Speaking as a peasant, that makes no sense."

"He's betrothed to someone else."

"So he's cheating. What's his name?"

"Albrecht."

"Is he hot enough to make up for the crappy name?"

"*Anyway*. Another gent has been pining after Giselle, and he thinks Albrecht is up to no good. When a hunting party with Albrecht's fiancé arrives, the secret is revealed."

"Wait, who's Mr Third-Wheel?"

Javier hesitated. "Hilarion."

Ethan guffawed so loudly that someone shushed them. He coughed. "Hilarion's not getting laid with a name like that."

"The story's set in Germany, they don't have English names." Javier pouted. "*I* don't have an English name."

"Sorry, but if you were called Hilarion, I don't think I could take you seriously either."

"Mum named me after grandpère, so thank her. By the way, both Albrecht and Hilarion are being played by my friends tonight."

A melodious chime, followed by a voice commanding all to silence their mobile devices. Javier watched Ethan switch off his phone with visible concern.

Ethan raised a questioning eyebrow.

"What if someone needs you?" asked Javier. "You're a healer."

"We're not on-call twenty-four-seven. You're not turning yours off?"

"Oh, it's been off since you arrived for dinner."

The lights dimmed leaving only the stage aglow, jewel bright. Ethan could feel Javier's attention, magnetic in the thick, velvet dark. They shared an armrest, shoulder to shoulder. The curtains rose with a swell of strings.

"Are you going to stare at me all night?" Ethan asked. Even without turning, he was willing to put money on Javier blushing.

"Sorry," Javier whispered.

"You're gonna miss what's happening."

"I already know how the story goes."

"Oh. Carry on then."

The shusher coughed, pointedly. On stage, a man was being dramatically indecisive about knocking on a door. The dancer took off his belt and sword with a flourish, turning this way and that.

Ethan hadn't expected people to start stripping five minutes in. Perhaps Javier was cannier than Ethan gave him credit for.

"He's saying 'tell me Jeeves, do I look hot in this?'" Ethan whispered.

Javier made a strangled noise, between a laugh and a shush. "His friend is telling him to break off his affair with Giselle."

The lady behind them coughed again, sending Ethan into a fit of undignified sniggers. Javier had a fist over his mouth.

Eventually they settled down, the live orchestral music sanding the edges from the day. Ethan rolled his neck against the back of his chair, the major thirds and tenths filling his lungs.

On stage, everyone had straight limbs and narrow hips. The women were weightless in their floaty skirts, anchored only by the points of their shoes. Perhaps it was the dark theatre, the comfortable seat, the warm line of Javier's presence...whatever it was, Ethan found himself biting back yawns.

He must have fallen asleep at some point because next thing Ethan knew, Giselle was stabbing herself with a sword.

"What!" Ethan jerked upright, almost clocking Javier under the chin.

"For pity's sake," someone hissed.

The strings were frenetic. Albrecht was sobbing over a dead body at the front of the stage. He tried to knife Hilarion, only to be stopped by Jeeves.

"Shit." Ethan rubbed his eyes. "What did I miss?"

"You just dozed off," whispered Javier. His left collar was flattened, like someone had fallen asleep on his shoulder.

Ethan could feel a matching imprint on his cheek. *Fuck.*

The curtains came down on a tragic tableau: everyone weeping, Giselle limp save for her pointed feet. The auditorium lights returned amidst applause.

"So." Javier smiled, cherubic. "What was your favourite part?"

Ethan slapped a hand over his eyes. "You said this was a love story!"

"People die from heartbreak, you know."

"I can't believe I missed the entire ballet."

Jav patted Ethan's arm. "That was just Act One."

Ethan flung a hand at the stage. "But she's *dead*."

THEY TOOK intermission in a green salon.

"We don't have to stay for Act Two," said Javier, sipping from a tall glass of water because that was what he was. "If you're tired. Or bored."

"I'm not bored." Ethan cleared his throat. "Ballet music is relaxing. The seat was comfy."

Javier touched Ethan's elbow with the back of his hand, careful. All his movements were constrained with a reserve uncharacteristic of a man who sent giant bouquets of flowers. "It's nice of you to humour me."

"Yes, well. I'm not sure what kind of romance is happening in Act Two if the main character is dead."

"Oh, she comes back. Would you like more cheesecake?"

"Don't mention necrophilia and change the subject."

Javier choked. "She comes back as a ghost! They dance and that's it."

"It's a ballet. Dancing is a euphemism for everything. You'd think a duke would have access to a healer."

"Not for a broken heart." Then, evidently convinced of Ethan's boredom, Javier said, "Would you like to visit backstage? I have a staff pass, so I can show you around. Or we can leave too."

Ethan didn't know how to explain that his body had been conditioned to sleep at any opportunity. The music and warm seats beat the on-call rooms at St Ophie's. "I don't mind. It's your evening too."

"I've seen *Giselle* a thousand times." Javier guided Ethan effortlessly through the crowd. "There's still ten minutes of intermission."

Ethan tossed his recyclable cup across the room. It dropped into the bin with a neat, ringing sound – eliciting a gasp of disapproval from a nearby grandmother.

"Good aim," said Javier.

"I'll have you know I can pop a headshot in a hundred yards," said Ethan. "VR airsoft."

"Then you and Rina would get along."

They ventured down a panelled hallway, through a few locked doors. Soon they were greeted by a cacophony of sound: discordant brass and low, thumping noises vibrating from the bowels of the opera house. The air was misted with hairspray. They stopped next to a door with a paper sign bearing '*Albrecht / Hilarion*' and a scrawled smiley face.

Javier knocked.

"Decent!" someone called.

The small room was bracketed by giant mirrors framed with lightbulbs. One occupant held a makeup brush while his companion perched on a stool, sipping water.

"Jav!" the first exclaimed. "You made it!" He pulled Javier into a vicious one-armed hug. His features were heavily obscured by stage makeup, but he appeared South-East Asian, dark hair stiff with gel.

Ethan blinked at the twang of his American accent.

"Who else would rate your jetés?" said Javier. "Aww, I missed you too."

"Since three days ago?" said the other friend. He stood a full head taller than everyone else, complexion inky dark.

Javier stepped aside, exposing Ethan to scrutiny. "This is Ethan. Ethan: Carter and Elijah. Or Albrecht and Hilarion."

"Nice to meet you," said Ethan.

Neither Elijah nor Carter moved to shake Ethan's hand. Knowing Javier, he had probably schooled them on healer etiquette.

"So *this* is the famous Ethan," said Carter. "Heard you saved Rina's life. Jav has been talking about you non-stop." He thumped Javier on the left pectoral.

Javier cleared his throat. "Aren't you meant to be heading to the wings?"

"Yeah, Carter," said Elijah. "Save some dignity for me to destroy."

"You enjoying the show so far, Ethan?" asked Carter.

"Yes," said Ethan, ignoring Javier's grin.

"Staying for Act Two?" asked Elijah.

"I thought I'd show him around backstage," said Javier.

Elijah frowned. "What, and miss my death scene?"

"Does *anyone* survive in this ballet?" Ethan wondered.

"Yep, me," said Carter, pulling on a flowy shirt.

"So Mr Cheater gets off while everyone else dies?"

"Giselle forgives Albrecht," said Javier. "He really did love her."

"Giselle should have blackmailed him and become a duchess," said Ethan.

"I like you," Elijah declared.

Javier looked a little lost. "Why *does* Albrecht get a happy ending?"

Carter bowed with a flourish. "Rich, white, and a man."

Elijah confiscated his friend's powder brush. "Any more foundation and it's gonna cake off."

"I don't want to be shiny. We can't all have your good skin." Carter shoved Javier playfully on his way out. "Behave yourselves!"

"Nice to meet you Ethan," said Elijah.

And suddenly Javier and Ethan were alone in the dressing room.

"Your friends seem nice," Ethan offered.

Javier's eyes were still on the closed door. "I'm glad Carter got the lead this season. Elijah's played Hilarion before, but..."

"You miss it."

"Yes, well. Do you still want to look around?"

He sounded so hopeful that Ethan couldn't help but smile. "Give us the tour then."

Javier's melancholy faded with each piece of trivia. He walked Ethan through a corridor filled with props on wheels, a fitting room stuffed with hangers and fabric, studios of dancers warming up.

Everyone knew Javier by name.

"The orchestra pit is through here. The floor's on hydraulics. And see that trapdoor? Giselle is lowered through, at the end, when her ghost returns to the grave." Javier checked his watch. "There's still twenty minutes or so 'til then." He led them up a flight of fire-stairs and out into a pitch-black hallway, pushing open a heavy set of swinging doors. "It's about to get crowded when the Wilis come off stage."

Soon, they were above the stage itself, ensconced by enormous drapes that reached into the rafters. The heavy thud of wood and feet betrayed the gravity that was inaudible to the audience. Dancers and stage crew rushed amongst the wings. The choreographed chaos reminded Ethan of the emergency department.

"Let's go up to the catwalk," whispered Javier. "There's no set changes in the last scene, so we won't disturb anyone."

They ascended two flights of steep metal rungs. Ethan winced every time the frame rattled and echoed, while Javier practically floated on the balls of his feet. At least the view was fantastic – almost enough to distract Ethan from the yawning void as they tread across the ribs of this giant, hollow beast.

Predictably, Ethan tripped. He hissed, arms windmilling.

"Careful!" Javier caught him beneath the armpits and lifted Ethan neatly onto the landing.

Ethan's heart thumped loudly in his throat. "How many stories up does this go?"

"Fifteen-ish. They store entire backdrops out of sight up here. See *Don Giovanni* with the windows?"

Dark plaster sheets, the size of warehouse walls, hung in front of and above them. It felt like being inside a doll's house.

"Imagine being crushed underneath that," said Ethan. "Cool."

The music soaked them to their waists, roaring up from the stage like inter-Level gale. Javier leaned over the railing like a handsome death wish, enraptured by the stage lights upon his friends on the stage below.

Ethan's weak knees had nothing to do with vertigo.

"Aren't they beautiful?" said Javier in hushed, reverent tones. "Oh, don't go too far out. Come back to her, come back...there we are."

Below them, Carter lifted a ballerina afloat, the arch of her back forming a pause. It was heady, being suspended here above the stage lights: the rush, the height, the infatuation. Javier's honest joy was so radiant that it burned haloes into Ethan's retinas. He took an involuntary step forward.

Javier turned, beaming. "Are you enjoying yourself?"

"Yeah," said Ethan, "I am." Then he pulled Javier in by the lapels and kissed him.

Ethan swallowed the first sharp intake of surprise, pressing his tongue against the soft give of Javier's lower lip. He tasted like lemon water and mints, pliant with surprise.

For a moment it was like kissing a statue, Javier's eyes wide and staring. Then he stuttered to life, tilting his head to slot their mouths together, returning the kiss with enthusiasm. Javier let go of the railing and leaned Ethan backwards, one hand on his nape and the other anchoring the dip of his spine. Ethan's heel lost traction with the metal flooring, but Javier wasn't phased, holding him upright with one looped arm.

Ethan's skin was numb with oxytocin, heart thudding, lungs full. "Fucking *finally*," he said, in between each kiss. "I was beginning to think you weren't interested."

Javier mouthed a reverent line down Ethan's throat, eyes closed.

"Oi." Ethan tweaked his nose. "Look at me when I'm kissing you."

"Sorry. Was asleep."

Ethan burst out laughing. He muffled the sound by another open-mouthed kiss. "Tou-fucking-ché." He backed Javier up against the railing, hip to hip, pulse to pulse. "Guess I'll have to make this more exciting."

They both missed the end of *Giselle*.

NINE

1 Madeleine Avenue, Upper Chelsea, Level 22.
Sunday, 17 October.

Jav's baby sister threw herself onto the couch in an explosion of purple tulle.

"Rina!" Maddy yelled. No answer. "*Ree-naaaah.*"

Despite the time difference between London and Sydney, Maddy's jetlag was nowhere to be found. She had dumped her luggage at their parents' house and caught up with five hundred of her closest friends before crashing at Rina and Jav's flat before dinner.

Maddy floated Jav's phone out of his hand to use as a second mirror.

"*I* can do your braids for you," Jav protested half-heartedly, used to the perils of telekinetic siblings.

"You have butter fingers," said Maddy, still texting. "Make Rina give me bobby pins. And Giulia says to hurry up, they're already at Uncle Harry's."

Jav stretched across the couch, with an upside-down view of the aquarium and stairs. "Rina," he hollered. "Maddy needs hair pins!"

A door slammed. Rina appeared at the top of the staircase, perfume in hand. "I'm not a courier pigeon."

Maddy groaned. "You're coming downstairs anyway. *Rina*."

Jav yawned, rotating his ankles. No one felt irritated. In fact, Rina had been radiating smugness ever since she and Peter came home at 1 am, drenched in smoke and lust.

Maddy poked him in the cheek. "Hey. Do something. Rina's bullying me."

"She is not. And give my phone back, please, I was texting Stephen."

Maddy squished herself between Jav and the back of the couch. "You seem happy. I bet it's because I'm home."

"Good bet," said Jav, chest tight with fondness.

There were twelve years between them, but sometimes Jav felt closest to Maddy out of his three sisters. A year abroad hadn't changed her, the easy hugs and unthinking affection – while more of Rina slipped through his fingers every day.

Speaking of the devil: Maddy leapt off the couch as Rina appeared. "Pins?" she demanded, palm held out.

"Left them on the dresser for you."

"You could've just — argh!" Maddy stormed upstairs.

Rina had a pair of stilettos looped around one pinkie finger. Her asymmetric dress framed a gold necklace (a birthday present from Uncle Harry, their godfather). She lay a hand on Jav's forehead. "What's wrong?"

Jav sat up. "What were you doing out so late?"

"Told you. Chatting to Bobby."

"I thought we were avoiding him."

Rina tutted. "You're the one who didn't want to come with."

"You said you'd stop seeing Langley."

"Charlie was there."

"Oh, so two Langleys for the price of one? What a bargain."

"Bobby won't kill me in front of his precious nephew, son, or whatever it is legally"

Jav pulled a face. "I hate Charlie. Twenty per cent water and eighty per cent chauvinist."

"I hate him too, but Bobby's easier to play when I'm a potential daughter in law."

"Don't even joke about that. You know Peter will poison Charlie if you ever get married."

Rina laughed. "Peter will do as he's told."

Jav pulled her down to sit next to him. "You're on edge. What else aren't you telling me?"

They were interrupted by Maddy's shout from upstairs. "They're not here. Rina, seriously!"

"Jav's dresser, not mine," Rina shouted back, eyes still on Jav. Doors slammed in rapid succession. "I'm happy because you're happy. Mister 'my date went alright'." Jav projected a flat scepticism. She made kissy noises, palming Jav's face when he didn't smile back. "The whole house reeks of dopamine. Maybe you're getting confused with a feedback loop."

"If you don't want to tell me, then don't. But I know what's yours and what's mine."

"What's *ours*." His twin drew a circle on Jav's palm with an index finger, undeterred.

Jav pulled his hand away and crossed his arms.

Rina sat back. "Fine. We figured out who hired the shooter."

"What?! Who—?"

"*Shhh.*"

"How are you so calm?" Jav hissed, glancing upstairs. "Have you told the police?"

Rina yanked him close by the wrists. "Obviously not. I was going to tell *you* eventually, but I didn't want to ruin your good mood."

"Fuck my mood!" Jav flushed hot-cold with shock. "Well? Who was it? Is Maddy in any danger? Giulia? You need to tell mum—"

Rina's grip tightened, excitement like nails on chalk. "No one's in any danger," she said, machine-gun rapid. "We're taking care of it. There's not enough evidence for the police, so you can't tell anyone, okay? Not Giulia, not mum or dad, not Stephen. You can't trust anybody right now, except me and Peter. Wouldn't want to accidentally tip off someone dangerous, would you?"

Jav shook his head, numb. Rina rested her forehead against his, unblinking. Her tile-grey calm was inexorable, flattening Jav's pulse until it slowed.

"So not Langley, then?" he asked, hoarse. "Was it a Sixty-Fourther?"

"Peter didn't want to tell you at all. But I knew you'd worry yourself to death." She pressed her thumb gently against his Adam's apple, like a sedative. "You've been having nightmares."

"But..."

"Promise me you won't say anything."

"Rina, I really think we—"

"*Promise.*"

Jav searched her expression but found nothing but himself, staring back, uncertain. "Okay," he croaked. "I promise."

"Ready!" Maddy flounced down the stairs, pausing on the threshold. She looked between her siblings. "What happened?"

"Jav stubbed his toe, and then his heart," said Rina. "Give him a hug, he's missed your vapid chirpiness."

"Ha, fuck you too," said Maddy, but dutifully came over. She slapped a freezing hand to Jav's cheek. "Happy thoughts: direct transmission!"

"Alright, alright." Jav swallowed his unease and tried to rally his composure. "Shall we get going?"

"I'm driving," said Rina.

Maddy abandoned her brother for the door. "Shotgun!"

The Boltons, Upper Chelsea, Level 21. Twenty minutes later.

FOR AS LONG AS Jav could remember, his parents and godparents took turns hosting 'family dinner' every other week. Someone was always absent, but Jav loved basking in the hum of comfortable familiarity.

Tonight, everyone was present, even Giulia and Nath.

Nath sat furthest away from Jav, wearing empathic dampeners on both wrists. Like Giulia's bracelets, they were for the wearer's benefit, against Jav's aptitude. Science understood empaths a lot less than it did firestarters and telekinetics, and empath dampeners were just non-localised, long-distance suppressors. The best empath dampener was a solid wall. As it was, Jav could still feel the foggy echo of distaste, but one didn't need to be an empath to see it in Nath's and Giulia's body language.

The sight hurt less over the years, but still stung.

Harold Mansfield rang his glass with a dessert spoon. "I do believe it's time for a toast."

Stephen slouched until he almost slid beneath the table. "Dad, *no*."

"Let your father have his moment," said Harper Mansfield. She refilled her champagne and turned to Jav's mother. "Marie?"

Marie Sainte-Ophie nodded. "I'll need it for whatever's coming next."

Maddy held out her glass. "Me too, please and thank you, Aunty Harper."

"You're underage," said Giulia.

"Only until April."

"So? You've had two drinks already."

Maddy swivelled to the nearest authority up the food chain. "Daddy!"

"We're at home," said Thomas Arden, fond. "Won't hurt, Giulia."

Uncle Harry beamed as bright as a Christmas ballet. "Firstly, we're so grateful that Rina is safe and sound."

Rina had been shot outside Yellowstone, a building built and managed by Ascenda – the Mansfield family firm. Jav wondered if Nath had to deal with any blowback after the incident. It'd certainly explain his bad mood.

Beside Nath, Giulia was distracted. Her dark hair had half-escaped her corporate bun, and she was tucking a strand of it behind her ear, over and over. The Ardens were evenly split: Giulia and Maddy took after dad, while Jav and Rina took after mum.

"I lost ten years, when Giulia called," said dad. "And I'm already ancient."

Rina rested her cheek against his shoulder. "Don't worry, I'm good as new."

"Yes, the healers are worth our tax dollars," said Uncle Harry. "Unlike our law enforcement."

"They've made no headway with the shooter then, I take it," said Nath.

"If it's not a Sixty-Fourther, I would be very surprised," said dad. "They've been making so much noise lately."

"Innocent until proven guilty," Rina hummed, returning to her food. Jav raised an eyebrow. She met his gaze. "Could've been anyone."

"You and Jav should stay with mum and I, until I am satisfied with your...security arrangements." Dad leaned back in his chair. "Won't it be nice to spend more time with Maddy, now that she's home?"

"No," chimed Rina and Maddy in unison.

Uncle Harry chortled. "Well, that was my second toast – pumpkin's back home! It's been too quiet without you, sweetie."

"Yeah. Peace and quiet," Rina muttered.

Uncle Harry cleared his throat. "What was the third thing...Ah. Our good friends in Westminster." He raised his glass at Thomas. "Good show, bringing that vote home. I don't think anyone expected a substantial cut, but the Sixty-Fourthers have been brazen. They must be feeling the pressure in Whitehall."

Dad threw back his glass in lieu of answering. Parliament had voted to maintain the CM15 subsidies for two more years.

"Maybe the news coverage about trafficking glass finally knocked them off their high horse," said Rina, so sugary smug that it left Jav no room for dessert.

Giulia snorted. "If they cut the subsidy ahead of schedule, water bills go up – then we'll have a real riot on our hands. Before the election? I don't think so."

"We're just delaying the inevitable," said Nath. "Reallocating CM15 subsidy to fund fusive purification is hardly enough to keep pace with the retrofitting costs. Meanwhile, the subsidy's gone down, CM15's more expensive...what do they think is going to happen to their water bill?"

"They had to cut something, or else people start getting anxious about the deficit. Taxes. Both."

Nath snorted. "At least that'd be more realistic. Now we're the ones who must play pretend, then draw up proposals to fit! When costs blow out – and they will – Ascenda's the villain."

Auntie Harper *tsk*'d. "Price it in, my dear. These projects take time. More time, more to go around. Be patient."

"We have to win the tender first." A vein twitched in Nath's neck. Not brave enough to roll his eyes at his mother, he turned to Giulia. "I'd be more confident, except who knows what the press will dig up next?"

Jav braced himself for the spike of irritation.

Giulia narrowed her eyes. "Don't be shy. Say what you mean."

"Nath's never been shot before." Rina licked her spoon. "Not as fun as it sounds."

Nath opened his mouth to retort – but stopped when Thomas cleared his throat.

"Now, now," said dad. "Rina was at the wrong place at the wrong time. As for the press, poor Jav can't be in two places at once."

Nath's expression grew constipated. "I'm just concerned that all the pent-up frustration about CM15 will jeopardise Ascenda's bid by association."

"Watch your tone," barked Uncle Harry.

"I'm well aware of the prevailing narrative," said dad, unphased. "Why else have we invested in so many alt-purification start-ups? And fusive projects." It took a lot to tip his temper, especially when it came to family. Jav couldn't remember the last time dad was agitated – not even when Rina was six and accidentally locked Jav in a bathroom because she melted the door handle. "Percentage points matter very little if they award the tender to a hostile firm." Thomas turned to his wife. "Your mother hardly needs more ammunition against me, right darling?"

"Distance and time have not made her heart fonder, no," said mum.

Since Arden Pharma supplied all the CM15, it was the only subcontractor for water works, be it public or private development. There was no guarantee that a foreign construction firm would be so chummy, should one win the tender – especially if Arden Pharma could no longer offer the cheapest CM15 once the government subsidy drained away. Theoretically, that foreign firm could bring in a competing CM15 manufacturer. A supplier like Sainte-Ophie Biotech, whose matriarch had an axe to grind against Beatrice Arden.

If the future really was fusive, the fight over the remaining CM15 market could get ugly unless the Ardens and Sainte-Ophies came to an understanding. Jav couldn't believe it all came down to stupid brunches with his cousin Marc. Jav pinched the bridge of his nose.

Maddy noticed. "I thought dinner was a work-free zone," she admonished the table at large.

Dad chuckled. "Sorry sweet pea. No more boring talk."

"*I* thought dinner was a phone-free zone," said Nath, "but Stephen has been texting for an hour straight, *mother.*"

"Some of us have a wedding to plan." Stephen high-fived Jav without looking up from said phone.

"Oh, when's Clara's flight landing?" asked Auntie Harper.

"Tuesday evening," said Stephen. "Two more sleeps."

"Isn't it 6 am for Clara right now?" Jav sighed. "I wish someone loved *me* enough to message me that early."

Rina grinned. "Don't doctors start at the crack of dawn? Is Ethan neglecting you?"

Pin-drop silence.

"Who the hell is Ethan?" Maddy demanded. "You've never mentioned an Ethan before."

"He's a friend," said Jav quickly.

"One that Jav's been seeing every night." Rina wiggled her eyebrows.

Maddy's dessert spoon shot across the room and into a window. Giulia spilled her wine with a curse.

"You have a boyfriend and didn't tell me?!" Maddy felt both outraged and delighted. "*I* tell you everything! *Everything.*"

"I don't have a boyfriend." Jav glared at Rina, who blew him a kiss across the table.

"Then why is it a secret?" asked Maddy. "Who else knew? Stephen, when did this happen?"

"Eh, three weeks ago?"

"Less than," said Jav, betrayed.

"You talk about him so much it feels like three weeks."

"Oh, that's rich, coming from you."

"Aha!" Maddy thumped the table. "So you *have* been dating."

"Your brother can do as he likes," said dad, bemused. He glanced at Giulia. "I assume we've vetted."

Jav sighed. "It was just dinner, let's not get too paranoid."

"Five dates this week already," Rina corrected.

"Rina."

"He's been playing jazz covers of *So This Is Love* on repeat."

"*Rina.*"

"Oh, by the way, Mummy, Ethan's a healer."

Marie's laser interest refocused on Jav. "Really? Which clinic?"

"St Ophie's Hospital. He was Rina's consulting healer."

"He. With a Y chromosome?" asked Mum.

"I think so," said Jav.

"How anomalous, especially one strong enough for clinical practice. What's his surname; do we know the family?"

"Faulkner," said Jav. "And no?"

Mum nodded. "Sounds like a nice young man."

"We don't know that he's *nice*," said Maddy. "We don't know anything about him. Is he hot? Show me a photo."

"I shall be perfectly happy with ugly grandchildren if they were healers," said Mum.

Jav buried his face in his hands.

"He saved my life," said Rina. "That's one redeeming feature, right?"

"Invite him round for dinner," mum commanded. "That's the least we can do."

"You just want DNA samples," said Giulia.

Auntie Harper laughed into her dessert.

Maddy waved a hand in front of Jav's face. "He*llo*. Are you withholding photos because he's hideous?"

"He has eyes like a frog," Rina announced.

"He does *not*," said Jav, indignant. "Some people have the bone structure to pull off deep-set eyes."

"Yeah, nah, just found him on the hospital website." Maddy floated her phone over to Aunty Harper and mum. "Look. Eww."

"He does look a bit depressed," said Stephen.

Jav didn't want to jeopardise his position as chief wedding planner for Stephen's nuptials, so merely crossed his arms and sulked.

Mum raised her glass to him. "Good job."

"You never say nice things about *my* boyfriends," Maddy complained.

"When you start dating healers instead of musicians, we can revisit my opinion. If your brother can find—"

"Technically I found him," said Rina.

Jav huffed. "And *I* introduced Stephen to Clara, but you never hear me getting any bloody credit."

JAV AND STEPHEN escaped in the name of wedding planning.

"Help." Stephen was lying on the floor, having fallen trying to pick up his VR headset with his toes. "I've strained something."

Jav set down their drinks and threw the headset at Stephen. He missed. "You're gonna have to be more limber for the groomsmen dance."

"I can't perform in the bedroom if I pull my groyne."

"You won't be performing anywhere if you mess this up for me. I've spent months on the choreography."

"Sorry, who's getting married?" Stephen pulled on his VR glove and selected a zombie first-person-shooter. Jav was too tired to protest. At least VR gave Stephen his adrenaline rush without being detained for joyflying. "No splits."

"I'll consider it. Are you still going to that Aston Martin expo this week?"

"Dunno, Clara'll probably be tired. Why?"

Jav kept his eyes on the screen. "Can you forward me the details?"

Stephen raised his eyebrows: Jav didn't bring up cars on his own. "Why?"

"Ethan might want—"

"I fucking knew it." Stephen almost lost both eyeballs with how fast he rolled them. "You whinge so loud whenever *I* invite you. Now that blow jobs are on the line—"

"Don't be crass."

"Is this why Rina said you wanted biking lessons? Is Ethan a gearhead?"

Rina, you traitor. "We went to a ballet on Thursday and he fell asleep." Jav glared as Stephen started cackling. "I want to do something that he's interested in and — will you stop laughing!"

"Ethan hates ballet?" crowed Stephen. "Ha!"

"He doesn't hate it. He's a doctor so he's tired...*stop laughing.*"

Stephen's mirth tickled the back of Jav's throat, diluting the mortification of boring his date unconscious. If they hadn't made out afterwards in the wings for ten minutes straight, Jav would've been too embarrassed to keep in touch.

That said, skin contact rendered empath suppressors useless. Jav stepped around the possibility that Ethan might have been caught up in Jav's euphoria. He cleared his throat. "So can Ethan come along or not?"

Stephen jammed VR goggles over his eyes. "Your surname's on every prescription bottle. Just walk in."

THREE IN-GAME DEATHS LATER, Jav bid his own escape to the bathroom: VR made him nauseous. Jav opened the bathroom door – and promptly tried to slam it shut again as he detected Nath's presence barrelling down the hallway. Jav wasn't fast enough.

"A word," said Nath, yanking Jav out of the bathroom by the elbow.

Jav lunged for the living room. "Actually, Stephen's—"

Nath shoved him into a study, kicking the door shut behind them. This close, dampeners did shit-all. Jav winced at Nath's roil of stress, strung tight as a violin string between eyes and teeth.

"Uh," said Jav. "What the hell."

"We need to talk about your sister."

"Which one?"

"You fucking know which one." Nath's gaze fell to Jav's bare wrists. "Put your suppressors back on. I can't have you messing with my head."

Nath was Jav's least favourite Mansfield. He wore cortisol in a permanent noose about his neck; cynicism etched his brow into hawkish severity. And though he and Stephen looked alike, you couldn't mistake one for the other in temperament.

Unhurried, Jav fished out his cufflinks. "Only because your foul mood is so loud. *There.* Happy?"

"You need to get Rina under control before she tanks Ascenda's bid all on her own."

"I dunno what you mean."

"Don't play dumb, that doesn't work on me."

"But I am dumb. Can I leave now?"

"No," spat Nath. "Rina only listens to you."

Jav burst out laughing.

Nath scowled. "I don't care what your father says. Public sentiment is too volatile. We won't get Project Earthflown if Arden Pharma gets embroiled in some glass trafficking scandal – Ascenda will be tainted by association."

"Okay."

"Okay?"

"Yes. You're right about everything." Unequivocal agreement usually appeased Giulia. "*Now* can I go?"

"Let me put this in terms you can understand." Nath leaned against the edge of the desk. "Our long-term interests are aligned – and I'm not talking about Ascenda and Arden Pharma. I mean everyone under this roof. Mum and dad gave you all stakes in Ascenda." Nath paced, agitated. "If Ascenda wins the tender, Arden Pharma remains in the CM15 pilot seat – you decide where and how slowly to land. Manufactured dependency. Rina should concentrate on that instead of fraternising with Langley."

Here we go again. "Charlie? You think I control who Rina dates?"

"I'm talking about Robert Langley, but his nephew is the same. Everyone knows how glass gets around. And I have it on good authority that Langley is funding half the anti-fusive lobbyists."

"Maybe they're just worried about losing logistics business?"

"No, I'm sure they've done the maths. Cheap glass needs cheap CM15. Arden Pharma will survive without CM15, but one cannot phase out CM15 from glass production."

Ignorance was bliss, and the truth greatly impeded Jav's acting.

"Even your parents have planned for a CM15 phase-out," Nath continued. "A *year* ago, I tried explaining to Rina that it was in her best financial interest to cut ties with Langley. Next thing I know, she's dating Charles and flaunting it all over the social pages."

Jav dragged a hand down his cheek. "Oh my god, so that was *your* fault."

"I beg your pardon?"

"She's wanted to piss you off and now we're all suffering Charles' awful company. Thanks for nothing."

Nath stared, mouth thin with contempt. "What was Rina doing on Level 9 when that boy died? You must know." He narrowed his eyes at Jav's silence. "Rina's dalliance with Langley will come back to bite all of us. The SIA probes. The police inquiries. The company she keeps – people talk."

"I don't know what you're saying."

"Of course not. And when she gets arrested for running a glass cartel, I'm sure *you'll* be just fine."

Jav sighed. "Look. I know you take Ascenda stuff super seri—"

"Don't fucking patronise me," Nath snarled.

"I'm not! But Rina was shot by Sixty-Fourthers and you're accusing—"

"I thought they didn't know who shot her yet." Nath's alarm was a slap to the face.

Jav shrugged. "I just assumed..."

For a frozen moment, Nath was wild-eyed. Then the tension left his shoulders in a rush. "I'm worried too, you know. Rina's meddling with dangerous people. Would hate for either of you to get caught in the crosshairs. Talk some sense into her."

Before Jav could respond, the study door flew open, startling them both.

"There you are." Rina leaned against the door frame, hand on hip. "Stephen thought you had indigestion."

Jav exhaled in relief. *Rescued!* "No, just Nath."

Nath's adrenaline hummed, a drill behind the eyes.

Rina's smile broadened to show pearly whites. "What did I interrupt? Sibling meeting?"

"No," said Nath. "We're done here."

"Boy talk? I can leave."

"For heaven's sake," Nath muttered, moving towards the door.

What a coward. Talk to Giulia like this and see what happens.

Rina reached for Jav's hand. Then she gasped, plucking off a cufflink. "This isn't even on – the battery's flat, *silly*."

Nath blanched. His eyes flicked between the twins, before clocking Jav in the shoulder as he shoved past.

"You should see a healer about those eye bags," Rina called. "I've got sleeping pills if you need some." A door slammed in answer. She raised both eyebrows. "What on earth were you chatting about? He practically ran away."

"Yes. From you." Jav rubbed his eyes.

"I'm flattered. Do tell me more." Rina linked their arms and proffered the cufflink with a flourish, smirking.

Jav pocketed the suppressor. "That was mean," he said reproachfully. "This was turned on the whole time."

"Oh, I know *that*."

TEN

Bergenia Residences, Lower Lambeth, Level 9.
Wednesday, 20 October.

Night shifts meant that Vegas was home to judge Ethan's schedule for the day. She flung open the sliding door to his bedroom. "Rise and shine, it's time for school!"

Ethan clutched his covers pre-emptively. "Piss off, it's freezing."

"Aren't you gonna be late?" The mattress dipped as she sat down.

"For?"

Vegas whipped the duvet off Ethan's face. "I assume Javier's taking you to Paris for breakfast or whatever it is today."

"No."

Clad in pyjama bottoms and Ollie's jumper, Vegas squinted. Then she stuck a frozen foot under Ethan's covers.

Ethan hissed. "*Fine*, we're having dinner later."

"Ha. Which number date is this?"

"Is it a 'date'?"

"What would you call dinner, opera, then hanky-panky?"

"It was a ballet, barely any hanky, and no panky. Hands above the waist the whole bloody time. Then he dropped me home and — oi, this is *my* blanket."

Vegas shoved him aside to make room. "Your bed's warmer. So, no updates? No dick?"

"He kisses like a choir boy."

"I guess it's only been two weeks-ish." Vegas turned to face him, cheek on his pillow. "Not like you to play hard to get."

Ethan snorted. "I'm not, trust me. We've had, like, ten thousand da —" Vegas's eyebrows shot up "—*meals* together and he seems keen. The way he looks at me. The stuff he says. And you'd think, after all the flowers...I don't get it."

"Maybe he's saving himself for marriage."

Ethan reflected on Javier's careful manners, telegraphing every move for permission. "Then why the wining and dining? It's not like we're gonna see each other once I'm back at work."

"Did Javier say that?"

Dinner with no adjectives; no strings. Different guy; same story. Ethan wrinkled his nose. "Sort of."

Vegas pursed her mouth. "Did *you* say that?"

"I told him I didn't have time to date."

"Uh, déjà vu. You told him you were too busy to date, and now you complain that he hasn't been using the right labels. Is this like how you told Nick, 'no strings', then angsted over him not romancing you properly?"

"Nick never messages me for anything except—"

"Aha!" Vegas propped herself up on one elbow. "Then sex isn't mandatory on Ethan's dating Venn diagram. Quality time and food could seal the deal. Or sex plus quality time, I guess."

"You can't have sex when you're hungry," Ethan muttered.

"Are you gonna keep seeing Javier?" Vegas yanked the entire blanket away. "What was that?"

"I *said* 'for a few more days'." Ethan could feel the judgement of Vegas's gaze on the back of his neck.

"You and Nick have been playing commitment-chicken for two years now. If you blink first, Nick deserves to know."

"Nick hasn't told *me* about everyone he sleeps with." Ethan hesitated. "Not that it's any of my business."

Vegas hummed. "I don't think he is seeing anyone else. Ollie would have mentioned it."

"Well, it's been No-llie season for months, so who knows. Nick's been busy too." Ethan sat up, hunting around for warmer clothes to avoid eye contact. "Javier seems the type to want proper dates and all that. And once I'm back on-call and doing nights? It won't work out." When his head popped free of his jumper, Vegas was still staring at him. "*What?*"

"Nothing. Just déjà vu."

"Like you and Ollie?" Ethan retorted – then immediately felt guilty. "Sorry, I didn't mean it like that."

"At some point you have to use words, instead of assuming."

"What, and get humiliated?" Ethan backpedalled at Vegas' frown, which was growing sadder by the second. "I'm not under any illusions, that's all. I know what I'm like; no one survives it full-time. Well, except you."

Vegas unrolled herself from the duvet and lifted a corner. "For pity's sake, c'mere."

Gratefully, Ethan dove back under the covers. Communication could wait.

Upper Mayfair, Level 19. Twelve hours later.

PERHAPS SENSING THE END of a good run, Javier seemed determined to leave a lasting impression by checking off Ethan's entire bucket list. It made the prospect of Javier's absence downright dreadful. But when else was Ethan going to sit in an Aston Martin concept flier?

"Did you see his face while I was in there?" Ethan swiped through the photos as they returned to Jav's car. "Can't believe he let me."

Javier pressed a hand to the dashboard, which lit up for the biometrics. "No, I relate: you, looking the way you do. He's only mortal."

"Ha. Props to you for saying that with a straight face."

Their car emerged from the building and into a howling storm, rocking on its axis, windscreen instantly opaque with horizontal rain.

Ethan whistled. "Should we be flying in this?"

The chassis jolted as they entered a wind tunnel that screamed upwards between two buildings, funnelled from the Level below.

"We could switch to a solid route, but that'll take a lot longer. Sorry, I didn't check the forecast. This flier isn't the most stable."

Ethan patted the upholstery. "Don't listen to him, it's not your fault that you were built for speed and not a hurricane." He turned back to Javier. "How far are we from yours?"

"Much closer than Level 9. We could wait out the storm with some cocktails and stuff?"

"Hmm. I do love 'stuff'."

Predictably, Javier went pink. The interior of the car felt too warm, fizzing beneath the skin, low ceiling sloped and intimate. Ethan wondered if Javier would combust if he kissed him. He leaned in to test the hypothesis.

Javier cleared his throat. "You'll finally meet Rina."

"While she's awake." Ethan sat back as Javier busied himself with his phone. *You're doing this on purpose, you sly bastard.* "Will she mind us interrupting?"

"The flat's big enough, we won't get in her way." Javier paused, wrinkling his nose. His typing intensified.

"Bad news?" asked Ethan.

"No? What makes you say that?"

"Oh, I thought you were pouting but there's a speck of — here, let me—" Ethan yanked Javier in by the lapel and kissed him.

There was a thud as Javier dropped his phone and it slid into the footwell. *Good,* thought Ethan, tilting his face to better investigate Javier's tonsils. The seatbelt was cutting into Ethan's collarbone. He let go of Javier's neck to depress the catch.

Javier caught his wrist. "The car will get angry if you do that."

"The car—" Ethan burst out laughing. *You're too sweet for anyone's health.*

They traded kisses as the car's stabilisers battled the wind, teeth to teeth, nose to cheek.

As soon as they pulled into the garage, Ethan undid his seatbelt and swung a leg over Javier's hip. It would have been smooth if he didn't hit his head on the ceiling.

"Fuck!" Ethan slapped blindly at the side of Javier's seat. "Where's the thingie to go back? Bloody hell."

Javier ran a hand through Ethan's hair and left it atop of his head. "The 'thingie'? I thought you knew your way around cars."

Ethan huffed. "Trouble with these racing models. Low ceilings." Javier's eyes were creased soft, as if looking at a baby animal. *Well, that won't do.* Ethan rolled his hips, smug when it elicited a high-pitched noise. He swallowed the gasp with a kiss. "You," he bit Jav's lower lip, "are unreal."

Javier's hand on Ethan's neck, pressing down his spine – a tentative line of warm pressure. Before the hand could pass the waist, they were interrupted by Javier's phone ringing through the car speakers.

Ethan jerked, hitting his head on the roof a second time. "Bloody hell!"

"Sorry. Rina." Javier couldn't seem to settle on laughing or aww-ing. "She's probably wondering where we are." They both stared at the 'incoming call' hologram until it blinked away. "I'll get out of the car. Make sure we aren't too high off the ground."

Ethan buried his face in the cook of Javier's neck. "We're not finished here."

"Are you gonna be okay with the ceiling while I'm gone?"

"Oi," laughed Ethan, and kissed him some more.

It took them another ten minutes to leave the car.

"LOOK WHO IT IS," someone drawled as soon as they stepped out of the lift.

Javier's response was lost as Ethan stared, speechless, between the water feature in the foyer and the two-storied aquarium in the living room beyond. The glass curved along the staircase, seamless and defying physics. It cast an ever-shifting lattice of refracted light on the couches below, shadows lapping like waves against the expansive floor-to-ceiling windows on the opposite end of the room.

There were a *lot* of fish.

"Yes, I know," laughed Corinna Arden, who was suddenly *right there*. Ethan realised he had spoken out loud – but before he could clear the kaleidoscope of fish-scales from his retinas, Corinna kissed him twice on both cheeks. "It's *so* lovely to finally meet you while I'm conscious, Dr Faulkner! Or is it *Mr* Faulkner? Jav says you're a surgeon, but I think healers formally retain the doctor title, right?" They were close enough to bump noses and Ethan didn't dare blink for fear that Corinna's gaze devoured him alive. "You must tell me your preferences."

Ethan rocked back on his heels, stumbling. "Just Ethan's fine." He cleared his throat. "You seem better."

"Mmhm." Corinna's smile widened. "Thanks to you."

"It was a team effort," said Ethan. "We would have preferred checking on you overnight, but *someone* moved you against my advice."

Javier looked abashed.

"Aww, don't blame Jav. Giulia probably yelled at him over the phone and he panicked." Corinna pouted. "You're not still mad at him, are you?"

"Furious." Ethan's deadpan must have been defective because Javier's dimples reappeared.

Javier nodded at the flying helmet on a nearby chair. "Going storm chasing?"

"If the wind hasn't died off," said Corinna. "You took your sweet time."

"Uh huh." Javier herded Ethan towards the cluster of coffee tables bathed in aquarium blue. "Let Ethan sit down first."

Corinna threw herself onto a sofa. "Why? I assume you two won't remain vertical for much longer."

"*Rina.*" Javier turned to Ethan. "Fancy a drink?"

"I'd love a drink, thanks." Ethan sat gingerly. The sofa was a dangerous shade of pale.

"Anything in particular?"

"Something sweet."

From this angle, Ethan could see tall shadows through the windows and realised that they bordered a huge indoor garden, complete with a koi pond and — "Are those *trees*?"

"Yeah, the view's great from the conservatory when the storm shields are down," said Corinna. "Stay for breakfast and Jav can give you a tour."

"Rina, stop it." Javier called from the wet bar.

Corinna had her back to the aquarium and her unblinking attention reminded Ethan of the fish behind her. She followed his gaze. "Do you like them?"

There was clearly a right and wrong answer.

"Yes. Uh. That's a lot of water." Ethan wondered if all oligarchs could afford this kind of excess, or whether one must control an entire nation's water supply.

Corinna tilted her head. "It's not potable, you know."

"Oh." Ethan cleared his throat, relieved. "Then—"

"They're saltwater fish."

"...Right." Patients were much easier than this – if someone needed a healer, they were generally unconscious. "They must be hard to take care of?"

"I lose a few every now and then. Sometimes they eat each other. I have to count them every morning."

"Uh."

"Kidding, they're all tagged. The fat one by the coral is Jav-574."

Ethan wished she would blink more often. "You named them all Jav?"

"I gave Rina the first fish in her collection. We were six." Human-Javier had returned. He passed Ethan a lychee martini.

Corinna raised an eyebrow. "Ahem, where's mine?"

"You can't drink and fly," said Javier.

"No more hospital visits, please," Ethan agreed.

Corinna sighed with gusto. "I *suppose*. Well, charming to meet you, Ethan. Mummy wants you at family dinner next Friday. She will be upset if you don't show."

"Rina," said Javier, expression exasperated.

Ah, there it is. How telling. Ethan swallowed his disappointment. "That's nice of her, but I'm back at work next week. I'll have to check the roster."

"I'm sure we can make it happen." Corinna rose to her feet. "Alright, I'm off." She plucked the lychee out of Javier's cocktail glass and sashayed towards the lobby. As she pulled on her boots, a tall figure materialised from nowhere.

Ethan froze.

The man proffered Corinna's flight helmet to her. He saluted Ethan, smirking, and nodded once. "Doctor."

Then they were both gone.

"Who—" Ethan turned to Javier. "Was he there the whole time?"

Javier threw back his drink. "Probably. Can't get rid of him; like a bad smell."

"I've never met a ghost before. Is everyone in your family an aptee?"

"Peter's not family, he's Rina's...something. But no, Giulia's not an aptee. And neither am I, unfortunately."

"Why's it unfortunate?"

The question seemed to catch Javier off guard. "Unexpected is a better word. Dad's a watercaller, mum's a firestarter, Maddy's telekinetic. Mum was very deliberate about what she wanted – it's her field of expertise. Editing, I mean." Javier fiddled with his cufflinks. "Dad said she practically slept in the lab while Rina and I were, um, in progress. We were both meant to be healers, but nobody has cracked the code yet." He laughed, stilted. "Sorry, I'm rambling."

"Don't be sorry," said Ethan. Here, surrounded by water and every excess – the same attitudes. "If it helps, healers are overrated."

Javier stared. He spun his empty cocktail glass by the stem. "What do you think of Rina?"

That you live and die by her approval. "Seems cool."

Javier cast him a knowing look. "She's a bit direct, but I think you'd get along. She likes you already, I can tell."

"She's met me for ten minutes."

"Well, you saved her life."

"Hmm." Ethan tipped the lychee into his mouth. "Is that why *you* like me?" Judging by the way Javier went stock-still, Ethan's nonchalance wasn't as smooth as he'd hoped.

Javier joined Ethan on the sofa. "You know this hasn't been about —" He reached for Ethan's hand, and Ethan let him have it. "That's not to say I'm not grateful for what you did, I can't even imagine how — if you hadn't been there—"

For someone with an uncanny talent for saying all the right things, Javier was lost for words. *You really are a piss-poor liar. But bless you for trying.* Ethan set down his drink and kissed Javier to spare him the indignity.

"Doesn't matter," said Ethan, between open-mouthed presses. "Don't look so tragic, I was just teasing." He leaned back against the arm of the sofa, trying to coax Javier down with him.

Javier propped himself up with one hand, hair falling into his eyes. "This isn't about Rina."

"Okay."

"Wait, I'm serious." Javier resisted when Ethan clasped a hand to his nape.

"Then why are you making me work so hard, instead of kissing me?" Ethan flopped back, squinting up at Javier's backlit features. The aquarium haloed his hair. Forget white-collar dealings and drug cartels – it was surely a crime to look so earnest.

Javier wet his lips. "Listen, I think you're wonderful company. You make me laugh and you always mean the things you say. Do you know how rare that is?"

Ethan burst out laughing. "Stop," he wheezed. *Don't make this harder than it needs to be.* "That's sweet. But I wasn't fishing for compliments."

"...I know that." Javier sounded plaintive.

A flash of lightning arced through the storm shields, splashing bright across the glass and walls. Javier's pulse sped up beneath the pad of Ethan's thumb. The drumroll of thunder shook the shadows by their seams.

Javier's gaze didn't falter, despite the flush in his cheeks. "As long as you know that we're not dating because of some misplaced gratitude."

"Dating," Ethan repeated. *Say, therefore I am.* Was it usually this simple? He couldn't mask his disbelief.

Javier's eyebrows shot up. "Have I been too presumptuous? Or not presumptuous enough?"

"Yes," said Ethan, then immediately, "no?" He frowned. "Wait."

To his dismay, Javier actually waited instead of interrupting in mercy.

Ethan scrubbed a hand over his face. "Look. I'm back at work next week."

"I know."

"My schedule's unpredictable."

"Mine's flexible."

"And I'm usually too tired to be interesting. Especially after work."

"That's fine?"

"No, as in, I just want to eat, then crash. By myself."

Javier considered him for a moment. "I hope I haven't given you reason to think I'm the sort of man who would be so easily inconvenienced."

Ethan snorted. "That's what you say now." *Everyone is fine with it at the start; resentment takes time to bloom.* "Full disclosure, that's all."

Something passed over Javier's face, there and gone like a ripple on water. He kissed the corner of Ethan's mouth. "Well, if you give me a bit of time, I can say it again later. As many times as you'd like."

Ethan made a hiccupping-cough of relief. He hooked one leg behind Javier's knees, trying to collapse the full body's worth of air between them. Javier responded by flipping them around so that Ethan was half wedged against the back of the sofa, lying atop Javier like a blanket.

"Oi, I was comfy down there," Ethan complained.

"Sorry, I can barely feel my hand." Javier wiggled his fingers and bopped Ethan on the nose.

Ethan retaliated by grabbing said hand, pressing his mouth to the palm and – maintaining eye contact – dragging that kiss along the length of Javier's index finger. Javier's eyes grew wider as Ethan reached his cuticles.

"Better?" asked Ethan. It took every ounce of self-control not to start wheezing at Javier's slack-jawed expression.

Jav held out his other hand. "I gave you the wrong one."

"Oh no. We can't possibly have that."

ELEVEN

The Sentinel Studios, Upper Bloomsbury, Level 13.
Thursday, 21 October.

When it came to an unfinished story, Florence likened Ollie to a fox with a possum: one of them was getting stuck in a bin. "And you're both classified as pests," she said.

"Tim was left-handed! If he's never done glass before, why would he mainline with his non-dominant hand? Why does nobody *care*?"

A week had passed since Ollie brought his hunch to Ian: that Tim Hersch was a homicide case, not an accidental overdose. That hunch had turned into full-blown suspicion when Ollie's questioning about traffic cameras on Levels 9 and 4 lead to the following exchange:

"Were all the cameras malfunctioning? Did the cab's internal records show anything?"

"No comment," Ian said through a mouthful of Ethan-delivered salad.

"I talked to residents in the buildings on either side of that street. In line of sight of Tim's cab. Nada." Ollie crossed his arms. "I think someone got Tim before he left Level 9."

Ethan bore little resemblance to his dad, but they defaulted to identical *you're an idiot but I'm too tired to bother* expressions. Ian had been wearing his for the last half hour.

"Let this go, Ollie."

"Okay."

Ian narrowed his eyes. "Really?"

"Nope."

That was last Thursday. Ollie had since taken more photos of the street where Tim was found (in the name of maths and angles) and compiled more neighbours who might have seen something.

"It was buttfuck-o-clock, of course they were asleep," said Violet, the intern. "FYI: Damien's looking for you."

Damien was Ollie's editor.

"I was out chatting to witnesses," said Ollie.

"I told him that." Violet swivelled on her chair. "Damien said you've got other assignments. *And* he wants to talk to you in his office."

Ollie didn't look up from Tim's toxicology report. "Did he say when?"

"Nah."

"Then it can wait." Ollie grabbed his satchel. "I need to see a doctor."

"For a rash?" quipped Julian, who was walking by.

"For a story, you spoon!"

OLLIE DETOURED to buy strawberry pralines: they were Vegas's favourite. He walked twice around their block before summoning enough nerve to call. Vegas had night shifts: he prayed she was already awake.

Vegas answered on the sixth ring. A long draw of static.

"Hey." Ollie cleared his throat, looking up at the building façade. He counted the windows. The light was on, butter yellow against the watery London dusk.

"What," said Vegas.

"You busy?"

"I'm always busy. I'm working."

Ollie checked his phone calendar. "Oh. I thought you had night's this week. Did they change it up again?"

Silence.

When Vegas replied, she sounded pleased that Ollie remembered her schedule. "Okay fine, I'm at home. Gotta head in soon though."

"I'm outside." Ollie winked at the intercom camera.

Vegas hung up. The door buzzed open.

Ethan and Vegas lived three blocks from St Ophie's Hospital in a renovated tower, its worn façade stained by London rain. Its south-facing side had the rare luxury of unobstructed light in the mornings, thanks to the inter-Level motorway and air space for emergency vehicles. Nearby, a cluster of light-rail and pedestrian lifts threaded directly to the Levels above and below.

At this hour, the lobby was deserted; just cacti and the drone-delivery lockers. Ollie stepped into a lift and pressed for the top floor.

Vegas was only here by the grace of Ethan's lease. Healers at public hospitals had first pick of residential units nearby. A chunk of their rent or mortgage got covered, and the rest was pre-tax. It was a cushy arrangement, and the main reason why Vegas and Ollie could never justify moving in together.

Nine years and counting.

Ollie knocked, wiping his shoes on the cat-print welcome mat.

Vegas opened the door, arms crossed, feet slippered. Her hair was loose around her shoulders, one cheek creased with a recent pillow. A heavy ache slid the length of Ollie's spine.

"What do you want?" she asked.

It had been a month since their 'break up'. They texted sporadically, but Ollie couldn't tell if she was still angry. He was grateful for the

Hersch story: it kept his mind busy and his body out of his lonely studio.

Ollie proffered the pralines. "Here."

Vegas wrinkled her nose. Ollie knew she was trying not to smile.

"You skived off work to bring me chocolates?" She took the box and stepped back to let him in.

"Maybe."

Vegas harrumphed, pulling mugs from the shelf and starting an English breakfast tea without asking. The thin roller-door that lead to Ethan's room sat ajar and quiet.

Ollie jerked his chin towards it. "I thought Ethan's still on leave."

The boiling water hissed, an ellipsis between words and their intent.

Vegas passed Ollie his mug and poured herself juice from the fridge. "If you want to talk to him, don't bother. He'll ignore you."

"No. I wanted to talk to you." The tea burned his oesophagus.

Vegas held his gaze as she chugged her juice in one go. "Then talk."

Ollie dealt in words for a living – but for all the times they had argued, broken-up, and mended again, he still struggled for the right things to say. Honesty was rarely the panacea that people envisioned. But the ensuing quiet left them orbiting, waiting for a catalyst to knock them closer or further apart.

Ollie took a deep breath. "I wanted someone to look over an autopsy."

"For god's sake, of *course*—"

"I promised Ian I wouldn't talk to you about it! But it was the best excuse I had to come see you during work hours. I couldn't wait."

Perhaps Ollie should have just apologised in text and gauged her mood that way. But they had done that before and look where they were now. "I've missed you." He swallowed. "Are we still fighting?"

Vegas took a glass, filled a quarter from the filter tap, and thrust it towards him. "Gargle."

"Why?"

Vegas's lips pursed into an angry strawberry.

Ollie hastily took the glass and gargled. "There, happy? What—"

"I hate the taste of English Breakfast, and you know it," Vegas hissed, and slammed Ollie against the nearest wall, kissing him so hard that their teeth clicked.

Ollie grabbed her by the waist, spinning them around so he could hoist her onto the kitchen counter. Vegas had one hand fisted in his shirt and one on his neck, slotted against him like a key into home. She hooked her ankles behind his back and pulled him in, pressing flush and evaporating all the blood from his brain.

"Fuck," Ollie gasped. "Guess we're not fighting then?"

"You're such an asshole." Vegas shoved his jacket off his arms. "I missed your stupid face. Nobody drank your horrible tea."

Ollie slid a palm up her back, unhooking her bra, then lifted his arms so Vegas could yank his shirt over his head.

"Couch," said Ollie and Vegas locked her ankles around his waist, kissing him still, lips bruising. She yelped with laughter as he carried her from the kitchen, dropping her onto the couch cushions and climbing over.

Vegas feathered his hair. "Did you cut it again?"

"Yeah. Buzzed it."

"In winter? Your place has lousy insulation."

"But you like my hair short." Ollie palmed the swell of her breast as she licked into the next kiss.

Vegas 'accidentally' kicked him in the shins as she shimmied out of her pyjamas. She yanked off his trousers, taking the opportunity to flip him onto his back, straddling his hips.

Ollie stared up at her. Being relieved and turned on at the same time was both familiar and thrilling. "We good?" he asked, hands on her waist.

Vegas leaned forwards, hair falling in a curtain around their faces. "I don't know. Are you sorry for guilt-tripping me?"

"Look who's talking."

"That doesn't sound very apologetic." Vegas slid one index finger along his jaw, over his collarbone, across his pectoral...then twisted his left nipple, hard.

"Ow! Fuck!"

"It takes more than chocolate."

"Yes, yes, alright! Damn, I can't regrow these, you know."

"You don't need either of them, Oliver Taika Everett Roskopf."

Ollie groaned, entire body a livewire. "We do this a lot. And I know it goes both ways but...I just...well."

They stared at each other for a moment, nose to nose.

"I missed you. It was shit," said Vegas in stilted honesty. Another pause. "Okay, enough chit chat. Show me how sorry you are."

They both missed the scrape of the key and the beep of the biosensor on the door. They did not miss Ethan's howl of disgust.

"No! What the fuck. *No.*"

Vegas screeched with mirth, still astride Ollie, mid-coitus. She had her back to the door, and from his vantage point, Ollie could see Ethan had one hand slapped over his eyes.

"Vegas, what the hell?" Ethan shouted. "That's the family couch! *I* use that couch! We agreed...!" He petered off into a moan of dismay.

"Just go to your room, oh my lord," said Vegas, giggling.

"No, I'm leaving. Fuck this. Fuck you, Ollie."

Vegas snickered. "What do you think we're trying to—"

"Don't *turn around*, I can see your boobs—"

"You're a doctor. You've seen boobs before."

"I don't want to see *yours!*"

"We also fucked in the kitchen," lied Ollie.

Ethan almost ricocheted off the wall in his haste to leave. He vanished into his bedroom, and they could hear him rustling, through the thin partition. Thirty seconds later, he reemerged, bag in hand, gaze averted, speaking into his headphones. "—still close by? Thank god, come rescue me. No, I'm fine, tell you later."

"Remember, your curfew's at ten," called Vegas.

"Fuck you, I'm running away," said Ethan.

The squeak of shoes against the floorboard, the jingle of keys. The front door slammed.

Vegas shifted her hips, apparently keen to send Ollie into cardiac arrest. She grinned, biting her lip, cheeks flushed. "I've got work in twenty."

"Don't worry," Ollie managed. "I'm punctual when it counts."

Six days later, Wednesday, 27 October.

BEING BACK in Vegas's good books made dreary days helium light. Despite the numerous dead-end leads and scrapped drafts, Ollie was in a toweringly good mood all week.

As he stepped out of the lifts on Level 6, his phone pinged.

> 18:01 · FLORENCE — Where are you?

> 18:02 · OLIVER — In bed. What are you wearing? ;)

> 18:02 · FLORENCE— Can you send me your spreadsheet on glass overdose stats from Tuesday?

> 18:03 · OLIVER — Later tonight ok? I'm about to see a mechanic.

> 18:03 · FLORENCE — Is that what we're calling it now. (Tonight is great, thanks!)

> 18:03 · OLIVER — FOR A STORY. (You're welcome.)

> 18:04 · OLIVER — I have questions about autocabs, like the one Tim was in.

18:06 · FLORENCE — What did Vegas say
about the left-handed thing?

> 18:07 · OLIVER — Turns out some people do
> mainline with their non-dominant hand. Not
> conclusive enough for Ian. Vegas said
> nothing else stood out, but she isn't a
> pathologist.
>
> 18:08 · OLIVER — I'm gonna see if I can
> eliminate some theories re the cab, since
> the traffic cameras were a dead end.
>
> 18:08 · OLIVER — Have you heard from
> Martin at all this week?

18:08 · FLORENCE — No, sorry.

Ollie cursed, glancing both ways before dashing across the street. Martin had promised to talk to Tim's friends but hadn't been in touch.

> 18:15 · OLIVER— Hi Martin, just checking in.
> Have updates re tox report. Call me when
> you can.

It was probably time he dropped by for a visit anyway.

TOM'S GARAGE sat two blocks from the off-ramp, overshadowed by the Level above. The air rang with traffic and the buzz of old electromagnetic rails – a deep, immortal tuning-fork.

A talk-show burbled from hidden speakers in the cramped waiting room. Muffled rock music filtered from the main workshop. Ollie rang the buzzer at the abandoned front desk.

A moment later, a girl popped her head around the staff-only door. She had grease on her chin. "Hey there." She raised her voice over the general din. "You have an appointment?"

"Yeah, Tom's expecting me."

She tapped the side of her headphones. "*Tommy? Yeah, a bloke's here to see ya.*" To Ollie, she said, "He'll be out in a minute."

Through the clear cut-out in the door, Ollie spotted a two-seater flier resting on a half-elevated platform. Further in, a row of familiar black cabs.

When Tom finally appeared, he gave Ollie a spine-shattering clap to the shoulder. "Ollie! Can't chat for long, gotta help Ben with a racer. How are you?"

"Same old." Ollie followed Tom into the garage proper. Fliers and cars sat with their guts exposed, waiting for surgery. "How's married life?"

"Good!" Tom beamed. "Kate's expecting."

"Oh shit, no way?" Ollie tried to keep the mild horror from his voice. "That's big news. Congratulations."

Tom stood half a head over Ollie and was built like a boxer. His voice carried with the practice of someone used to speaking above machinery. And like all the other men that Ethan had dated, he was blonde.

A small office overlooked the main garage, housing mismatched furniture beneath a low ceiling.

Tom kicked a squeaky chair towards Ollie. "You said you had questions about cabs."

"Yeah. But you must keep this to yourself."

"Are *you* gonna keep it to yourself?"

"Have you heard about the guy with a cab full of CM15? From a few weeks ago? Well, he's dead."

"That story you wrote?"

Ollie paused. "You've read it?"

"Vegas sent the article in our group chat. She shares links to everything with your name on it."

Something clenched, lead heavy in the pit of Ollie's stomach. He tried to school his expression into nonchalance. Judging by the shape of Tom's eyebrow, Ollie failed.

"I didn't read it," Tom added. "No offence."

"None taken." Pulling out his phone, Ollie swiped through a few photos of Tim's cab for Tom to examine.

"Hm. Most autocabs are registered to the same two holding companies. The actual registrant might be different, but it's one of two if you go up the food chain. They use the same couple of insurers. It's steady work." Tom swiped to the next photo, eyes shrewd. "What do you want?"

"You can't tell Ian if he comes knocking."

"I'm not crossing Ethan's old man."

"I just need your opinion on a hypothetical."

Tom tapped the photo of Tim. "Doesn't seem hypothetical."

"Listen, this whole story is suss. Too many convenient vectors." *Including the tip I received.* "Cab routes are all logged, right?"

"Yeah, normally tracked live," said Tom. "Helps with congestion. There's receivers all over London to help, 'cause GPS can get scrambled on the lower Levels. Why?"

Ollie knew that the SIA had already tracked Hersch's route from Level 9 to Level 4, and must have the location records. If they proceeded on the assumption that no one approached the cab on Level 4, then either the cab must have stopped on the way there, or someone got Hersch before he got into the car on Level 9.

"How secure are these records? Could the ping-rate be altered retrospectively? Or faked?"

Tom shrugged. "Depends on how long the record is kept. Driverless models have the longest. But I'm more of a hardware than a software guy." He floated Ollie's phone free of his slack fingers.

Ollie snatched it back out of the air. Telekinetics were such show-offs. "Oi, don't scramble it!"

Tom laughed. "Calm down, they're all insulated."

"Mine's old," Ollie muttered.

"Couldn't the police figure out if someone tampered with location records?"

"You'd hope so, but I'm not sure they're looking that hard."

"I'm sure they have actual experts examining all the other records that get captured in an auto-cab."

Ollie's ears perked up. "Such as?"

"Autocabs log every time a door opens or closes. All models alert emergency services after a crash."

"Interesting. Can *that* be altered? Or is it a mechanical clicker counter?"

"Physical tampering is no good unless the digital record is also altered to match."

"But tampering *is* possible." Ollie drummed his fingers on his knee. He'd been so embroiled in the misaligned circumstances of Tim Hersch's death that he'd forgotten the initial possibility: that Tim had been up to no good.

"I don't know how you'll get access, but the EMS alerts are harder to fudge. They're logged live and it depends on which catchment area the vehicle is in. If this guy died in the car and no alert was flagged – that's telling."

Realisation dawned on Ollie. "What if he was already dead when he got in the cab? Would the car know?"

Tom squinted. "How would a dead person hail a cab by himself?"

"Exactly."

OLLIE'S PHONE CALL went to Martin's voicemail again, so he got off the tube a few stops early to pay him a visit.

At 7.30 pm, the air clung to skin and lungs, the collective condensation of a city heaving for breath.

No one answered the intercom.

Ollie redialled. "C'mon mate. Pick up." The dial-tone went to voicemail. "Bugger."

He paced with indecision. Rain started to fall, building quickly to a roar. Ollie flattened himself against the lobby entrance. Maybe he could call the ad agency's public number and catch Martin at the office. Then Ollie remembered that Martin was taking bereavement leave, devoting every waking hour to the how and why of his son's death.

"Call me anytime you have news," Martin had said, gaze bloodshot but clear. "Don't care when. Just call."

That was over a week ago.

"You alright, dear?"

Ollie looked around. An old lady smiled at him, groceries in one hand, enormous umbrella in the other. She eyed Ollie's shivering form with a mix of suspicion and sympathy.

"I'm fine, ma'am, thank you." Ollie stepped out of her way,

deliberately into the rain. "Trying to check on a friend who isn't well. Do you need a hand?"

"No, no." She gestured Ollie inside, shaking her umbrella. "This old thing never closes properly."

"They're designed so you have to buy new ones."

"Too right!" She tottered to the mailboxes.

Ollie tried to catch her flat number: if she was on the same floor as Martin, maybe he could tailgate. "Sorry, I've been rude. I'm Oliver."

The lady shook his hand, eyes crinkling. "Meredith. Who did you say you're visiting?"

"Martin, he's on the fourth floor."

Meredith stopped short. "Oh dear. You haven't heard...?"

"You know Mr Hersch?" asked Ollie.

"I thought you were friends."

"Work friends." Ollie thought fast. "I'm a copywriter at the agency. Martin hasn't been feeling well, so."

Meredith lay a hand on his wrist. "Dear, I'm not sure I'm the best person to be saying this, but Martin passed away."

It was a few moments before Ollie's tongue unfroze. "What?" he croaked. "When?"

"The police came last week," said Meredith, mouth pursed with the sympathy of a neighbour but not a friend. "I was heading out when they arrived."

"What happened? An accident? Did you see anything?"

"We had that freak storm. A grade five upstairs, but we get the southerlies down here. Howled like anything! Alicia – that's Martin's neighbour – said she saw his windows were open. Alicia knew him better than me. I'm down the other end of the hall."

"Right," said Ollie, faintly.

"Apparently he drank himself to death, the poor man." Meredith paused. "Do you need to sit down, dear?"

"I'm fine. I...thanks for telling me."

Meredith patted his arm again. "I'm sorry for breaking the news to you like this. Will you be alright by yourself?"

"Yeah. Thanks." Disoriented by the casual way Meredith had recounted the events, Ollie stared at the timestamp on his phone.

> 01:12 · MARTIN — Not much news. Had
> coffee with them this morning.

'Them' being Tim's university friends. Martin insisted on removing most details from their texts and refused to talk over the phone. Protective. Ollie had asked Martin for patience. *These things take time, unfortunately. We've got to stick with it.* As it turned out, Martin knew better.

They didn't have time for patience and other such virtues.

When Ollie could hear again, the old lady had vanished into the lifts – leaving him alone with only the weight of the blinking surveillance camera and a few long, empty minutes.

TWELVE

Special Investigations Agency, Central London Precinct, Level 10.
The next evening, Thursday, 28 October.

I t was hard to sleep after that. Martin's death clung to Ollie's conscience every time he walked to the station, past the spot where he found Tim. The space pulled his gaze in; the gaping maw of an unanswered question.

"I told you," Nick said, "Ian's busy. *I'm* busy."

Ollie crossed his arms. "We spoke on Monday. You didn't think to mention that Martin was murdered in his bloody flat?"

"For fuck's sake." Nick shunted Ollie into the nearest interview room. "Have some discretion."

Tim's Arden Pharma uniform and the vials of stolen CM15, the syringe in the front seat – it had all painted such a clear picture. And maybe that was it. Maybe that picture was a tad sharp, ends tied a little too neat. Initially Ollie thought Tim and his activist friends might have run afoul of Langley or some other glass-trafficking intermediary. Martin's death suggested something more.

Nick sighed. "Before you say anything else: I'm not denying, confirming, or otherwise reacting to anything you're about to try on. But I will tell you something for free."

"Yeah?"

"Stop speculating."

Ollie sat on the edge of the desk. "Martin's neighbour told me that he drank himself to death. That true?" No response. "What did the toxicology report say?"

"You know I can't talk to the press about on-going investigations."

"At least it's *on-going*. Because an overdose is one thing, but two in a row?"

Nick scrubbed a hand over his face. "This conversation is over."

"Fine with me, I wanna talk to Ian."

"Make an appointment."

"I was in contact with Martin before he went quiet. He had been talking to Sixty-Fourthers about his son's death. You think there's nothing here?" Silence. "Well, this is disappointing. Martin's theories look a lot less paranoid this side of the grave."

"What theories?"

"Are we going on record now?"

"No."

Ollie kicked out the metal chair next to the table. "I guess I'll wait for Ian then. No need to keep me company."

"As if," said Nick. "I'm escorting you out."

"You can *try*—" Ollie's phone lit up on the table with a rattling buzz. It was a text from one Ethan Faulkner.

> 18:06 · ETHAN — Where the fuck are you.
>
> 18:06 · ETHAN — You're late. Vegas is upset. Get here or else.

"Wow," said Ollie. "Look at that. Sentences."

Nick snorted. "This is pretty verbose, for Ethan. Usually, he's just emojis."

> 18:07 · ETHAN — Will castrate you if she cries. We are out of ice cream. Shithead.

"I think Ethan missed out on some critical socialisation, being rushed through school," said Ollie.

"He saves people every day. I'd say he's doing alright."

"Don't suck his dick too hard, you might get injured."

"That's not how healing works."

> 18:08 · ETHAN — Not saving any food for you.
>
> 18:08 · ETHAN — There's calamari. Your favourite.
>
> 18:09 · ETHAN — HELLO? Are you ignoring me???

"Well?" said Nick, nodding at the screen. "Are you? Sounds like Vegas isn't happy."

Ollie pocketed the phone without answering Ethan. He wanted to stay and ambush Ian at dinner time but didn't want to step on the familiar relationship landmine. *Priorities.*

At some point, Ollie would be late to one thing too many, and upset Vegas. Exhaustion and career progression went hand in hand, but so did pots and kettles. He wasn't keen to restart the cycle again so soon – even though he felt off about being so happy with Vegas while Martin lay cold and dead on the other end of his phone.

"We're not done here," said Ollie.

Nick raised both eyebrows. "Piss off before I text Vegas myself."

Bergenia Residences, Lower Lambeth, Level 9.

BY THE TIME Ollie swiped himself into the building (Vegas reinstated his key-fob privileges), it was 6.45 pm. He caught his reflection in the lift mirror and winced at the eyebags. If he wasn't careful, he'd start resembling Ethan. The familiar soundtrack of Vegas and Ethan's favourite first-person VR shooter greeted Ollie at the front door.

"Finally!" Vegas was in sweatpants and her Queen's College Med Revue shirt, wine glasses in hand. She didn't seem upset at Ollie's tardiness, stepping in for a kiss.

"Hey you." Ollie sank his fingers into her hair. Vegas tasted of stale coffee and well-loved habits. "Sorry I'm late."

"You haven't missed much. Oi, Ollie's here!"

"Damn," called Ethan. "I mean, hi."

"Go wash your hands before dinner," Ollie shot back, toeing off his shoes.

He froze in his tracks.

There, next to Ethan, was the last man that Ollie expected to see on their living room couch.

"Hello," said Javier Arden. He smiled, all straight teeth and slate-blonde hair. His sleeves were buttoned-up to the wrists like a sociopath.

The silence barrelled past polite and into awkward.

Javier started to rise; hand outstretched for a handshake.

Without looking away from the screen, Ethan pushed Javier back down with a hand on the thigh. "Nope," he said, taking out three zombies.

"You must be Vegas's boyfriend," said Javier. "I'm Javier."

Disbelief threw Ollie's senses into overdrive, his depth of field shaved paper thin as his mind whirred. Javier's guileless smile was garish when superimposed on Martin's features, Tim's autopsy report between them, loose threads everywhere. Martin's words rang in his ear: *For all I know, Langley and the Ardens are in on it.*

And now Javier Arden was sitting in their living room. *Pretend you don't know him!* Ollie's inner voices always sounded like Florence or Vegas. *Don't bungle this. Figure out why he's here.*

The real Vegas shot him a pointed look. "Earth to Ollie?"

"Have you tried turning him on and off again?" asked Ethan.

"Not in public," Vegas grinned.

Later, Ollie would blame the shock and sleep deprivation for what came out of his mouth. "What the hell happened to Nick?!"

Vegas spluttered on her wine.

Ethan shot Ollie a wide-eyed, homicidal stare. "I *assume* he's at work."

Javier looked between them. His socks matched the colour of his shirt. Someone who put this much effort into their appearance always had ulterior motives.

"Are we expecting more company?" asked Javier.

"No," said Ethan. "Ollie just hates me."

Vegas yanked Ethan into a hug. "You know we love you."

"Do we though," said Ollie.

"Let me up," Ethan protested, muffled from where Vegas had his face trapped in her cleavage. A hand flailed. "Jav!"

"Jav can't save you, he's helping me with the wine," said Vegas, making loud kissy noises as Ethan squirmed.

Javier popped the cork on an expensive-looking bottle. He poured with a practised hand; watch on one wrist, gold band on the other.

"*Jav?*" Ollie mouthed, when Javier had his back turned. Vegas shrugged. Ethan used the distraction to wrench himself free. Ollie rallied his composure. "Sorry, you caught me by surprise. Ethan doesn't have friends." He held out a hand. "Ollie."

Javier shook it, still smiling. It was disconcerting in a way that Ollie couldn't define. This initial nasty surprise had evaporated like rain on chrome rails.

"Hope I'm not ruining your usual rhythm of things too much," said Javier.

"With this wine, you're welcome to come over every day," said Vegas.

"Move," said Ollie, kicking Ethan in the shins.

"No."

"My legs are too long for the beanbag. You're short."

"Am not. *You* use the bloody beanbag."

"I'm happy to sit on the beanbag," said Javier.

"*No*," sighed Ethan, retrieving the onigiri-print beanbag and settling between Javier's knees.

Food was an ever-present motif in the flat. A burrito-print blanket was draped over the back of the couch, the pink donut floor cushion being Vegas' favourite.

"Jav brought fresh calamari and salmon," said Vegas.

She and Ethan were so easily won over by food. Ollie slowly began assembling his taco. Javier did the same without rolling up his white sleeves. Untrustworthy behaviour. Wariness scraped against an impatient, burning curiosity.

They ate wordlessly to the backdrop of in-game pause music.

Ollie wondered how Florence was going to react. He waved a hand between Jav and Ethan. "So, are you two...?"

Ethan was hunched over an overstuffed fish taco like a gremlin. "What."

"Fucking," said Ollie.

"Classy," Vegas laughed, handing a napkin to a spluttering Javier.

"*Dating*," Ethan corrected.

Ollie frowned, affronted on Nick's behalf. Ethan and Nick had been together for two years, yet Nick rarely came to game nights.

Javier's mere presence was insulting and out of character. "Since when?"

Ethan wiped lime juice off his chin with one hand. "Did you need five business days' notice?"

"Someone else might need notice," said Ollie pointedly.

"It's been a month or so," said Javier, in a tone that suggested he knew the exact date and hour and was counting down to an anniversary. He was still smiling, the conniving bastard.

"How did you meet Ethan?" asked Ollie.

"The hospital." A sappy look came over Javier's face. "Ethan and Vegas saved my sister's life."

Ollie turned to Ethan, mock surprised. "A patient?"

"Briefly." Ethan bumped Jav's knee. "Extremely brief. Right, babe?"

Javier appeared both thrilled at the pet name and abashed at Ethan's tone. "I'm sorry." He folded himself in half to kiss Ethan on the cheek. "Won't happen again."

"Jav got her transferred to Highgate, and Ethan is not over it," said Vegas.

"It was dangerous," said Ethan.

"Well, I hope your sister's alright," said Ollie.

Javier nodded. "She's doing great, thanks."

"Must have been pretty bad to get Ethan involved," Ollie continued. "Car crash or something?"

"Or something," said Javier. "I never want to go through anything like that again."

"What hap—"

"And bonus: you met me," said Ethan.

"I *did*," Javier agreed, hearts in his eyes.

Ollie wondered if he had hit his head and this was all a bad hallucination. His hand itched to activate the dot mics in his pocket.

"Ahem, where's my credit?" Vegas sipped her wine. "Jav, did you know Ethan threw your first card away?"

Javier's pout was large enough to shelve a pot plant.

"It was an accident," said Ethan.

"And then you 'accidentally' blocked his number."

That sounded more in character. Ethan muttered something under his breath that sounded suspiciously like *and that's not the only thing that's blocked.*

"All's well that ends well." Javier cleared his throat. "So, Oliver. Vegas said you write?"

"The Sentinel." Ollie wrote prolifically on the glass epidemic and CM15-adjacent issues. Javier must know, especially as Ollie broke the story that preceded Corinna Arden's hospital visit. He scrutinised Javier's expression. Ollie's anxiety about Ethan and Vegas, spurred by the spectre of two dead bodies, made double-bluffing impossible.

"How impressive," said Javier.

"Is it?" drawled Ethan.

Javier blinked.

"Yes," said Ollie, "he's always this petty. It's not too late to change your mind."

"Says the man who gets returned for a refund on a quarterly basis—"

Vegas threw a crumpled napkin at Ethan across the table. It hit him square on the nose. "Boys, play nice."

"Did you go to Queen's with Ethan and Vegas?" asked Javier.

"We overlapped a bit."

Javier's bland curiosity made Ollie antsy. He shrugged to mask his unease. "There aren't too many jobs that pay you for writing and being nosy."

"Ollie narrowly escaped being a lawyer," said Vegas.

"You mean I narrowly escaped being soullessly boring."

"Alas! I could be a pampered housewife."

Ethan rolled his eyes. "Then you should have gone out with any one of the visiting surgeons that have asked me for your number. But *no.* You want—" he gestured at Ollie with a half-eaten taco "—whatever this is. I never send you anyone below an eight."

"Ethan," said Vegas, "we've been through this. Dominic was gay."

"Why would he ask for your number then?"

"He wanted *yours* but you gave him mine and demanded a valid passport and a years' worth of bank statements."

"I was gonna get dad to run a background check."

"To see if he's gay?"

"To see if he's a *criminal*."

Ollie choked on his salad. The dossier the SIA had on Javier's family was far larger than any random doctor that Ethan wanted to play matchmaker with. To his credit, Javier barely reacted.

"Who's this Dominic person?" asked Ollie. "Do you hand out Vegas's number to all and sundry?"

"Obviously not, he was in orthopaedics," said Ethan.

"And?"

"Ethan enjoys the gun show," said Vegas, as if that explained anything. She nodded at Ethan. "Your gaydar's shit."

"My gaydar is perfectly profitable, thank you." Ethan made jazz-hands at Javier, who looked like he very much wanted to know where Ethan rated *him* out of ten.

"Let me find a photo." After a moment, Vegas brandished her phone screen at Javier and Ollie.

There was a photo of a man in his early forties. He had a square jaw, green eyes, and most importantly, brown hair.

"Ah," said Ollie.

"Exactly," said Vegas, vindicated.

Ethan leaned against Javier's leg, one elbow resting on his knee. "Well?"

"I'm glad I'm not competing with a surgeon," Javier said diplomatically.

"Seems a bit old for Vegas anyway," said Ollie.

"*You're* old," Ethan shot back. "The point is, I've found heaps of men – piles of them – who all have better résumés than you."

Vegas stroked Ollie's ankle. "At least *I* found a man who likes to eat p—"

"Al*right*!" Ollie turned to Javier. "Were you a Queen's College alum?"

"No. I'm the odd one out it seems."

"Oxbridge?"

"Heavens, no."

"Boat-shoes not for you?"

Javier laughed. "I didn't follow the usual university track with my previous career."

"Jav teaches at the Royal Ballet," said Ethan, patting Javier's right calf.

"Ethan can send you the videos he binge-watches at 3 am," said Vegas.

"It's good content," said Ethan.

"I don't care what you wank off to," said Vegas. "Wear headphones, so I don't have to wank alongside—"

"Oh my god." Ethan got ungracefully to his feet. "Jav is never visiting again."

"Why am I the one being punished?" Jav protested. "Did you really watch my old ballet videos?"

"Yes." Ethan promptly tripped over the beanbag, knocking into the dining table. He swore all the way to the bathroom.

The door clicked shut. Jav looked from Ollie to Vegas.

"Yeah, it's like this all the time," said Vegas.

Ollie couldn't take it anymore. When he heard the toilet whirr, he rolled over the back of the couch. "Next in the queue." He caught the bathroom door handle as it unlocked – shoving Ethan backwards and kicking the door closed with one foot.

Ethan's face cycled through the first three stages of outrage in an instant.

"What the fuck do you think you're doing?" Ollie hissed.

"What are *you* doing?" Ethan shot back, much too loud.

Ollie jabbed a thumb over his shoulder. "Do you know who that is?"

"Jav?"

"Yes, *Jav*," snapped Ollie. "Javier Arden." He reached past Ethan to grab the hand sanitiser, scoring a thumbnail beneath the small print: Arden Pharmaceuticals. "*This* Arden. Come on now, you're a doctor."

Ethan's expression didn't shift but he leaned back against the sink and crossed his arms. "So?"

"So?" echoed Ollie, blood thrumming in his ears. "*So,* you knew who he was, and you still slept with him?"

"This house is a politics-free zone," said Ethan, like the privileged brat that he was. "You're so dramatic."

Ollie waved a hand under the dryer so the sound would mask their voices. It was hard to swallow the mounting urgency lodged at the base of his throat. "There's been a lot of coincidence involving that man's sister. The night Corinna Arden was shot, one of her warehouse employees was found shortly after, dead. Ostensibly a glass overdose, but I've been investigating discrepancies with the deceased's father. Who, I found out last night, is now *also* dead – by alcohol poisoning, if you can believe it? And now—"

"This is also a conspiracy-free zone."

"Did you and Nick have a fight or something?"

Ethan looked constipated. "None of your business."

"I know for a fact that Nick didn't sign off on this."

"*Sign off*—! What kind of—! I don't need his—"

"And he doesn't need *you*. If you've broken up, great! Nick can do much better, but at least shagging Nick won't get you poisoned."

"Oh please, Jav is harmless."

Time was running out. Ollie could only trap Ethan in the bathroom for so long. If Ethan refused to see sense..."Harmless, huh. You think your dad would agree?"

"...Dad wouldn't have an opinion because it's none of his business either."

"Great, so you won't mind if I let him know what's going on. Can't be too careful."

A pause, made stark when the dryer cut out.

This time, Ethan waved his hand under the sensor. "You wouldn't."

At last – uncertainty. "So you agree that Arden is dodgy."

Ethan tilted his head. "Look. I know about the stuff."

"The stuff."

"Dad's glass files. CM15 rorts. When has there *not* been stuff? But Jav doesn't work for Arden Pharma, and even if he did, have you met him? Wouldn't hurt a fly."

"There's a lot of money at stake. If the Ardens are getting personally involved, he's dating you just to—"

They both jumped when the bathroom door flew open.

"It's okay," Vegas called over her shoulder. "They've both still got trousers on." She turned back to Ethan and Ollie. "Got lost, did we?"

Ethan and Ollie glared at each other. A mere few feet separated them from the living room – and Javier's coiffed head.

"Ollie is worried about a rash on his dick," Ethan said loudly. "Horrific. We should quarantine him."

Vegas herded them back to the living room. "I'll have to examine that later."

Ollie wiggled his eyebrows. "Thanks, Dr Kelsey."

"Gross." Ethan pulled a face. "Are you staying the night?"

"Me?" asked Jav, inflection hopeful.

"No, me," said Ollie.

"Jav can stay if he wants," Ethan said with a toddler's devotion to contrarianism.

Ollie broke out in metaphorical hives at the thought of Javier being alone with Vegas and Ethan.

Perhaps sensing Ollie's allergic reaction, Jav said, "If a full house is inconvenient—"

"We can all wear headphones in bed," said Vegas sweetly.

Javier went pink. Ollie had to hand it to him: he was a convincing actor.

Then Ethan threw a spanner in the works. "I could stay over at your place," he said to Javier.

"No!" Ollie exclaimed. Everyone stared at him. "You've got day shift tomorrow," he added, lamely.

"I'll give you a lift to work in the morning," said Javier.

"The car drives itself," said Ethan. "Just shove me in and off I go."

"People will notice if he's not at work," Ollie tried. "You can count all of St Ophie's healers on one hand."

Ethan gathered the dirty plates from the coffee table. "Alarms exist."

"So we're not doing any actual gaming then?" asked Ollie.

Ethan began loading the dishcleaner – no doubt rushing to separate Javier and Ollie. "Yeah. Getting late."

Goddammit.

Vegas poured herself another glass. "Ethan likes to be in bed by nine so don't keep him up too long, Jav."

"Fuck *off*," said Ethan.

Logically, Ollie knew that Ethan wasn't in any immediate danger.

Given this whole affair was a month old, Javier was probably keeping an eye on things. Ollie couldn't look away from Vegas and the wineglass in her hand. He thought of Martin's neighbour: *They said he drank himself to death.*

Ethan slid open the roller-door to his bedroom, reappearing moments later with a familiar satchel.

Javier cleared his throat. "Thanks for having me for dinner. I know you're all busy. Really lovely to meet everyone."

Vegas leaned backwards on the beanbag, shaking Javier's hand upside-down. "Remember our deal. There's more photos where those came from."

"What photos?" Ethan demanded. "What deal?"

"I'm a man of my word," said Javier solemnly.

"Jav."

"...You were a very cute toddler."

Ethan rounded on Vegas. "I want a cut of whatever he bribed you with."

Javier offered his hand to Ollie. "Hope we'll be seeing more of each other. You can trounce me in VR-anything. Ethan can attest."

Ollie shook Jav's hand, feeling ill. "Sure."

"We're out of eggs," said Vegas.

"Make Ollie do groceries, he ate the last two." Ethan threaded his arms through the jacket that Javier was holding out for him.

The man was laying it on thick, but this post-personality-transplant Ethan seemed to enjoy the performance.

"Be careful," Ollie tried. "It's foggy out. Don't get blindsided."

Ethan rolled his eyes. "Thanks channel four."

The door closed with a soft click.

"Wow," said Vegas from her beanbag. "You *really* didn't like Jav, huh."

"You don't say!" Ollie exploded.

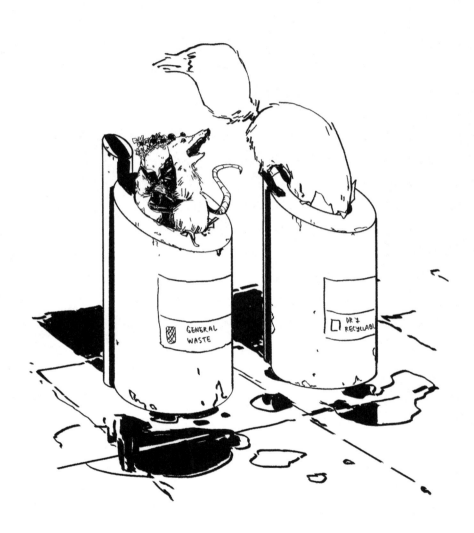

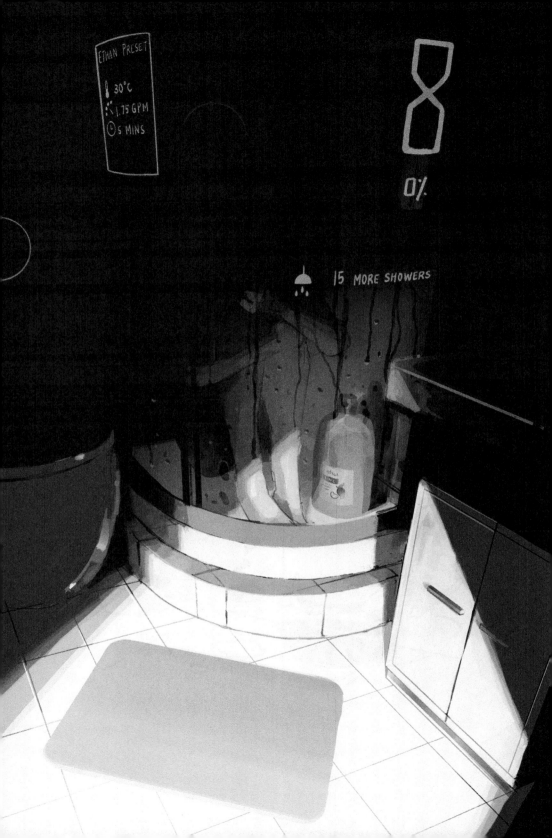

THIRTEEN

Bergenia Residences, Lower Lambeth, Level 9.
Friday, 12 November.

Ethan subscribed to the The-Other-Shoe-Dropping theory in the Nothing-Good-Ever-Lasts school of thought. So, when a fortnight went by uninterrupted by angry fathers, Ethan wasn't relieved. Ollie was clearly saving his blackmail for a rainy day.

"Aren't you supposed to be out?" asked Vegas.

Ethan didn't look up. "No."

Life defaulted to resignation. Time ground apathy into guilt's fine dust. Inertia was equally reliable: to sleep and to wake, watch a bruise bloom dark and vanish. Like his body, each new day reset itself in tireless monotony, leaving no souvenir of the day before.

Ethan wasn't depressed. Probably situational depression; logical depression, however oxymoronic. *Just tired*, he told his therapist during mandatory counselling sessions.

Javier contrasted monotony like a hailstorm in sunshine. His presence warped the passage of time, minutes unevenly spaced between contentment and the heady fondness of being so wanted. They dinnered three times a week: still too novel to be routine. They even lunched. Lunch! A ten-minute window that Jav dashed through with alarming determination.

Perhaps Ethan owed his good mood to sleeping eight hours a night. Or the simple spice of new things – the rush would wear off soon. Ethan realised, with a bit of panic, he was dreading it.

"You said something about Kew Gardens," Vegas continued, memory like a steel trap.

"Cancelled."

"Jav cancelled?"

Ethan shifted guiltily on the couch. "No. Me."

"Why?"

"Tired."

"What about your dinner date last week?"

"...Exhaustion is cumulative."

Vegas levelled an unimpressed look before stomping to the bathroom. Ethan resisted the urge to check his messages. He'd been a coward and cancelled on Javier with less than an hour's notice.

> 18.21 · JAVIER — Rest up. Do you have dinner at home? Let me send you something.

Ethan had left him on 'read'. *Six weeks wasn't long.* No use waiting to see if Jav would get annoyed. Better to know now. Cut losses. Prevention is better than cure.

Eight minutes later (shower timers defaulted to five minutes, which was never enough), Vegas emerged in clean pyjamas and a scowl. She clattered about the kitchen, returning with a packet of cherry tomatoes. "Why're you self-sabotaging? Did Jav say something weird?"

"No."

"Did he do something?"

"No, everything's fine." Ethan stared at his unfinished sketch. Vegas waited, hands on hips. No interruptions came to the rescue. "I'm managing his expectations."

"By ghosting? Again? We just had this conversation about Nick."

"Yes, well."

"It's not nice to test people."

Ethan flushed. "You test Ollie all the time. And grade him on a curve."

"We've been—" Vegas waved "—forever. He always comes back."

"How nice for you."

"Ethan."

"Vegas." He stole a handful of tomatoes.

"Destroying relationships on purpose is not more admirable than doing it by accident."

"I'm not *trying* to fuck up. Just giving full disclosure."

"Have you tried using words?"

Ethan snorted. "You say upfront that you've got unpredictable hours, that you're gonna be tired. They say, 'I support you'. Everyone thinks it'll be okay until they experience it. Then the resentment comes out, right, you're the one who isn't invested, you're the one who doesn't put enough effort—"

"Ethan."

"—so fine, you say 'maybe let's take a break', and they go, 'I just want you to be happy'. Then they leave. Not this fake-leaving that you and Ollie do. They're relieved for an out. I'm cutting to the chase."

Vegas groaned into the nearest cushion. "Why do you talk as if you've had your heart broken ten times—"

Ethan went red. "Who said anything about br—"

"—when you're actually a foetus, and this is all about Tom."

"This isn't about Tom. I've dated other people."

Vegas raised both eyebrows. "You said you and Nick weren't dating."

"...Fine. I've *slept* with other people."

"You sure Nick's on the same page?"

"He hates labels. I mean, have you ever seen him around at breakfast? No. How else should I interpret it? And before you say anything, I'm not asking Ollie." Ethan stared at the blank television. "I want to see if Jav's okay with it, like he keeps saying he is. See if he'll stay."

"No," said Vegas, years' worth of patience wrapped in one syllable. "You want to see if he'll leave."

"Same thing."

"It really isn't."

They lapsed back into silence.

"We already know what happens when you're immature by accident," said Vegas. "Don't be immature on purpose and expect different results."

"If Jav can't handle me cancelling—"

"You're gonna keep at it until he gives up?"

"Well, I'd rather know now than later."

Vegas walloped him with a cushion. "Stop testing people. I know you have abandonment issues, but you can't actively be your worst just to see if people will put up with it. Plus, it's not fair on poor Jav. He's sweet on you."

Ethan made a noise of agreement. Jav was sweet in general. "Ollie thinks he's gonna kill us in our sleep."

"Ollie says Jav has ulterior motives because of Ian's investigations. The dead protestor had him spooked."

Javier and nefariousness felt oxymoronic. "And? What do you think?"

"I think Ollie lives in a crime noir." Vegas yawned. "I haven't seen you smile this much for ages. It's creepy."

"I'm glad I creep you out," said Ethan, dehydrated from all the sincerity.

"Yeah, yeah. Keep it up while you can. Ian's gonna have a fit."

St Ophie's General Hospital, Level 9. The next afternoon.

BETH, A SENIOR ICU registrar, was brisk. Medicine was a bloody business, and time its currency. "New mum, thirty-five, non-aptee.

Standard editing, so no allergies. O&G noticed mild bleeding eight hours after delivery. Got worse this morning."

The ICU nurse ushered the patient's husband out of the room. The man stared at the VM light on Ethan's temple as they passed, gaze fervent with hope. This misplaced faith still unnerved him – *wouldn't dread be more appropriate?* A healer in the ICU meant something had gone wrong, fast.

"Clotting factors didn't work?" Ethan asked. "These numbers aren't good."

"She's circling the drain. The lab called two hours ago, saying her PTTs and PTs are long. We transfused her again, but she started bleeding from her IV site. Desatting and hypotensive. Have you dealt with disseminated intravascular coagulation before?"

Ethan shook his head. "Not solo." DIC: a once-uncommon condition that now occurred with worrying frequency. *There's something in the water. Something in the air. Something healers can't fix.* One day, there would be nothing left except water, bone, and plastic. "I don't know how her plasminogens will react to my transference. Might get stuck in a loop. This is a two-plus healer job."

"She doesn't have that kind of cover. We can't transfer to a clinic. I hoped you'd be able to lay hands on, at least."

The heart monitor stuttered as the ICU nurse returned.

Ethan pressed a palm below the patient's IV tape – and hissed. *Pain between his legs, wound tight at the base of his gut, along his stomach...*his skin crawled as every site fought to close: the sutures, IV sites, everything. As soon as one sealed, another frayed open. "There's internal bleeding, but if I push, the extra clot—"

"Risks sending her into shock," Beth finished.

Their patient coughed wetly. The perforations were gossamer thin, a thousand pinholes beneath skin and nerves. Ethan tried to smooth over her lungs, but by the time he finished, her nose was bleeding again, capillaries inking rough and awful.

He coughed. "Sites keep reopening. Call Niharika, she's more experienced."

The patient's heart monitor sped up.

"Niharika is with Mr Besanko," said the nurse. "Louise is already red."

"Then I'll buy her some time while you prep the third transfusion," said Ethan.

Beth frowned. "You're not her consulting physician."

"If I stop, she might go into shock." *For the love of god, please stop talking – I can't keep this up for much longer.*

"She might go into shock if you *continue,* and I'd have run out your clock as well."

The patient's brow was damped with the effort of breathing, eyes flickering between fever and lucidity. "...Henry?"

"Easy, breathe," said Beth. "Your husband's just outside."

The air rushed from the room: the fresh units of blood had arrived. The patient's eyes darted from one face to another, glassy. She mouthed the same words, over and over. *My boy.*

"She wants her baby," said Ethan, going cold. "Maybe someone can bring him over, so she can at least—"

The patient exhaled all at once, the tension leaving her neck and shoulders. Ethan choked. Someone flung an arm across his chest, pushing him away from the bed. As he lost skin contact, his vision flipped into photo-negatives before snapping back into colour.

Beth's voice, saying, "I'll start compressions. Paul, ED kit."

"Here. BP 49."

"Ready."

"Clear!"

Ethan's palms burned in the aftershock. He glanced at the monitor. "She's losing too much blood. I'll—"

"I'm not pushing you into red." Beth didn't look up, palm over palm, metronomic. Their patient's head lolled with the force of each compression, brow smooth at last.

Static roared in Ethan's ears. His eyes stung hot, and he stamped down on a wild lurch from his chest into his throat. *Get it together, you're a fucking professional.* He reached out, bare handed.

"Emergency paged for you, Dr Faulkner," said a nurse, stopping Ethan in his tracks. "Abbey's waiting to brief, if you're able to take it."

Ethan tore his eyes away from their patient's face. "Your call."

"Go. You're our last resort anyway." Beth spared a quick smile. "And I *really* don't want to be the one that ran out your clock."

The moment Ethan was out of the room, he ducked into an alcove, out of sight. He scrubbed his hands clean, pressing the heels of his hands against his eyes. Beth was just being prudent. *This isn't about you. Have some bloody perspective.* Inhaling unsteadily, he wiped his face and accepted the pending call on his earpiece.

"Dr Faulkner! Dr Kelsey requested a consult, if your VM is okay."

"Amber six-ish." Ethan walked back into the ICU reception, past the central nurses' station. "Heading to you now."

A shout cut across the lobby. "Wait, Doctor!"

Ethan turned and his heart plummeted. "Hang on," he said into his earpiece.

It was their patient's husband: the man rushed over, wide-eyed. "Is everything okay? Can I see her now?"

Ethan was rooted to the tiles. He'd never been very good at this part of patient care, and his hesitation did not go unnoticed. "Dr Taylor and her team are still looking after your wife. If you take a seat, they'll—"

"Why aren't you in there with them?"

Ethan never had the stomach for platitudes. He could see his dad, getting the call at work. Could hear everyone saying, hushed but confident: *I'm sure she'll be okay. She's a healer.* How it must have felt, when they were all wrong. No hope was worth the grief that came after.

"I'm afraid a healer isn't useful in all scenarios," said Ethan. "Resuscitation—"

"*Resuscitation?* Then they need you!"

"I need to go to the emergency department," Ethan started – and realised immediately it was the wrong thing to say.

The man's face contorted.

"Dr Faulkner." Abbey was still on the line. "If you can't come down, I'll tell Dr Kelsey—"

"I'll be right th— whoa!" The man had grabbed Ethan by the upper arm. "Let go," Ethan said sharply. He tried to twist out of the grip. They were about the same height, but the man was broader, stride bolstered by panic, hands vice-like in desperation. "I said *let go.*"

The husband marched them to his wife's unit, shouldering the door open before the reception nurses had caught up. Someone shouted for security.

Ethan brought his fist down on the hand around his arm. The man yanked him forwards by the front of his scrubs, shaking from hand to shoulder. Ethan could feel *an open ulcer inside his lip, a two-day old cut on his chin—*

"Please help. Please help her."

Ethan threw himself backwards, heels skidding, one foot connecting with something. Gravity slid up his spine in a stomach-lurching swoop.

They both went down, hard – Ethan's head bounced against the tile with a *crack*. The ceiling lights sunburst on impact, whiting his vision against the sharp pain and the taste of blood. *Bit my tongue.* There was a pressure around his throat, hands fisted in Ethan's scrubs, catching the wire of his VM.

Sound flooded back faster than vision.

"I know there's other people here, but I'm begging you—" Then, abruptly the hands were gone. Security uniforms blocked Ethan's view, but not the desperate voice: "She needs a healer, stay with her, *please—*"

Ethan flinched at a pencil light being shone into his eyes.

Hands tilted his chin forwards. Someone pressed the lump at the back of his head. "I need a gel pack for this goose egg."

"Healers don't need — oww!"

The nurse hoisted him off the floor. The vertigo made Ethan dry retch, staggering until he was sat down. *Has the waiting room always been this loud?* A cup of water appeared in his hands.

"Does anything else hurt?" the other nurse asked. "Ankles? Back?"

"No. The bruises'll be gone in a minute." Ethan jabbed himself in the ear – and realised his earpiece was missing. "Shit. Where...?" One of the gel pads for his VM had been pulled loose, the plastic tab caught on his collar.

"You're going nowhere with that concussion. Plus, your VM's red."

Both nurses hovered as if Ethan might make a run for it. Defeated, he wondered where security had taken the patient's husband.

A nurse brandished a portable scanner over Ethan's skull. After thirty seconds, it trilled. "Hmm. You should be supervised for at least twenty-four hours. If you prefer to go home, I can call your emergency contact to come pick you up."

"But I live three steps that way," said Ethan, pointing at the exit.

"Or you can stay here overnight."

Ethan sighed. His emergency contact was Vegas, who was on-shift. Unable to stand the scrutiny and sympathy for a moment longer, he texted her – and quickly switched numbers to feign a response. He presented the screen to the nurse.

"Dr Kelsey's downstairs. She'll be up soon. I'll just wait here."

The nurse seemed reluctant but nodded. "Please sign out properly, okay?" she said, handing him a fresh gel pack.

Ethan attempted a smile. He waited a few minutes for her to disappear from sight, and another for the nearest staff to be preoccupied with triage. Then he slipped out.

LONDON HAD NEVER BEEN SUNNY; certainly not below Level 10. It was scalding bright now, saturated with sound and dust. Wind scraped the spine, a nail through the sole, rough enough to sand enamel from teeth.

It was a relief to get home.

Ethan toed off his shoes. Realising he was still in scrubs, he stripped, dumping them into the 'contaminated' hamper. He stood in his socks and underwear. Listened to the hum of the refrigerator.

Somewhere, a door slammed – Ethan flinched.

Maybe a shower would help.

Their shower unit was an ugly, airless pod. Ethan tapped the console for his pre-set and the clear doors fogged opaque like the ICU windows. Ten seconds later, the shower chimed, hissing.

Ethan stepped in, closing his eyes against the mist. He imagined the heat washing off the stains beneath his eyes and the man's grip from his arms. He tried inhaling slowly but dissolved into coughs, lungs stuttering in memory of another struggling chest. The echo left him weak kneed.

It was easier to cry alone. No people or mirrors to bear witness. Ethan sobbed into his fist, the swell of pointlessness and frustration bursting a dam in his throat. The exhaust fan drowned out the sound. Ethan wanted to scream, to manifest some tangible evidence of the shredding hurt. He managed a few croaky gasps, the sound withering like rot.

Even encased in solitude and steam, it felt performative.

Ethan cried into the shower spray, biting his lip until he tasted blood, eyes stinging with water. Eventually he shifted against the wall of this white coffin, folding down to sit, knees pressed against his chest. The water-steam pelted the back of his neck, numbing his nerves with heat. Ethan rested his forehead on his knees and breathed in the tiny dark space created by his own limbs.

His heart gradually slowed.

The water timer chimed a warning. Twenty seconds later, the flow stopped. Ethan remained curled up. He wished the water could run forever, scouring him clean of skin and sensation.

Steam sank past his shoulders, settling into the drain and goose-pimpling his neck. It was comfortable like this, with nowhere to go. He concentrated on the pressure of his kneecaps against his eyes. He breathed slowly, counting the stars inside his eyelids.

Ethan must have dozed off at some point – because the next thing he knew, he was jolted by rapid knocking.

"...are you in there? Ethan?" That didn't sound like Vegas. "Darling?"

"Hang on," Ethan croaked.

"Oh, thank god!" Jav exclaimed. "Are you alright? Can you open the door, please?"

When Ethan tried to stand, the spike of pins and needles would have toppled him – but the narrow shower saved him from a second concussion. He cursed.

"Did you hurt yourself?" Another pause. "I'm coming in."

"No," Ethan blurted. Wrapping a towel around his waist, he checked the mirror for tears. Eyes bloodshot, but explainable by the shower. Bruises gone.

He opened the bathroom door.

Jav's face was five centimetres away. His shoulders slumped at the sight of Ethan. "Oh, thank heavens!"

They stared at each other.

"What are you doing here?" asked Ethan.

"Checking in on you." Jav's eyes darted, cataloguing.

"No, I mean, how did you get in?"

Jav held up a kitty keyring. "Vegas said you'd gone home with a concussion. I got here as fast as I could, but you weren't answering your phone or the intercom." If gentle fretting could be bottled, this would be its scent: skin-warmed oak and bergamot. "I called Vegas. Detoured to the hospital for her keys."

"Oh. Sorry. I didn't hear anything."

Jav's hands hovered. The perpetual tentativeness would be frustrating if he wasn't so earnest. Ethan wanted him to do something, anything – just so Ethan didn't have to wonder anymore.

"You don't feel well," said Jav. "Does your head hurt? Let's sit down."

"Should I get dressed? Or are you getting undressed."

Jav's mouth twitched, but not enough to wipe the anxiety away. Wordlessly, Ethan shuffled to his bedroom. The curtains were still drawn, the bed unmade. When his head emerged from a t-shirt, it was to the sight of Jav in the doorway, watching.

"I slipped over at work. Nothing to worry about." Ethan sat heavily on the duvet. "What."

Jav perched next to him. "Vegas said someone assaulted you at work."

Ethan laughed, too loud for the small room, and Jav's shoulders tensed. "Not quite. Vegas wasn't there."

"What happened then?"

A baby lost their mum. "A disagreement."

Jav wore polite disbelief as handsomely as he wore everything else but his hair was an uncharacteristic mess, lower lip red from worrying teeth. Ethan leaned in to kiss him.

Jav acquiesced once, twice, then held Ethan still by the elbows. "Don't distract me. A disagreement about?"

"Whether or not I should go through a door."

"So they knocked you around? Who the *hell*—"

"If you must know, I tripped and took them down with me. We had a patient I couldn't...assist. Her husband got emotional."

Jav's fingers curled and uncurled, palpably upset.

To Ethan's horror, an answering lump swelled in his own throat. He never cried in front of others, except Vegas – not thanks to self-control but paralysing inhibition. The force of his emotions always felt unjustified, curdling into embarrassment. He and Vegas would talk about random topics until the immediate roar bled out.

Ethan didn't want to cry now either, but his eyes stung, chest strained tight as a drum.

Jav ran a hand up and down Ethan's arm. "I don't know what happened, but—"

"Then drop it."

The palm stilled, but Jav didn't move away. "I'm sorry."

"No, *I'm* sorry." Ethan pressed his knuckles against the bridge of his nose. "You should leave. I'm not good company right now."

"I don't care about that."

The tenderness made Ethan panic for something tangible to hold, lest he lose his composure. He wished Jav would squeeze all the emotion from him like blood from stone. He'd rather be empty than be filled with *this*. "You really should go."

"Ethan."

Inhaling took conscious effort. Ethan wanted to be alone so he could cry without caring whether that was selfish or not. He dug his nails into the sides of his wrists. "Don't you teach on Tuesdays?"

"Ethan," Jav repeated, gently. "May I hug you, please?"

Ethan drew back. "If you have to ask, then I don't know what the fuck we're even doing! Stop *asking* all the bloody time and put your words wh—"

Jav pulled him in, forcing all the air from Ethan's lungs in one swoop. The skin contact made him flush cold then hot. Every muscle seized, before whiplashing like a snapped piano string. The shift was so abrupt that it took another second before Ethan realised that he was bawling.

"Oh, love."

"Sorry," Ethan gulped between sobs. "This isn't...I'm just tired. I'm so tired." He'd never felt this hysterical and absent at the same time. He tried to bite back each wet breath, and might as well have tried conquering hiccups.

"It's okay," Jav tucked Ethan's face against his neck "Shhh, I'm here."

Ethan was an hourglass without a base, but Jav didn't seem to care. He pressed a cheek against Ethan's head, pouring affection in, heedless of it draining into the floor through the soles of Ethan's feet.

Jav's voice was carved from patience and worn cotton. "You can say anything, it's okay."

But Ethan never knew what he wanted, or should, hear. He could barely articulate why he was crying, so what's the point?

"It's alright to be upset," Jav continued. "It must be hard seeing patients who—"

"No. I knew what I signed up for. By the time they're...they're just bodies. Flesh." Confronted by Jav's soft hands, Ethan had to explain. "I don't know why I'm so upset. It's not about dying. You get used to it, when you can literally feel the moment second hand. Often the heart just does flip-squeeze, like—" He thumped Jav over the heart. "Bleeding out is different. Sometimes the heart just gives up." His hands shook. "If *I* died, I'm not sure I'd know the difference. I think it'd feel the same, except I wouldn't have to be there, after. God, *I'm so tired.*"

Ethan's breakdowns were often violent bouts that left him wishing he could fall asleep with a promise of being dead in the morning. "I thought I could buy her some time. But I made it worse."

Jav's eyes were bright with tears. "Ethan..."

Who knew sympathy was this hard to bear? "Should have known not to trigger it. I suppose all tools malfunction at some point."

"You're not a *thing*. This isn't your fault."

"It's my fault but I don't feel guilty." Ethan laughed. Breathing through a blocked nose was hell. "What kind of person...? You all think we're in this for the right reasons, to help people. But nothing matters because — *stop looking at me like that.*"

Jav pressed his palm harder between Ethan's shoulder blades, perhaps to mask the tremors through their paper-lungs.

But once a man began negotiating with his shadow, he never slept again. "This is literally the point of me. To do *this*. What else am I good for? What use am I?" Ethan lapsed into sobs again, throat clogged with self-loathing, eyes squeezed shut against Jav's collar. "A baby lost their mum today and I'm talking about *me*. I haven't thought about my mum for years. I don't remember...what kind of right do I have, now—!"

Jav clasped the back of Ethan's neck, and the skin contact rendered him boneless. Ethan went loose at the seams.

"Oh darling, don't say that. You'll break my heart. Shh, it's okay."

"I don't even know what I'm trying to prove," Ethan hiccupped, exhausted. "This is why I said you should go."

"You're not selfish for hurting." Jav slotted the pad of his thumb in the divot behind Ethan's ear, turning Ethan's cheek so he could breathe easier.

Ethan cried and cried. He gave up trying to be quiet, heaving gasps and coughs. Jav murmured something in his ear, words unfocused, perhaps not even in English.

Slowly, Ethan became aware that he was being rocked back and forth. Ankles locked together, Jav's arms looped tight, Ethan's left hand curled against Jav's heartbeat. It ticked a steady metronome against the jump of his own pulse. He inhaled the scent of Jav's cologne; the resin that clung to his callouses.

Gradually Ethan's breathing evened out. Shadows blurred the shape of the room, refracted through tears and exhaustion. Outside, traffic blared, acoustics whipped hard by the wind.

"You're more than your aptitude," said Jav.

Ethan tried to snort. It came out as a disgusting sniffle-cough. "It's the start and end to my intros."

"Well, healers are so rare...but you're not a utility."

"I'm lucky. Could have been worse. Could have been born in the Middle Ages. Burned at the stake for being a witch."

"Darling, really."

"A ghost at any point before the 21st century. An empath during the Holocaust. Or the Cold War. An empath, in general." Jav's chest went still but when Ethan looked up, the tension vanished. "I'm not complaining about my lot in life. We get a lot of perks. And people think you're a good person, by default."

"I wish I knew you felt this way," said Jav, regretting curling his consonants. "All the times I asked about healer stuff. You're more than that. To me."

You're too sweet to survive. "It's fine. Being a doctor is my entire personality." Ethan sighed. "Sorry for the melodrama."

"I don't think you're melodramatic," Jav carded Ethan's damp hair with one hand "But we don't have to talk about this right now, if you don't want to."

Ethan let himself be petted for a few minutes. He must have fallen too quiet because Jav's hand paused.

"Sweetheart? I'm not supposed to let you fall asleep," said Jav. Ethan grunted. "You have a concussion."

"...Are you feeling for the swelling?"

"Maybe."

"Lump's gone. Accelerated healing."

"Vegas told me to keep you awake. I'll make you something mild. Soup?"

"I don't want soup. I want a nap."

"Soup it is."

"Well, I'm not moving." Ethan reached for his pillow.

"Good idea." Jav swept Ethan into a bridal carry in one fluid motion, moving with the grace of someone who had never been felled by debilitating pins and needles. He deposited Ethan neatly at the dining table. Covered him with a throw blanket.

"What," said Ethan.

Jav began investigating the kitchen cupboards, bending to rummage through the drawers. "Where do you keep stock?"

"A stock of what?"

Jav shot him an unimpressed look. "Chicken stock."

"I think we have powdered soup packets, somewhere."

"You're not eating powdered anything." Jav opened the fridge. "Oh good, eggs."

Ethan recalled a dinner party where Jav's friends had cooked up a seven-course meal for everyone, while Jav 'helped'. "Should you be cooking without Carter and Elijah?"

"I messed up Elijah's pan *once*." Jav laid out spring onions, mushrooms, frozen crab sticks, and eggs on the chopping board. "I bought him a new one, but he never lets me forget it. How does Taiwanese steamed egg sound? Carter taught me. Where are your knives?"

"I'll do the cutting, thank you," said Ethan, having once witnessed Jav almost take off an entire knuckle when chopping carrots.

Jav pouted. "I'll go slowly. Don't stand, you have a concussion."

"Yet it'll still be safer." Ethan made quick work of the vegetables, then watched Jav crack two eggs – and spend an eternity fishing for shell shards. "...Can you wake me up when you're done?"

"*No.*" Jav began (trying to) beat the eggs with chopsticks. "Stay awake."

The flat came with a multipurpose cooker, which steamed the egg while Jav watched, nose pressed to the window. Eventually, Jav set the steamed egg in front of Ethan, brandishing a large spoon. "Careful, it's hot."

Two months of relentless sweetness had rotted Ethan's teeth and reservations away, leaving behind exposed nerves and anxious honesty. The avoidance was in self-preservation. Ethan couldn't keep a clear head, not with Jav sitting across, so close, knocking knees, ankles, and hearts.

"Thank you." Ethan picked up the spoon.

The egg was mostly smooth, with a few lumps to keep life interesting. It was the emotional equivalent of baby food.

"Carter has this magic chicken soup," said Jav, chin in hand as if there was nowhere else he'd rather be. His cheek dimpled while he chattered, and the very sight wrecked Ethan's pulse. "...gogi and bamboo shoots and white melon? Gourd? Can't remember. It's a clear broth. Carter refuses to give me the recipe. Eli says there isn't one, but *he* knows, so there must be one! Anyway, steamed egg is also good 'under the weather' food."

Shit. Panic rose in a cold flush. *I think I love you.* Out loud, Ethan said, "I think we should take a break."

Jav froze. Then he leaned back in his chair. "Oh," he said, as calm as you please. "Okay."

Ethan's stomach dropped through the floor. "Okay?" he echoed, voice shooting up two octaves. "*Okay?*"

"You don't have to finish it all now. Though it's probably best not to keep it overnight."

"Wait." Ethan's heart bruised the lining of his soul, it was beating so hard. "What are you talking about?"

Jav reached across the table. He unravelled Ethan's white-knuckled grip on the spoon with the patience of someone who knew they were bad at cracking eggs and was willing to spend hours picking out every single shard of shell.

Ethan relinquished the spoon with a *clink*.

"The steamed egg, of course." Jav nodded at the unfinished bowl. "Why, what were *you* talking about?"

"...The egg." The words barely made it out past the lump of relief in Ethan's throat. *Say, therefore it is.*

Jav smiled, dimples and all. "Don't worry. It'll keep."

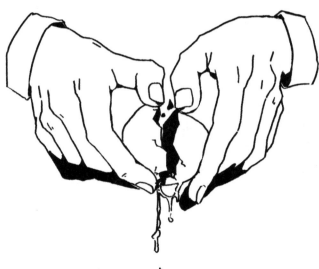

FOURTEEN

As it turned out, Ethan's emotional baseline had masked a sinew-deep compression which, when removed, loosened his affection into something spontaneous and sweet. *That, or you're love-sick, and Ethan is simply reflecting it back.* Jav wore that guilt on his wrists, fastened next to the suppressors. Doubt coated his teeth after every kiss: *whose feelings were they?*

But all the doubt in the world could not blunt the force of his want. This realisation had struck him in the second act of *Carmen*, with Ethan asleep on his shoulder. Jav wanted to be selfish. What good was honesty if it meant losing this? Ethan's toothbrush on his sink, spare clothes in each other's drawers, being gazed at with promise yet asked for nothing.

If virtue must be discarded on the altar of happiness, then so be it.

7 Kensington Palace Gardens, Level 16.
Wednesday, 24 November.

PERHAPS THANKS to Jav's quick response to Ethan's incident in the hospital, Vegas didn't share her boyfriend's obvious contempt for Jav – and she accepted an invitation to a family thank-you dinner. Jav picked her and Ethan up from St Ophie's Hospital after work.

"I wanted an excuse to not wear anything fancy," said Ethan.

"You put a lot of effort into not putting any effort in," laughed Jav. He ushered them through the lobby, around a life-sized statue of Medusa standing on a glass-covered water feature. She held the head of Perseus in one hand and a blade in the other.

"Wow," said Vegas.

"Dad installed this for mum when they got engaged," said Jav. "It's Garbarti's original. Her favourite."

Vegas snorted. "Nothing more romantic than a man's severed head."

"I dunno." Ethan peered at the decapitated cross-section. "I like my men with cervical vertebrae."

They passed through arching double doors and into the formal dining room.

Jav's mother made a beeline towards them. "At last!" She stopped in front of Ethan, eyes agleam. "I've been telling Jav to invite you over for so long. Welcome to the gene pool."

"*Mum.*"

"Uh, thanks." Ethan blinked rapidly between air kisses. "St Ophie's is short staffed—"

"Yes, very noble, staying with a public institution." Marie waved a hand. "I was so surprised when Jav found himself a healer. Do you have any siblings?"

"No, I'm an only child."

"Pity. Your mother's a healer, I presume?"

"Yes, she was."

"Oh. I'm so sorry."

"It's okay, I was six," said Ethan. "Can't remember very much."

Marie made a sympathetic noise, her bright focus unwavering.

It was difficult growing up, unable to read her – until Jav reconciled the dissonance between her affectionate words and her unflinching disinterest. Love felt differently for everyone.

"We're delighted to meet you both," said Jav's father, squeezing a word in edgewise. "This is Marie, and I'm Thomas." He shook Vegas's hand, then Ethan's – taking care to clasp Ethan by the wrist, over his sleeve. "Dr Faulkner; Dr Kelsey."

Marie finally noticed their second guest. "My dear. Are you a healer as well?"

"No," laughed Vegas, "not an aptee."

"Ah." Marie's attention swivelled back to Ethan.

"We're indebted to both of you," said Thomas warmly. "Rina was fortunate to be in good hands."

"Such good hands." Rina appeared behind Vegas's shoulder like a ghost. She kissed Vegas on both cheeks. "Nice to meet you while I'm conscious!"

Vegas grinned. "And with your organs where they belong."

Marie sat Ethan down beside her at the table. "You must tell me: were you edited in vivo? In vitro?"

Jav face-palmed.

"When your work is your life," said Thomas, smiling. "You were all meant to be healers, originally."

"I think it's too late for a refund now, dad. You'd think it's her first time meeting a healer. Aunty Meredith's a healer."

"It's not the same when you can't engage in transference healing. She might ask for a blood sample."

Jav boggled. "Did mum say that? Did you tell her no?"

"Mmhm."

"Is that 'mmhm, I didn't tell her no', or 'mmhm, I told her no'."

"Yes," said Thomas with a straight face.

"*Dad*."

"Locate your younger sister, please. It's rather rude that she missed greeting our guests. Rude enough that Giulia couldn't make it."

Before Jav could respond, the double-doors burst open.

"Good evening family!" Maddy announced.

All of Jav's sisters possessed a genetic flair for drama, but Maddy had been practising since the day she leapt out of her incubator. She might have been wearing a neon dressing gown back then as well.

"Sweet pea," sighed Thomas, "what are you wearing? We have guests."

Maddy hugged him around the neck. "What's for dinner?" Her gaze landed on Vegas, and Maddy's phone – which had been hovering beside her – clattered to the floor in surprise.

"Vegas, Ethan: this is Madeleine," said Jav. "Maddy—"

"You never said we were having guests," Maddy accused.

"I absolutely did."

"Guests. Plural. I would've gotten dressed."

Jav knew she wanted to emphasise her disinterest. Given her pink cheeks and radioactive mortification, she had played herself.

"Nice to meet you," said Vegas, smiling.

Maddy stood, frozen in her blue slippers. She didn't so much as glance at Ethan. "I'm Maddy." She blushed.

"You're in time for entrees," said Jav.

"Maddy's doing her A-levels," said Rina.

Maddy shot Rina an acidic glare. "You're in my seat."

"Sit next to me," said Jav.

"No, you're boring." Maddy made a show of eyeing Ethan up and down. "*You're* not as ugly in person as you are in photos."

"Maddy!" exclaimed Jav, as Vegas laughed uproariously.

The chef and her assistants brought in the entrees.

"Don't be mean, pumpkin," said dad, no admonishment in his tone.

"It'll come back to bite," said mum. "If Jav is smart about it, he'll look thirty when he's sixty and you'll be off seeing a healer every week to keep those wrinkles at bay."

"I'll just pay one to hug me," said Maddy sourly.

Across the table, Vegas and Rina were bent close together like a pair of conspiring magpies. Self-satisfied glee dripped from Rina's every pore. Jav turned to Maddy. She was staring at her food in between furtive glances at Vegas over the floral arrangements.

"So. How was school?"

The napkin flew up between their faces.

"I'm mad."

Jav swatted the napkin out of the air. "You're the one who decided to dress for a pyjama party."

"That's all Ethan deserves," said Maddy. "Someone must put him in his place. Mum's a lost cause: she has a hard-on for anything healer related."

"Please don't say 'mum' and 'hard-on' in the same sentence."

"Dad's biased because Ethan saved Rina's life, or whatever."

"Are you feeling neglected because you're not the centre of attention for one single meal?"

"Giulia's not here, so it's up to me." Maddy narrowed her eyes, looking pointedly at Jav's right hand, and then the absence of his left hand next to his plate. "Ahem. I can see seven people at this table, but only twelve hands."

Without pausing in his conversation with mum, Ethan let go of Jav's wrist to slide his palm up Jav's thigh. Jav hid his laugh in a bite of food, then jumped when Ethan yelped. A small dessert fork had leapt off the table and jabbed Ethan in the back of the hand.

"What on earth is happening over there?" asked Vegas.

"Some casual maiming," said Jav.

"Without me?" said Rina.

Ethan held out his hand, skin unblemished. "No harm done."

"Big up," Maddy muttered. "It's a dictionary of aptitudes around this fucking table."

"Language," said dad.

"I'm not an aptee." Vegas nodded at Maddy. "Telekinetic?"

Rina gestured between herself and Jav. "After us, mum decided to get one of each, but Maddy was so annoying that we never completed the full set."

"At least I wasn't copy-pasted," Maddy retorted.

Rina conjured a flame, rolling the blue orb between her knuckles like a poker-chip. The nearest jug of water floated off the table in response.

Jav grabbed it. "Hey. *Guests.*"

Maddy turned to Ethan. "Edwin, don't you think Rina looks copy-pasted?"

"...Only because Mrs Arden looks so young." Ethan immediately shovelled a spoonful of food to ward off further questions.

Marie laughed. "How sweet. Though it's Ms Sainte-Ophie – keeps the papers and patents clear."

"And your mother's blood pressure high, no doubt," dad chuckled. He turned to Ethan. "The twins took after Marie while Maddy had the unfortunate luck of taking after me."

"Luck had nothing to do with it," said mum. "Two for me, two for you."

"And I'm forever grateful, dear."

Mum tapped the lip of her water glass. Dad filled it with a glance, then swapped the glass with one from the filtered carafe. It was a little routine they had for as long as Jav could remember. Sometimes dad would simply frost the glass over. Other times, he would conjure water from the air for mum's amusement – then hand her something safe to drink.

Jav wanted his own rituals, trading handfuls of habits and affections until one lover was indistinguishable from the other.

"Do you feel left out?" Ethan asked Jav. "Not being an aptee."

Despite the well-trodden lie, Jav's anxiety spiked. "It's not so bad. Giulia isn't an aptee either."

"I had hoped she'd be a watercaller, like Thomas," said mum, "but that's my mistake for doing things the traditional way. With due respect, I cannot believe your mother took that risk, even if you turned out wonderfully."

Ethan choked on his food. "That's what my gran says. Mum didn't tell her that I was a healer until we were home from the hospital." He coughed again. Jav handed him a spare napkin. "Thanks babe."

"Mum, please stop interrogating Ethan so he can finish his main course."

"Yes, let's talk about something else," said Maddy. "So, Edward—"

"Ethan."

"That's what I said, Edmund. Any hobbies besides gold-digging?"

"Only at the weekends," said Ethan.

Later that evening.

THEY RETURNED TO JAV and Rina's place, which was much closer than Level 9. After some obligatory compliments about Rina's aquarium, she and Vegas disappeared to the balcony pool, absorbed in a fierce debate about VR airsoft battles. At least Rina wasn't out with Peter or any of the Langleys.

"What matters is that mum likes you," said Jav, languid after their long bath. They were in front of the bathroom vanity. "Maddy just loves drama."

"Uh huh." Ethan leaned in for a kiss.

Jav put a hand on his shoulder. "Facemask still drying."

"When can I wash it off?"

"Fifteen more minutes."

"Fifteen?" Ethan whined, "I'll be dead by then."

"At least your pores will be hydrated. Don't pull faces, it needs to set."

"I have healer pores."

"Don't care. I saw you washing your face with *soap*. Healers aren't invincible—"

"Against soap?"

"Against dehydration."

"Shouldn't have washed my face in the first place..."

"Ethan."

"I'm tired. I want to lie down."

"For the love of..." Jav capped his eye cream; his own routine could wait. "Stop pouting, you're creasing the clay. How about a massage?"

Ethan side-eyed him. "A sexy massage?"

"No, a..." Jav tapped the mirror to bring up the time, "...fourteen-minute massage."

"I don't need that long to suck you off."

"There will be no sucking of any kind. You'll ruin the mask."

They both started to laugh. There was no dignity involved, noses scrunched, shoulders shaking: it was infectious.

"Your priorities," Ethan hiccupped. "Never, in my entire life, have I had to work so hard to blow—"

"Stop talking, you're cracking the—! That's it, we're reapplying."

"Babe, *no*."

TWO-AND-A-BIT MONTHS WAS NOTHING.

Guilt festered in the quiet, and it was quietest while Ethan was asleep beside him. When left alone with warm skin and steady breaths, all doubts became dangerous.

Time ticked as it passed, louder than all the mechanical time-pieces in his drawer. Most of the watches housed empath suppressors, gifts from Jav's sisters, marking each birthday. They spun quietly on their stands, round and around, keeping Jav's secrets as well as the time.

Maybe love would always sound like bated breath, punctuated by gasps when overcome with a reckless fervour to confess. To shake Ethan awake and tell him everything. Jav could imagine it now: Ethan's ever-steady fondness, matter of fact, unflappable. He would look at Jav with that same look he wore to bed, smile, and say—

— then the feeling would pass.

Jav would put on his suppressors and pray that they appeased his conscience for one more day.

THOUGH ETHAN NEVER FELT upset when Jav turned him down, they were quickly reaching the critical mass of deflections. There was no doubt Ethan *noticed*, if the thrum of pleasant frustration was anything to go by. He had yet to comment – but kept leaving the metaphorical door open, as if Jav was an indecisive housecat.

None of it dampened Ethan's enthusiasm when they made out. And since skin contact made empathic suppressors and dampeners useless, it also rendered artificial any moral distinctions while one had fingers in hair, mouth to throat, hand to heart.

Lucas had thought so, and that had been the end of that.

*And yet...*It was a matter of consent. They couldn't venture further when Ethan didn't *know*. They showered together, took long baths overlooking London through the tilt-shift lens of the angled glass. Lay in bed, curled like speech marks around a secret.

You're not telling him because you know you're in the wrong. The longer this goes on, the worse it'll be. The more you'll lose.

"Hey," said Ethan late one night. "Can I ask you something?"

They were snuggled under the covers. A remake of *Alice in Wonderland* played quietly on the opposite wall. Jav hummed, distracted by the way Ethan's damp hair curled against his ears.

"You'd tell me if I was making you uncomfortable, right?"

"You don't make me uncomfortable," said Jav.

Ethan shifted onto one elbow to face Jav. "I meant anytime I suggest we have sex."

Jav's stomach dropped through the floor – Ethan's brows immediately shot up. He realised that Ethan must have felt that second-hand. A cold flush ran down Jav's neck.

Ethan squeezed his hand. "See? *This* is why I'm asking."

"I'm not uncomfortable." Jav wavered under Ethan's steady stare of gentle scepticism. "Really! I don't want to take advantage of you."

Ethan blinked slowly, a universal 'come again?'. "Look. Tact is not my strong suit. But I wanna make sure I'm not pressuring you. Or overstepping."

"You're not."

"Hmm. 'Cause I'm not gonna lie, it's sometimes a bit confusing. With the mixed signals." Ethan combed a hand through his own hair. "Sorry, is that a douchey thing to say? It's fine if you don't want to have sex. As in, ever. If you're asexual, or just don't feel like it with me..." He cleared his throat. "What I'm *trying* to say is, you don't have to give me a reason. Right? If you're feeling off and just too nice to tell me—"

"You don't—"

"—but I'd appreciate if we could be honest."

Jav bit back a wince. Judging by the twitch of Ethan's mouth, he failed.

"You don't have to let me down gently," said Ethan.

A mix of guilt and trepidation clogged Jav's throat. In truth, he had never found sex itself to be tremendously appealing. But whether that was due to an uneasy conscience or an 'unusually needy' (Rina's words) desire for emotional honesty – Jav didn't know. These thoughts were mortifying, even alone in his skull. It reminded him of Peter and Lucas, both of whom made Jav rather nauseous.

Ethan was still watching him with patient eyes.

Jav swallowed. "It's not you, it's—"

"Please don't finish that sentence," groaned Ethan. They stared at each other, shoulder to shoulder, legs tangled under the duvet. "Look. We don't have to talk about any of this. Should I...is it better if I back off a bit? And you can tell me if you ever, you know."

Ethan's brand of anxiety was tricky to read. Hesitation was plain in tight corners of his eyes, but not reflected in his aura. There was no telltale aftertaste of resentment either.

Just be honest. Oh, if only. "Ethan. I think you're very handsome. You make such beautiful lines—"

"Spoken like a man who doesn't wanna fuck me."

Jav spluttered.

"I'm just *saying*." Ethan coughed. "Sorry. It's gonna take a while to train myself out of these quips."

Oh, sweetheart. Jav could spot the pattern now: Ethan was giving him another out.

"Do I act like someone who finds you unattractive?" asked Jav.

Ethan shrank into his own shoulders, gaze averted.

"I want to spend every minute with you," Jav continued. "I could watch you do nothing all day and be utterly fulfilled. Am I making any sense?"

Ethan's cheeks were rather red by now, but he settled back against the pillows, shifting so that he and Jav shared a dip in the mattress. He felt mollified. "Yeah. Ball's in your court, then?"

"There's no rush, right?"

That seemed to be the right thing to say, because Ethan's smile went all the way to his eyes. "Of course not," he said.

Their next kiss tasted like toothpaste and soda-water, free of expectations and softened by relief.

ETHAN AVOIDED STAYING over if he was on-call in the wee hours.

But every now and then, Jav would wake to an empty bed and a dark grey sky. He'd turn his face into Ethan's pillow and sulk. Surely Ethan had his pick of private clinics, government loans be damned. There was no reason for a healer to be working such awful hours – and no reason for Jav to be alone in the mornings.

Then Ethan started leaving him notes.

They appeared on Jav's bedside table. Then the bathroom mirror, the vanity, the door. One morning Jav woke to a sticky-note on his cheek, crinkling against the pillow as he turned over. Hastily, he smoothed out the crumpled half and was greeted by a rabbit holding a pocket watch.

Beside the drawing, a scrawled note:

Have to go in early. Might be too tired for dinner out :(
Will text you later. Hope your classes go ok! —E.

The rabbit looked rather cross.

"I'm sorry you've suffered a crease," said Jav. "Let me make it up to you."

On his way to shower, he slid the rabbit into a scrapbook with Ethan's other drawings; fragments of affection to remember him by when things inevitably came to an end.

1 Madeleine Avenue, Upper Chelsea. Wednesday, 1 December.

RINA DIDN'T LIKE GIVING people automatic access to their penthouse, family or not, but there was a whitelist of who could access the garage versus the private lobby.

Stephen was currently jeopardising his position on both lists by blasting the intercom non-stop. "I bought a new car!"

Jav hung up. A second later, his phone rang.

"It's dark out, we can take her for a test flight!"

Jav sighed. "When did you even get this thing? I thought you were doing honeymoon logistics. You said you didn't want my help."

"Yeah."

There was a guilty pause. Jav sipped his tea.

"...I bought it over the phone," Stephen admitted. "I was stressed."

"Aaand there it is."

"C'mon, quick lap round the block."

"No."

"Fifteen minutes, tops. Sent you a photo."

Jav gestured to accept the attachment. It flashed above the stone counter. "Oh, hell no. Is that floor transparent? *Nein. Wǒ bù yào.*"

"It's more fun with you in the passenger seat! Pleeease?"

"Fun for you. Terrifying for me."

"Potayto, potahto; adrenaline, endorphins!"

"You will lose your licence if we get caught again. Plus, I get carsick."

"Don't you wanna learn how to dive? For Ethan. We could drop you off at his place, after. Eh? *Eh?*"

Jav hesitated.

"C'mon I need this. Nath has been fucking insufferable, Charlie has started texting me, *and* I'm freaking out about the wedding. Pretty please?"

"...Fifteen minutes, no more."

"Woo! By the way, we're flying with the top down, so empty your pockets and leave anything that might get loose."

Jav frowned. "Now, hang on just a—"

"I've got your jacket and goggles already. See you soon!"

THEY MADE IT twenty minutes before police-sirens started.

"I," Jav shouted over the howling wind, "am going to kill you!"

Stephen cackled, pulling out of a sharp dive and into a stomach-lurching turn. The tailfin flicked hard left before straightening out. Jav's organs slid to one side of his body.

The London lights stretched, hyper-sharp between the shriek of terror and a heady, joyous high that radiated from Stephen as he floored the accelerator. The car *vroom*'ed, throwing Jav against his seat as the nose of the car veered a terrifying ninety-degrees up.

Jav clutched his seat. "No, no, *no*."

Their reflection rippled across the dark surface of the nearest building, a hair's breadth from the safety lattice, the underside of the car luminous against the windows as they rocketed heavenward. The moment stretched, taffy like, the wind wiping the world silent.

Then Stephen flipped them over and Jav *oofed* as the harness slammed into his ribs. The sirens blared, red-blue lights refracting against windows to cast every brutalist tower into a cathedral.

"Oopsie-daisies," Stephen sang, no trace of contrition.

The endorphins and adrenaline made for an infectious empathetic loop. Jav knew it was why Stephen liked flying with him so much, and Jav would be lying if he said he didn't enjoy the thrill. He could only laugh, wheezing and gasping.

Stephen slotted them into a legal-flying zone. A police cruiser tailed from behind, while another officer flanked them on a solo-flier.

"We're in so much shit. Your mum will be furious." Jav was too light-headed to project any disapproval, heart still in his throat.

London yawned, cavernous between their shoes.

"No regrets!" Stephen slapped the call-hailing icon on the dash with one gloved hand. "Ayyy, good evening officers."

The cop did not sound amused. "Mr Mansfield—"

"Wow," said Jav, "look at that. They just know who you are now."

"I didn't realise the rego went through that fast," said Stephen.

"You're a bloody criminal, that's what you are," said Jav.

"Traffic rules aren't proper laws."

"I'm texting Arthur."

The speakers crackled indignantly. "—excuse me! Sir!"

"Oops." Stephen winked at Jav. "Sorry, ma'am, trying to find a park."

"Accept my hailing instructions as your vehicle is not accepting it automatically. That alone is cause for suspension—"

Stephen rolled his eyes. "The dealer must have made a mistake. I only got this car today. Shall we rendezvous at the precinct?"

"You will land your vehicle *now*."

"Right you are, ma'am. Chat soon—"

"You will remain on this line until we arrive at the Level 10 precinct, Mr Mansfield!"

"Okay, okay. Landing now. Jeez."

The police cruiser tailed them so closely that their headlights spilled onto their faces.

Jav slid lower in his seat, stabbing a button to raise the roof of the convertible. He smacked Stephen across the chest with a fist. "Ethan might be free for a late dinner at his place. If I miss it because of this..."

Soon, they were pulling into the precinct's loading zone. The officer on the solo flier immediately leapt from her bike while another clamped their car.

"Relax." Stephen shoved his goggles onto the top of his head. "This part never takes long."

Public lobby to the City of London Police and SIA Central London Precinct, Level 10. A few minutes later.

NEITHER JAV NOR STEPHEN had ever been cuffed, but the wrath on the officer's face made Jav wonder if perhaps today was the day.

"Aww, it's been ages since we were last here," said Stephen, too loudly, as they were escorted into the lobby. "Did you fix your coffee machine?"

Jav stood close, using Stephen as a buffer for the general ooze of stress and anticipation in the air. He only had a suppressor-watch on.

"Section thirty-fours," the officer said to her colleague, "I'll be right back." She vanished through a pair of sliding doors.

"Can't you write up the ticket so we can go?" Stephen waved at Jav. "My mate has a hot date to get to."

"You may both take a seat," another officer replied tersely.

Jav eyed the grubby upholstery and remained standing.

Stephen sat, noisily. "Don't you have actual criminals to find?"

The officer was irate. "You were doing two-fifty in a no-fly zone! You could have killed someone, including yourselves. Not to mention the illegal mods that—"

"Babe? What are you doing here?"

Jav spun around.

It was Ethan. He held a take-out bag in one hand, satchel in the other.

Stephen waved. "Oh hey, look who it is! We were just talking about you."

"Really." Ethan stepped into Jav's personal space. "Hello you. I was gonna text. Why are you here?"

"Joyflying," said Jav.

"Without me? How could you."

Jav kissed him in apology. But before he could reply, a flare of shock hit him in the side of the neck. He flinched, and Ethan jerked backwards – a split second before a familiar voice thundered:

"What *the hell* is going on here?"

It was Ian Garner.

Jav had been so distracted by Ethan's sudden appearance that he hadn't noticed the looming presence approaching behind Ethan.

Ian was positively apoplectic, mouth working, speechless.

Ethan turned around, and – to Jav's absolute horror – said, "Oh. Hey dad."

Jav made a strangled noise.

"What," said Ian, slowly, "is going on?"

Ethan held up his bag. "Food delivery. Beep beep..."

"Do you know this man?" Ian pointed at Jav.

Ethan squinted. "Nah. I snog all the men in reception when I'm here." He felt calm, apparently oblivious to Jav's panic. Ethan tried looping the take-out bag around his father's wrist. "The noodles are gonna clump if you don't eat them now."

Ian didn't seem concerned with noodle integrity. "Do you know who this is?" he demanded.

"...Do you really think I go around kissing men I don't know?"

"Do *I* look like I'm in the mood for your jokes right now?!"

Ethan glanced at Jav, then back at Ian.

Jav was too scared to exhale or exhibit any other signs of life.

"I guess you were gonna find out sooner or later," sighed Ethan. "Jav's my boyfriend."

The entire lobby was eavesdropping. Jav couldn't look away from Ian's poker face, the heat of his incandescent contempt spiked with alarm.

"Your boyfriend," Ian repeated. "Since when?"

Ethan's eyes were big and innocent. Judging by Ian's frown, it wasn't working. "Why? You were fine with everyone else I dated."

"Oh, you dated other criminals, did you?" Ian barked.

"I was the one flying," Stephen piped up. "Jav was just a passenger."

Ian only had eyes for his son. "How long has this been going on?"

"Dunno."

"Young man—"

"I'm not having a public row."

"How long?"

Ethan pulled out his pager. "Oh no, I have to dash. People are dying..."

"You told me you were heading home. Ethan! *Ethan Bliant Faulkner*, you come back here this instant—!"

Ethan ducked around Jav, shoulder clipping the glass doors with a wince-worthy bang as he sprinted out of the lobby. Jav felt a little abandoned. Ian stared at the entrance through which his son had absconded. Standing in the blast-zone of his fury was like being next to an open freezer.

Ian rounded on Jav. "*You.*"

Jav gulped.

"Hang on," said Stephen, exhibiting a wholesale disregard for their lives. "If you're Ethan's dad, why didn't you take your wife's surname? Isn't that what usually happens when people marry healers?"

FIFTEEN

In the end, Arthur rescued him. The lawyer's mild manners dripped with disdain. "Luckily you weren't driving, or they'd have an excuse to keep you, like Mr Mansfield."

They stepped out together onto the noisy street.

"Will Stephen be alright?" asked Jav.

"Yes, like the last hundred times. Did Garner speak to you about anything unrelated to traffic violations?"

"Now, Mr Arden. I'm a patient man, so I'll ask again: what on earth are you doing with my son?"

"No," Jav lied. "I called you, then—"

"Kept your mouth shut?"

"...Kept my mouth shut."

"Good. Go home and stay out of trouble." Arthur opened the door of a nondescript black flier with opaque windows.

"You need a ride upstairs?"

"I'll make my own way back. Have a good evening." Arthur slammed the door shut, leaving Jav in the sudden quiet.

The driver's partition slid down to reveal Peter's smirking profile.

Jav immediately grabbed the door handle. "No thanks, I'll walk." The door remained stubbornly shut as they peeled away from the kerb.

"Up twelve Levels?" said Peter. "You'd get kidnapped. Stop yanking, the child-safety lock is on."

"Fuck you," snarled Jav. "I'll take a cab, let me out."

"As much as I'd like to eject you, Rina sent me." Peter swivelled his seat to face him. "What's got your knickers in a twist?"

"Wait. You must have known."

"Known...?"

"That Ian was Ethan's father!" Jav shouted.

"Oh. Caught up, have you?"

"He should be Ian *Faulkner*, not Ian Garner." Jav wanted to strangle Peter. He stabbed Rina's profile on his phone instead. "What kind of disrespectful man marries a healer and doesn't take her surname?"

"Not that I don't find your old-fashioned sensibilities fascinating but dialling Rina over and over isn't going to make her pick up."

RINA WAS FLOATING in the pool.

The penthouse storm-shields were retracted in deference to the mild weather, navy sky yawning above shimmering water. Piano music played on the speakers, echoing against tile and glass. Peaceful.

"Rina." Jav threw open the balcony doors and strode to the edge of the water. He was so annoyed he didn't pause to take off his shoes. "Corinna, we need to talk."

His twin didn't move from her star-fish position. "You're pissy."

"He's found out who Ian Garner is," said Peter.

A splash. "Ha."

Jav threw up his hands. "You both knew. And no one thought to warn me?"

The air popped as Rina conjured a ball of flame above her hand, suspending it above the water like a sunset. She dove beneath the surface and the flame sank in a wash of steam, lingering and refracting the light when she emerged at the edge of the pool.

Jav stepped backwards, out of grab-and-drag range.

Rina pouted. "Towel."

"Ian interrogated me for an hour because he thinks I have nefarious intentions," said Jav.

"He's not wrong." Rina yawned. "Why else would I tell you to make nice with Ethan in the first place? Good job on that, by the way."

Before Jav could respond, Peter phased into view, proffering a fluffy towel like a butler instead of the flea-infested mercenary Rina had rescued against Jav's better judgement. He could always sense Peter's shit-eating presence, whether the ghost was visible or not. Faint heat, ozone, dry static on skin. Smug.

Rina hoisted herself from the pool, selkie-like with her slick hair and one-piece. She gave Peter a sultry look beneath her lashes as she sashayed indoors. Jav wanted to shove Peter into the pool. Instead, he trailed them to the wet bar.

"Tell me what happened," said Rina.

Jav grunted. "Stephen and I had to visit the precinct after flying. Ethan was there with dinner for his dad. For Ian bloody *Garner*."

Rina sniggered. "Were you snogging in public? Please tell me Ian had a heart attack. Giulia would *love* that."

"The kiss was perfectly polite, thank you for your concern."

"I didn't see the good doctor," said Peter. "Did he run away?"

"Yes, he *ran away*," snapped Jav. "I would have too, if I didn't think Ian would tase me before I got to the door!"

Rina burst out laughing, high and chalky. She grabbed Jav's wrist to share the mirth, but he didn't want to be mollified. He wrenched his hand away, poured himself two fingers of amber, and threw it back. Poured himself another.

"Wish I had been there to see Ian's expression," said Rina. "Was he scared?"

"No. More shocked. Angry." Jav glowered. "Ian doesn't like me – and now he'll *never* like me."

Rina nodded at Peter. "Maybe this will finally get him off our backs. That man is like a dog with a bone."

"The conflict of interest may come in handy," said Peter. "As long as Barbie here keeps things rolling."

"Was Ethan upset?" asked Rina.

"Maybe," Jav said through gritted teeth. "Given that his dad thinks I'm a criminal."

"You *were* speeding," said Peter.

Jav slapped his glass down. "Can you fuck off?"

"Call Ethan and check," said Rina.

"I'm not calling him. I will finish my drink, then I'm going to run a bath and drown myself." Jav held up a warning finger. "Whatever's going on, leave Ethan out of it."

After years of staring at her fish, Rina had plenty of practice not blinking. She perched on the arm of a chaise. "Leave Ethan out of your bed?"

"I'm serious. Ethan's got nothing to do with the investigation, and—"

"How do you know he's got nothing to do with the investigation?"

Jav froze. "What?"

"I *said,*" Rina fished a cherry from her glass, unhurried, "how do you know that Ethan's got nothing to do with the investigation? Did you two discuss it?"

Doubt unfurled like a weed. "Of course not."

"Maybe Ethan's in this for the same reasons you are," said Rina. "*Someone* told him to make nice."

Jav stared at Rina, speechless. *It's not that you've made a fool of me, it's that you're so entertained.* It hurt. He turned on his heels, striding past the aquarium, up the stairs – away from Peter's low chuckling.

Jav pushed open his bedroom door, eyes stinging. He waved at his mirror to activate the room controls, and to start a bath. Shook out an extra dose of painkillers with unsteady hands. Perhaps the alcohol had been a bad idea.

As Jav stripped out of his clothes, his phone rang, muffled by the duvet. *Ethan.* He stood in his briefs, stalled by indecision. Which was worse? Ethan calling to break up because he believed Jav unsavoury...or because the charade was over?

Make nice, Rina had said. If Ian *had* told his son to 'make nice' for the sake of an investigation, the man was a phenomenal actor. Ian's dismay had been visceral. Jav clung to that fact. It was almost impossible to feign emotion at the chemical level. People were often dissonant: their faces and bodies made all the right cues, while their heart and nerves told a different story. Anyone could perform the manifestation of emotion, but they'd feel different underneath (or not at all).

No, thought Jav fervently, Ian's reaction had been genuine.

On the bed, the phone went quiet. He flinched as the bedroom door banged open. It was Rina.

"I'm about to take a bath," Jav said flatly.

Rina leaned against the doorframe, having replaced her cocktail with a bowl of raspberries. "Good. I'm freezing."

"You're not invited." Dropping his watch on the vanity, Jav strode through his walk-in closet to the bathroom.

Undeterred, Rina followed. "About Ethan: I was just teasing."

The bathtub sat in a bed of moss, half-sunken into the floor against a floor-to-ceiling window. The ceramic framed a mirror of the inky London night, steam curling above the warm water.

"Turn around," said Jav.

"Oh please. We were in the womb together."

"I have it on good authority that we had separate test tubes."

Rina's cheek bulged with raspberries. "Incubators, you mean."

"Whatever." Resigned, Jav stripped, ducking beneath the shower spray before stepping into the bath. The hot water bit through flesh to bone, cutting all his nerves at the spine. He tipped his head back, closing his eyes.

Rina balanced herself on the edge of the bathtub and stuck both legs in. She flicked water with a finger. "Could be hotter."

Jav stared back wordlessly.

She continued to demolish her raspberries. It was quiet, save for the piano music from Jav's wind-down playlist and the swish of water around Rina's legs.

"Berry?" she offered.

Jav wiped the bubbles from his face, sinking lower so the water lapped his neck. "I know you're bad at reading the room, but I really don't want to talk right now."

"Is this about Ethan?"

"Rina, not now."

"You're still pissy then."

Jav closed his eyes. "It's been ten minutes."

"I *said* I was sorry."

"You didn't."

"Well, I said it just now."

"Fine. Apology accepted. Please leave me alone."

More chewing noises. "It wasn't like Ian's identity was a secret. It's easier for you to act normally around Ethan if you didn't know. You overthink things and get nervous."

"So it's my fault."

"Peter thought you'd get spooked. That'd be bad if Ethan *was* a snitch."

Jav blinked at the pendant lights draped above the bath. "You really think Ethan's working for the SIA?"

"Maybe."

"No. Ian was shocked when he saw us. Didn't feel fake."

"Who knows, Marc might have got to Ethan before you did. The Sainte-Ophies can make Ethan's career difficult. Either way, don't get too attached."

Jav laughed. It hurt. "I think it's a bit late for that." He rested his cheek against cool ceramic. The window was angled so that light refracted outwards, obscuring Rina's reflection with the city lights. "Promise you're not going to drag Ethan into your mess."

"If Ethan minds his own business, he'll be fine."

"*Rina.*"

"You can't be suckered by a pretty face, Jav. Ethan's not even good looking."

Jav wrapped a hand around her ankle beneath the water, projecting a chest-sinking sobriety through his palm. "If anything happens to him, I will be very upset. Extremely, horribly, miserably upset. You won't enjoy it."

Rina hissed, annoyed. "Don't assume it'll be my fault. Garner's been on the glass beat longer than we've been alive. He's got more enemies than I do."

"I didn't say it would be your fault, it'll be *my* fault for *making nice.* I'm involved because you're involved. I wish you would just stop. I wish you left Peter to Robert, then he'd be dead. And I wish you would take me seriously for one goddamn second when I say how much Ethan means to me!"

Rina narrowed her eyes. "You've only known him a few months. You got over Lucas just fine."

"I got over—?" Jav sat up, stomach churning. "He passed away and you didn't tell me th—!"

"Well, you're fine now, aren't you?"

"After ten fucking years, sure!"

"It was never gonna work out between the two of you. You said that yourself."

"So I'm meant to be alone forever?"

"Don't be stupid. You have me."

"When it suits you."

They glared at each other stonily across the water.

After a while, Rina said, "I didn't know you were gonna get this invested." *You and me both,* thought Jav. "How long do you expect it to last? You haven't told Ethan about your empathy, have you?"

"Is he going to have a car accident if I say yes?"

Rina frowned, apparently concerned – but emotion and light could both refract. Sometimes Jav wondered if that's all he knew of her.

"I don't know what you mean," she said. "I'm just looking out for you."

Jav exhaled slowly. "Ethan doesn't know."

Rina studied his expression, fingers and teeth stained red. Finally, she said, "Let's keep it that way. You know what'll happen if it gets out. I just want you to be happy." Then she smiled, abrupt as spring rain. "Now, don't kill me, but I have a teensy, tiny favour to ask."

The next evening.

"...AND *THEN* SHE SAID she's skipping the gala because Charlie Douchebag Langley somehow got a seat at our table. It's next Wednesday. We've been taking tango lessons for six months!"

Elijah looked like he wanted to join his soufflés inside the oven. Stephen was shelling edamame beans, while Carter bounced between four live stove-tops. A wok sizzled with paella, filling the kitchen with seafood steam.

As usual, Jav was the only one who didn't have a task. "Well?" he demanded, when it became clear that no further reactions were forthcoming.

"Why are they still dating?" asked Carter. "Rina never invites Charlie to hang out with us."

"Dating," echoed Stephen, making air-quotes with his fingers.

Rina mostly kept Charlie around because of his uncle, Robert Langley – and to keep Nath's blood pressure up. Though there would be no Langley if they had never met Peter. It was all Peter's fault.

There was absolutely nothing attractive about Charlie, and Jav would have been worried about him being a threat to Rina if the guy wasn't so transparently in lust with her. He was handsy, wore too much cologne, and radiated smug self-satisfaction whenever she paid him any attention. An absolute bore of a man.

Jav stared enviously at Stephen's bowl of edamame.

"You look constipated," said Eli, closing the oven.

"Because you won't let me help with dinner," said Jav.

Eli and Carter exchanged a look.

"You're helping plenty," said Elijah.

Jav sighed. "I'll make drinks. Sorry for whinging, it's just...we usually wipe the floor with our routine. It's our *thing*. Now months of practice, down the drain."

Carter checked on the Moreton Bay bugs, sympathy caramelising. "Maybe Clara can talk her into it."

Jav shook his head. "Charlie's been clingy. I don't want to put Rina in an uncomfortable position."

"Can you bail?"

"No, it wouldn't look good for the Foundation if we're both absent." Jav took his feelings out on the muddler, pulping the mint. Carter rounded the kitchen island to hug him. It was like being blasted with an oven light; Carter's sunny disposition always threatened a severe tan.

"Maybe one of Maddy's three million online followers can go with you," said Eli. "She can auction you off for a good cause."

"Har har har," said Jav. "No mojito for you."

1 Madeleine Avenue, Upper Chelsea.
The next day, Friday, 3 December.

JAV AND ETHAN RETIRED to the penthouse after a quick dinner out. Rina and Peter were nowhere to be seen. Jav tried not to think too hard about what they were up to.

"Headache?" asked Ethan.

Jav paused, one hand on the painkillers in his bedside drawer. "Much better now that you're here."

Ethan held out his palm for the pills, which Jav relinquished after a moment's hesitation. Ethan turned the bottle over, thumb on the small print. "These are pretty strong. Are they just for your migraines?"

"Yeah." That wasn't a lie: migraines were a daily by-product of wearing suppressors or being in crowds for too long. Jav had relied on painkillers since he was a child.

Ethan tossed the bottle back into the drawer with a careless flick of the wrist. "You have me now. Shut your eyes." He swung a leg over Jav's waist to straddle his hips – and almost tipped off the bed.

Jav steadied him. "I thought you said healers can't cure migraines."

"Do as you're told."

"Yes, doctor."

Ethan made a noise like a cat being stepped on and retaliated by rolling his hips back. Jav wheezed, arching up, only to be pushed down into the pillow. He held Ethan by his bony knees, lest he topple off and break his neck.

Ethan's hands were cool against Jav's face. He ran his thumbs beneath Jav's eyes, a gentle pressure along symmetrical divots of bone and affection. Static gathered at each point of skin contact. In the span of a few exhales, the migraine was pulled through nerves and skin.

Neither of them spoke for several minutes, lulled by the late hour. Jav ran his hands from Ethan's knees up to his hips, relishing in the easy weight of another soul against his.

"How's your head now?" Ethan asked.

Jav kept his eyes shut. "Better." He turned into Ethan's right hand; kissed his palm.

"Really?"

"Mhmm."

"Then I have some bad news and some good news," said Ethan. Jav raised an eyebrow but kept his eyes closed. "The bad news is that you're right: headaches can't be 'healed', as such. Depends on what's causing the headache."

"And the good news?"

"Placebo works on you."

Jav walked his fingers along Ethan's spine. "I wouldn't call you a placebo."

"Healer-related placebo is a well-documented phenomenon. Normally more reliable if it's a woman administering that placebo."

"Maybe if you wear your black healer coat..."

"You've been watching too much *Healer's Anatomy*. Here, the coat's grey."

Jav pouted. "I've never seen you wear it."

"Too conspicuous."

"*I* think you'd look dashing in grey."

"Is this a healer fetish?"

Jav spluttered. "No! And you made such a deal about my dance shorts, so you can't talk."

"Oooh." Ethan grinned. "That's different."

"How? It's something I wear for my profession."

"Your profession is to look hot." Ethan paused. "And artistic."

Laughing, Jav pulled him close by the waist. Ethan immediately hooked their ankles together, kissing Jav hard on the mouth. It was a long while before they resurfaced.

"My point is," Ethan continued, "I'm worried about your painkillers. You take them so often. I didn't know they were this strong."

"Don't worry. I'm used to it."

"That's not comforting. I hope your doctor routinely reassesses. And don't think I didn't see those sleeping pills."

The Arden family doctor was one of the very few people who knew about Jav's empathy. When Jav was younger, it had been a daily struggle to manage his migraines. Full-strength suppressors had been his only ticket out of the house.

"I do have regular check-ups," said Jav.

"As long as you're not grabbing these out of the back of a truck."

Jav laughed, but it came out strained.

Ethan seemed to take pity. "What's this gala that Maddy mentioned? She said something about an incest tango."

"Oh lord."

"Something I should know?"

"There's no incest."

"That's nice."

"Maddy has too many followers online. Bad influence. When did she even manage to impart so much slander?"

"Before we left for dinner, while you were in the bathroom."

Jav sighed. "The gala is a charity fundraiser for performing arts scholarships, mostly. There's dancing, dinner, awards. A silent auction. Rina and I attend every year." He rubbed the back of his neck. "I never mentioned it because I thought you'd get bored. It's a few hours long. Rina's bailed because Charlie is going."

"Charlie?"

"Rina's not-boyfriend."

"The one she hates?"

"Yep. Wouldn't want to subject you to...that." Jav didn't want anyone to suffer Charlie's lack of charm, but he also rather fancied spending an evening with Ethan. If they held hands, Jav might not need his suppressors at full strength.

Ethan hummed. "I feel bad about throwing you under the bus with dad."

Jav winced. They hadn't spoken about the encounter since it happened. Ethan never brought it back up. But seeing as Ethan was cuddling him in bed, Jav counted it as a win.

"Have you talked since?" asked Jav. *Do you think I'm a criminal or just criminal-adjacent?*

"We'll talk when we talk." Ethan cleared his throat. "I hope he didn't give you too much grief, after I left."

"Not at all." Jav's voice skipped up an octave.

Gentle friction of disbelief. Jav recognised that particular blend – and relaxed into his pillow. Clara felt like this whenever Stephen did something idiotic but, in her eyes, loveable.

"Well," said Ethan. "Let me make it up to you anyway."

It would have taken a saint to refuse.

Royal Charlotte Hall, Upper Kensington, Level 12.
Wednesday, 8 December.

AS THE NIGHT of the gala arrived, anticipation eroded Jav's disappointment with Rina's absence. It was also difficult to remain annoyed whilst being kissed within an inch of your life.

"You know," said Ethan, breath warm against Jav's pulse, "I really like your navy-officer get-up."

"Really? I hadn't noticed." Jav's head hit the seat as Ethan's hands trailed south. The car chimed: they were nearing the Royal Charlotte Hall. "Um. We could still go home."

Ethan grinned. "I don't need to go anywhere to finish what we've started."

On Prince Consort Road, the noise of the crowd washed over the car like rain. Jav could see the flash-pop of lights through the one-way windows as security hailed them to a stop.

"Last chance," said Jav, passing Ethan a pair of mirrored sunglasses.

Ethan squared his shoulders. "Just promise I won't have to talk too much."

"Promise." Jav kissed him for good luck and swung the door upwards and open.

Sound and light flooded into the car, the crowds' emotions sparking Jav's nerves alight. There was an audible pause in the onlookers – followed by a crescendo of shouting as the press realised: no, that wasn't Corinna's well-stilettoed foot.

"Javier! Javier, this way!"

"Mr Arden, over here!"

Jav held out his hand. "Watch your step."

"My dad's gonna fucking kill me," Ethan muttered.

THEY MADE THEIR WAY up the grand staircase, fingers laced together.

"Javier! Javier, who's your friend?"

"One photo!"

Ethan's amusement was a shot of liquor, a pleasant blur. "Have I been pronouncing your name wrong this whole time?"

"No, grandpère is French, so it's a soft 'j'. But either works."

"Whatever you say, *Havier*."

They reached the top of the steps in short order. Journalists milled about in cocktail dresses and suits, radiating zest.

One made a beeline for them. "Javier, I adore your shoes. Let me guess...Hermes?"

"Perseus, actually." Jav tried to recall Maddy's fashion-week coverage. The journalists' lapel pin read 'The Sentinel'. "How's your evening going, Mia?"

She laughed, which surely meant Jav got her name right. "Wonderful! I must confess, we were all guessing what the Arden twins were coming as. You always bring the theme as a pair. But I don't think I've had the pleasure...?"

Ethan was staring at a new arrival – clad in plaster and not much else. Jav tugged on his hand.

"Hmm? Oh, hi."

"I was just saying what a surprise it is to see Javier alone this year!" Mia smiled as bright as her sequined dress. "As in, without Corinna."

"Ethan's here indulging me," said Jav.

"I'm here for the free food."

"Darling, I'll take what I can get."

Mia's eyes darted to their clasped hands. "Well, you make a very handsome pair. Any plans for the after-party?"

"Looking forward to the fireworks," said Jav. "I think we're holding up the procession, so we should shuffle on. Lovely to chat, Mia."

They stepped past floor-length gowns and curious looks until they reached the main salon. An attendant ushered them through oversized doors and into a cavernous auditorium. Round tables sparkled with tableware.

Ethan pulled off his sunglasses with tangible relief. "I don't know how you maintain that smile. How's your head?"

"I have my favourite placebo, so I'm fine." Jav squeezed Ethan's hand.

"Perseus was decapitated by Medusa. So that's always an option if your migraine flares up."

"After three hours with Charlie, a beheading would be a kindness."

"Don't worry, I have an escape plan." Ethan lifted his jacket to reveal a pager clipped to his belt. "Anytime we want to leave, I'll get an emergency call," he stage-whispered. "The perils of dating a doctor."

"...I love you."

A chorus of hellos rose as Ethan and Jav approached their table which bordered the dance floor, overladen with linen and olive wreaths. Charles Langley was slouched next to Rina's place setting – and the look on his face was priceless. He rose loudly to his feet, reaching to thump Jav on the back.

"What's all this?" Charlie exclaimed. "Where's your better half?"

"Right here," said Ethan, taking Rina's seat like a man taking a bullet.

Jav shrugged off Charlie's hand under the guise of pulling out his chair. "Good to see you. Rina sends her apologies; she's not well." Not his best lie: they both knew Rina never apologised for anything.

Charlie's face puckered. "I thought I'd surprise her. Haven't seen her in yonks."

"Mmhm." Jav shook hands around the table before taking his seat next to Ethan. "Lady Hartford. Let me guess...Athena?"

"Correct." Lady Hartford possessed a complexion of someone who saw a healer regularly, but not enough to counter her alcoholic excess. "I hope your sister feels better soon."

Ethan was preoccupied with the champagne selection. His barefaced disinterest took the wind out of Charlie's sails.

"Well?" Charlie harrumphed. "Aren't you going to introduce us, Javier?"

"Ethan," said Ethan, and promptly drained his glass.

If Ethan planned to drink his way out of conversations, he would be drunk before the second course.

"Charlie." Charlie shook Ethan's bare hand – rude. "Rina's my girlfriend. My uncle knew her grandmother quite well. Old family friends. You know how it is."

"Do I," said Ethan.

"Were you not feeling the theme, Ethan?" asked Lady Hartford.

Ethan blinked, then fished out a pen. "No, I'm in theme."

Trust doctors to carry ink pens, Jav thought fondly. He watched Ethan draw two circling snakes on a palm and recognised the 'healing hand' from watching *Healer's Anatomy*. The symbol was an almost-universal representation for healers – one that the Spanish appropriated from the Hopi tribe of Arizona. Ethan's snakes were smiling.

"I'm Asclepius," Ethan announced.

"Ethan is a cardiothoracic surgeon at St Ophie's Hospital," Jav added.

"How appropriate," said Lady Hartford. "If I was a healer, it'd do wonders for my skin."

"I *am* a healer," said Ethan.

A murmur rose around the table.

"If only we all had such admirable callings in life," said Charlie.

"Thanks," said Ethan. "Uh. What do you do, then?"

"A bit of this, a bit of that," said Charlie. "Family's in logistics. We handle things for Arden Pharma. They say you shouldn't mix business with pleasure, but sometimes that's the *best* way to do business."

"Right." Ethan shot Jav a glance that said, 'oh lord, I see what you mean'.

"A surgeon, at your age?" Lady Hartford glittered with interest. "I know this is gauche to ask, but...well, it's so hard to tell with healers."

Ethan seized the opportunity. "I'm eighty-five this December. Jav got catfished. Right, cupcake?"

"My love, you don't look a day over fifty," said Jav.

"That's a long time in public service, doctor," chuckled Lord Hartford.

Charlie leaned over Ethan to smack Jav's arm. "Bit out of your league, eh Javvers?"

"I could say the same for you," Jav retorted. He should try being nicer to the man, but it was difficult when Charlie's every facet grated on his nerves. He caught Ethan mouthing 'Javvers' to himself, eyes glued to the menu card.

Charlie turned to Ethan. "We go way back, you know."

"If by 'way back' you mean a few years," said Jav.

"He doesn't think anyone is posh enough for Rina," Charlie continued, elbowing Ethan as if they were old chums. "I've managed to stick around though. It's only a matter of time before I'm his brother-in-law, eh? Then we'll have another wedding to look forward to! How's Mansfield doing these days?"

Jav gritted his teeth.

Ethan leaned in. "*Psst.* Where are the entrées? I'm starving."

ETHAN LASTED THREE COURSES, four speeches, and twenty minutes into the dancing. Three hours next to Charlie. He was currently stealing sliced figs off Jav's plate while Charlie bragged about winning a rare single malt at auction.

"If you have a migraine, we could initiate the emergency protocol," Ethan whispered to Jav. "There's much nicer things that we could be—"

"You don't strike me as a man who's partial to scotch." Charlie interrupted. "Do healers have higher alcohol tolerance?"

Jav snorted.

Ethan stared between them, then dove for his pager. "Sorry. Someone's dying."

"I'll drive you to the hospital," said Jav immediately.

Ten minutes later they were in the Bugatti.

Jav had to pour Ethan into the car, but once there, Ethan shoved Jav down and climbed into his lap. He smacked blindly at the control panel to tilt the seat back, kissing Jav with teeth and zero grace.

Why was this a bad idea? It was hard to recall. His ears rang with Ethan's effervescence, giddy with their escape.

"Aren't you glad I came prepared?" Ethan punctuated each word with a kiss. "Charlie would *not* shut up." He shoved Jav's suit jacket off his shoulders, making short work of the buttons.

"We almost made it the whole evening."

"I was on my best behaviour. I think I deserve a reward." Ethan sucked a hickey into Jav's collarbone, even though his love bites never lasted.

Jav wished he could have a souvenir. "You promised me a waltz."

"Can't dance."

"It's a simple rhythm—"

Ethan rolled his hips. "Nothing wrong with my rhythm."

Jav choked on a laugh. "Incorrigible."

"I wanna suck you off," Ethan said, vowels worn smooth by alcohol.

For someone so uncoordinated below the waist, Ethan retained admirable fine-motor skills. The pearl-shank buttons on Jav's waistcoat proved no match.

Jav realised, belatedly, that Ethan was waiting for an answer. "Um."

Ethan ran both palms up Jav's abdomen. Then – in a move that might have toppled Rome – he licked his lips. The sheer *want* felt foreign, like heat injected straight into Jav's veins.

"I'm good at it, you know," said Ethan, perhaps mistaking Jav's moral dilemma for doubt.

He doesn't know about your empathy! But they were so close, and Ethan's smile so inviting. It was difficult to thread that thought to its logical conclusion.

"If you're sure that you..." Jav yelped as Ethan yanked his trousers and pants down in one go.

"Yes, I'm *sure*." Ethan rolled his eyes, scooting backwards. "Been wanting to suck you off ever since I saw this sweet ride."

"I knew it was about the car you — *fuck*!" Jav made a noise of disbelief as Ethan took him into his mouth...and kept going. "Shit, *shit*," he hissed, head hitting the car-seat.

The sensation liquefied his spine, a bright roiling pleasure making his toes curl. His hips jerked, helpless, and Ethan pressed a commanding hand on Jav's bare thigh to hold him still, all the while keeping eye contact as he deliberately swallowed several times without coming up for air.

Jav scrambled for sanity, fist to mouth, the nerve-searing heat at odds with the gentle way Ethan was patting Jav's right knee with his other hand. Jav choked on air. Ethan's satisfaction soaked into Jav's every pore, intoxicating.

"Sweet — god, Ethan. *Ethan.*" Jav sank one hand into Ethan's hair, then let go immediately because surely that was bad manners? Something molten rose up, clutching his lungs and dragging a hot, lovely sensation down to his sternum.

Jav could barely keep his eyes open. There was no way he wasn't projecting. And maybe it was the empathic feedback loop of oxytocin and dopamine. Maybe it was the obscene way Jav was hitting the back of Ethan's throat, combined with the press of Ethan's tongue as he hummed what sounded suspiciously like *God Save The Queen*.

"Ethan," Jav gasped. "Ethan, wait, *wait*, sorry I'm close...if you...i-if you — *Ethan*." He went blind for a few gut-punching, stuttering seconds. Static roared in his ears, leaving him gasping and helium light.

Slowly, Jav became aware of the sweat on his brow, the pin-point pressure of Ethan's fingers, and the tickle of breath on bare skin. He twitched as Ethan finally pulled back, wiping his mouth with the back of his hand. *Good lord.*

Ethan's pupils were blown dark. He looked as dazed as Jav felt, cheek pressed to Jav's right knee. The two of them must have made an indecent picture.

"What the fuck?" said Ethan.

Jav wheezed. "Sorry. I tried to warn you. Um."

"No, not that. Please, I'm not like you Kensington boys." Ethan thumbed the corner of his lip. "We've better table manners where I grew up."

Jav made a high-pitched noise. "Shall I return the favour...?"

For some reason, Ethan flushed red. "Actually. I already — I'm done." A pause. "This has never happened before."

They stared at each other.

"What?" Ethan's blush deepened. "You're hot, but not *that* hot. I've never...at the same time, just from—!" They stared some more, breathless. "Let's just say this suit is ruined, okay?"

Ethan didn't *feel* upset. Of course, as far as Ethan was concerned, it was a tipsy coincidence.

Jav knew better. Guilt crept back, dulled by oxytocin. "I'm sorry."

"Why?" Ethan demanded. "Hey, car, how long 'til we're home?" The dashboard chirped: *approximately ten minutes*. "The only way to test for a fluke is with the scientific method."

Jav didn't know whether to laugh or cry. He settled for not lying. "You're going to be the death of me."

"Nonsense. Healers are famously good for your health."

SIXTEEN

The Sentinel Studios, Upper Bloomsbury, Level 13.
The next morning, Thursday, 9 December.

The last thing Ollie expected to see at work was a giant photo of Ethan's face. But there he was, next to Javier Arden's blonde head on the 'Arts and Culture' page.

Ollie yanked the meeting-room door open. "What the hell!"

Everyone turned to look at him.

"We have this room until ten," said Mia Hyun, raised eyebrows promising slow evisceration. "We've been up all night—"

"Reporting on cutting-edge exfoliation? Where did you get that photo?"

"From the gala last night," one of the interns piped up. Ollie assumed he was an intern because he looked the most caffeinated. "Javier Arden didn't do a twin-look with his sister this year."

"What gala?" asked Ollie.

The intern's laugh devolved into coughing when he realised Oliver wasn't joking. "Uh. The Fashion Council gala. Theme was 'Mortal Gods'. We're pulling together the night's best looks."

"And you put *Ethan* on the landing page?" Ollie whipped out his phone and snapped a picture of the screen. "Ta."

"Wait. You know this guy?" Mia called down the corridor. "Ollie, come back you piece of shit, I'm talking to you!"

OLLIE HAD BEEN at a dead end for some weeks now.

Vegas always said that what Ollie lacked in patience, he made up for in persistence. But Ollie's best lead was lying in a morgue. Without the actual cab to examine, Tom couldn't tell Ollie anything the investigators wouldn't already know. To top it off, Javier Arden was now haunting Ollie's every step.

He stared at the photo of Ethan and Javier. *God, I hope Nick already knows about this.* Ian likely hadn't caught wind of the gala yet. Last time they spoke, Ian was livid that Ollie didn't tell him about Ethan and Javier sooner – and ignored every call since.

"Why is Ian mad at me, when *you've* known about this since the beginning?" Ollie had whined to Vegas. "You're the one who set them up."

"I'm his favourite child," Vegas had replied, while Ethan sulked in the corner.

Would sending Ian the gala photo redeem Ollie – or send Ian further down the spiral of fatherly rage?

A shadow fell over his lap.

"Why the pout?" It was Florence, tablet in one hand, stilettos in the other.

"Life," said Ollie. "You look fancy."

"It's the double-espresso. The Water Secretary has a presser in two hours."

"Fun."

"What are you angsting about?"

"Murder."

Florence leaned against his desk. "Anybody I like?"

"No."

"So Javier hasn't killed Vegas, Ethan or any of your estranged family members? Or you."

"Was that in order of descending priority?"

"That's right, turtledove. Still working on the Hersch story, then."

Ollie chewed on the end of his stylus. "Yup."

"Didn't the official report say alcohol poisoning?"

"Oh, it was *some* kind of poisoning," Ollie muttered. "Makes sense, since everything seems to be Arden Pharma adjacent—"

Florence yanked Ollie to his feet, frog-marching them into the nearest empty room. There was barely enough room for a chair and her squint. "Did you get any sleep last night?"

"Have I lost my usual dewy complexion?"

"You should talk to someone."

"What do you think I've been trying to do this whole time?" Ollie yawned. "The issue is no one seems to want to talk to *me*: Martin's colleagues at the ad agency, no help, Tim's friends, lips sealed. Violet even joined some student union servers with her uni email."

"I meant a therapist."

"You think Martin told his therapist—?"

"For you, dipshit."

"Pass."

"Ollie."

"I'm *fine*."

"You're obsessing, and not constructively. I'm worried you're going to have a breakdown and shove Julian's hand into the coffee grinder."

"That's specific. Are *you* going to maim Julian?"

Florence deflated. "I swear, if they don't announce fusive numbers I shall stab everyone at the briefing and then myself. My mascara is baked in. My pores—"

"...I'll take that as a 'yes'," said Ollie.

"The French refuse to budge on CM15 tariffs. We *just* greenlit CM15 funding for the next two years, but every pundit is speculating that the government will axe the CM15 subsidy regime early – instead of waiting for Project Earthflown to get to phase three or whatever the fusive roll-out targets are."

Ollie massaged his migraine. "Did they find the extra votes somehow?"

"Not yet. Sainte-Ophie Biotech is the only real contender and too many would rather die of thirst than let the French in the market. God forbid our elected representatives be bought by some foreign pharmaceutical company, when every patriot knows Westminster should be owned by a *British* pharma company."

"Who cares. Half the buildings in London already have pharma names slapped on. Look at St Ophie's Hospital."

"They're public – but the Sainte-Ophies funded both relocations after the floods, so. I suppose moot point."

"If Project Earthflown is election fodder, wouldn't giving it to a foreign firm defeat the nationalist angle?"

Florence snorted. "I'm sure they'll award the tender to Ascenda. They're the largest British construction firm. Then Arden Pharma will get all the water subcontracting work as usual. Don't forget, the transition to fusive-powered infrastructure will take decades. Plenty of CM15 pie left, and worth fighting over."

And that's assuming the fusive roll-out and CM15 phase-out happens in lockstep – an utter fantasy. "Water rates will shoot up at the first sign of CM15 subsidies being rolled back," said Ollie. "No one is brave enough to own that in an election year."

"We don't have much goodwill left. The next Sixty-Fourther protest might turn violent."

"Remember that Arden Pharma email about Corinna Arden being shot? You thought they leaked it on purpose."

"It did shift the news-cycle for forty-eight hours, in their favour. Bit of a windfall, at least."

"A windfall *by design*." Ollie would have paced if there was room.

"You said Corinna Arden needed a healer. There are less convoluted – and less fatal – ways to misdirect the press."

"I'm not saying she got *shot* on purpose. But she wasn't there by accident. And if the shooter was working with Hersch, why didn't they check in on the guy who had the goods?"

"Got spooked?" Florence suggested. "I'd be scared. Though abuela would get to me before the police had a chance."

"Tim Hersch had no priors, just attended protests, wrote for the student union. And suddenly he's trafficking CM15? He wasn't even right-handed. Tim was at the wrong place at the wrong time. Saw something he shouldn't have. Became a loose end."

"Make up your mind – who was at the wrong place at the wrong time? Corinna or Hersch?"

"We're in the European capital of glass. Who is the largest and only manufacturer of CM15 here?"

"Neither CM15 nor glass was invented yesterday. I agree the circumstances are a bit suss—"

"Know what else is *suss*? Father of the deceased starts talking to a journalist. The next thing you know, he's dead in his flat. That journalist talks to the police. Bam: Javier Arden himself appears!" Ollie succumbed to gravity, sliding until he hit the floor. He put his head between his knees and moaned.

Florence patted his hair. "I agree it's all a bit spooky—"

"Spooky?" Ollie shouted, muffled. "*Spooky?*"

"It's been almost two months and Javier hasn't done anything nefarious."

"That we know of!"

"You said Javier and Ethan were already seeing each other *before* Martin died. Taco night might have been a coincidence. Have you talked to Ethan again?"

"He's been avoiding me. Apparently Javier flooded the hospital with flowers and took him out for dinner that same week." Ollie jolted upright. "Shit, that's how Javier knew I had been talking to Martin. He's probably bugged the flat! I've taken work calls there. Shit. *Shit.*"

Florence stared. "Seems a risky move, given Ian visits?"

"That's two...no, three birds, in one stone." An unbearable itch threaded its way to Ollie's jugular. "I didn't think of the timeline until just now, about the Earthflown bid."

"The public consultation."

"Yeah, that. It's so close to the general election. When we wrote that first article, it was days before the CM15 subsidy vote, and you said 'wow, the timing is sure handy dandy'—"

"I sound nothing like that."

"—So what's Javier still *doing here*? The subsidies got renewed. Security audit looks dead in the water. Tim's been written off as an overdose. Martin drank himself to death." Ollie rubbed his eyes with the heel of one hand. "But there's plenty of time before the Earthflown tender is locked in, and I bet there are a *lot* of skeletons that the Ardens would prefer remain buried before the election."

"Look. Legal has kittens every time somebody links Arden Pharma directly with the glass trade—"

"Legal can kiss my ass—"

"—their pockets are so bloody deep!"

"Something happened the night Corinna Arden was shot. They flew her out of St Ophie's, like *that*." Ollie snapped his fingers. "Vegas said the police interviewed half of A&E. Ethan was hauled in front of a disciplinary panel, so the transfer must have been dodgy. Which brings me to another thing: why haven't they caught the shooter? Corinna Arden isn't a nobody. If a Sixty-Fourther *was* responsible, you'd think the Ardens would exploit that angle."

"What has this got to do with Javier dating Ethan? If Ethan knows something fishy about Corinna's injuries, then so do half the medical staff."

"Ah, but *they* don't have a father in the SIA." Ollie gestured between the two of them. "Or friends who broke the story in question."

"And you think Javier will poison Ethan's morning coffee if you write something incriminating?"

"He snogged Ethan, at the SIA precinct, in front of *Ian* – the lead investigator on Corinna's case; a man who has been on the glass beat for thirty years."

Florence snorted. "Alright, that's pretty ballsy."

"Ian called *me* for once. He was not happy. The Ardens got rid of Tim, Martin, most of the surveillance tapes...I guess Ethan and Vegas are loose ends."

"And us." A long pause. "We need to update our flow-chart. If it's any comfort, healers are hard to kill?"

"Vegas isn't a healer," said Ollie.

"Maybe she should move in with me…"

"Oh, stop it."

"In all seriousness, I don't think Arden would dare touch Ethan. Healers wear those health monitors, right? Alarms blare if he so much as stubs his toe. What does Vegas think about all this?"

"She thinks Javier's sweet," Ollie muttered. "Bastard's been bribing her with expensive alcohol and cat-themed kitchenware."

"Aww."

"No, not *aww*. What's wrong with you?"

"Well, we have to persuade Ethan then."

Wordlessly, Ollie brandished his phone, the photo of Javier and Ethan still on the screen.

Florence scrunched up her face. "I'm sorry, *what*."

"Yeah, Ethan's a lost cause."

***

Later that evening.

VEGAS SEEMED SHOCKED to find Ollie in the A&E lobby. "You're early," she said, accepting a kiss. "Is that udon?"

"Figured you'd want to eat at home." Ollied traded the takeaway bag for her satchel.

Vegas prodded happily at the soup container all the way home. The air stuck to their throats, cold with the promise of frost, pinking their nose and ears by the time they arrived. Years of familiarity were worn into the lines of this flat. It was unsettling to think that there might be something here, listening.

"So." Vegas set the table as Ollie rummaged for white wine. "What's the occasion?"

"Nothing. Thought it'd be nice to have a night in." Ollie poured the broth into the two bowls. When he looked up, Vegas was still staring. "What?"

"Waiting for you to tell me what you need help with."

"I got you an extra egg."

"Yes. Very suspicious." Vegas stretched, plopping both feet into Ollie's lap and almost incapacitating him with one heel.

"Oww! Don't we want kids someday?"

"Oh shush," said Vegas, chopsticks in her mouth. "Ay 'ove oou."

"I love you too," said Ollie. They ate in companionable silence. Outside, it started to rain. "Can I have a bite of the egg?"

"No."

The next morning, Friday, 10 December.

IN DEFERENCE TO VEGAS'S sleep (and their last big fight), Ollie slept with one earbud in whenever he stayed the night. Notification chimes now woke him with a direct jolt to the brainstem via his ear canal. Ollie inhaled a mouthful of Vegas's long hair and fumbled for his phone.

> 08:02 · VIOLET — I have bad news.

> > 08:03 · OLIVER — Can't call, can text. What news? :(

> 08:03 · VIOLET — You know how we set up keyword alerts for Tim Hersch etc in October? Tiff set alerts for the court register + lists, just in case. There's a hearing re police raid on a 64er stash house. They pleaded guilty. Tim Hersch was named.

Ollie sat up, fully awake.

> > 08:04 · OLIVER — When did this happen? Yesterday?

> 08:04 · VIOLET — There's been a few hearings and there's a delay before each transcript is uploaded. This one was from Monday. Sentencing 9am today.

"Ollie?"

He winced. "Shit, didn't mean to wake you."

"S'fine." Vegas yawned. "Have work soon anyway. What's wrong?"

"Plot twist on a story." Ollie kissed her forehead. "Sorry, gotta reply. It's the intern."

> 08:06 · OLIVER — Do we know if it's open to the public as usual?

> 08:06 · VIOLET — Yep and I forwarded the transcript. You're welcome.

Beneath the text was a screenshot of the court registry website, complete with the room number.

"Have to run to court." Ollie cast about for his jeans and found them wedged beneath the door. His shirt was in the kitchen. When he returned, Vegas had sat up, cocooned from chin to ankle.

"You're going to court like that?" she asked, squinting adorably when he pulled on the blinds.

"I don't have time to go home and change."

Vegas sighed and made a big show of getting out of bed, dragging the blanket with her. She slid open Ethan's partition door with a bang. "You can borrow."

Ethan's room barely fitted a chest of drawers and bare-bones clothes rack. Jackets and shirts hung on mismatched hangers, bookended by fancy monogrammed garment bags.

Vegas held out a blazer. "Maybe this was yours first and *Ethan* borrowed it? Who knows — *oww*." She broke off with a hiss.

Ollie paused. "You okay?"

"Yeah, just stepped on something. God, Ethan's such a slob." Vegas bent, patting around the rug, then under the bed (brave, given whose room they were in). She straightened triumphantly. "Ah-ha!" She grabbed his hand, fastening cufflinks to Ollie's sleeves. "Dapper's a good look on you."

They stood nose to nose, and she kissed him, soft and inviting.

Ollie yanked her closer by the waist "I've gotta go now-ish. S'gonna take me at least thirty minutes."

Vegas bit his lower lip. "Fine. Whatever. Shower time."

The cufflinks felt heavier than they looked, each gold face depicting a tiny bird with silver beaks and gem inlays for eyes.

"When did Ethan start wearing shit like this?" asked Ollie.

Vegas poked her head around the corner. "Oh, no, those are definitely Jav's." She laughed at Ollie's disgust. "I'm sure he won't mind. Have fun!"

OLLIE TOOK THE PEDESTRIAN STAIRS up to Level 10, then a bus across the city. He spent the journey scrolling through the court transcript that Violet had sent.

If Tim Hersch had been fleecing CM15 on the job, where did that leave things? Maybe it *had* been a post-heist high. Ollie tabbed through a key-word search, but the entire proceeding was focused on a separate instance of theft. The co-defendants appeared to be young Sixty-Fourthers, and the 'stash house' was a residential building on Level 4. Perhaps there'd be more information in the earlier transcripts.

Overhead, the bus announced that they were approaching Ludgate Circus. He'd have to continue searching later.

Like other buildings that once housed the machinery of government, the Old Bailey moved upwards through the decades as London left its brick and sandstone roots to rot. This Level 10 iteration had shed much of its original visage, but still sprawled solemn in the watered-down sunlight.

Ollie detoured to the locker service outside the main entrance, passing over his phone and tablet to the clerk in return for a docket. With fifteen minutes to spare, he joined the short queue at security.

"Morning," said the lady manning one scanner. "No phones, cameras, or any other kind of electronics. Shoes et cetera in the trays."

The scanner beeped as Ollie stepped through it. The security guard waved at him back. Perplexed, Ollie patted himself down. Had he forgotten a spare stick-on camera or mic?

"Anything in your pockets? Keys?" Security looked at her screen then pointed at his wrist. "In the tray, please."

Ollie mentally cursed the cufflinks. "Sorry."

By the time he reached the lifts, he had minutes to spare. He sandwiched his notebook under an arm to put the cufflinks back on, fumbling with his non-dominant hand.

Someone jostled him as he stepped out of the lift, and Ollie almost dropped a cufflink. "Heaven's sake," he muttered, taking a quick left, counting the numbers on the doors as he went.

He struggled with the slim metal toggle, pressing on the face of the cufflink to pin it in place. Instead, the embossed face shifted under his thumb with a distinct *click*.

For a second, he thought he might have snapped the stupid thing. The toggle was no longer parallel with the bird's feet. Conscious of the time, Ollie pressed the cufflink between thumb and forefinger, trying to recreate the twisting motion.

And as he did so, a green glow brushed against the pad of his thumb, there and gone.

Ollie stared at the cufflink. "Well, how 'bout that."

The bird stared back with one tiny emerald eye.

The Queen's Head, Upper Lambeth, Level 10.
Many hours later.

THE PUB WAS CHEERFULLY NOISY, befitting a Friday.

Nick dropped the cufflinks into the white box. The lid hissed as it sealed shut – blocking any transmissions in or out. "There. Happy?"

Ollie exhaled with explosive relief. "I can't believe you made me wait all day. I was about to gnaw my hand off."

"I think what you meant to say was: Thanks for doing me yet another favour. Dinner's on me."

"I said I'd shout drinks."

"Cool, I'll just take this." Nick swept the case into his jacket pocket, scraping his chair back to stand. "Good chat."

"Alright, *alright*, you miserable sod. Don't leave. *Thank* you."

Nick sat. "I'll have the steak with mashed pumpkin. With cider."

Ollie dutifully went to the bar. When he returned, drinks in hand, Nick had shed his jacket and was looking marginally less grumpy. *Was it an amicable breakup? Goddamn your poker face.* Thus far, Ollie had taken the coward's route by avoiding the topic of Ethan entirely.

"So." Nick tapped the case in his pocket. "These look expensive. Stole them, did you?"

"One could say I 'nicked' them. Eh?"

Nick took a long sip of his drink, throat working, unamused.

"It was a lost and found situation," Ollie conceded. "They were on the floor. Vegas found them under Ethan's bed."

Nick raised his eyebrows. "You think someone broke in and planted listening devices beneath Ethan's bed."

Invited in, more like. "Not break in, per se."

"Ethan doesn't wear cufflinks."

Ollie edged around the Javier-shaped sinkhole, reluctant to be the bearer of awkward news. "Can you get someone to check these out? See what they are?"

"Not so fast. What makes you think they're more than cufflinks? Besides your unhealthy paranoia."

Ollie ignored the jibe. "I noticed some kind of biometric sensor. It's big enough to house a decent recording unit so I chucked it in a Faraday bag and locked it in one of the recording studios for most of today."

Nick eyed Ollie with a shrewd, knowing look that only came from the kind of friend who spent years holding your head above the toilet and making pasta for you to cry into when Vegas dumped you (again). "I *do* know someone who might be able to help."

"Great—!"

"But I'm not risking my neck or jeopardising potential evidence." Nick set down his glass. "Tell me how you really found them."

"Aren't you concerned that someone bugged Ethan?"

"By giving him cufflinks? Why not dot-mic his satchel? Tap his phone? There are so many less conspicuous ways."

Their food arrived, an interruption of gravy-laden steak and a basket of chips. The meat was grown-not-born, but you couldn't tell the difference on a night like this. Ollie gathered a giant forkful of food to stall for time while Nick methodically worked his way from vegetables to protein.

There was no way around it. Ollie dunked a chip into the tomato sauce and took a deep breath. "Have you talked to Ethan recently?"

"No."

Ollie waited. Nick kept eating.

"Okay..." *Best get it over with.* Ollie cleared his throat. "Ethan's been seeing some guy. That's who the cufflinks belong to."

"Are we talking about Javier Arden, or someone else?"

"Oh, thank god. Yes. Arden." Ollie backtracked rapidly as Nick narrowed his eyes. "I mean, good that you already know. Not good that Ethan's, uh. Well. You never told me you broke up."

Nick smiled, no teeth. "Don't feel left out. I wasn't told either."

Ollie winced. *Onwards and forwards.* "They're Javier's cufflinks. And given everything that's happened in the past couple months, I thought the timing of how they met was too convenient."

Nick set down his knife and fork. Wiped his mouth with a paper napkin. "Timing," he repeated. "Out of curiosity, when was that exactly?"

"Uhhh." Ollie knew that the brighter Nick's expression, the more upset he was. Right now, he resembled a toothpaste commercial. "A few weeks?"

Nick waited.

"Since October," Ollie admitted. "Vegas said they started going out when Ethan was on leave."

"We're in December. You didn't think to, oh, I don't know, give me a heads up? Maybe while you were hounding me about Hersch?"

"I only found out recently. Recently-ish. And speaking of Hersch—"

Nick's mouth flattened. "No."

"Did we know that Tim Hersch was skimming CM15? Or did that allegation only come out in court?"

"You have the gall to ask, after not telling me about Ethan for months?"

Ollie dragged a hand down his cheek. "I'm sorry! Honestly, I thought you might have seen it on social media already, or the tabloids, since they've—"

"You wanted me to find out *via the news*?"

"No! I just mean —" The conversation was derailing faster than Ollie anticipated. "Look. Ethan has the emotional intelligence of a teaspoon. We both knew this was going to end in tears, right? I figured you wouldn't want to talk about it."

Nick's expression smoothed over. "Fair enough. Ethan can do what – and who – he wants. None of my business; certainly none of yours."

"Did he not even text you?" asked Ollie. *Surely Vegas would have said something.*

Nick shrugged. "No strings."

"Bullshit. You two have been – whatever you've been – for over two years. That's *some* strings."

Nick narrowed his eyes. "You know how you thought I wouldn't want to talk about it? You were right."

"I'm just saying! I didn't think either of you were sleeping around."

Nick's chin went up. "I *wasn't* sleeping around."

"Exactly." Ollie chewed the inside of his mouth. "How did you find out?"

"Gossip travels fast around the precinct. And Ian pulled me into his office last week to ask whether Ethan and I 'had a fight'."

Ollie sucked in a breath through his teeth.

"Exactly." Nick stabbed his last piece of steak.

There was a long silence.

"And how're you holding up?" asked Ollie.

"Never better."

Ollie stared at him for a full two minutes before going to the bar for more alcohol.

Nick accepted the fresh bottle. "So. To be clear, you stole—"

"They were lying on t—"

"*Stole* these cufflinks from Ethan's place, cufflinks that belong to Javier water-magnate Arden. And you'd like me to figure out if they are secret recording devices. Because reasons." Nick took a sip. "How am I doing so far?"

"If I say 'great', will you help me?"

"No."

"Why not?"

"Because I'm not gonna be 'that guy'."

"The guy who steps in when a douchebag is using their boyfriend as part of some conspiracy?"

Nick flushed. "No, the 'jealous guy' who is trying to interfere with his ex."

Something sour and sympathetic twisted in Ollie's stomach.

"I'm not like that." Nick ran a hand through his hair. "Ethan will think I'm helping you because...well. I'm not that."

"Ethan doesn't need to know," said Ollie. "Plausible deniability. I could have asked anyone to look at these."

"Great, ask them, not me."

Trust Nick to call his bluff a hundred per cent of the time. The perils of pickling a friendship over two decades. "Fine! I don't know anyone else, and this looks custom. I need your help. Please?"

Nick took a deep breath but didn't respond.

"I know you think I'm just paranoid—" Ollie ignored Nick's snort "—if these turn out to be overpriced cufflinks: fantastic. In fact, I'd be overjoyed. Because the alternative is that the Ardens are more personally involved than Florence and I thought. We knew that any transition away from CM15 will be seismic for their bottom line. But someone resorted to *shooting* Corinna Arden two months ago. All those 'malfunctioning' surveillance cameras, Martin Hersch conveniently dropping dead... Doesn't any of that smell off to you?"

"Get to the point," said Nick.

"The *point*: I think some very rich people are very nervous. So nervous, in fact, they're willing to gas the entire place, rather than risk anything coming out of the woodwork."

"Why are we the pests in your analogy?"

Perhaps the breakup was a blessing in disguise. Ethan's contrarian attitude had clearly been a terrible influence on Nick over the years.

"They don't want anyone looking too hard or speaking too loudly," said Ollie. "That's the police, the SIA, the press. Glass trafficking is under Ian's purview, yeah?"

Nick stared. "This is a stretch, even for you."

"There've been multiple investigations about the glass market and CM15 supply. The Ardens have had so many audits about missing stock—"

"And in case you haven't noticed, none of that has exactly *gone* anywhere. Plus, Ian isn't the only one working on these matters."

"*He's* the one who interviewed the Arden twins after Corinna got shot. Reckon something spooked them. Maybe Ethan is insurance."

"They were a little evasive, but that's not unusual."

Ollie paused. "You've seen the interview tapes?"

"I was there," said Nick, with vengeful nonchalance.

"What?! Why didn't you tell me?"

"And how does that make you feel?"

"Forgive me Father for I have sinned. You *knew* I was working on this story..." Ollie whined. Nick made a show of examining his cuticles. "So, what did you think of humpty and dumpty?"

"No comment," said Nick.

"As *people*, good lord, throw me a bone."

Nick shrugged. "A little rehearsed. Polite enough."

"Fake as hell, I thought."

"You've met them too?"

"Only Javier." Ollie prayed Nick wouldn't ask where.

Nick's lip curled, letting some colour slip. "He didn't seem to be the sharpest scalpel on the tray."

"If these cufflinks aren't dodgy, I'll drop them in Ethan's drawer next time I'm over there. No one would know they were even gone. And if they're bugs...well." Ollie pinched the bridge of his nose. "Cross that bridge when we get to it."

Nick traced the condensation on his glass with the pad of his thumb. "I'll help you, on two conditions."

"Go on."

"First, this stays between us. If Ethan asks, you lie. If *Vegas* asks, you lie. Got it?"

Ollie pulled a face. "Fine."

Nick tapped the white box in his pocket. "Second, if this turns out to affect any on-going investigations, we give them to Ian. Ah-ah!" He raised a finger. "I'm not done. *If* that happens, you will do as you're told. That includes publishing *nothing* until we say so. *And* you tell me immediately if you find anything that might put Ethan in hot water."

Ollie made a show of counting on his fingers. "That's four conditions."

"Or I give these to Ian tonight," said Nick.

The Sentinel Studios, Upper Bloomsbury, Level 13.
Five days later, Thursday, 16 December.

FLORENCE POKED OLLIE'S CHEEK with her stylus. "We only have this meeting room for another five minutes."

Ollie was face down in transcripts, annotated by one of their resident court reporters. Ollie and Florence had to bribe her with fancy Australian coffee. It hadn't been worth the trouble.

"Maybe you were right, the first time around," said Florence. "If Tim Hersch et al were skimming CM15, maybe he *did* overdose by accident. Or ran afoul of bigger fish."

"And you think those bigger fish ate Martin alive? What about Corinna Arden getting shot right before the subsidy vote?"

"I doubt dying from a gunshot wound was some kind of four-dimensional chess move."

Someone knocked on the meeting room door and Ollie's phone chose that moment to start vibrating. He straightened when he saw who it was. "Hey, gimme a sec."

"Can't chat long," said Nick. "I have a jewellery update."

"Already?" said Ollie. "Okay, hit me." Florence smacked him on the ass with her tablet. He yelped. "No, not *you*."

"Sorry?" said Nick.

"Nothing, ignore that," said Ollie. "What's the update?"

"They're not recording devices," said Nick.

"Wait, really? Then...?"

"It'll be easier to talk in person. I should be back at the Level 10 precinct soon. You free?"

"I can be free. I'll need to swing by to pick them up, right?"

Nick laughed, humourless. "Yeah. About that."

SIA, Central London Precinct, Level 10. A few hours later.

NICK ELBOWED the interview-room door shut. "This is off the record."

Ollie collapsed into one of the chairs. "Only because I love you."

Reaching into his pocket, Nick dropped the cufflinks on the table with a *click*.

"So," said Ollie. "Not bugs then?"

"Not normal cufflinks either," said Nick. "You were right about the sensors." He held a cufflink between thumb and forefinger, press-twisting the embossed face. Citron flickered against his thumb. "Biometrics. My buddy took these apart. At first, she thought they housed a jammer, which isn't necessarily *better* than a surveillance device."

"Stop teasing and get to the punchline."

"They're aptitude suppressors." Nick set the cufflink next to its sibling on the table. "Clearly custom."

"Aren't they a bit small for suppressors? And Javier Arden isn't an aptee..." Ollie dove for his phone. "Or *is* he?"

"Once we realised this was aptee tech, we tried to figure out what kind – which is where things got interesting."

Ollie frowned, still scrolling. "The internet says Javier is *not* an aptee."

"By the way, you owe me. I used up a lot of favours for this."

"I'll suck you off later. What kind of suppressor is it?"

Nick rolled his eyes. "Suppressors aren't one-size-fits-all: depends on the type of suppressor, the aptitude they were designed for, and the aptee's Xu's Scale rating. We also know a lot more about certain aptitudes than others. You slap a commercial firestarter suppressor on a healer and nada. Firestarters, we've got a handle on, so their suppressors are most effective." He wrapped a hand around one wrist. "Suppressors have limited proximity. Dampeners have longer range, used in non-wearables. Aircraft, tube stations, et cetera. Consumer-grades are usually bracelets and cuffs."

Ollie made a mental note to check his Yellowstone notes. Had Corinna Arden been wearing suppressors when she was shot?

"So suppressors are stronger, but only affect the person wearing them," Nick continued. "Current dampeners only work on firestarters and telekinetics, but nothing is watertight. That's why firestarters must wear suppressors *and* sit next to dampeners on commercial flights, for example."

Ollie flicked one of the cufflinks. It rocked back and forth, gleaming like a gamble. "So this is a custom suppressor, not a dampener. Why would Javier wear one if he's not an aptee?"

"Emphasis on custom. They're empath suppressors. Distinct mechanisms from firestarters and telekinetic wearables, apparently."

Ollie's eyebrows shot up. "And a non-aptee would wear something like this because...?"

Nick shrugged. "The same reason anyone wears empath dampeners. Paranoia. You'd be surprised how many politicians have these. They're mandated for jury hearings even though a camera and wall would do."

"A second ago, you said these were empath *suppressors*."

"They're usually marketed as dampeners. Point is, most people who wear these things aren't experts. It's not the same as localising a firestarter or telekinetic. Or a ghost." Nick rubbed his eyes. "Apparently there's next to no range on this pair, so it's probably a vanity piece. Would explain the form over function. The kind we use for interviews are more like chunky headbands."

Unless range wasn't the point! Ollie's nerves buzzed with the alternatives.

Nick tilted his head. He resembled the birds on the cufflinks in that moment, green-eyed and growing more cynical by the minute. "I was hoping you'd look less excited."

"I have a new theory," said Ollie.

"Of course you do."

"Range wouldn't matter if their owner was the empath."

Nick scrubbed a hand over his face. "Why do you always jump to these conclusions? There are far more paranoid people—" he raised his eyebrows at Ollie "—than there are empaths."

"That we know of."

"Lots of rich folks wear empath dampeners. Suppressors. Whatever."

Nick was probably right. Javier Arden was far more likely a paranoid bastard than an empath. But now that the possibility was seeded in Ollie's brain, it'd certainly explain Ethan's newfound romantic impulses.

Ollie glared at the cufflinks. "If I managed to get some DNA samples—"

"That's illegal."

"What if we *accidentally* found some DNA samples."

"What if you didn't tell all this to someone in law enforcement."

"I said *if*," Ollie muttered. "Look, you're probably right."

"...But?" Nick packed years of exasperation into one syllable.

"This is gonna eat me alive," Ollie announced, leaping out of his seat and swiping both cufflinks.

Nick jumped up. "Don't do anything illegal!"

"Me? Perish the thought." Ollie yanked the door open. "I'm just going to ask him."

SEVENTEEN

Friday, 17 December.

Time passed strangely when not tracked minute by minute against green, amber, and red. "Are you still thinking of going back to emergency early?" asked Jav.

Ethan hummed, noncommittal. The floor of the carriage shook as they rounded a bend, windows rattling, lungs against brittle bone. Jav's gaze snapped up as the lights flickered.

"Are you sure you've been on the Tube before?" asked Ethan, amused.

"Of course." A metallic shriek. "...Is it meant to be making that sound?"

"Old rails and runners. It'll be better once we're past Level 7."

"Flying is safer," Jav muttered.

"We'd have to walk, after."

"We walked for fifteen minutes anyway! Where were the buses? Uncle Harry must prioritise this neighbourhood in the bid proposal."

Bless. "Too narrow for buses. Bill's Chicken was worth it, right?"

Watching Jav eat fried chicken from a paper bag had been fantastic entertainment. He still wore plum spice on his nose, and Ethan wasn't about to say anything.

"It was okay," Jav conceded. "For grown-not-born chicken."

Ethan laughed. "You're such a snob."

"The texture lacks the fibre of born protein. Stop sniggering, I'm not a picky eater!"

"Sure, hun."

Jav tilted his head in a way that suggested he'd very much like a kiss for these trying times, please and thank you. Ethan obliged. Behind him, the carriage doors whooshed open as they pulled up to a platform awash with rain.

"This is us," said Jav.

"We've got four more stops."

Jav looped an arm around Ethan's waist, scooping him through the doorway. "I called the car."

"..."

"No vehicle should sound like they're in *pain*," Jav whispered, as if the Tube could overhear. "How do you know it's safe? No one knows."

"Can you imagine the PR nightmare if a carriage detached? The paperwork. If that's not incentive to keep things safe, I don't know what is."

"If the fall doesn't kill us, the radiation would finish us off."

"Everyone dies at some point." Ethan frowned. "Wait, did you say *radiation*?"

Since Ethan had day shifts that week, it was easier for Jav to stay the night on Level 9. An extra pair of shoes greeted them at the door. *Ollie.*

Ethan banged on Vegas's bedroom door. "Jav and I bags the shower."

An answering *thump*. "Okay!" Vegas sounded suspiciously out of breath. "Hi, Jav!"

There was a muffled curse. Another thud.

"Hi Vegas. Oliver." Jav set down his overnight bag and began conjuring fancy toiletries like a magician.

"We have shampoo already," said Ethan, holding out a bottle.

Jav accepted gingerly, as if handling toxic waste. "We've been dating for almost four months. It's high time that I saved you from...this."

"Uh huh. Arden Pharma owns that brand."

Jav almost dropped the industrial-sized bottle on his foot in horror. "Good lord! Wait. This means Giulia can recall it."

"Don't you dare, that's my favourite flavour."

"Flavour? *Flavour*?" Jav's voice rose – because of course he was soft-spoken until it came to skincare. "Three-in-one is a crime and I refuse to aid or abett."

A loud thud. Ollie's muffled voice floated through Vegas's bedroom door. "What crime?"

The next morning.

JAV WOKE EARLY to fetch their breakfast from the drone locker. "I know you skip lunch, so you must eat properly *now.*"

"You're an angel," said Ethan groggily.

Jav beamed to his ears.

Since Nick rarely stayed for breakfast and Ollie was always late for dinner, the kitchen was rarely crowded. Ethan didn't mind this: being pressed knee-to-knee, elbows knocking tea and coffee. Watery sunlight streamed through the window as they ate. Vegas was devouring a salmon bagel. Even Ollie seemed to appreciate his ham and cheese croissant. Neither were bickering.

Ethan shovelled food on autopilot, sleep fogged. He noticed Jav's staring in his periphery. "Wot?"

"Nothing." Jav carded his fingers through Ethan's hair. "You're very fluffy this morning."

"Your shampoo, your fault."

Vegas drained her coffee. "Jav, you've truly ruined me for all other bagels." She stretched, taking her plates to the washer. "Okey-dokey, be right back: bathroom."

Ollie sipped his tea. "Yeah, thanks for breakfast. Nice of you."

Jav blinked. "You're welcome."

Ollie was sporting an innocent expression, which usually meant he was up to no good.

"Before I forget." Ollie rummaged in his pocket. "I think this belongs to you." He dropped something small and shiny into Jav's palm.

It was one of Jav's many cufflinks.

"Oh," said Jav. "Thanks."

"No problem. Looks expensive." Ollie shrugged. "Didn't know you were an empath though."

The temperature in the room fell. *What the fuck?* Ethan stared at Ollie, mortified – and almost missed the wide-eyed panic that flashed across Jav's face.

"Not sure what you mean." Jav's palm was still lying open on the table. "I'm not an aptee."

Ollie's gaze was fixed on Jav's face. "But that's an empath suppressor."

A pause. Jav laughed. "I see the misunderstanding. I have a lot of cufflinks, and some have empathy dampeners built in. I've lost track, to be honest."

"Really. Short-range suppressors?" asked Ollie. "They wouldn't have much effect on any empaths in the vicinity, surely – just the wearer."

Ethan kicked Ollie under the table. "Since when were you an expert on aptee suppressors?"

Poor Jav looked increasingly uncomfortable.

"I consulted someone," said Ollie, not looking away from Jav.

"When?" asked Ethan. "Did you *steal—*"

"What's he done now?" Vegas had returned from the bathroom. She took one look at the cufflink and her stare sharpened. "I thought we agreed not to bring this up."

Ethan rounded on her. "You knew about this?"

"I think the question is whether *you* knew," Ollie said to Ethan.

"About your kleptomania?" said Ethan. "Where's the other cufflink?"

"Dunno," said Ollie.

Jav's stress grew palpable. His expression remained politely confused, but Ethan recognised the anxious turn of his mouth, the twitch of his hand. It triggered a kernel of indignant anger in Ethan's stomach.

"You *lost*—" he started.

"No, this is my fault," Vegas cut in. "Ollie stayed the other night and had court in the morning. I grabbed a shirt from your room so he wouldn't look like a blob. I stepped on the cufflinks. Figured you wouldn't mind him borrowing. I didn't know he was going to lose *someone else's jewellery.*"

"Don't worry about it," said Jav, quiet.

Vegas shook her head. "I'm sorry. And Ollie is too. Right?"

Ollie was still looking at Jav like he was trying to scan his brain. "I mustn't have put it back on properly." Then he hissed.

For someone wearing fluffy cat slippers, Vegas had sharp toes.

"Sorry," Ollie added grudgingly.

"I'm gonna head in." Vegas yanked Ollie up by the arm. "This one's gonna be late for work if he doesn't skedaddle." She didn't give Ollie a chance to say more, just grabbed his satchel, her bag, and shoved him out the front door. "I'll see you after rounds, yeah?"

"Yep, my first surgery isn't until ten," said Ethan.

The front door slammed shut.

Jav was still holding the lone cufflink like a communion wafer. Ethan nudged him by the knee – and Jav flinched so violently that he almost upset a glass of water. The cufflink clattered across the table.

"I'm sorry about Ollie." Ethan nodded at the cufflink, embarrassed. "Were those emotionally significant?"

Jav stared at him like Ethan was some ghastly apparition. "*What?*"

And there it was again, the same hair-raising temperature fluctuation. *Weird.* "You know. Sentimental value."

"Oh, right — I'm. No."

Carefully, Ethan laid a hand on Jav's wrist. His pulse was racing. "Are you okay?"

Jav pulled away.

Ethan raised his eyebrows. "Babe?"

"Yes?" Jav suddenly smiled, too bright for the silence. "Sorry, I probably needed more sleep than I thought. Rina's been stressed. My head's not all here. Didn't expect Oliver to. Well."

"I'll chat to him." Ethan swallowed. "Can't believe he said all that."

"It's a reasonable misunderstanding." Jav chewed his lip. "But plenty of people wear these. People who aren't empaths."

Not for the first time, Ethan wondered if Jav felt displaced, growing up in a family of aptees. With a mother renowned in her research in the field of aptitude genomics, no less. Jav's eldest sister wasn't an aptee either, but from what Jav had told him, they weren't very close.

Ethan chose his next words with care. "Ollie's not a bigot. Just... nosy. I don't know what possessed him to spout off like that. He has his paranoid moments." He attempted a smile. "We all have them, right? Mr Anything-below-Level-5-shall-give-me-radiation-poisoning?"

Jav's gaze darted all over Ethan's face. Ethan swallowed, nervous. *Shit. If Ollie has fucked this up for me, I'm gonna kill him.*

Eventually, Jav said, "That's what Giulia and mum told me, and they're scientists."

"I'm pretty sure they said that to stop you wandering off and getting ransomed for a billion pounds." Ethan nudged the cufflink with his thumb. "Speaking of a billion pounds, I assume that's how much these cost...?"

"Don't worry about it." Jav's lower lip was chewed raw. "I should get rid of a few pairs anyway. Running out of drawer space."

"You do seem to have a hoarding problem," Ethan tried. "Like a little magpie. So much jewellery."

"That's a myth, you know. Birds prefer food."

"Same."

Finally, Jav smiled – strained but soft. "Yes." He stood, gathering up the plates and cutlery. "Come on, it's almost eight-thirty."

Who's the king of deflection now? Ethan pointed at his own forehead. "Aren't we forgetting something?" He hoped the petulance would make Jav laugh. Ethan ran his foot up Jav's right leg like people did in the movies but had to clutch the table before he fell off his stool. "Could have slipped and died, just now. You never know what can happen—"

He didn't even see Jav set the dishes aside: Ethan's back hit the wall.

Jav had hoisted him up by the waist, a hand under his thigh and one tilting Ethan's face so Jav could kiss him with bruising urgency.

Now that's more like it! Ethan clasped Jav by the nape of his neck, kissing away the abrasion on his bottom lip. Surprise flooded his veins with static. Jav responded by thrusting one thigh between Ethan's legs, pinning him more securely against the wall. He kissed Ethan's pulse, edged with teeth and promise.

"*Hello,*" gasped Ethan. "Where's all this been?"

Jav paused, pupils dark, lashes close enough to count. "I guess we're in a rush."

Ethan blinked away a hot prickle behind his eyes. *Lord,* he thought, distracted by Jav's thigh against his groyne. *Have I turned into the kind of person who cries when they're horny? Maybe Jav is an empath.* Ethan compensated by pulling Jav flush against him, mouth at his ear, hand fisted at his neck. "If I had known time pressure was what got you revving. You're the one who wanted to take it slow, remember?"

Jav's laugh sounded like stones skittering off the bypass, rattling against bone and steel. If you couldn't hear the splash, perhaps they'd never hit the sea. "Darling, please don't believe a word I say."

The next evening, Sunday, 19 December.

"Do you think all that mould in Ollie's flat has affected his brain?" asked Ethan.

He and Vegas were having dinner on the couch.

"Maybe."

"Jav thinks there's radioactive pollution below Level 5. Ollie would be in the blast zone."

Vegas's cheek bulged with broccoli. "I didn't peg Javier as a tin-hatter."

"And I didn't peg Ollie as such a rude shithead."

"*I* peg Ollie—" Vegas caught the cashew nut that Ethan threw at her.

Once they finished eating, Ethan voiced the doubt that had been niggling him since Ollie's confrontation at breakfast. "Does Ollie actually think Jav's an empath? Or is he trying to get back at me for... stuff." One might have thought that Ollie, who complained loudly about Ethan and Nick's ill-defined relationship, would be happy to hear the end of it. Alas, Ollie was never happy with anything.

Vegas shrugged. "He wasn't sure. That's why he wanted to ask Jav directly."

"I wouldn't call what Ollie did 'asking'."

"I told him not to. That stuff's private."

"Exactly! It's not something you share. Or expect to be shared."

"You know, Ollie cares about you a lot. You should have seen how worked up he was. He's worried you're being taken advantage of."

Ethan choked on his water. Vegas thumped him on the back with more violence than medically necessary.

"I have not been fucked enough to have been 'taken advantage of'. I have not been fucked *at all*."

"My heart bleeds. Ollie thinks Jav's here because of Ian's work."

Unfortunately, that wasn't an outlandish thought. Although he and dad had a no-work-talk rule, Ethan knew things from sheer exposure. Dad was chest-deep in glass and CM15 trafficking – had been, long since before mum passed away.

"How did Ollie make the leap from empath suppressors to dad?"

"He thought the cufflinks were secret recording devices at first, and that Jav had bugged the flat," said Vegas. "When he realised they were empath suppressors, he figured Jav was an undue influence."

That's prejudice talking. "If I were a betting man, I'd put my money on Jav being paranoid, not him being an empath. He spent an hour showing me 'evidence' about radiation poisoning on Level 1. He had screenshots about average life expectancies and everything."

"Oh dear."

"Do *you* think Jav's an empath?"

"I wouldn't know. Like Jav said: lots of people wear empath dampeners. Heaps of duds online."

"If Jav *is* an empath, then those suppressors must be strong as hell because there is *no* way he doesn't know how much I want to—"

Vegas flattened a pillow over Ethan's face. "Oh, we *all* know. I'm not an empath and even I know, because you whinge constantly. *Constantly.* Oi!" They tussled. By the time Ethan re-emerged, he was wheezing like a respirator and had lost possession of the burrito blanket. "Pathetic. How are you gonna pass your next physical? They'll be extra stringent after your recent naughty behaviour."

"Ughhh."

A long pause.

"Would it change things, if Jav was an empath?" Vegas asked.

Ethan studied his fingernails. "Not sure. Do you know of any empaths? Personally."

Vegas pursed her lips as she indexed her voluminous contact list. "Not that I'm aware of. Would be statistically rare anyway."

"As if you'd self-report."

"Yeah, most stats come from the US and Greater China."

"I've worked with *one* empathic anaesthetist, but that's it," said Ethan. "Dr Walsh. She was brought in for an elective. I wore empath dampeners when we were in the OR together but they went above my glasses."

Vegas leaned forwards, curious. "How did it feel?"

"Slippery? But that might have been placebo. She told me skin contact helps localise the empathic influence."

"Yeah, otherwise the entire team would zonk out, right?"

"I guess the dampeners were enough? From what she said, we basically know fuck-all about empathy. We don't know that much about healers, either. Healer suppressors don't exist."

"I think they're called gloves."

Ethan squinted. "That's technically healer dampeners. If *I* got stabbed in the chest, healer suppressors would be helpful. Instead of stabbing me over and over to relieve the pressure—"

"I'll happily stab you as many times as it takes."

"Cheers." Ethan fiddled with the empty food cartons. "Haven't talked to Dr Walsh since. I think she's consulting at Highgate Private. She said hospitals were awful places, empathically speaking. Everyone is stressed or in pain."

Vegas winced. "Damn. Are all empaths depressed, you think?"

"Dr Walsh wore strong suppressors whenever she wasn't in the OR.

Told me she always had the worst migraine and had to...take special painkillers..." Ethan trailed off. He thought about Jav's reliance on pain medication. *Huh.* But there were numerous reasons for taking analgesics.

Vegas poured herself a glass of water. "Maybe the amazing sex balances it out."

"What do you mean?" asked Ethan.

"Orgasm feedback loops." Vegas mistook Ethan's squint for confusion, rather than slow-dawning realisation. She rolled her eyes. "Have you not seen season four of *Healer's Anatomy*?"

1 Madeleine Avenue, Upper Chelsea, Level 22.
A few days later, Tuesday, 21 December.

THERE WAS NOTHING Ethan hated more than Ollie being right. But the more he thought about it, the more obvious it became: Jav was an empath.

But were Ethan's memories proving Ollie right – or feeding an illusory pattern perception? He tried to gather more data but there was no ethical way to trial an orgasm-loop. In any case, Jav was now keeping the Holy Spirit between himself and Ethan after his unexpected bout of passion.

In the days leading up to Christmas, Ethan read about empath studies, wrapped presents, and tried pain-based empathic litmus tests. One evening, he resorted to silently stabbing himself with a fork – behind a couch but within line of sight – while Jav worked on his best-man speech. Walls would have ruined the experiment.

Jav had leapt up instantly, which was interesting.

"How's the draft coming along?" Ethan asked, once Jav stopped fretting. They sat on the couch, Ethan's feet in Jav's lap.

"I'm worried no one will laugh at my jokes," said Jav.

"You can practise on me. When's the wedding again?"

"March. First one's in Taipei on the 19th. The London one is the week after."

"Why two weddings? Sounds like effort."

"Most of Clara's family is in Taiwan. And why *not* have two weddings?"

"I'm tired just thinking about it."

"One for each person."

Ethan snorted. "I'm pretty sure the point of marriage is that you share. Do you have to write two best-man speeches, or can you recycle?"

Jav massaged Ethan's ankle, digging in his thumbs into the groove of Ethan's sole. "I'm only writing one speech because I'm the second-best man, first. Carter gets to go first. The real best man."

"Isn't that a good thing? *Fuck me*, that feels...yeah, right there..." Ethan wriggled his toes. "What was I saying? Oh, right. Everyone's probably way more chill by the second wedding."

"Stephen and I have known each other our entire lives," Jav muttered. "Mum timed it so we would be born in the same hour, so neither of us would be lonely. Isn't that cute? I mean, I had Rina, but Stephen only has Nath, so."

"Your mum sounds organised."

"You can time things very precisely with incubators. Aunty Harper refused to tell mum whether Stephen was a boy or girl, so mum made one of each. Anyway. For the record, Stephen and I swore an oath as children that we would be best men at each other's weddings. Wedding*s*. Plural. All of them."

"Vegas and I made a pact to get married and adopt a cat, if Ollie didn't propose by the time she's thirty. Yet, no cat to be seen." Ethan tried to focus on whether he could feel any emotions that didn't 'belong' to him but couldn't sense anything other than his peroneals screaming with relief.

Jav's hands stilled. "Would you like to go to Stephen's wedding with me? I know you might not be able to plan this far ahead, but we could save you a spot?"

Bless your heart. "If your mum can schedule your birth down to the hour, I can schedule some annual leave," said Ethan, touched. "Can you text me the date, so I don't forget?"

Something flared between his ribs, crisp, like inhaling frost amidst an embrace. But try as he might, Ethan could not tell whether it was empathic, the throw blanket, or the soft look of surprise in Jav's eyes.

Certainty wasn't worth the doubt. Probably.

The next evening, Wednesday, 22 December.

JAV ALSO INVITED ETHAN to Christmas lunch with his family.

Ethan turned him down. "It's nice of your parents to include me, but dad's coming to ours for Christmas lunch..." *And he really hates you.*

"No, of course," Jav replied, pink cheeked. "At least you're coming to pre-Christmas dinner. Elijah is taking names for airsoft battle, and no-one wants me on their team."

With Vegas working every night past New Years, Ethan decided to stay with Jav until Christmas Eve. It would minimise any exposure to Ollie and increase opportunities to administer empathic litmus tests.

They detoured to Ethan's flat before dinner, Jav's car flying laps around the block as they waited in the lobby for the lift.

"We're not going anywhere posh," Jav said. "You look fine as you are."

"What a ringing endorsement." Ethan tugged Jav closer by the belt.

"Adjectives must be adjusted to scale." Jav looped an arm behind Ethan to keep him upright as they traded kisses. "Your 'fine' equals 'radiant' for us mortals."

"Do you practise these lines in front of a mirror?" Ethan leaned in. "I have a confession," he whispered, pausing for dramatic effect. "I stepped in some puke earlier."

Jav burst out laughing as the lift dinged on arrival "Well, aren't you charming—" He broke off, arms going stiff with surprise.

Ethan spun around. Nick and Ollie stared back.

Time stretched, viscous and mortifying. The lift door started to close.

Ollie stuck his foot out. "You're not supposed to be here."

"What the f— *I'm* not supposed to—!" Ethan spluttered. "I live here. *You're* not supposed to be here!"

The lift made a reproachful noise. Everyone ignored it.

"Vegas said you were out 'til Christmas," said Ollie. "And I half live here."

"Like a squatter." Ethan's ears burned hot. He realised Jav still had an arm around his waist and there was nowhere for Ethan to go – certainly not forwards, closer to Nick's unwavering gaze. "What are you two even doing? Vegas's at work."

Ollie looked to Nick, who returned a stare of chilly indifference. The lift made another, more urgent, noise.

"Maybe we should let them step out," said Jav, finally taking his hand off Ethan's waist.

They all shuffled into the lobby proper. The lift slammed shut, leaving the four of them in uncomfortable silence.

Ethan turned to Ollie. "Well?"

"I left some work stuff here. Nick and I were gonna grab a pint after work, so we rendezvoused."

"You can't just invite people over," said Ethan, trying to pave over the churn in his stomach.

Nick snorted. "Nothing I haven't seen before." He caught Ethan's gaze and held it at gunpoint. "I can't believe that cardboard is still up. You should replace those blinds."

Ethan flushed. "Whatever. Jav, this is Nick. Nick; Javier."

"We've met," said Nick dismissively.

What?

Jav was wearing his polite mild-as-mayonnaise smile. "Perhaps briefly."

"Perhaps," said Nick, a dry twist to his mouth. "Must be hard keeping track."

Something flickered across Jav's eyes, but his smile could have weathered a hurricane.

"Okay," said Ethan, drawing out the vowel. "We have a reservation—"

"Ollie, I'll catch up," Nick said. "Want a quick word with Ethan."

"Your funeral," said Ollie and fled.

Ethan stuck his hands in his pockets. "Look," he started, hoping someone else would interrupt him.

Nobody did.

Nick glanced at Jav and nodded towards the street. "You mind?"

After a long moment, Jav held out a hand for Ethan's bag. "I'll grab your things while you two catch up."

"But I need to get changed for—"

"You can get changed in the car." Jav winked – Ethan didn't even know he could wink! – and took Ethan's duffle. Resigned, Ethan patted his pockets for his keys. "It's alright, I have my key." Jav flashed a toothpaste-commercial smile at Nick. "See you both in a bit."

And suddenly it was just Ethan and Nick in the empty foyer.

When it became clear that Nick wasn't going to break the silence, Ethan said, "So. Um. How's things?"

Nick's stare usually preceded one of them being slammed against the nearest flat surface. The inertia was disconcerting. Ethan crossed and uncrossed his arms.

"Fine," Nick said eventually. "It's been a while."

Ethan's stomach knotted tight. He put a hand on his neck, realised what he was doing, and shoved it back into pocket. "Yeah. Sorry I didn't text back. I got caught up."

"For four months?"

Ethan stared at the floor.

"That's a third of a year," said Nick.

"I procrastinated." Ethan rocked back on his heels. "Too much time passed, and I figured it would be weird. I meant to."

Nick raised his eyebrows. "Is that also why you've been sprinting out of the precinct every time you visit? To avoid me?"

"I haven't been avoiding—" That was a blatant lie. "It's not—"

"Not what I think it is?"

Silence.

A couple of other residents came in from the street and everyone exchanged nods. All too soon, Ethan and Nick were alone once more.

"I would have appreciated a break-up text," Nick said, quietly.

Ethan didn't know how to react. They had never used dating terminology before. "What's there to break up?" he asked – and immediately regretted it as genuine hurt flashed across Nick's face. Something slick and awful slid down the length of Ethan's spine.

Nick seemed at a loss. "Right. My mistake. I assumed that the guy I'd been seeing for two-and-some years would at least tell me to bugger off when he got bored."

"I didn't get *bored*," Ethan said, stilted. Bizarre, that a person bleeding out on a gurney was less stressful. "I just meant it's not as if we were in a proper relationship. I thought we had no strings—"

"You're the one who said 'no strings'."

"You agreed!"

"That was a long time ago." Nick's voice rose in volume, words bitten to the quick. "I figured we had moved past — I thought things had changed."

Ethan chewed the inside of his lip. "You could have said something."

"*I* could have said—?" Nick stepped closer, joints stiff, involuntary. "I was respecting boundaries that *you* set. I know your job is unpredictable. I didn't want to push, in case you...in case it... nevermind."

"No," said Ethan, crossing his arms. "In case what?"

"Triggered a knee-jerk reaction."

Ethan reared back. "What's that supposed to mean?"

"A flight response."

"As in fight or flight?"

"No," said Nick, expression as flat as his tone. "According to Ollie, you only have a flight response."

"If Professor Ollie says so, it must be true."

"You don't exactly invite—!" Nick was wound so tightly that every sentence jerked like someone tightening violin pegs. "You always change the subject. We've been doing this for so long, I thought we were on the same fucking page."

"How was I meant to know that you wanted something different? I can't read your mind—"

"Yet you expect everyone around you to read yours! I didn't want to risk ruining what we had, okay?"

"Well, maybe I didn't want to risk it either!"

Nick laughed. The sound clattered to the floor; a plate smashing on tile. "Oh, spare me. You're *seeing someone else.*"

"And I should have told you, I'm sorry." Ethan scrubbed his face with both hands. "I didn't plan on—"

"Do you know what it was like, finding out third-hand that your boyfriend was—"

"Oh, so *now* we're using labels? I thought the whole point was to keep it casual. Convenient."

A sudden hush.

Nick's mouth opened and closed, eyes creased as if he had been struck. "Convenient," he echoed. "Right."

"Wait." Ethan could barely see out of the hole he had been digging for himself. "That came out wrong."

Nick shook his head. "You're selfish, you know that? I'd like to think I don't have much of an ego, but you sure know how to take someone's pride and—" he mimed balling something up in a fist and throwing it to the floor, grinding his heel into the tile "—like that."

"I said I'm sorry." They were so close that Ethan could see a cut near Nick's hairline. The injury was still slightly wet, new. Out of habit, Ethan *tsk*'d, reaching to wipe the injury away.

Nick caught Ethan's bare wrist in one hand. His thumb dug into Ethan's pulse like a brand, and the cut on his temple smoothed over between one blink and the next. Nick's grip tightened – for a second, Ethan thought Nick was going to kiss him.

Then the moment passed.

Nick let go. "It's not about what I want. Though I think you owe me the bare courtesy of a text."

"Yes, I should've messaged you first." Ethan looked around the deserted lobby. "I really am sorry. I didn't know you'd care." *I didn't want to embarrass myself. Make things awkward.*

"No, it's clear that *you* didn't care." Nick sounded like he was scraping out the inside of his lungs with a spoon. "God. Why do I bother."

"Good question. Why bother." Ethan's throat grew tight. "There are heaps of people with better schedules and more time to spend with their...their whatevers—"

"This isn't about your bloody schedule, and you know it—"

"—never invite me to anything with your other friends—"

"—how tired you were, what was I supposed to—"

Ethan threw up his hands. "Why are you saying all this to me now?"

"Because *I love you!*" Nick shouted. "Though god knows why."

The words rang, too loud, unplanned.

Ethan couldn't move. They were both breathing hard, wide-eyed. Nick seemed shocked at the words that just came out of his own mouth. The silence could have lasted forever: awful and heavy.

Then Nick took a step back. It felt like being nudged out of orbit. If Ethan hadn't been rooted to the floor, he might have stumbled.

All the fight drained from Nick's shoulders. "I shouldn't have said that. Thought I'd be fine, but seeing—" He took a deep breath. "Forget it."

"Nick—"

"You're right." Nick's eyes scanned Ethan's features, lingering. "Too little, too late, and all that."

"Wait—"

"Take care of yourself."

"Nick, wait!"

But there were drawbacks to keeping exits so close, always counting the distance between *us* and *what if.* They were only three steps to the door. And before Ethan could move, Nick was gone.

LATER, ETHAN TRIED to call. When that failed, he tried messaging.

21:46 · ETHAN — I'm sorry.

21:48 · ETHAN — You caught me off guard, I really am sorry.

23:30 · ETHAN — Can we please talk?

He waited, wide awake, into the early hours. But for the first time that Ethan could remember, Nick did not answer.

LIKE MOST NICE THINGS, Ethan had Vegas to thank for their family Christmas tradition.

He still remembered Christmas with mum: a loud kitchen, multi-coloured lights, laughter close to his face. Dad tried his best in the subsequent quiet, sad years – but the attempts made her absence harder. By the time Ethan went to university, he and Ian weren't on speaking terms, and Ethan spent every holiday in Edinburgh with gran.

"More bubbles!" Vegas hiccupped. "Ollie, pass— no, don't *pour*. Gimme that bottle." Her sparkling enthusiasm (and gift for bulldozing awkward silences) made Christmas actually pleasant.

They were crammed into Ethan's flat: dad, Ollie, Vegas, Ethan, and a battered Christmas tree. Dad would get tipsy on sparkling wine. Ollie micromanaged the music. Vegas always – without fail – cried.

This year, lunch started off tense. Ethan and his dad hadn't spoken much since Ian's run-in with Jav at the precinct. Meanwhile, Ollie had been standoffish after Ethan's confrontation with Nick. Good food eventually thawed everyone out.

Then dad brought up New Years.

"I don't understand why Ethan gets the time off, but you don't," Ian said for the hundredth time. "You work too hard."

"I'll get time in lieu," said Vegas.

"We should all have dinner out. On the third, maybe? When are you back on day shifts, sweetheart?"

"The third. But Ethan will be at the North Pole with Jav!"

Ian's expression shuttered at the mention of Jav. He set his drink down. Vegas mouthed 'oops' and dissolved into giggles.

"The North Pole, really?" asked Ollie.

"We're spending a couple nights in Reykjavik to see the aurora. And we'll be back after the fourth," said Ethan hastily. "Belated new year's dinner sounds great, dad."

"Arden is a bad influence!" Ian burst out. "Will it just be the two of you?"

"No," lied Ethan. "His sister is chaperoning us." Ian looked like he couldn't decide if this was better or worse. Ethan leapt to his feet. "Dessert?"

· · ·

MUCH LATER, Vegas came to find him. She looked exhausted but happy, hair streaked with tinsel. Drunk carolling floated up from the street. It was four in the morning.

"Hey." She passed him a mug. "Can't sleep?"

"Thinking," said Ethan. The cocoa was barely visible under a mountain of marshmallows.

Vegas dumped the burrito blanket over their legs. "Wanna talk about it?"

They sipped their cocoa. The TV played cat videos on mute, the only light source in the flat. Ollie's snores could be heard through the door.

"Thanks for tolerating me for another year," said Ethan.

"I'm here for the perks." Vegas patted his knee. "Seriously, what's wrong? You've been extra mopey the three whole times I've seen you this week."

"Nothing's wrong."

"It's about Nick."

Ethan nodded, wordless. Of course, Ollie had already debriefed Vegas. She was the perfect counterweight to Ollie's freneticism. Perhaps that was why they never fell out of orbit, all these years. Then again, Ollie was in the word-smithing business. He probably knew the right things to say – or when to risk saying the wrong things, instead of clinging to the fatal quiet.

"What did Ollie tell you?" asked Ethan.

"He and Nick got wasted a few nights ago. So it was more of a rant."

"You were right. I fucked up."

Vegas sighed. "It got worse the longer you put it off."

"Why did you tell Ollie I was commitment-phobic?"

"Nick said that?"

"Nick said Ollie told him. I assume you and Ollie've been gossiping."

"Ollie has eyes and ears too." Vegas sipped her drink. "You dumped Tom because he wanted more time than you could give. And you ghosted Nick because you assumed he didn't want what you did."

"He never *said*—"

"And you were so sure that you didn't ask?"

All of Ethan's marshmallows had decomposed. "I don't think either of us were sure." He swallowed. "Jav just told me what he wanted. I didn't have to second guess."

"He said what *you* wanted. And even then, you still weren't sure, or else you'd have broken things off with Nick right away." Vegas narrowed her eyes. "I hope."

If I had known there was anything to break off... "Do you think I've been acting differently? Since I met Jav, I mean."

"...You really believe he's an empath?" asked Vegas.

Ethan swallowed. "So I *have* been weird? You're the only one who'd know."

"I mean, you seem happier." Vegas yawned. "Chirpier."

"Well, I've been on probation so it might be the extra sleep. I never expected that I'd...that we..." *You're the one who hedged your bets like the chips were people. If your pride is worth more than two years of routine, then what are you worth to anyone?* Ethan exhaled. "I should have told Nick."

"You need to apologise."

"I think he's blocked me."

Vegas squeezed him in a hug. She smelled of the fancy bergamot conditioner Jav left in their bathroom. "We'll figure it out."

"Hey," Ethan said into her shoulder.

"Mmhm?"

"How do you know if someone makes you happy, or if they're *making* you happy. Or if *you* make them happy, so you think they make you happy?"

"All three options sound pretty good, honestly."

Ethan stared at the ceiling. "I suppose it would be hard to tell the difference."

EIGHTEEN

With enough time, all hanging swords became yokes; the threat worn thin by worry, like water on a prayer wheel. But even three decades of dread could not prepare Jav for this moment. It had always felt so theoretical: a risk to be managed by lawyers and comms. Enough to wake him in a cold sweat, but a nightmare that faded with morning.

As Jav grew older, his secret became a chore to be maintained. Knowing that someone *actually* suspected the truth, however...

Jav kept the lone cufflink hidden amongst its siblings. Out of sight, out of mind. Rina still didn't know about Oliver's accusations. She would be furious, and Jav had no defence. How could he have been so complacent? So careless? He wondered what lengths Rina might go to keep his secret – and realised he wasn't brave enough to find out.

Ethan's non-reaction left Jav floundering. How could Ethan not have noticed Jav's screaming panic? In the days that followed, Jav teetered between relief and dread, waiting for Ethan to call out the lie and leave.

But Ethan never mentioned the cufflinks again. He behaved so normally that, had it been any other secret, Jav might have thanked his lucky stars and clung to ignorance. He suspected Ethan's apparent amnesia had more to do with their run-in with Nick Holt. Nick had been radioactive with dislike, joining the growing list of Ethan's friends and family that Jav had wronged. And knowing how close Vegas and Ollie were to each other, it was only a matter of time before her goodwill ran out.

Yet, Ethan said nothing.

Besides the uptick in clumsy accidents around the penthouse, Ethan felt as he always did: smile mirroring affection, consistent, calm. Jav waited for the tell-tale wariness that trailed Nath and Giulia whenever Jav walked into a room. Instead, Ethan would tilt his head, ask what Jav was frowning about, and lean in to kiss that reason away.

A week passed without fanfare. Then a fortnight.

They spent three glorious evenings flying through the aurora borealis, Ethan sprinting around the aircraft's observatory deck, projecting exhilaration that belonged only to those in love, in the sky, or – for a lucky few – both. *This is worth it,* Jav had thought, knees weak. *I'll gladly take the consequences, just let me have this for a little bit longer.*

By the time they returned from Reykjavik, Jav's heart had convinced his brain that everything would be alright.

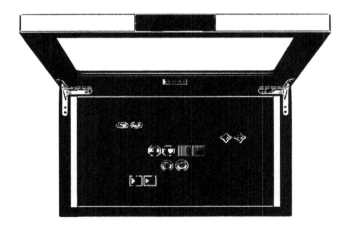

Two Finches, Upper Chelsea, Level 22. Sunday, 9 January.

ETHAN HAD A FAVOURITE breakfast spot on Jav's street.

The mere fact was a miracle because Ethan hated getting out of bed. Nestled in a tree-lined boulevard, the Two Finches sat between a hair salon and a florist. The shopfront featured an old-fashioned awning above a glass window, through which Ethan loved people watching.

"There's other dishes on the menu," said Jav, as Ethan demolished his truffle omelette. "Non-egg dishes."

Outside, the crisp winter morning boasted a rare cloudless sky. Inside the cafe, the air sparkled with flour.

Ethan scraped his fork in a way that suggested he wanted to lick his plate clean. "You recommended it."

"Two months ago. Don't you want to try something else?"

"But I *know* this one's good."

"I'm worried about your cholesterol."

"Aha! There's always an agenda."

"I just want you to pass your next physical." Jav speared a piece of fruit. "Have some pomelo."

Ethan opened his mouth, whether to respond or to accept the food, Jav never found out because they were interrupted by a *crash*.

Jav spun around.

A grey courier pod had wrapped itself around a lamp post at the mouth of the boulevard. Beside it, a two-seater car was on the kerb, tipped on its left, wheels in the air. And there was Ethan, sprinting out the door.

"Bugger," said Jav, and followed suit.

A lady was screaming at the top of her lungs whilst being helped out of the upturned car. "My baby girl! What if the car explodes?!" There was blood beneath her nose.

Jav almost vomited from her panic.

Ethan had one knee braced against the car's headrest, shoulders up against the windshield. His voice was muffled but stern: "—going to be okay. Deep breath — miss? Miss! Can you count to ten for me?"

A wail that sounded like 'mummy'. The woman lurched forwards.

"He's a doctor." Jav caught her by the elbow, offering a handkerchief "Here."

The woman batted him aside. "Tilly? Tilly!"

Jav wrapped a hand around her bare wrist using Ethan as an anchor to project calm. She gasped into silence, mid-sob.

Jav smiled, all eyes, no teeth. "I'm Javier and that's Dr Faulkner, a healer at St Ophie's Hospital. Everything is going to be okay. What's your name?"

"Amelia." She swayed on her feet, pupils blown.

Oh dear. Maybe he had overdone it. "Amelia, your daughter is—"

"Mummy? MUMMY!"

Amelia's panic spiked, making Jav wince.

Ethan stuck his head out of the car. "Has anyone called an ambulance?"

"Is she okay?" cried Amelia. "Tilly, mummy's here!"

"She'll be fine," Ethan replied, brisk. He pointed at the nearest bystander, a man holding a latte. "You! Call nine-nine-nine."

Latte Guy spilled his drink in his haste to comply. Jav couldn't blame him.

A moment later, Ethan re-emerged with the toddler in his arms: she had one hand fisted in his hair, the other smacking him across the nose. As soon as she spotted her mother, Tilly's crying intensified. She kicked Ethan in the stomach and shrieked into his ear.

Having both hands occupied with a toddler, Ethan wobbled, lost his balance, and tipped backwards into the car. The onlookers gasped. "Babe, some help please?!"

Jav rushed over. Ethan lay, limbs akimbo with the toddler on his chest. He had managed to break his fall with his own back, rather than Tilly's – who had a fistful of Ethan's nose, face bright red with the effort of crying.

It was the most adorable thing Jav had ever seen.

"Take her, would you?" Ethan wheezed. "And *calm her down*, sweet mercy."

"Do I need to keep her neck still?" asked Jav, thinking about spine injuries and *Healer's Anatomy*. "Or just grab?"

"Grab. Grab is fine." Ethan looked like he wanted to lob Tilly out the window.

Jav picked her up, summoning that morning's sleepy memory of Ethan buried in pillows.

The toddler hiccupped, falling quiet. She stared at Jav with huge eyes. "Buh."

"Fucking unbelievable," Ethan muttered.

"Language." Jav scooped Tilly against his chest. "Hel*lo*. You're *such* a brave girl." Tilly's face wobbled but there wasn't a single bruise. Ethan was so efficient. "Let's get you out of this silly car, eh?" Jav wiggled his eyebrows. Tilly returned a smile full of milk teeth. "That's right, mummy's waiting," he sing-songed. "Upsies-daisies."

The toddler vibrated with shock, no room for stranger-danger. Babies and toddlers were so easy to read; so easy to love. Jav smiled at her until his face ached, skin numb with cold air and dopamine. Tilly's forehead drooped against his neck, fast asleep. *Oops.*

Amelia rushed over. "Did she hit her head? Why is she unconscious?"

"Maybe too much excitement." Jav pushed a gentle tickle of oxytocin at the toddler, to nudge her awake – before relinquishing her to Amelia. He then turned to help Ethan, who was climbing out of the car with all the grace of a cat escaping a bathtub.

Amelia almost collapsed with relief (and Jav with her) when Tilly stirred awake.

Ethan dusted himself off. "You two should still get a proper scan done, but I didn't feel anything serious."

"Thank you so much," said Amelia.

Tilly reached for Jav. "Bubuh!"

"Quite right," cooed Jav.

"I called the ambulance," said Latte Guy, as a police cruiser and ambulance pulled up. He seemed to be waiting for Ethan's approval.

"Be faster next time," said Ethan, eyes fixed on Jav. The intent in his gaze faded the world into static.

Better than any suppressor, Jav thought, even when Ethan turned to deal with the paramedics. Every few seconds, he'd glance over and pin Jav to his own shadow.

"The sun must have interfered with the car's sensors," said the officer. "But it still shouldn't have swerved like this. What mode were you on, ma'am?"

"Driverless. Almost home so the wheels were down."

"If this is a family car, then I assume the baby's registered," said Ethan.

Amelia nodded.

"The AI prioritises children," Ethan continued. "It turned so the impact would be on the adult's side. Low sun often messes with sensors, but this two-seater is last year's model. The firmware shouldn't have errored out, even with the narrow street."

A pause.

"What kind of doctor did you say you were?" asked the officer.

JAV AND ETHAN barely made it back to the penthouse.

"That was—" Ethan pushed Jav against the lift wall, kissing him hard "—very impressive."

"What?" Jav managed, overwhelmed by the heat of Ethan's enthusiasm.

They staggered out of the lift and into the flat. Ethan kicked his shoes off, and began stripping Jav with determined efficiency: scarf, coat, sweater.

"You worked so *fast*." Ethan wiggled his fingers near his temple. "Wait. Tell me if you don't — is this okay?"

Jav nodded, trying to remember his list of unused excuses.

Ethan's smirk bloomed into a grin. "Bedroom. Unless you'd rather live dangerously. I'm not the one with a sister in the house."

"Good lord, you're so..."

"Yes?" Ethan prompted. Jav kissed him on the nose, cheeks, each eyelid. "Stop stalling, come *on*."

Jav looped an arm beneath Ethan's arse to carry him before Ethan's socks on wooden steps resulted in a concussion. Ethan's pulse spiked with a pleasant curl of heat in Jav's stomach. They fell through the door to Jav's bedroom and straight onto the mattress.

"You—" Ethan snapped his fingers "—and she was out like a light."

You could have been an anaesthetist. I barely felt it. Impressive localisation."

Jav was so distracted that it took several seconds for his brain to catch up with his ears. His heart stuttered. *Did Ethan mean...?*

Ethan was still talking, oblivious to the ice settling around Jav's heart. "I haven't worked with many empaths, but I know it takes decades of training. They make everyone in theatre wear dampeners, but you can still kinda sense it. I don't think I felt you at all. Maybe a bit of relief? But that was probably the lack of screaming...Jav?"

Jav couldn't breathe.

Ethan's smile faded. "Babe, what's wrong?"

"I'm — I don't know what you mean. I'm not—" Static roared in Jav's ears, a decades-old noose tightening around his throat. *Of course he knows. Of course he knows, you stupid, stupid man!* The world blurred, Jav's depth of field sliced so thin he could only see Ethan's eyes.

One thought replayed, siren loud. *He knows. Oh god, he knows. It's over.*

"I'm sorry," said Ethan, after a moment. "I shouldn't have brought it up. I just thought, after...Let's pretend I never said anything."

Jav stared, light-headed.

"Hun?" said Ethan. "Please breathe. You're kinda freaking me out."

"I'm not an empath." The words were tasteless from a lifetime of recital. "I'm not an aptee."

"Okay." Ethan smiled, but he felt resigned.

They stared at each other, suspended, heartstrings taut with the gravity of what might happen next.

Jav opened his mouth – and the dam broke. Tears poured down his face, silent at first then dissolving rapidly into half-aborted sobs.

Ethan jerked backwards. "Sorry, shit, please don't cry—"

The loss of skin contact made Jav sob harder. "No, *I'm* sorry. I should have told you earlier. I'm sorry. I'm sorry." He didn't have suppressors on. Jav practically tipped Ethan off the bed in his haste. Stumbling to the walk-in, hands shaking, he grabbed the first cuff he saw.

Ethan followed. "What are you doing?"

"Suppressors. I forgot them before, I usually w-wear..." Jav wiped his eyes furiously. "Have to put these on or you'll—"

"Alright, okay." Ethan grabbed Jav's hand. "Slow down. Deep breaths."

Ethan usually rang clear as a tuning fork, but Jav could barely feel him through his own fog of panic.

"Jav. *Hey.*" Ethan dug his fingers into Jav's arms, ten points of pressure. "Look at me."

"I-I'm sorry, I'm sorry, I didn't th—" Jav pressed a fist to his mouth.

"You're okay." Ethan pulled Jav into the bathroom. Backed him into a chair. "*Sit.*"

Jav sat.

Ethan stepped in between Jav's knees, turning Jav's face with a hand on his chin. Jav felt a *push* behind his eyes, the sensation rattling soul against bone. The abrupt temperature change made him exhale all at once. It took a moment before Jav realised that Ethan had removed Jav's left cuff and was working on the other, one handed.

"No!" Jav tried to pull away. "I have to wear them or you'll feel whatever I'm feeling. And then you won't *know.*"

Ethan didn't respond, just folded Jav close, carding his fingers through Jav's hair. Jav shuddered at the skin contact.

"Deep breaths." Ethan sounded entirely unaffected – heartbeat a little fast, but metronomic. Reliable.

Jav closed his eyes, letting the rhythm of Ethan's breathing tug him from the panic spiral. He pressed his eyes against Ethan's naval until red and white imprints appeared in constellations. Ethan stroked Jav's hair, brushing it back from his forehead with slow, deliberate repetition. They stayed like that for a long while, the sunlight warming the moss rug.

"There," Ethan said quietly. "Better?"

Jav nodded, eyes still closed.

"Let's forget I said anything," Ethan continued. "Shouldn't have mentioned it so casual, like. It's private."

Jav looked up. "...What?"

"Pretend this never happened." Nervousness clouded Ethan's aura.

The vignette brushed Jav's nerves like piano wire across an open wound. "I don't want to ruin...I should have minded my own business."

Could we pretend? The thought was seductive as it was fleeting. At some point, doubt would overcome faith. They had to confront Jav's ugly truth, it was a matter of time. *But that's the point. You could have* more *time.*

"No," Jav croaked. "We can't pretend. It won't work out."

All the colour drained from Ethan's face. "Are you breaking up with me?"

"Am I — no? Wait. Are *you*?"

"*No*. Just. We should talk."

They stared at each other.

Then Ethan snorted. "Don't scare me like that." He herded Jav out of the bathroom and onto the bed, vanishing briefly to fetch some water. "Here. Emotions dehydrate you."

Jav accepted the glass. He was grateful for something to hold, though wary of swallowing anything that could be thrown up. Ethan sat down beside him, hands loose in his lap. The windows in the bedroom were set at half opacity, muted and drowsy.

Several minutes passed, unhurried.

"What did you want to talk about?" asked Ethan gently.

"Me being an empath."

"Okay."

Ethan was wearing his polite-doctor expression. *That stare alone could anchor a ship.* Jav hoped he would continue talking, but it soon became clear that Ethan was prepared to wait him out.

Jav took a deep breath. "Before we start, I need my suppressors on."

"Mmhm. Why?"

"Otherwise you'd..." Jav frowned. "So you can trust your own thoughts and feelings while we talk. That you're not being influenced."

"Right. Lots to unpack here. But even if I accept your premise, there are other ways for us to talk without empathic influence." Ethan made air quotes with his fingers, the same way he did when they argued about Lower Level radiation. "I could go downstairs. Chat to you on the phone."

"Yes, let's—"

"Not do that."

"Then I need to wear—"

"We should just talk normally. Like how we are doing now."

"*No.*" Jav scrubbed both hands over his face. "You don't understand, I can't always control what I'm projecting. And if you're not sure that your thoughts are *yours*—"

"Whose else would they be?"

"You know what I mean. Emotions influence thoughts."

"Everything influences thoughts. Look. I *want* you to know what I'm feeling. Feature not a bug, right? I'm not great with words."

"But how would you know I'm not manipulating you?" asked Jav.

Ethan snorted. "Doesn't matter."

"Doesn't matter?" The whole conversation had long since deviated from the script in Jav's head. "How are you so calm? You don't feel—" He shut his mouth.

"I don't feel what?"

Jav dug his fingernails into his palms. "Angry."

There was something close to pity in Ethan's eyes. "I'm not angry. Maybe we should be worried about *me* influencing *you*. I read that empathic projection takes more effort than empathic reception, which would explain why we're not both sobbing right now."

How long have you known? Jav wondered.

"Do you want me to wear suppressors so you can trust *your* emotions?" Ethan offered.

"No!" Jav hesitated. No one had ever framed it like that before. "I don't know."

"I think you should tell me what you want."

"I want to know what you're feeling," Jav blurted. "But I also want you to trust that your feelings are yours."

"I trust you more than I trust my emotions, frankly."

Jav immediately thought of Rina and Peter; about Ethan's father; about stories planted in the paper. Guilt scoured his throat raw. *Secrets upon secrets. One day they'll bury us alive.* "But you'll always be second-guessing. You will wonder—"

"Are you talking about me, or someone else?" asked Ethan, sharply.

Jav flushed, sick to his stomach.

Ethan's expression softened. "Look, there's plenty of toxic relationships without an empath in sight." When Jav didn't respond, he scooted closer. "This isn't the sort of thing you can prove definitively. Not even with a live-MRI study. And if you need that kind of proof, there's no trust. If there's no trust, it's not gonna last – empath or no empath."

God, thought Jav, overcome with a reckless ache, *I love you so much.*

Ethan cocked his head. "Now, let's say there's some probability that my emotions have, at one point or another, been affected by your empathy. Given how much time we spend together, it's safe to say that the probability is not zero."

"Yes," Jav croaked.

"Then the question becomes whether I care about that non-zero probability. And I've decided that I don't."

Jav's eyes almost fell out of their sockets. "You don't care. You *don't care* that an empath might be influencing you."

"We're yet to see what this empath is influencing me for. Not money or sex, apparently. Is it eternal youth? If so, I have some bad news."

Jav knew Ethan was joking, but he couldn't shake the memory of Ethan crying his heart out, devastated after a patient had passed away. They never spoke about that incident again, but Ethan's words still haunted like heartache. '*This is literally the point of me.*'

Something must have shown on Jav's face.

"I'm kidding." Ethan sighed. "See, I told you I'm no good at this. Words."

"You're not your aptitude." Jav stared at Ethan's hands, mere centimetres away. "Do you really think—"

"No, relax. And this isn't about me."

They lapsed into silence again, the weight of Ethan's expectant gaze curving Jav's spine like a flower after heavy rain.

"If it helps, it feels different when emotions are...external? Sorta?" Ethan tilted his head. "Are you scared I might tell someone? Is that what this is about?"

Jav opened his mouth, but all that came out was a wheeze.

Ethan's expression cleared. He pried the glass from Jav's clawed fingers, setting it on the floor; circled Jav's wrist where a watch usually rested. "Jav. I would never. We could fight, say goodbye tomorrow, and I won't say a word. Not to Vegas, not to dad, not a soul." He sounded as certain as the shore waiting for the tide. "Do you trust me?"

Jav's eyes burned. He nodded – and when Ethan lifted his arms for a hug, Jav pulled him in and held on tight. "I'm sorry I didn't tell you sooner. I wanted to, I wanted to tell you so badly," he sobbed. "I was scared that you'd hate me. The longer I waited, the worse it got, and I didn't know how to fix it, I couldn't—"

"It's okay. I'd be scared too." Ethan felt as steady as his words, a benediction. "Shh. Breathe."

Jav laughed, wet and hiccupping. But Ethan wasn't the only one who had suspected. "What about Oliver...?"

"He hasn't published anything, so maybe Vegas talked some sense into — hun, *calm down*. Nobody's outing empaths. You're not a judge or running for PM, so who cares?"

Jav should be more panicked, but the confession had wrung him dry. He nodded against Ethan's neck, inhaling the too-harsh-soap scent. It clashed horribly with Jav's cologne. Jav loved it.

At some point, they lay down across the bed, hands clasped, heartbeats in sync.

"Can I ask you something?"

"Anything," said Jav.

Ethan ran a thumb over the back of Jav's knuckles. "Would you have told me, eventually, do you think?"

Jav nodded. "I'd have to."

"What do you mean?" Ethan felt surprised at Jav's lack of hesitation.

"I should have told you already. I was scared of how you'd react. But you can't consent if you don't know. I should have told you, before... um."

"Consent?" A pause. Ethan's eyes widened. "Wait..."

"I should have stopped you, that time in the car," Jav said miserably. "If you had only wanted because *I* wanted, then that's rape—"

Ethan sat bolt upright. "Hang on. Firstly, *I* wanted to suck you off. Does that mean you only said 'yes' because you were under the influence? *My* influence? My horny energy? Aura? What's the terminology?"

Jav choked. "No, I wanted. You. I mean. It was consensual."

"Not by your logic!" For the first time that day, Ethan didn't feel calm at all. "Especially since you told me that you're ace spec. *Shit.* I'm sorry. Should *I* wear empathic suppressors? Dampeners? Should I ask this stuff over the phone?"

Jav started to laugh, and once he began, he couldn't stop. It took a few minutes for him to regain the power of speech. "Thank you, darling." He wiped his eyes.

Ethan huffed, alarm fading. "The latest literature suggests that empathic reception is easier than projection, so I'm worried."

"You hereby have my consent for all of the things, going forwards," said Jav. "Do I have yours?"

"Yes, but that's not the point. What if you wanna say 'no' and I'm. Well."

"Then I'll say no. And you'll trust me, right?"

Ethan snorted. "...Well played." A long pause. "You're sweet for getting so philosophical about consent. I can tell why your mum lied to you about radiation in Lower London."

"What?"

"You heard me." Ethan sat up. "You know, we have this the wrong way around."

"Wrong way what?"

"It's always spies and espionage, empaths making others feel this or that..." Ethan's tone remained mild, but Jav could feel the weight of his heart on his sleeve. "Earlier you said I'd doubt whether my emotions were genuinely mine. Honestly, the person I'm worried about having second guesses is you."

Jav tried and failed to parse Ethan's unreadable calm. It tasted sweeter than resignation, but twice as heavy. "What do you mean?"

"I mean that one day, if you realise you love somebody, I hope you won't second guess yourself." Ethan's voice wavered. "I hope you never wonder if you loved them for them, or if they loved you so much that it fooled you into it. I hope that difference won't matter to you. Because it doesn't matter to me."

Static filled the room, a storm against glass, applause after the last act.

"...You love me?" asked Jav.

Ethan offered a tentative smile and held out both hands, palms up. Jav didn't need skin contact to know – but he pulled close nevertheless, a hand in his hair, the other on his face. He kissed Ethan's forehead, his nose, both cheeks, the arch of his throat.

"*God*," Jav managed, "I didn't think I'd ever find someone like you."

Ethan fisted both hands in Jav's shirt, giddy with the tidal pull of certainty. "How do you always say exactly what I..."

Jav had spent most of his life trying to stand in the undertow. It was a relief to be swept off his feet.

NINETEEN

A week passed. Then another. Jav still hadn't told Rina. There never seemed to be a good time to face her volcanic reaction. Each new day post-confession felt euphoric, his conscience buoyed by Ethan's unassuming acceptance. Jav felt like a kite cut loose and he wasn't ready to come back down to earth.

"She won't take it well," he explained to Ethan one night. "I'm waiting until she's in the right mood."

"I can play dumb as long as you need. Did you talk to your physician about changing painkillers?" Ethan had wasted no time investigating gentler alternatives for Jav's now not-so-mysterious migraine.

"I'm trialling them this week," said Jav, and was awarded with a pleased nudge.

"Good. Hopefully that breaks the cycle. And you can try your suppressors on half-strength while we're out."

"It's easier when I have someone to focus on." Jav palmed the small of Ethan's back, sliding his hand under the soft t-shirt and luxuriating in the lack of guilt. "Skin contact helps."

"Then kiss me more often."

"Oh, I was thinking we'd hold hands." Jav wheezed at Ethan's indignant pout. As it turned out, kissing cured that too.

Arden Pharmaceuticals, Upper Mayfair, Level 14.
Friday, 28 January.

JAV'S RADIANT good mood did not go unnoticed.

Giulia shook her cuffs. "I can feel you, even with these on."

"Oh. Sorry." Jav lowered his tablet and glanced at the closed meeting-room door. "I'm trying new painkillers. Not supposed to have my suppressors on full. I could go to another room and use the hologram?"

To his surprise, Giulia shook her head. "I assume mum knows you're trying new meds?"

"Yeah. She said she didn't realise my migraines were so bad, still."

"You're happier lately."

Jav shrugged. "Yes."

"And less joined at the hip with Rina." Before Jav could process that observation, Giulia added, "Faulkner's good for you."

Jav blinked. "Really?"

Giulia had met Ethan at a few family dinners, but she had never indicated that she even remembered his name. Before Jav could prod for details, Nath's photo flashed above Giulia's phone.

She dismissed it with a wave. "Nath's insufferable – I think no one in this stupid family remembers that I'm meant to be in the lab. But PR falls to me. Holding Rina's leash falls to me. Nath probably wants to read our press release before it goes out. I don't think so."

Jav made a sympathetic noise and kept his mouth shut.

Giulia sighed. "Alright. Let's run through your speech again with the edits I made. No need to hammer the nail in our own coffin. The fact the Arden Foundation is investing so much in fusive projects should speak volumes." She rolled her neck. "And tank our market cap."

Jav wiggled his tablet. "Once more, from the top?"

Three days later, Monday, 31 January.

THE PRESS EVENT itself went off without a hitch: the Arden Foundation supported many artistic institutions, and this wasn't Jav's first rodeo. Their donation went towards retrofitting the Royal Ballet Schools and the opera house for a fusive future. The business pages salivated over the fact that Arden Pharmaceuticals appeared to be hedging their bets.

"You'd think it's the first time we've done this," Giulia had said. "If it doesn't get Nath off my back, then nothing will."

Since Giulia was satisfied with Jav's performance, he was now free to focus on what was truly important: Valentine's Day.

"We've only been dating for four months," said Jav. "Almost five months, by Feb fourteenth."

"Feels longer," said Stephen.

Jav propped his elbows on the side of the pool, the water heated against the late January chill. "I sometimes forget that we haven't been together for years..."

"Sure feels like you've been talking about him for years."

Jav glared. "Ethan can't wear watches or jewellery at work. What should I get him?"

"Easy. Two-seater flier."

"That's over the top."

Stephen hoisted himself out of the pool. "He said the same thing about the flowers, yet here we are."

Jav wavered. "A car is too intense before six-months. Plus, I commissioned little Ducati models for his birthday. I don't wanna double-up thematically."

Stephen just tossed him a towel. "C'mon. Everyone will be here in fifteen minutes."

"Help me figure out Ethan's present."

"God, you have such a planning fetish." Stephen made a beeline for the kitchen. "There's still two more weeks to find a present."

Jav trailed after his friend. "And you've only got two months until your wedding, which is *not* enough time for these idiots to learn the choreography since nobody has put in any bloody effort!"

"That's because the routine is twenty minutes." Stephen was raiding the fridge, baba ganoush in hand.

Jav slammed the fridge door shut. "Clara is marrying you for the *rest of her life* and you can't handle a twenty-minute dance? Shame on you."

Two weeks later, Monday, 14 February.

ETHAN WORKED all Valentine's Day, so it ended up being a quiet affair. They had the penthouse to themselves since Rina was busy with Charlie. It didn't bother Jav as much as it might once have: it was difficult to feel hard-done-by while cuddling on a chaise, basking in the aquarium's glow.

"Sorry I couldn't get the day off," said Ethan, pressing hot, open-mouthed kisses to the hollow of Jav's throat. "This is nice though, right? Staying in. Lazy, like."

"I do love this." Jav ran a hand through Ethan's hair. "I love *you*."

Ethan's aura hummed; a tuning fork struck just right. "I can tell. Can you?"

"Can I what?"

"Tell. Empathically."

Jav turned, wedging Ethan against the back of the sofa lest he roll off. "Sometimes. Emotions aren't unequivocal."

"What does it feel like? I mean, how do you distinguish...Is it a spectrum? A sliding scale?"

Jav smiled at Ethan's stop and starts, the way he walked circles around the L-word, like a cat looking for a good spot to nap in. "Love feels different to lust, if that's what you're asking."

"What about love *and* lust?"

"Humans aren't radios. You can play more than one channel at once."

"It's all oxytocin and dopamine, I suppose. Do they all feel," Ethan waved a hand, "different types of happy?"

"You can love someone and be miserable. But love often feels happy, yes."

"You feel happy," said Ethan, unknowingly echoing Giulia.

"Because I am." *And you're not worried that you can tell? You don't wonder if...* Jav's heart strained so full it threatened to fracture his ribs.

"S'nice." Ethan buried his face in the crook of Jav's neck. Then, as if he was the one with a secret, said, "*Loveyoutoo.*"

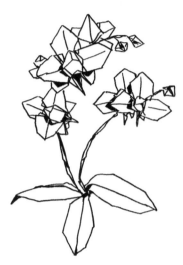

Bless. "I can't believe you found a loophole in your own no-flower rule." Ethan had gifted him a bouquet of origami orchids, reminiscent of Jav's first faux pas. "These must have taken hours to fold—"

Suddenly, the lift doors opened.

Fury hit Jav like a wall of heat. Ethan, who was plastered along Jav's side, jerked away in alarm.

Peter was shouting. Peter was shouting *at Rina.* "—know what possessed you to say—!"

"What the fuck was I meant to do? We were in public, people were filming!" Rina shouted back. "This was Bobby's idea, I know it. Oh, when I get my hands around his old wrinkly neck..."

They were nose to nose, Peter radiating frustration, his visage fading in and out like a mirage. The ghost rarely lost control like this, and whether it was his anger or Rina's fire, it raked across Jav's cornea.

Rina jabbed a finger in Peter's face. "Charlie has outlived his usefulness—"

Jav cleared his throat, thrusting out a deliberate calm. "What's happened?"

Rina and Peter turned, in sync.

"Your sister—" Peter started.

Without warning, Rina swept the nearest vase off its stand in a burst of porcelain. "Charlie proposed!"

"He *what*?!" Jav shouted, bolting upright and dislodging Ethan. "Are you okay?"

Rina threw her heels at the wall in response.

"She said 'yes'," spat Peter.

Jav's eyes almost popped out of his skull. "You said what?!" Even Ethan's amusement wasn't helping. "*Why*?"

"Because her ego is the size of—"

"If Bobby thinks he can back me into a corner, he has another think coming," Rina hissed. Her pulse points shimmered with blue fire, an incandescent silhouette of smoking satin. "Fuck his lobbyists, fuck convenience. I'm going to get Charlie back for this. I'll pretend everything's fine, get him in bed, and burn through his chest until I'm *holding his ribs*."

Perhaps sensing Jav's dismay, Ethan lay a palm over Jav's wrist. His free hand was in the chocolate box. The juxtaposition didn't help stem Javier's mounting hysteria. He stood up. "But *why* did you say yes?"

"I wasn't going to give him the satisfaction," said Rina.

"Of being rejected?!"

"He was banking on you saying yes!" Peter shouted. "Whatever our reassurances to Robert, they're evidently not enough. Perhaps Marc has stabbed us in the back. Maybe Robert suspects on his own – but this was clearly a bid for your literal fucking commitment!"

"Well, I've called his bluff, haven't I?" snarled Rina.

Peter opened his mouth – then stopped, gaze falling to Ethan. "Ah," said the ghost, posture easing from one blink to the next. "We've interrupted your evening."

They all turned towards the chaise.

"That's okay," Ethan said around a cheek full of chocolate. "It sounds like you've had a big night."

Rina hissed like a cat. Exasperated, Jav grabbed her wrist. She yanked her arm back but Jav held on, grasping for their familiar calm. It splashed on her flames, before Rina's skin burned white with spite.

Jav let go with a wince. "Maybe we should call Giulia. She'll know what to do."

"Don't you dare," spat Rina. "She's been spending far too much time with Nath—"

Peter cleared his throat. "We promised Jav the place to himself."

"We can move upstairs." Jav turned to Rina, conscious of Ethan's curious stare. "We'll figure out a way for you to say no. Or I can talk to Charlie—"

Peter snorted, but Rina's eyes flashed. "Yes. Put the fear of god into him. Or the fear of me."

"He's clearly acting out of desperation," said Peter. "We should tread carefully until we know what Robert knows—"

"And let him think I'm worried?" Rina turned an inky smile upon Ethan, who was unwrapping another praline. "Do me a favour, would you? Keep my brother suitably distracted so he doesn't call our parents about this little hiccup."

Ethan licked chocolate off his hand, pulling his index finger out of his mouth with an obscene *pop*. "We'll be pretty busy, yeah." He wiggled his eyebrows at Jav.

Jav flushed, skin prickling from all the conflicting emotions in the room. He flexed his fingers, wet and painful from the burn.

"Yes. Enjoy yourselves." Rina bit each syllable like she wanted to break their necks. She swept out of the living room.

"I'll handle this. Don't talk to anybody," said Peter and vanished.

Distantly, another crash of porcelain, followed by a long pause. It was broken by the crinkle of foil wrappers.

"I hope you don't mind," said Ethan, "but I've finished all the hazelnut ones."

Jav succumbed to laughter, collapsing back onto the chaise. "Please, never change."

ETHAN WAS A LOT less amused when he saw Jav's second-degree burn.

"It's fine." Jav baulked at the way the mood went from pillow-soft to sterile. "Doesn't hurt much."

Ethan didn't reply right away. He uncurled Jav's fingers gently and skin smoothed over before Jav's hand was fully open. The pain vanished behind Jav's cuticles, leaving only a faint itch.

Ethan traced the lines of Jav's palm with an index finger. "Does this happen often?"

"Rina has great control, usually."

"Hmm. No excuse for lashing out."

Jav looked down at his unblemished skin, disoriented by Ethan's chill. "Well, lucky you're here, right?" He nudged Ethan with his empathy, wanting a smile. Then Jav realised what he was doing and pulled back guiltily.

Ethan didn't seem to notice the fumble. "Will you tell me if this happens again?"

"It was an accident."

"You're very flammable. Rina should know better."

Jav leaned in for a kiss. Ethan tasted of pralines. "I think you're flammable too," he said, trying to change the topic. If he dwelled for much longer, Rina's terrible engagement was going to overwhelm him. Jav had been looking forward to Valentine's Day with a partner for *years* – he was going to enjoy tonight and panic later. "Flammable, as in hot."

"I gathered, thanks." Ethan turned away when Jav tried to kiss him again, brow furrowed. "Are you able to bunk with Stephen if Rina... loses her temper again? If you don't feel comfortable telling me, I mean."

"Rina doesn't usually bring drama home. She goes out to blow off steam. I help her calm down, after."

"Oh, so we have a routine for these unanticipated 'accidents'?"

Jav opened his mouth, then closed it again. "I just meant that she doesn't normally...I pushed her—"

"So she burned you."

"By *accident*." Jav pulled Ethan closer, hoping for a deflection. "It still feels tingly," he said, holding up his now-uninjured hand.

Something finally gave; Ethan relented. "I suppose we can't have that. Let me check." He cupped Jav's face in both hands and proceeded to thoroughly investigate his tonsils. After a few minutes, both breathless, Ethan announced, "Inconclusive. Clothes off."

Later that week.

THANKS TO RINA, the family dinner was rescheduled and chaotic.

Giulia even arrived early. "What the actual hell, Javier! You said you'd keep me informed of any bullshit *before* it happens."

Rina rounded on her twin. "What? You snitch!"

"I didn't say anything," Jav shouted back. "I didn't know anything *to* say."

Between Giulia and Nath, Jav's phone had been blowing up for the past two days. He had muted them both so he wouldn't miss Ethan's messages.

Giulia threw her bag onto the nearest chair. "I don't care, I'm holding you both responsible."

"That's not fair," said Jav. "I hate Charlie as much as—"

"I hate Charlie the most!" Rina hollered.

"Then why did you say yes?" Giulia slammed a fist on the table. "Because you thought I wasn't stressed enough? Jav memorised an entire binder for our Covent Garden presser and you've flushed all that goodwill down the toilet!"

"*Charlie* was the one who—"

"Your engagement is all over the tabloids, all over social media. Why are you always in the papers?"

It was at that moment their father walked into the dining room. He didn't feel angry or frustrated – just worried. All three Arden siblings turned in unison.

Thomas Arden sighed. "Girls. Indoor voices, please."

Giulia opened her mouth, but Rina beat her to the punch.

"Daddy!" she cried, tears welling on command. "Charlie proposed in public, and I panicked!"

Giulia pointed at Jav. "Stop helping her with those crocodile tears."

"I'm not *doing* anything!"

1 Madeleine Avenue, Upper Chelsea, Level 22.
Monday, 21 February.

RINA COLD-SHOULDERED JAV for the rest of the week.

"I can't believe you took Giulia's side. I'm never telling you anything again."

You never tell me anything, these days. Sometimes I don't know who you are. I miss my sister. "Do whatever you want, I'm going to bed."

It had been a month since Ethan resumed consulting for the emergency department. His shifts oscillated between night streaks and alternating days-and-nights. Jav assured him everything was fine – and it was. But the irregularity contrasted the languid evenings they had enjoyed together for the past five months. Just enough to establish a routine for Jav to now miss.

He thumbed through photos to console himself, pausing on one taken at the Kew Conservatory. Ethan had dirt on his hands from where he'd tripped, moments before. Jav made the photo his phone wallpaper.

The sun had set half an hour ago. Yawning, he climbed off the wicker swing, still engrossed in the photo album. He barely registered a looming, invisible presence before an arm whipped across his chest.

Peter clamped a hand over Jav's mouth before his shriek could leave his throat. "Shhh. Rina sent me."

"Fuck off!" Jav's expletives were muffled by Peter's bruising hand, pinning them flush. Jav stomped on Peter's toes with zero effect.

"Now, isn't this familiar?" Peter chuckled, breath warm on Jav's neck, amusement dulling the blade of adrenaline.

All the hairs on Jav's arm stood on end. He threw an elbow back into Peter's stomach in lieu of throwing up.

Peter didn't budge. "We have a visitor. Rina wants to know whether he's lying or not. One might describe it as a matter of life or death. Are you going to help, or are you going to be an infant?"

Jav twisted, trying to wrench his wrists free. This time, Peter let him go.

"Where are they?" asked Jav, heart still thudding.

"Breakfast bar. But you'll need to stay out of sight."

"That's not how it works." Jav held up a hand when Peter moved to follow. "And I can't concentrate with you hovering. Go upstairs or something."

Peter shrugged. "Very well." He phased from sight.

Long shadows pooled on the living room floor, broken only by the ever-shifting water shadows from the aquarium. Jav stuck close to the stairs, careful to stay beyond the light spilling from the kitchen. Empathic senses did not travel through walls, but Rina knew that – having positioned Nath with his back to the lobby.

But Jav didn't need to see or hear Nath's voice to pick him out of a crowd. Chemically speaking, emotions were emotions. Familiarity bred recognition though, of consistent baselines and reactions – like an accent or timbre of someone's voice.

"...a coincidence?" Nath was saying. "That Charles proposes, two weeks after Arden Pharma backs the Covent Garden fusive project?"

"I'm the victim here," drawled Rina.

"It looks like you're in Robert Langley's pocket."

"Bobby needs me more than I need him. He would be in *my* pocket, if this dress had any."

"You must know how this looks," said Nath.

"Phenomenal for my cleavage?"

Nath's anger jerked like an unsteady hand. "Is everything a joke to you? Whatever your petty grievances against me, a fortune is on the line! Wash your hands of glass before it—"

"Glass has many proven therapeutic uses."

Nath barked out a laugh. "Fine. Let's talk purely in terms of CM15 then. It's on its way out."

"No. We'll always need CM15. We can afford to lose a little margin now. When Arden Pharma is the last one standing, they'll come crawling on their knees."

The silence spilt across the floor, oozing.

When Nath spoke again, his quiet voice was at odds with the thunderous volume of his distaste. "What exactly does Robert Langley have on you?"

"A leech of a nephew, apparently."

Breathing required a conscious effort he couldn't spare; Jav felt lightheaded.

"Your arrangement must involve some mutually assured destruction," said Nath. "Otherwise, Charlie wouldn't have resorted to marriage to keep you in line."

That sparked a swell of irritation. "Just because Stephen's having a politically advantageous wedding doesn't mean I will."

Silence.

"Did Langley find out about Javier? Is that his leverage?"

Forget Nath's emotions. Jav wasn't sure that he could trust his own thumping heart, throat clogged with the effort of not projecting his nausea.

Rina's attention hardened to a razor's edge. "Getting ideas, are we?"

"If you tell me what's going on, maybe I can help."

"How about you tell *me* what you actually want?"

"Break off your engagement."

"Hmm. I rather fancy keeping Charlie on his toes. Think I'll wait a bit longer. See what happens."

"Then I want you to relinquish your stake in Ascenda."

"...Nah. And don't bother bullying Jav. We vote in a bloc."

"It's *my* family's business, I'm not going to stand for this conflict of interest," snapped Nath, voice rising. "My father—"

"Thinks of me as the daughter he never had, but do go on."

"I could go to the authorities."

Jav flinched at Rina's peal of laughter. He felt like a moth, trapped against a burning lamp.

"Oh, *Nathaniel*," said Rina, vowels punctuated by the wheeze of genuine mirth. "Don't be silly. Of course you won't."

"I have evidence of—"

"You have fuck all. Tattling would mean a scandal for Ascenda if Arden Pharma gets dragged through the mud. Save your bluster for someone who cares."

A clink, followed by the pop of a cork. Rina, pouring herself a drink.

"Do you think I'm bluffing?" asked Nath.

"If you thought backstabbing my family would help, you'd have done it a year ago. You wouldn't have waited this long." Rina underlined the pause, the hum of a finger caressing the rim of crystal flute. "You certainly wouldn't have resorted to having me shot."

Jav pressed a fist to his mouth. *Nath hired the shooter? It was Nath this whole time?* Second-hand fear clawed at his veins, looping tight with shock, impossible to untangle who they belonged to.

When Nath spoke, he sounded like someone had a knee to his throat. "I don't know what you mean."

"How funny, neither do I. The real question is, do you think *I'm* bluffing?"

Nath didn't answer immediately, his fear-anxiety making the room swim in and out of focus. The silence stretched on, underscored by Rina's satisfaction. She must have been happy with whatever expression Nath was wearing.

"I'm so glad we understand each other," she said. "Honestly, I'd hate to ruin Stephen's wedding."

"I don't know what you're suggesting," said Nath, words soaked in cortisol. "I had nothing to do with the shooting, how could you accuse—"

"That's not what your Sixty-Fourther told us."

Nath's alarm made Jav bite his lip so hard that he tasted blood.

"Sloppy," Rina sing-songed. "Very sloppy, Nath."

"I don't know what you're—"

"Yes, yes. But there's plenty who *do* know what I'm talking about. Dwell on that, the next time you feel like threatening me or Jav."

Silence stretched like skin across the knuckles of a clenched fist. Rina luxuriated in the tension, threading the seconds between her fingers and winding them into tight, suffocating minutes.

"What do you want from me?" asked Nath.

"Want?" Rina tutted. "Nothing, of course. We're family."

Jav waited. Surely his veins would calcify from sheer dread.

"I see," Nath bit out. "Well. It's getting late."

"Mmhm. You know what they say about late and never."

There was a tell-tale shift in the air; Peter stood on the other side of the lobby. Jav stepped backwards as Nath and Rina moved out of the kitchen.

Nath froze at the sight of Jav.

Rina made a show of being startled. "I thought you were out with

Ethan!" She looped an arm through Nath's elbow. "Look who dropped by for a visit."

Up close, Nath's aura was tinged green with stress.

Jav mustered a smile. "Ethan's working. Sorry I didn't say hi earlier. Fell asleep reading in the garden." He clasped both hands behind his back to hide the shaking.

Peter was fully visible now. He called the lift and offered Nath a mock-bow. "After you."

Nath looked between Jav and Rina. "See you both at the dress rehearsal."

The door closed after Nath and Peter with a weighty *click*, leaving Jav alone with the fish and Rina. The wind whistled against the windows. Jav had forgotten to close the conservatory doors.

"Now you know why I didn't tell you," Rina said quietly.

"Uncle Harry and Aunty Harper," Jav began, voice catching on his teeth. "Stephen's my — *Nath is family*. How could he have...how could he—?"

Rina pulled him closer by his hands. "So Nath was lying, then? When he denied hiring the shooter. You felt him lying?"

"I-I'm not sure." *What's Peter going to do to Nath if I say 'yes'?*

She pressed her thumbs to his wrists, one on each pulse. "You're usually so good at detecting this stuff."

"Truth and lies aren't emotions."

Rina narrowed her eyes. "You always said you could tell—"

"When people are lying, yes, but you don't feel whether something is a lie. You feel what the speaker is feeling when they make that statement. Depending on how this compares to their baseline, you might infer—"

"Then *infer*," said Rina, impatience slick as ice and twice as deadly.

"It's never for certain. Just because someone feels scared or nervous doesn't mean — *oww!*" Jav wrenched his hand back, heart thumping in his throat from the flash of heat. *Fuck, I hope that won't leave any marks.* They stared at each other, separated by déjà vu.

Rina flexed her fingers. "I didn't know what to think when we suspected Nath. You're the only person that can *check*. And that I trust."

"Then why didn't you tell me earlier?"

"Nath's family. Would you have believed me if it was 'he said she said'?"

Guilt reared its ugly head, a wild thing that swept in and cut free the tethers of reason and sinew. Jav pulled her into a hug. "*Of course* I'd believe...you didn't think I would hear you out?"

"I knew you'd be upset." Rina's hand pressed between his shoulder blades, rubbing a comforting circle. "You're upset *now*. Feels shit."

Jav breathed in the familiar scent of her hair. Closing his eyes, he confessed, "Nath was terrified."

"The whole time?"

"Spiked, when you confronted him. He wasn't expecting it. Felt angry too, frustrated. Mostly scared." Jav swallowed. "But it doesn't necessarily mean that Nath was *lying*." This came out as a plea, thready and unconvincing. "You were accusing him of trying to *kill* you, Rina. I'd be scared too, knowing that Peter would chop me into little pieces, after."

Rina hummed.

"God." Jav's voice cracked. "What are we going to tell Stephen?"

"Nothing." Rina cupped Jav's face with one hand. "Stephen's naive. If he goes to our parents, or, God forbid, the police, then we'd have nothing to keep Nath's mouth shut. You don't want that to happen, do you?" Jav shook his head, numb. "Plus, like you said: we're not a hundred per cent sure."

"You think the Sixty-Fourthers—"

"Bobby's the only person who knew what Peter and I had planned that evening. Well, Charlie might have known, but Bobby pulls all the strings. Bobby lent us the cab. Could still be him, I suppose. Peter has his suspicions."

"You *suppose*—"

Rina tapped Jav on the nose. "All the more reason not to blab. Promise?"

"Please stop seeing Charlie. And Robert. All the Langleys. It's not *worth it*."

"We don't want Nath getting any other bright ideas about your empathy. Though I don't think he'd risk Uncle Harry disowning him."

"Maybe we should at least talk to Aunty Harper. Or mum?"

Rina shook him by the arms. "I know this is hard to understand, but Nath is family, and he *tried to have me killed.* Project Earthflown is worth more than what we'd lose in CM15 and glass, combined. You think Giulia wouldn't do the same if the tables were turned?"

"Absolutely not—!"

"Because *I* would," Rina continued, chin at a stubborn angle. "We'll need to deal with Nath sooner or later."

"Don't say that," Jav whispered. "Rina, you *can't*, Nath—"

"Threatened you." Then her expression softened, switch-fast. "If he outs you, it's all over. You'll be under house arrest at best, or sedatives every time you want to go anywhere exciting. You can kiss the Royal Ballet goodbye. Is that what you want?"

Unbidden, Ethan's voice: '*You clearly miss it.*' "What if the police find out?" asked Jav.

"How? From you tattling? Nath tried to have me killed!"

"We don't *know* that. You just said—"

"Promise me you'll keep quiet," hissed Rina. Jav stared, unable to feel anything except the sweeping chassis of her spiteful resolve. His silence only made her more furious. "If I can't trust you, if I don't have time to figure this out—"

"No, no, I won't breathe a word. Don't do anything rash."

"Don't patronise me!" Rina spat. "I've kept your secret for almost thirty years, and now, when all I'm asking—" She turned on her heels and stormed up the stairs.

Jav's entire body went cold with her dismissal. "Rina!" he ran after her. "Rina, I'm sorry, I just meant—"

The slam of her door made him flinch to a halt. The bang echoed on the glass and wood, like a gunshot might have done. Long after the tremors dissipated, Jav stood alone, unable to move.

TWENTY

Somewhere on Level 10.
A month earlier ↺ Thursday, 20 January.

"What you need," Ollie announced, "is a clean break." Nick stared resolutely into the holographic distance as the treadmill whirred beneath his feet. He showed no signs of slowing. Ollie had long since given up, sipping water while Nick took out his feelings on the lousiest terrain mode.

Ollie waved. "Oi, you listening? Block him."

"Like you blocked Vegas?" Nick shot back. "Oh wait."

"Block Vegas too. She and Ethan switch accounts all the time since they share subscriptions. When you're as wise as me—"

"I'll be winded after a ten-minute jog, apparently."

Ollie swiped at the dashboard settings to create a sudden hill on the terrain modulator. Nick leapt over it without breaking his stride.

Show-off.

"I finished a whole route with you," Ollie muttered. "At least twenty minutes."

"Wow, that's an entire relationship cycle for you."

"Hey. Vegas and I've been great lately."

Nick pulled a face. "Sorry. I'm just not in the mood for I-told-you-sos."

"I didn't say that." Ollie leaned against the safety rail which shuddered with Nick's footfalls. "You hungry yet?"

"Nope."

"Let's get dinner."

"No thanks."

"I'll buy you a drink if you stop running."

"You just want to watch me cry, so no."

Ollie squashed himself between the edge of the treadmill and the wall, into Nick's line of sight. "There's nothing wrong with a good cry. God knows you've seen me bawl enough times."

Nick glared at him. "I *have* been a good friend, haven't I? Unlike some people."

Ollie chewed on his water-bottle strap. Around them, people filtered out for dinner. A woman paused as she passed, giving Nick's backside an appreciative once-over. She looked as if she might interrupt in the name of flirting, so Ollie scowled at her until she left.

Nick seemed oblivious. *Still* running. "You could have told me earlier."

"I know, I'm sorry." Guilt settled, a sticky film against Ollie's conscience. *Better disclose everything now.* "Ethan asked me yesterday what we were doing at his place. You know. Before Christmas."

"And you told him we were sweeping the flat for surveillance devices?"

"Obviously not. C'mon."

At least Nick sounded more winded now. Maybe they'll have dinner before Ollie's stomach devoured his other organs. Nick tapped the dashboard of the treadmill, slowing to a jogging pace, the latticed material smoothing out to match the holographic sand dunes flattening into the horizon.

There was a pixelated metaphor about futility, somewhere.

"Do you think I took him for granted?" Nick asked, abruptly.

Ollie squinted. "Ethan cheated on you."

"No, we had no str—"

"Mate, you've got strings as far as the eye can see."

"Why wouldn't he just text me?" Nick's mouth flattened, unhappy. "If it was no big deal. If we had an open relationship—"

"There's a difference between 'no strings' and 'open'. Did you guys specify?"

"No, we did not bloody *specify*. There weren't any terms and conditions."

"Maybe there should've been."

"Next time I'll reuse the contract you've got with Vegas."

Ollie crossed his arms. "Ours has special clauses that you have no interest in."

"Expiration clauses?"

"Oi. At least Vegas and I are on the same page."

That shut Nick up, which, Ollie realised a split second too late, was the opposite of what he wanted. Nick's eyes were unfocused as he walked in place. The terrain was smooth now, the treadmill's wind-down timer nearing zero.

"Look, the truth always gets out." Ollie glanced around. The hum of air conditioning masked their voices. "Florence reckons that Javier's doing pre-emptive scandal control. Public submissions are open for the Earthflown tender, so he's—"

"Christ, Ollie, can you not pretend to care about something else for *one* second—"

"This affects you!"

"How," snapped Nick.

"At some point, the facts are gonna reach a critical mass where even Ethan can't ignore them. I think he's in denial about Javier being an empath—"

Nick thumped the dashboard, stumbling as the treadmill whined to a halt. He ducked under the safety railing and strode towards the changing rooms.

Ollie jogged to catch up. "Hey. Nick, c'mon. I think Vegas will be able to persuade Ethan, once I've convinced her."

Nick rounded on him. "And what would that accomplish? Relationships aren't arguments you can win."

Tell that to Vegas...

"You can't 'persuade' someone if they don't care about—" Nick scrubbed a hand over his eyes. "Ethan didn't even think we had anything to break up!"

"So you're throwing in the towel?"

"There is no towel. This isn't up to me."

"Of course it is." Ollie wasn't sure how they got here: trying to save Nick's relationship with someone so patently terrible for him. "Where do you think I'd be if I took Vegas's words at face value every time we fought? Single and miserable."

Nick slammed his locker shut. At least he wasn't sprinting into the holographic nowhere. "Ethan and I've never had a fight."

Ollie rolled his eyes. "Congrats."

"No, I..." Nick looked at the floor. "I think that's the problem. You only fight when you feel strongly about something. Someone." He took a deep breath. "I'm gonna shower."

"Nick—"

"This conversation's over." Nick disappeared into a cubicle without another word.

"...Okay. I'll be right here." Ollie stared after his friend. Eventually he retreated outside and pulled up Vegas's icon on his watch, overcome with the need to hear her voice.

The Sentinel Studios, Upper Bloomsbury, Level 13.
Over a month later, Tuesday, 15 February.

FLORENCE WAS FROWNING SO SEVERELY that Ollie could feel her migraine from across the room. "Defamation risk?" she repeated.

"Damien said I'm flying close to the sun." Damien was his editor. Ollie chewed on his thumbnail. "They said we don't have enough to meet the public interest defence."

"That, and your subjects have very deep wallets. Damien might hang you out to dry."

Ollie kicked the table leg. "Nick won't go on the record. He's pissed that I didn't tell him about Ethan and Javier sooner."

"And you *should* have told him."

"I'm not responsible for Ethan's self-absorbed circus. Even Vegas is surprised how serious it got. And how quickly." *Out of character. Undue influence.* "Do you think your mum would defend me pro bono?"

"Again?"

They lapsed into the silence soaking into their soggy salads. Their room overlooked the arts-and-culture pod. Mia was holding court, having taken over the largest conference room.

"Look at them," said Florence. "So well exfoliated. Is that a wedding gown?"

"Covering only the most newsworthy events."

"Do you know what *I've* been covering?" Florence stabbed a piece of lettuce with her fork. "The Arden Foundation decided to drop a bomb on Friday. Giant donation to the Covent Garden fusive fund."

Clearly a distraction – but from what, exactly? "Green washing at its finest. Hey, maybe we chose the wrong career. Wedding coverage looks alright."

"I'm gonna propose to Vegas if you won't."

"Vegas thinks you're straight."

Florence laughed. "Now *that's* a defamation risk." She gathered her belongings and hip-chucked the door open.

Ollie followed. Distracted, he walked straight into Florence's back when she stopped without warning.

Florence pointed at the screen above Mia's head. "Why does Mia get all the leads? Did *you* know about Corinna Arden getting engaged to Charles Langley? Because I didn't."

Ollie almost broke his nose on the glass wall. "Since when? Bloody hell. Martin was right, they are all in bed together. Forget corporate incest: corporate *ménage à trois.*"

"But Langley is vocally anti-fusive, so it won't help with the greenwashing. You don't think it's true love, do you?"

"It's never true love." Ollie met Mia's gaze through the wall. She mouthed '*GO AWAY*', slicing her hand across her neck. He lunged for the door handle.

THE MEETING with his editor weighed on Ollie's paranoia all week.

"Don't be rash," were Florence's parting words. "If you're going to risk your career, do it properly."

Someone must be leaning on The Sentinel to shut him up. More than four months had passed since Ollie last spoke with Martin Hersch – five since Martin's son turned up dead in a cab. The lack of progress made time molasses slow. Events were coalescing fast around something unseen, and Ollie felt stuck on the side-lines. Truth asked for time that few could afford.

Being in Nick's bad books didn't help.

"You told me Ethan wasn't gonna be there, and now I look like a jealous idiot," Nick had said.

"He wasn't meant *to be home."*

"Whatever. I'm going to spend more time with people who don't only talk to me when they want something."

Ethan seemed to be avoiding Ollie too. They crossed paths just once, and Ollie witnessed the tail-end of a cringeworthy parenting lecture:

"All relationships take work," Ian said.

"I thought you said I worked too hard." Ethan edged along the office wall.

"Work and *patience*. You can't run away from every difficult conversation. When I was your age—"

"Vegas?" Ethan pointed at Ollie, standing in the doorway behind Ian. "What're you doing here?" When Ian turned to look, Ethan squeezed past like a bar of soap. "*Loveyoubye!*"

Bergenia Residences, Lower Lambeth, Level 9.
Sunday, 20 February.

WHEN VEGAS SUMMONED Ollie for late-night pizza dinner, he figured she had an unexpected night off. He should have known better.

"Does Vegas know you've been taking her name in vain?" Ollie peered exaggeratedly around the flat. "Stop using her phone number."

Ethan was cross legged on the couch, halfway through his own pizza. "Got you to pick up, didn't it? That one has extra mushrooms."

Ollie considered walking out, but Ethan had splurged for sourdough. He grabbed the box and collapsed onto the couch. "What's all this then?"

Ethan shrugged. "Thought we should have a chat."

"You wanted to chat." Ollie narrowed his eyes. "With me."

"Eh. 'Want' is a strong word."

Without Vegas, they ate in scratchy silence, the comfortable kind that nevertheless made its presence known. Despite their contrasting edges, Ethan had been a fixture in Ollie's life for almost a decade. And like the damp London weather, he got used to it.

Ollie helped himself to pear cider from the fridge. "Out with it then."

Ethan burped. "Vegas says you're worried about me."

"Adjacent – I'm worried about Vegas."

"Whatever. Is this real worry or journalism worry?"

"I'm worried that you'll become the third corpse in a story that already has two."

"A story *you're* writing." Ethan folded his pizza box. "Is it that hard to believe that someone might date me for non-nefarious reasons?"

"Well, Nick didn't have ulterior motives, but apparently you two were never dating. So, yes. Quite unbelievable." Ethan's expression puckered. *I hope that's guilt, you underdeveloped sociopath*, thought Ollie. "Have you apologised for cheating yet?"

"You just said there wasn't anything to cheat on. Not that it's any of your business."

Ollie crossed his arms and waited.

"Is that why you're not letting this Jav stuff go?" asked Ethan. "Because of Nick."

"If by 'this Jav stuff' you mean him sticking around to threaten me and Ian? Maybe. Regardless, you owe Nick an apology."

"Jav's never asked me about dad's work, or yours," said Ethan, pointedly ignoring the Nick part.

"His presence is enough of a warning. Not to mention a potential conflict of interest for Ian at the SIA. I think that's why he puts on such a sickly sweet schtick. That can't be natural."

"And *I* think you're just after a 'gotcha' quote. Jav didn't even know who dad was until recently."

"I find that hard to believe, seeing as Ian and Nick interviewed Jav and his sister after the shooting." Ollie knew Ethan well enough to catch his non-reaction as genuine surprise. *Ah. So you* didn't *know.* Ollie sipped his drink. "Did Javier tell you otherwise?"

"I haven't asked. Doesn't matter."

"Doesn't it? When did the wining and dining start?"

"None of your fucking business."

Ollie pulled out his phone. "Javier met Ian and Nick Friday afternoon, 8th of October. Check your calendar."

Ethan hesitated. Eventually, he said, "We made plans days before that."

Ollie sank back into the sofa. "Listen. I am pissed. Nick deserves better. But I don't *want* to be right about Javier, you know."

"Bullshit. You ambushed me in the loo, raving about Jav poisoning people. Just tell me what you want."

"The night Corinna was shot, an Arden employee ended up dead in a cab, five Levels away. Tampered camera footage, missing records, conveniently leaked emails. The police couldn't get a hold of Corinna for days because she had been transferred out of St Ophie's – against healer's orders, or so I hear." Ollie raised an eyebrow. "The victim's father got in touch with me. Next thing we know, he's dead too. I confronted Nick about it, told Florence: bam, Javier Arden's waiting for me on this very couch."

Ethan shook his head. "I'm the one who invited Jav over. And the hospital transfer was dangerous, but not *criminal*."

"Javier knows Ian is working on Corinna's case, he knows Florence and I are reporting on this. Why else is he going out of his way to make your relationship public? I mean, the Charlotte Hall Gala? Snogging you at the SIA precinct? Really?"

"Jav's just over-the-top. And Rina pulled out of the gala last minute—"

"Convenient."

"—so I offered to go. Wasn't Jav's idea. I felt bad because dad chewed him out at the station."

"Would you say you felt *unusually* sympathetic?" asked Ollie. No response. "For fuck's sake, Ethan, he's an empath."

"He's not."

"More likely than not."

"Tonnes of people wear empath dampeners."

"Suppressors—"

"Prove nothing," said Ethan, voice rising with frustration. "Don't throw these accusations around so casually."

"If I had something unequivocal, I wouldn't bother convincing you off the record – I'd have told Ian already and there'd be warrants, subpoenas, people getting detained."

Ethan's expression smoothed out, too blank – his performative apathy recalibrating. "Detained for what?"

"Questioning. Attempted or actual murder. Interference with SIA investigations. Failure to comply with statutory disclosure requirements." Ollie thumbed the dot-mic in his pocket, stretching his legs to mask the movement. "Y'know what I find interesting?"

"My love life?"

"You're remarkably unfazed by the prospect that the guy you're sleeping with—"

"Dating."

"—is an empath."

"He's not an empath. Even if he is, *I'm* not a bigot."

Ollie set down his empty glass. "Don't break your neck getting off that high horse. *I* have nothing against empaths, per se. But you need to see the bigger picture."

"*You're* fixated on Jav orchestrating some conspiracy via empathy.

Never mind that every paranoid person wears 'empath dampeners'. A whole industry that feeds off this misunderstanding—" Ethan sighed. "We need to address your urge to run around accusing people, which, and I cannot believe I have to say this, is not okay."

"Accuse? Being an empath isn't illegal. What *is* illegal: not declaring you're an empath during a police witness interview—"

"As if legal means *right*," snapped Ethan. He rubbed his eyes. "You're gonna ruin Jav's life over a hunch."

Ollie stared. Ethan, concerned about someone who was not himself, Vegas, or Ian? It was jarring to observe, and begged for pause. "You seem mighty worried for someone who thinks empaths are an improbability."

"Jav's in the public eye. Mere speculation will be bad enough."

"I'm sure he'll survive, being a trillionaire and all."

"Oh, because this country has such a wonderful record with empaths. If anything, his family's—"

"Obscene wealth? Political power? Notoriety?"

"Yes," said Ethan testily. "Paranoia against empaths transcends that stuff. Look at all the exceptions against empaths in the Equality Act."

'*That stuff*', thought Ollie, derisive. *Oh, to have the luxury of dismissing wealth.* It was strange though: Ethan had never been one for social justice trivia.

"People still talk about empaths like telepaths," Ethan continued. "Like we're still in the Middle Ages and burning healers for being witches. Would you have sold *me* out?"

"Dunno. Are you an empath sitting on the board of Europe's largest private foundation?"

Ethan went bug-eyed. "You think Jav sitting on some stupid board is the problem here? He wants to go back to ballet full time!"

"Uh huh."

"Your priorities are warped." Ethan ground his teeth, then changed tack. "A lot of weird timing happened. You and Jav got off on the wrong foot. But he wants to get along with my friends, you know."

"I thought we weren't friends," Ollie drawled.

"Can't you give him the benefit of the doubt? You said you *had* doubts, or else you'd have gone to dad already."

Ollie did have doubts. But Ollie also had Jav's 'lost' cufflink stashed in his studio, just in case. "I'm looking out for you."

"If Jav *is* an empath, the worst that happens is he dumps me. If Jav *isn't* an empath and you write a story..." Ethan exhaled. "That's not something you can take back."

"Two people have died and you're—"

"Not trying to diminish that, but I'm someone you actually *know*." Ethan raked fingers through his hair, agitated. "Tragedy happens to people every day, you can't carry it around with you. We have to triage. How do you think I walk in and out of the hospital, night in, night out?"

If Javier really was an empath, could Ethan become more empathetic over time? Or was disassociation something that calcified into your bones? Perhaps such apathy was a chronic condition, the same thing that made Ollie whip out a camera at the sight of a dead body.

"We're not all as lucky as you and Vegas," said Ethan. "Some of us didn't find our whoevers a million years ago."

"It can't be that serious already." Ollie sighed when Ethan simply stared at the rug. *Christ almighty.* "Even if Javier's not an empath, he's *involved*. Whether that's with Tim and Martin's deaths, whatever Corinna was up to, or via the Arden Foundation. When oligarchs have this much money to lose...He's involved."

Ethan's expression held steady. "That's not fair. You of all people should know about being part of unchosen families."

Blood is thicker than water, and twice as cheap.

"I haven't spoken to my dad in 15 years," said Ollie. "Whereas Javier attends press events on behalf of his family business. Complicity is a choice. There's no glass without CM15, and there's no CM15 if we all switch to fusive-powered water purification. Did you know Corinna Arden got engaged to a man whose family controls the largest cold-chain network this side of Europe? They've also been investigated for glass trafficking and have a vested interest in CM15 production remaining cheap."

"They, as in Charlie?"

What. "...You knew?"

"Rina was pissed off."

Ollie had not expected this many unexpected turns, even with

Ethan's Vegas-pizza-bait-and-switch. "Javier told you, I assume."

"Nah, I was there. She smashed a vase."

"You were at Charles Langley's engagement dinner?!"

Ethan pulled a face. "No. I was over for Valentine's Day when Rina came home, fuming. Literally on fire. Jav was horrified. Nobody was happy."

Ollie made a mental note to text Florence. Maybe Arden Pharma wasn't trying to have it both ways on fusive and CM15, after all. He needed another brain to debrief with. "Did Jav introduce you to every shitty rich person he knows?"

Ethan shook his head. "I met Charlie at that gala. Jav feels sorry for him since Rina's been stringing him along or something."

"Poor bloke," Ollie muttered.

"Nah, he was annoying," yawned Ethan. *Oblivious hypocrite.* "You should have seen Rina's tantrum."

Ollie could count on one hand everyone Ethan cared about. The healer possessed a streak of schadenfreude that bordered on mean – probably deficient socialisation, being rushed through primary and secondary education. Now Ethan was emotionally stunted, his ego driving every decision.

"Well," said Ollie, "I'm not sure there's much left to say."

"Don't make any hasty decisions," Ethan warned.

"Right back at you." As a gesture of goodwill, Ollie stacked the empty pizza boxes as he stood. "I'll take out the trash."

"Cheers. You might still fit in the chute, if you select the garbage option, not recycling."

"Hardy har har."

Ollie waited until he was out of the lobby before pulling out his phone. Shivering in the damp, he ended the voice recording, glancing back up at the lit window. *Speculation.* Ethan hadn't said anything directly incriminating, though his defensiveness...it'd be prudent to keep records. Vegas would be upset if she ever found out, but better sorry than lacking evidence.

Ollie stuffed the phone back in his pocket. He allowed himself a moment to compartmentalise, then began the lonely trek down to Level 4.

TWENTY-ONE

Thursday, 2 March.

There were few things more comforting than the transition from novel delight into treasured routine. Ethan couldn't remember when he began seeing Jav most nights of the week. But after six-ish months, Ethan's gaze automatically sought out the nearest sports-flier whenever he stepped out of the hospital. Thanks to Ethan's unpredictable schedule, Jav gave him an auth-key to call one of Jav's many cars whenever he clocked off. Ethan was sitting in one now, and he sent a text to Jav (*Almost there!*) before snapping the lid back onto his fruit cup.

Jav seemed convinced that Ethan would perish en route, and insisted on providing snacks.

"Not that I'm complaining, but the point is to have dinner *with* you."

"Healers have faster metabolism."

"Did you get that from *Healer's Anatomy*?" asked Ethan.

"I got it from watching you demolish Eli's challah loaf."

The car hovered above the tree-lined street, pausing within the landing bay for the security scanners. The building's shadow slid over the windshield like an exhausted eyelid. Going by the animated ellipses on Ethan's phone, Jav was still typing. He texted in full sentences complete with illustrative stickers every paragraph. Ethan smiled to himself.

The car let Ethan out next to the lobby, then peeled away towards a line of cloth-covered vehicles. It still boggled the mind to dedicate an entire floor of Upper Chelsea as a garage.

On his phone, Jav appeared to have abandoned his essay. *I'm here,* Ethan typed, standing still for the biometrics. Jav usually met him downstairs to assuage Rina's security concerns.

A few minutes passed. Ethan hesitated before typing: *Babe?*

Five more minutes passed without a response. This wasn't like Jav at all. Ethan frowned, holding a palm over the intercom. It rang twice.

"Ethan," said Rina.

"Hi, uh—"

"Hurry up." The intercom clicked once, and the lift doors opened without fanfare.

"Right," Ethan muttered and stepped in.

He found Jav's twin mercurial at best, oscillating between disinterest and predatory friendliness. Initially Ethan thought her a riot, before she left a handprint on Jav's wrist, blistering and raw. Perhaps Rina wasn't in a good mood today, given her 'Unfortunate Engagement Debacle'. At least he was getting Jav out of the house, away from any temper tantrums.

"Hey," Ethan called, toeing off his shoes.

Rina appeared like a ghost. "Finally." She tugged Ethan towards the kitchen. "Something's wrong with Jav."

"What do you mean 'something's wrong'—" Ethan stopped.

Jav lay on the floor, pale, eyes closed. His left arm was bent awkwardly, entire body stiff as a board as if he had toppled over where he stood.

Ethan stared, muscles seizing in unfamiliar panic. *This is why we can't treat family or loved ones.* Every breath scorched his nerve endings. The paralysis struck something he hadn't experienced, even as an intern: fear. *I can't do this, I can't do this, I can't—*

Then training took over. Ethan's dropped to his knees, hands automatically going to Jav's throat and wrist. There: a pulse. He exhaled in a rush, aware of the swelling on the back of Jav's skull, the raw skin, scrapes on his feet from a day in the studio—

Ethan yanked his aptitude inwards. "What happened? How long has he been like this?" Rina stood beside him, unnervingly calm. At least she wasn't in hysterics. "Have you called emergency services?"

"He passed out minutes ago. I was about to call triple-nine, but you arrived."

"Call them now." Ethan palmed Jav's forehead, tilting Jav's head back with some difficulty. Pinching Jav's nose, he pressed his mouth to Jav's and breathed out.

Jav's chest rose a little. *Thank fuck.*

Rina was talking to someone on the phone.

"Come on," Ethan muttered. He pinched Jav on the inner arm, desperate for a reaction. None. "Jav!"

"This isn't normal," said Rina, as if commenting on the weather.

"Yes, unless he's in status," gasped Ethan, inhaling for another rescue breath. Was her faith in healers so misinformed that she thought Jav immune to asphyxiation? Ethan flicked through a mental checklist while he continued the rescue breathing. *Jav wasn't on anti-psychotics. Tetanus, somehow? Unlikely.* Jav's joints were so stiff that Ethan could barely straighten his arm.

"No," said Rina. "I meant, when Jav takes sleeping pills, he doesn't pass out this fast. He gets sleepy around twenty minutes and starts stumbling by thirty."

Ethan's eyes almost fell out of his head. "Jav took *sleeping pills*?" he shouted. "Show me." He pressed another breath to Jav's mouth. "Ambulance?"

"They're still on the line," said Rina.

Her phone speakers emitted a familiar crackle before settling. "Ma'am?"

"ETA?" asked Ethan, curt.

"Ten minutes. Are you the healer?"

"Yes," said Ethan. "Can't chat – respiratory failure."

Rina held out a sheet of tablets for Ethan to examine. Ethan nodded. He could be angry later when Jav was safe and well.

"From the symptoms, this sounds like a seizure," the EMT continued. "Have you got lorazepam?"

"I'll get the first-aid kit," said Rina.

Ethan sealed another breath into Jav's mouth. "Patient took hypnotics recently, I'm not sure he's in status."

"Keep him breathing, we'll be there soon."

Rina returned with the type of first-aid kit that could only be found in the kitchen of a pharmaceutical scion. She flicked the case open. "Do we need lorazepam or not?"

A thought hit Ethan like ice. He lifted each of Jav's eyelids with the pad of his thumb – and cursed. Jav's pupils were the size of pinpricks. "Pen light."

Rina slapped one into his palm.

Jav's pupils were abnormally constricted. *Shit.* It was difficult to be certain. "I'm trying naloxone first." Ethan tore into the medical kit. It only took a few moments to find the right syringe and rip off the casing.

The EMT was still talking. "It's uncommon for someone who took hypnotics to be in status or displaying seizure symptoms. Sir?"

Ethan jabbed the syringe into the muscle of Jav's right thigh. For several long, agonising seconds, nothing happened. Then Jav gasped to life, jack-knifing upright – clocking Ethan in the nose.

Ethan fell on his arse, more from the empathic shock than the physical impact. He dropped the syringe. "Oh, thank fuck."

"Jav!" Rina cried and promptly hung up on the EMTs.

Jav dry heaved, shivering violently as he hacked and coughed. His eyes darted from Ethan to Rina then back again, glassy with shock.

Ethan clasped him by the neck and shoulder, keeping him upright. "Hey, *hey*, it's okay. Jav, look at me. You're alright. Breathe." Ethan willed his own pulse to slow. Maybe if he was calmer, it would help reset Jav's panic. "Breathe. Slowly does it. In...then out. In...out. That's it."

Rina snapped her fingers in front of Jav's face. "Focus. You're spiralling."

All the minor scrapes and bruises had been wiped clear from Jav's body, thanks to prolonged skin contact and Ethan's distraction. Jav shook with full-bodied tremors, brow damp with sweat. He stared up at Ethan, eyes dark against the bright tiles, lips slowly regaining colour with oxygen.

Furious relief crashed over Ethan. "How could you be so careless?" he shouted. "I told you not to take any of your old sleeping meds with these painkillers. You could have — if I wasn't—!" His voice slipped on the possibilities, shattering his composure when it fell. "God's sake, Jav, you scared the *shit* out of me!"

Jav clutched Ethan's wrist, an unsteady vice. "I didn't take any sleeping pills."

"You did." Ethan looked to Rina. "They reacted badly with your new meds."

"What new meds?" Rina demanded.

"We were going out for dinner," said Jav, lost. "Why would I take sleeping pills?"

"You never said anything about new medication," said Rina.

Jav's pulse jolted beneath Ethan's thumb, eyes darting everywhere except his sister.

"You told me he took sleeping pills," Ethan said to Rina.

"Jav has trouble sleeping. I know when he's stressed and needs help."

"I *beg* your pardon." Static crushed Ethan's ears. "You gave Jav sedatives *without him knowing*?!"

"It's never been an issue." Her knuckles were white around Jav's wrist. Ethan was abruptly reminded of the burns that might have remained, had he not been present the evening Rina lost her temper. "Wouldn't have *been* an issue if I had been aware of the switch. Jav? Does mum know?"

Eyes averted, Jav said nothing.

"Javier!"

"Yes, okay, mum knows! And I *was* going to tell you, I just…"

Ethan had never felt anger so visceral, hydrogen lungs struck alight. "What the hell is wrong with you? Do you have *any* idea — you could have killed him!"

"Because I wasn't told about the change!" Rina shot back.

"No! It's because you think it's okay to drug someone!"

Rina's lip curled. "Did you put Jav up to this? You're not his doctor."

"Jav is right here," said Ethan. "And I merely suggested that he talk to your family doctor about re-evaluating his pain meds."

"Why?" snapped Rina.

"I do have sleeping problems," said Jav, voice thready. "It's better when you're staying over, but if something's happening in the flat that might affect me, Rina—"

She cut him off with a warning glare.

Ethan clawed a hand down his cheek. "Christ almighty," he muttered.

"Please don't be angry," Jav pleaded. "I'm sorry I scared you."

"This isn't your fault." Disbelief had turned Ethan's nerves to ice. "Do you really not see what's wrong here?"

"You shouldn't be making suggestions about Jav's medication."

Rina's mild tone contrasted her knife-sharp sneer. "There's shit you don't—"

"He knows, Rina."

They both turned to Jav.

"Excuse me?" asked Rina, into pin-drop silence. Jav held her gaze. "Ethan. I need a private word with my brother."

Jav took a deep breath. "Ethan knows I'm an empath." Then he flinched.

Ethan yanked Rina's hand away, thinking she had burned Jav again – but realised it was an emotional recoil.

"Since when?" asked Rina.

"I was going to tell you, but with Charlie's proposal—"

"*Since when?*"

There was real trepidation in Jav's eyes now, hands still shaking from the naloxone.

"Have you told anyone?" Rina asked Ethan, turning a coin-flat gaze upon him.

"No," Ethan replied.

"Really."

Rina's phone rang, making them all jump. The intercom began flashing urgently on the wall.

When Rina didn't react, Ethan said, "You should get that. The ambulance."

Rina gestured over her phone without breaking their eye contact. "Yes?"

"Ms Arden, first responder mode doesn't seem to be en—"

"Sorry, must be a glitch." Rina stood, pressing a hand to the nearest intercom. A brief lattice of green swept her face and palm. "Come up."

"Thank you. What's the situation?"

"I'm fine," Jav croaked from the floor.

"He's stable for now," Ethan supplied, carding Jav's hair back from his clammy brow. "Naloxone worked; it wasn't a seizure."

A moment later, a clatter from the foyer announced the arrival of the EMTs. Rina and Ethan were politely but firmly pushed aside as the crew checked Jav over.

"I'm fine," Jav repeated. "Ethan's a real doctor."

"You're the family doctor?" an EMT asked.

"No. I'm his boyfriend who happens to be a doctor."

The other EMT nodded. "Do you have an ID with you?"

"Sure." Ethan reluctantly let go of Jav to retrieve his satchel.

"Will he be okay?" asked Rina.

Her eyebrows were furrowed in pitch-perfect anxiety, and the contrast with her fury mere minutes ago made Ethan's skin crawl.

"Someone mentioned sleeping medication?" asked one EMT. "Did you ingest anything else, sir? Alcohol?"

"Um..." Jav looked to Ethan.

"He's been on new analgesics for about five weeks," said Ethan. "He took some earlier and—"

"Forgot," Jav cut in. "Wanted a nap before dinner so I took some sleeping pills."

Ethan bit his tongue, frustrated.

"I didn't know he had switched pain meds," Rina added. "He went down like *that*. So scary."

The EMT made a disapproving noise. "I see."

"Does he need to go to a clinic?" asked Rina.

The other EMT returned Ethan's hospital ID. "Are you able to stay with him for the night?"

"I'm fine," Jav insisted.

Ethan might have been more convinced if Jav wasn't holding Ethan's hand in a vice grip. "Yes. We've got a full kit here. I'll keep an eye on him."

"Prelim work seems consistent with what you've said." The first EMT tapped through the reader. "Steer clear of any analgesics or hypnotics for at least forty-eight hours."

"I'll make sure," said Ethan.

The EMTs took another few minutes before gathering their kit and equipment. Ethan saw them ogling the aquarium as they left. All too soon, he, Rina and Jav were alone once more.

"I messaged Peter," said Rina, making Jav blanche. "So we can discuss our little situation."

"Rina, that's not—" Jav clapped a hand over his mouth. He wobbled to his feet, leaning heavily on the kitchen counter.

Ethan straightened. "Jav?"

Jav lurched away, shoulder hitting the wall as he stumbled out of the kitchen. A door slammed.

"Where do you think you're going?" called Rina. "Jav!"

Ethan elbowed the bathroom door open in time to see Jav throw up into the toilet. He sighed and knelt beside Jav to hold his hair out of his face as he vomited. "Oh, hun. It's okay. Let it out."

"What's wrong now?" Rina hovered, thoroughly unhelpful.

"*I* am," cried Jav, tears streaming down his face as he clutched the toilet seat. He hiccupped, then heaved again. "Ugh..."

"Don't talk." Ethan glared at Rina. "Get him some water." He rubbed firm circles between Jav's shoulder-blades. "Shhh. You'll be alright."

Jav was still trying to speak. "Don't. I'm..."

"Stop talking. Slow breaths."

"I t-think you should w-wait outside."

Ethan paused. "Why?" Perhaps his anger wasn't as well controlled as he had hoped.

"Because this is disgusting," Jav moaned. It echoed forlornly in the bowl. "I don't want you to smell...need mouthwash ..."

"I swear — no, don't *get up*. Honestly. I deal with much worse in the hospital. A bit of tidy vomit isn't going to make me squeamish."

Rina reappeared with a water bottle. "Here. Rinse."

"T-thanks." Jav gargled several times, looking even more clammy and pitiful than he did before the EMTs arrived.

Ethan snagged a fresh towel, wetting it under cold water. He still couldn't believe they had full-water taps in all the bathrooms. Jav leaned away from the toilet to press the cloth over his eyes. With the weight gone, the cover slid shut. The flush was comically loud in the sudden silence.

"I want a shower," said Jav.

"Let's get you upstairs," Ethan agreed. "Do you feel dizzy?"

"A bit."

"I think we should resolve our security risk first," said Rina.

Ethan helped Jav stand. "I'll sign an NDA later."

She laughed. "You think I want *paperwork*?"

"Rina, please," said Jav. "Not now."

Something ugly flashed across her features, a twist of flesh and teeth. "Oh, yes, *now*. Though you and I need a separate chat later, when Ethan's gone."

"You're out of your mind if you think I'm gonna leave him alone with you," said Ethan. "*Move*."

Rina didn't budge. "Listen here—"

"No. *You* listen to me. I don't know what kind of 'understanding' you had, but this stops now. Jav could have *died* if I didn't happen to be downstairs. All because you've dosed him so often that none of this felt scary enough to call triple-nine! You will *never* do this again. Do we understand each other?"

Ozone crackled about Rina's throat. At last, she bit out, "Quite."

Jav's eyes darted between his sister and Ethan. "I've always had problems sleeping," he croaked. "Rina means well."

Ethan shook his head. "Intention is cheap. Actions matter."

"How long have you known about Jav's empathy?" Rina demanded.

"Are we camping in the bathroom all night or are we going to let Jav rest and recover?"

"No one outside the family knows, for obvious reasons. No one."

"And?"

"What guarantee do we have that you won't blab? Or let something slip."

"Jav seems happy to take my word for it."

"That's because Jav doesn't know what's good for him," snarled Rina.

Ethan raised his eyebrows. "Is that why you gave him sleeping pills? For his own good?"

"Don't take this out on Ethan," Jav tried. "You're mad at me because I didn't tell you earlier—"

"Oh, you *think*?"

"—and I'm sorry, I am!"

"I try so hard to protect you and this is how you repay me," Rina hissed. "Didn't you learn anything the last time?"

Jav's hurt ran like a livewire through the palm of Ethan's hand. *Enough is enough.* Ethan shouldered past Rina, pushing Jav out of the bathroom. To his relief, Rina stepped aside – perhaps realising a line had been crossed. Ethan focused on shuffling Jav up the stairs, and being calm. *Jav doesn't need second-hand anger from you.*

"If this gets out, it'll be on your head," Rina called, words refracting off the aquarium glass.

Ethan paused on the landing. He thought of Ollie and his convictions. "I've no plans to tell anyone."

"Intention is cheap," Rina echoed. "I want insurance."

Jav squeezed his eyes shut. "Rina, *please.*"

"So that's it?" said Rina. "He promises not to tell, and you're happy."

"Yes," said Jav, mouth trembling. "It's *my* life, my secret, and my problem if—"

"Once it gets out, it'll be everybody's problem," said Rina.

"Maybe I can't live like this anymore!" Jav's voice rose with every word, until he was shouting. Ethan had never heard him raise his voice like this. "I'm sorry I didn't tell you sooner, I truly am. But you don't get to call me selfish when you do whatever you like and to hell with the consequences! I have begged you, *begged you* to stop seeing Charlie, but you refuse to admit that you're in over your head. Even when it almost got you killed. Do you know what it would do to me if you were gone? Do you *care*?"

Flames curled about Rina's hands, camouflaged by the veins of water-shadows cast by the aquarium. "Jav, let go of Ethan. He's getting you worked up."

Jav did not let go. Abruptly, he announced, "We're spending the night at mum and dad's."

Ethan blinked. "We are?"

"No," said Rina. "This conversation's not over."

"Peter's here," Jav said, stone faced. "So Ethan and I will be staying at mum and dad's."

"Peter?" Ethan scanned the empty living room.

"He's been here for the past ten minutes," said Jav. "Haven't you, Peter?"

A pause. Then the air wavered from the tell-tale heat, and a tall figure appeared at Rina's shoulder.

"I didn't want to interrupt a private conversation," said the ghost. He nodded to Ethan. "Maybe we should step out, doctor."

"Absolutely fucking not," said Jav. "We're leaving."

Rina crossed her arms. "Nobody is going anywhere until I say so."

"In case anyone's forgotten," said Ethan, "Jav wasn't breathing half an hour ago. He needs to rest." Extracting his hand from Jav's death grip, Ethan corralled him upstairs. "Make a list of what you want from me," he shot over his shoulder. "We can resume the threats later."

Bergenia Residences, Lower Lambeth, Level 9.
Two days later, Saturday, 4 March.

JAV WAS QUIET in the days following the incident.

Ethan spent two sleepless nights debating how to persuade Jav that Ethan's tiny flat was better than a psychopathic sister. Ollie would have to be quarantined, lest anyone got arrested. *Was it too soon to move in together?* Ethan had never thought this far along, and it was terrifying.

As it turned out, Jav wanted to keep Ethan as far away from Rina and Peter as possible.

"I knew she'd react badly," Jav fretted, over and over. "I should have told her earlier. Now Peter's involved and it's all my fault."

Because God forbid you keep anything to yourself. That, and whatever happened 'the last time'. Ethan resisted the urge to pry. "I suppose she can't see a reason to trust me yet."

"You saved her life!"

Ethan sighed. "That doesn't make me trustworthy. Just good at my job."

They were curled up in Ethan's bed, warm under the blankets and fairy lights. Vegas, bless her, had gone to Ollie's for the night so Ethan and Jav could have the flat to themselves.

"*I* trust you." Jav traced the shadow beneath Ethan's left eye with the pad of his thumb.

Ethan ceded a smile. "Love you too." He kissed Jav, hoping that would ease the searching anticipation in his face.

Jav tucked his nose against Ethan's neck. "Rina hasn't said anything else to you, has she?"

Ethan shook his head, and carded his fingers through Jav's shower-damp hair. Jav stayed quiet for so long that Ethan thought he'd fallen asleep. Perhaps they could stay here forever, behind paper-thin dividers and cramped furniture, affection piled high against leaky windows.

"I don't want anything to happen to you," Jav confessed, hushed.

"Nothing's gonna happen to me." Now that Ethan knew what to look out for, Jav's anxiety felt second-hand. "Hey. What's wrong?"

"I've dragged you into such a mess." Jav inhaled shakily.

Christ. Maybe Ollie was onto something. "Every family is messy in their own way." *Careful, Mr Not-Yet-Six-Month-Anniversary.* "Your secret isn't small. I get Rina's...worry. Except she almost killed you. So, frankly, she can trust me or blackmail me, but let's get on with it."

Jav sniffle-coughed against Ethan's t-shirt. Several minutes went by before he spoke again. "Will you tell me right away if Rina or Peter contact you?"

"Maybe we should cut to the chase. Meet up. Hash it out."

"Rina holds grudges."

"Good. Maybe she'll also remember how scary it was to almost kill her brother, you weren't breathing, you—"

"It was an *accident*."

Be patient, Ethan reminded himself: *Jav thinks Rina hung the moon.* "Have you told your parents yet?"

"About you knowing?"

"About Rina and the sleeping pills."

Jav sighed, sinking back on his pillow to stare at the ceiling.

Ethan propped himself up on one elbow, leaning over Jav to maintain eye contact. "Oi. Hello."

"Rina's holding this over me on purpose. Giulia might actually ask you to sign an NDA, if she finds out."

"Babe," Ethan said gently. "I think they need to know about what happened with Rina and the pills. This and all the other times." *And if no one reacts appropriately, we commence phase two: find a flat with Ethan.*

"I don't want to stress them out. Everyone's very busy with Proj—planning Stephen's wedding. Rina and I are flying out next week."

"Yes. Why do you think I'm worried?"

"She won't give me the wrong meds now that she knows about my new painkillers."

Ethan rubbed his eyes. "Jav, Rina should not be giving you sleeping pills *at all*."

"Yes," Jav agreed hastily, "that's what I meant."

"I know you two are close." Ethan picked his way through the metaphorical landmine. "But you stopped breathing and she didn't even call triple-nine."

"Rina's not in a good place right now. I don't want her to feel alienated. She needs me."

"And she won't have you if you're dead." Ethan thumbed Jav's hairline. "Do we need to stick a VM on you to make sure you're safe?"

"Like in *Healer's Anatomy*?"

"People who aren't healers wear VMs. Patients. Athletes."

"Okay, but the healer ones are special." Jav paused. "Do you have your set at home?"

"You can't wear mine; they're registered at work."

"Oh," said Jav, ears going pink, "I didn't mean for me..."

Ethan rolled his eyes. "My stats are logged automatically. So unless you want to explain the kind of vigorous 'healing' I'm doing offsite, off-shift, in the middle of the night..."

"Is that happening soon?" asked Jav, batting his eyelashes.

"Don't know," said Ethan. "Are you gonna tell your parents about Rina?"

Jav's smile faded as quickly as it appeared. "Ethan..." A long pause as he transparently debated whether to lie or not. "I'm not making excuses, but Rina's looking out for me. She was having guests over and thought they'd disturb me."

"So she put you to sleep."

"I don't want you to think badly of her." Jav's thrum of anxiety returned. "Growing up I never had to ask, she just *knew*. It's a twin thing."

Control is not a 'twin thing'. But Ethan held his tongue. His disbelief must have shown though, because Jav made a sad noise at the back of his throat.

"Please don't put me through this again," Ethan said, because maybe guilt would be more persuasive than reason.

"I'm s— I'll talk to someone. Maybe just mum. She's least likely to overreact."

Ethan wasn't sure how a parent might 'overreact' to the news that one sibling almost killed the other. "You staying with them still?"

"No, at Stephen's. I'm over there most of the day with wedding prep."

"Good." Ethan kissed him as positive reinforcement.

"I wish you could come with." Jav returned the kiss, making his way tentatively along Ethan's throat, eyes flicking up every few moments to meet Ethan's. "I'll miss you."

"It's only a week. You'll be too busy to miss me." Ethan tilted his head back. "Mmhm, I've never been to Taiwan."

"It gets larger every year. Quite amazing, from an engineering perspective. Clara can tell you all sorts of stories." Jav laboured over Ethan's pulse. "Also the food is fantastic. You'd love it."

"I have interests other than food."

"Oh?" Jav's eyes crinkled. "Such as?"

Ethan rolled his hips forward. "Exhibit A," he said, revelling in the answering spike of pleasure. It hooked into his lower spine, coiling in the pit of his stomach like a promise. "'A' stands for 'arse', in case you're wondering."

In response, Jav flipped Ethan onto his back – but ruined the movement by pausing to adjust Ethan's pillow. Jav's hair fell into his eyes; he braced an arm against the wall. "I thought A was for 'ace'."

"Dammit. I'll get better."

"It's okay, I'm just teasing. What's Exhibit B?"

"...Pass."

"Tell me."

"Buns."

Jav cast his eyes heavenward. "That's food."

Ethan grinned. "They could be. Wanna guess Exhibit C?"

They did not make it very far down the alphabet.

TWENTY-TWO

Bergenia Residences, Lower Lambeth, Level 9.
Saturday, 11 March.

V egas collapsed onto her bed. "Why are you moping? Jav's only been gone a day."

"Four days," Ethan corrected absently. He realised his mistake when Vegas laughed. "And I'm not moping, I'm worried."

"About the fight?" asked Vegas.

Her bedroom door stood ajar. Ethan could hear Ollie clattering about in the bathroom. It had been over a week since the sleeping pill debacle. Ethan initially told Vegas that the twins had had a fight, buying himself some time to think about whether he wanted Vegas (and thereby Ollie) to know about the incident. Ethan wasn't used to withholding anything from her and the omission itched.

"Jav almost had to go to the hospital," said Ethan.

Vegas sat up. "What?"

Things went quiet in the bathroom.

"Jav switched painkillers recently," said Ethan. "Rina gave him sleeping pills without him knowing." Vegas's jaw dropped. "Didn't mix well. I thought he had a seizure, at first."

"Oh, hun." Vegas pulled Ethan into a tight hug. "Why didn't you tell me sooner? She gave Jav pills without him knowing?"

"Apparently not the first time. Just the first time it's almost killed him."

"Good lord." A long pause. "I thought Rina was...quirky. But not, you know. This."

"I let her have a piece of my mind, after the EMTs left. She's pissed at Jav for not telling her about the new painkillers." *For Jav telling me that he's an empath, rather.* If only Rina had been equally furious about the painkillers. "Jav freaked out when I said we should report it. He promised he'd tell his parents but..." Ethan shrugged.

"Are you gonna tell dad?"

"Don't want to make it worse."

"You're not sure what Jav will do," Vegas observed knowingly.

Ethan nodded. "He lied to the EMTs, told them that he'd taken the sleeping pills himself. He won't say anything that'll get Rina into trouble. You should have seen how unfazed she was with Jav, on the floor, not breathing." *Is that what we seem like, to the patients?* "Should I tell dad?"

"Feels wrong not to tell someone."

"Dad has a knee-jerk reaction when it comes to anything Arden related. Same with Ollie. Plus, there's no point if Jav will just lie about the whole thing."

Vegas nodded. "You don't want to make him choose."

"Well. Family versus some guy you've been with for six months." Ethan attempted a laugh and failed.

"Wow, you do care."

Ethan flattened a pillow over his face. "I don't want to ruin everything."

"Look on the bright side. At least this evens the playing field."

"What field?"

"Ian hates Jav. Now Rina hates you." Vegas patted Ethan's head as he groaned into the pillow. "That's Ollie's, by the way."

Ethan flung the pillow at the wall.

Ollie chose that moment to stop eavesdropping and walk in. "Somebody say my name?"

I hope you heard all the important bits. "We were just bitching about you," said Ethan.

"Nice." Ollie pulled his shirt over his head, one handed. "Vegas and I are gonna have fun now. You staying or leaving?"

Ethan fell off the bed in his haste to exit.

Wednesday, 22 March.

JAV ET AL returned to London a few days after Stephen and Clara's first wedding. He was waiting for Ethan in the hospital lobby, flowers in one arm, umbrella in the other.

"Hello," said Ethan, off balance from the radiating warmth. It was like entering the orbit of a space heater. "You didn't have to wait inside."

Going by the dimples on Jav's face, empathic migraines weren't an issue today. *Everyone within a twenty-metre radius must be feeling this.*

Jav appeared oblivious to the effect he was having on their neighbours. "Did you miss me? Because *I* missed you..."

"Missed you like an afternoon nap."

Time apart didn't always make a heart fonder; Ethan knew that from experience. Was his brain just hooked on the dopamine rush of Jav's affection? It seemed that apathy couldn't compete with undiluted dopamine.

"I don't have a simile," said Jav. "What could I miss more than you?"

"Hmm, I still love naps the most. I'll blow you to make up the difference."

Jav went predictably pink.

Ethan accepted the flowers so they could link hands. "You make it so easy. C'mon then, tell me about being second-best man."

· · ·

Friday, 31 March.

To Ethan's relief, like Rina, Jav's anxiety was nowhere to be seen. A likely correlation – though certain not to last.

Enveloped in groomsmen duties (*"Best man duties!"*), Jav left Ethan to his own devices on the morning of the ceremony. Ethan's suit had arrived while Jav was overseas, a dove grey three-piece with evergreen lining and matching gloves.

A pastel purple convertible hovered outside Ethan's building. Its roof was up, material tinted like an oil spill. As Ethan approached, the door lifted to reveal Jav's younger sister who wore a floor-length dress with a slit rising past her knee.

Maddy gave Ethan an unimpressed once-over. "Get in then."

Ethan obeyed. "Does Jav know you're here?" he asked as the car took off.

Perfume clung to buttery leather.

"Obviously. I'm your babysitter."

"*Is* it obvious?"

"You'll be bullied, otherwise. Do you even speak Mandarin?"

"Nope."

"How did you get through your A-Levels?"

"Healers are exempt from secondary-language classes."

Usually, Ethan was terrible at small talk, but Maddy maintained an effortless stream of criticism as they journeyed to Level 2. The car's wheels lowered as they entered a no-fly zone. Some older roads couldn't draw sufficient power from the main grid, and others weren't retrofitted for repulsors.

"Didn't think this model was road ready." Ethan patted the dashboard. "Did you modify the chassis?"

"You're such a nerd, Edgar." Maddy was still cycling through non-Ethan 'E' names. "Yuck, it's so dark down here."

"I'm surprised Jav okayed this. What with the radiation."

Maddy turned in exaggerated slow-motion. "Are you enabling him?"

She cackled when Ethan showed her the necklace around his neck. "Ha. You piece of shit."

"Jav's convinced it'll help with 'toxins'. I figured the stress would be worse on his health than imaginary radiation."

"The venue was non-negotiable. St Paul's is the family church." At Ethan's blank look, she added, "Granny and poppy Mansfield helped relocate the cathedral."

St Paul's Cathedral was one of the only landmarks to have been fully relocated, stone by stone. The rest were abandoned to the floods. The old museums and grand galleries were so popular with urban divers and explorers that the police had regular human and drone patrols to save idiots from getting trapped.

Over the years, as London rose higher and higher, St Paul's was not further relocated. The initial move was already controversial, given the cost and the general state of crisis at the time. St Paul's was swallowed up, like shrapnel by the flesh of a city yearning for the sun. Today, thin shafts of light illuminated the cathedral dome, slicing through the four Levels of airspace.

Their car stopped near a tired green, crowded with suits and cocktail dresses. The media was roped off on either end of the short block.

"You go first and help me out," Maddy commanded. "These heels were not made for walking."

▬▬▬▬

St Paul's Cathedral, Lower City of London, Level 2.

LIVE CHERRY BLOSSOM trees filled the cathedral. Ethan had zero doubts who was responsible – the garden bursting from the transepts had Jav's name written all over it.

Maddy sat Ethan firmly between herself and Giulia. From the second row, Ethan enjoyed an unobstructed view of Jav bawling his eyes out as Stephen powered through his vows. Clara's composure was phenomenal – everyone in the front row succumbed to weepiness. Even Rina, standing two-over from Clara as a bridesmaid, looked rather emotional.

Jav's gaze found Ethan's amidst the choir music and Ethan received his first ever crying wink.

"I want the raw files," Maddy whispered. "Jav's gonna be ugly and blotchy in *all* of them."

Ethan quietly disagreed; he had never seen a more photogenic set of groomsmen. They paired off with the bridesmaids, following the happy couple down the aisle.

"Can you send me those photos?" asked Ethan.

"Mmhm. What's in it for me?"

Ethan offered her his arm as they shuffled out of the pew. "Vegas might be able to join, the next time Jav hosts a cooking night."

Maddy went beet red.

Somewhere above Red Sands Fort, off the east coast of England.
Two hours later.

IN CONTRAST to the ceremony on Level 2, the wedding reception was held, literally, in the sky. To get there, they travelled by flier, hurtling above the sea to where the aircraft eclipsed the moon. If Ethan squinted, he could just make out London's Levels in the distance – lights cascading towards the shoreline as the Levels rose and fell along flood-zone typography.

Ethan pressed his face to their flier's transparent roof as they flew into the shadow of the aircraft. "Jav never said anything about the Lotus! I saw photos online." Powered by fusive-cells, the giant aircraft relied on angled 'petals' that orbited the body. Telekinetic engineering at its finest.

Maddy snapped her hand-mirror closed. "He probably wanted to surprise you, given your flying fetish."

The ocean below them heaved with the force of the Lotus' propulsion, undulating with a hair-rising hum. Sea foam trailed every arriving flier in streaks of white.

"Have you flown on something like this before?" Ethan craned his neck, trying to catch a glimpse of the ship's engine as they flew into the underbelly of the Lotus.

"Nah, it's a prototype. Third-gen fusive cells are why our eardrums aren't bleeding. That's Clara's name on the hull, by the way. Real obvious who the favourite child is." They pulled up along a sweeping staircase and were immediately greeted by porters. Maddy dragged Ethan up the staircase by his elbow, having abandoned her stilettos for wedges. "No time for photos! Christ, how does Jav deal with you?"

The Lotus was dominated by a giant, circular ballroom at its core. The ceiling ran transparent, open to the night sky and holding the main floor as its equator. Round tables laden with flowers ringed a honey-wood dance floor. Thrillingly, the centre of that dance floor was transparent too, offering a dizzying glimpse into the guts of the ship and the ocean below.

The sheer scale and vastness of space left Ethan lightheaded.

A suspended gallery ran the circumference of this ballroom, overlooking the dance floor. Maddy and Ethan spent an enjoyable half-hour stalking the hor d'oeuvres (*"There's supposed to be aburi scallops and we're not leaving until I find them."*), avoiding small talk (*"Oh god, that's Marc, he is my least favourite cousin. Move, move!"*), and people watching (*"Huh, the PM did show up."*).

Jav's mother introduced Ethan to Clara's family, the extended Ardens, and the French cousins that Maddy had been trying to escape. Ethan soon gave up on remembering names.

"Mum hates her side of the fam," Maddy explained. "Mémé Marion didn't even come to mum and dad's wedding. She's not here today either, but Marc and Audrey are. Bleh."

A man – bearing a striking resemblance to Jav – was talking to Thomas Arden, a baby on his chest. The baby was dressed like a tulle marshmallow, complete with a tiny tiara. She stared at Ethan, thumb in her mouth.

Maddy grinned. "That's Marc and his spawn. Jav's always so bitchy to him and now regrets it, 'cause Marc won't let him play with Chloe."

The marshmallow – Chloe, presumably – waved at Ethan. Ethan waved back.

Charles was conspicuously absent from the plus-ones' table. Ethan wondered if Rina had broken off the engagement, and whether any vases survived the ordeal.

When the wedding party finally arrived, Jav dashed over. "Are you enjoying yourself?" he asked, hair and heart windswept. "Just dinner and speeches, then I'm all yours."

"Here," Ethan pulled him in by the lapel for a kiss, "have some placebo for the road. How's your head?"

Beside them, Maddy mimed gagging.

Five courses, several speeches, and an excessively professional groomsmen dance routine later, Stephen and Clara had their first waltz. Afterwards, the crowd spilled onto the dance floor, some retreating to the gallery for drinks and chatter.

At some point, Maddy vanished to dance and never returned. Ethan dithered, alone at his table. He rather fancied standing on the see-through floor and taking some photos – but didn't want to brave the crowd. He sipped his champagne, then quickly set it aside: a fancy reception full of Jav's relatives was not the time to get tipsy. He could see Jav's blond head on the other side of the dance floor, surrounded by friends. Ethan smiled.

A shadow fell across his lap.

"Been abandoned, have we?" Rina drained Ethan's champagne flute. "Come dance."

It was the first time they had spoken since the sleeping-pill incident.

Ethan leaned back in his chair. "Not a good idea."

"Why not?"

"Can't dance." He glanced at her stilettos. "And will ruin your shoes." *Plus, I'd rather drown in the Thames.*

"Nothing that can't be replaced." Rina adjusted her gold circlet, studded with jade. "The next one's a slow waltz. I'm sure you can manage."

Ethan shrugged. "Your funeral."

Jav had tried valiantly to teach Ethan how to dance after the gala. So far, Ethan's lack of rhythm was winning against Jav's optimism.

He and Rina stepped forwards at the same time.

"*I'm* leading," Rina admonished.

"Sorry."

One, two, three. One, two, three. Ethan wondered if Rina would explode something if he wrecked her shoes. They *were* very high above the sea.

They spun past a sky-filled window, Rina's gaze burning Ethan's face. "I've been thinking about how our last conversation ended."

"Have you been thinking about the part where Jav almost died?"

Rina twirled herself, deftly avoiding his feet. "If you hadn't been there, I would've called someone."

"Zero regrets then?"

"Oh, no, I feel *terrible*." Rina furrowed her brow in a perfect imitation of Jav's self-deprecation. It grated against her unfaltering stare. "Jav said he feels awful too, not telling me sooner." She slid her hand up Ethan's shoulders, clasping the back of his neck. "I can see why you think it's my fault."

"Can you." Thank god Ethan wasn't an empath, otherwise Rina would surely taste the bile of his contempt.

"I don't expect you to understand what Jav and I have. You're an only child."

"You might end up the same way if you don't look after the ones you've got."

Rina laughed "Let's clear the air. Get on the same page."

"As long as it says 'no drugging people without consent' on that page."

They completed a full circuit of the ballroom. The staff had shifted all the tables and chairs, exposing lovely parquetry and the transparent parts of the dance floor. Rina considered him. Ethan stared right back – and with his eyes off his feet, stepped repeatedly on her toes. He took petty delight in seeing her mouth twitch with annoyance.

"Ethan, I would hate for you to think me ungrateful for everything you've done." She stroked the dip behind his ear with her thumb, making the hair on Ethan's arm stand on end. "I suppose both Jav and I owe you one."

"So we're even? Or are you still looking for suitable blackmail?"

"Blackmail is such a strong word. Jav—"

"Can think for himself."

Rina smiled, teeth flashing like pearls sewn in red brocade. "You know, he only asked you to dinner because I suggested it. Jav's gun-shy."

It was only thanks to years of deadpan that Ethan's expression did not betray him. "Suppose I owe you a thank you, then."

"Oh, no, *no*." Rina tapped her fingers on the back of Ethan's neck, in time to the waltz. "You couldn't imagine what Jav was like, after I got shot. He was worried sick that you'd run off to the press – or worse. Wanted to make sure you felt...appreciated."

Ah, came Ollie's voice, *I did tell you.*

Ethan stamped down the doubt and on Rina's toes. *She just wants a rise out of you because she's not in control anymore.* "I'm not the sort to keep track," he said. "Too transactional."

"He feels indebted to you, for saving my life."

"If Jav didn't trust me, he wouldn't have told me."

The corner of Rina's lip curled like paper to a flame. "Ah. But he *didn't* tell you, did he?"

Ethan's heart skipped a beat. And even though Rina wasn't an empath, she seemed to know.

She wet her lips, eyes bright. "You guessed – clever – and Jav spilled the beans." She spun Ethan on the next crescendo, making him stumble. "He had no choice *but* to trust you."

Ethan opened his mouth, but the retort clogged his throat.

Rina slid her hand down the side of his neck and over his clavicle to lie, unnaturally warm, over Ethan's heart. "I'm glad this is in the right place, but my brother is very easy to love. As a doctor, I'm sure you know the mechanics. He can't help himself."

Ethan prayed his pulse didn't belie the constriction in his chest. "At least one of you has a functioning anterior insular cortex."

"Oh, *Ethan*." Rina threw back her head and laughed, high and derisive. They stood over the ocean now. "I do like you. Truly. I mean it."

The music unspooled. Rina shifted her hand and dipped him – or tried to. Not anticipating the sudden shift in gravity, Ethan's right leg failed to anchor him upright. Genuine surprise flashed across Rina's face. Ethan saw the exact moment where Rina decided she wasn't going to try salvage the move – then he landed flat on his back.

A chorus of gasps.

"Oops," said Rina.

"Sir!" someone exclaimed. "Are you alright?"

Ethan sat up. "I'm fine." He got to his feet in time to see Maddy elbowing her way over.

"My god, Edwin, can't even leave you alone for five seconds. Are you *drunk*?" Maddy turned to Rina, hands on hips. "What did you do?"

"Babysat," Rina replied sweetly. "It was your job, I believe."

"I'm sober," said Ethan.

Maddy wolf-whistled, windmilling one hand. "Oi. Jav!"

Ethan turned. "Wait, it's fine."

But it was too late. Jav – and half the bridal party – had been summoned. People parted across the dance floor and Jav was suddenly right there, radiant and definitely not sober.

"Hello!" Jav lifted Ethan with the force of his hug. "Where have you been?"

"Your stupid boyfriend fell on his arse," said Maddy.

"Oh *no*," cried Jav. "Why didn't you stop him?"

"It wasn't on purpose." Ethan swatted Jav's hands away. "What are you doing?"

"Checking for concussion." Jav stroked Ethan's hair clumsily. "Vegas told me how. Follow my finger."

"I will not."

"Concussion?" Carter had an arm around Elijah's neck, accent extra twangy thanks to inebriation. "Quick, someone call a healer!" He dissolved into giggles.

Clara rolled her eyes. She held out a hand to Rina. "Shall we? Stephen cannot jive at all. Let's go bother the band."

"With pleasure," said Rina.

"No, wait, what about me?" Stephen trailed after them.

They disappeared across the dance floor.

"Clara's right though," Jav stage whispered. "Stephen can't jive."

"Let's get you some water," Elijah said to Carter. He jerked his chin towards Jav, shooting Ethan a look. "This one has had too many as well. If you can't keep your own balance, I suggest finding a seat."

"Cheers," said Ethan.

"I don't want water," Carter whined as Elijah steered him towards the gallery. "I wanna foursome jive with Rina and Clara!"

Jav stared after them, blinking owlishly.

"Do you also want a foursome?" asked Ethan.

Jav turned back, circling Ethan's wrists with both hands. "Are you okay?"

"I just slipped."

"Not that. You feel..." Jav shook his head. "Wait, you were dancing? Without me?"

"Rina insisted. I wouldn't be too jealous. Pretty sure I annihilated her toes."

"Oh. What did she say? I'm sorry if—"

Ethan leaned up and pressed a kiss to Jav's frown. "Don't stress. I just wanted to see if we could smooth things over. Had a chat. We'll be alright."

"Oh. I'm so glad. Everyone's happy." Jav's eyes glistened comically. "I love weddings..."

Ethan returned the smile, a raw ache in his chest. "This is the first one I've been to. High bar." They were forehead to forehead, nose to nose. "Your speech turned out great, huh?"

"People laughed at my jokes!"

"Yes, very cute. Told you it'd be fine."

"You also said I'd get a dance..."

"I suppose I did promise." Clara and Rina spun past them at lightning speed, heels flashing. "You might have to ask for something easier."

Jav bounced on the balls of his feet, thrilled at Ethan's acquiescence. "I'll go request something we've danced to at home." He practically carried Ethan to a safe low-traffic corner. "I'll be right back. Don't dance with anyone else."

Ethan laughed, hiccupping from the pressure in his veins and the sting in his eyes. *If he loves you, does it matter why or how?* "Go on, I'll be here."

Why go searching for doubt? Ignorance was as blind as faith – and faith was a virtue.

TWENTY-THREE
—— PART I ——

1 Madeleine Avenue, Upper Chelsea, Level 22.
Monday, 10 April.

Anticipation warped yesterdays into lifetimes. If Jav didn't have Ethan, the weeks after Stephen's wedding would have been terribly lonely.

In deference to the looming election and scrutiny around the Earthflown tender, Clara and Stephen's honeymoon was a short, week-long affair in New Zealand. And even after he returned, business was business was business. Jav didn't see much of his best friend.

Change threw things off-kilter – like the time Carter lost his voice after his birthday bash and Elijah went mad with the silence. Perhaps it was Rina's lingering displeasure. Perhaps it was Peter's conspicuous absence.

When Jav asked Rina where her ghost was, Rina said, "You're always telling him to fuck off, so what's the problem?"

"He's fucked off...forever?"

"If you really wanted to know, he's babysitting Nath, et al."

Jav sighed. "Never mind, sorry I asked."

That more or less set the tone these days. Rina had never been partial to olive branches and grew more acerbic the longer Jav spent with Ethan. Yet, she still hadn't told anyone that Ethan knew about Jav's empathy. No doubt waiting for the right moment.

With ballet season in full swing, Carter and Elijah were too busy to hang out.

"What's stopping you from going back?" Ethan asked one evening.

They were watching videos in bed, Oliver and Vegas on the other side of the thin wall. Ethan only had one eye open, nose tucked under Jav's chin, a leg thrown over Jav's hip.

"Back where?" Jav yawned beneath the weight of Ethan's drowsy affection. *If only this could be bottled, we'd cure insomnia.*

"Ballet. You clearly miss it. Why not dance full time? It's not as if you have to work for a living. You can afford to do whatever makes you happy, so why don't you?"

Jav made a non-committal noise into Ethan's hair. "I was the only one off with my own thing. I wanted to spend more time with Giulia and Rina..."

The blink of Ethan's eyelashes tickled Jav's throat. "Elijah said most principals retire around forty. You've got me now, so let's double that."

Before Jav could respond, his phone flashed with an incoming call.

"Speak of the devil," Ethan groaned, squinting at the ID.

"Leave it," said Jav feeling impulsively brave. "I'll call her back later. If it's important Rina will make it known."

Ethan felt pleased, settling back against his pillow.

"Anyway. How about you?" asked Jav.

"Hmm?"

"Didn't you want to be a pilot? Are you doing what makes you happy?"

"I'm doing *someone* who makes me happy." Ethan waggled his eyebrows.

Perhaps one day Jav would earn an honest answer. "As flattering as that is..."

Ethan yanked him in by the neck. "I already have everything I want."

The next day. Tuesday, 11 April —— 3 pm.

THE EARTH SPUN FASTER with an election around the corner.

Ribbon cutting and endless PR events kept Jav busy at the Foundation. It spared Ethan the full force of Jav's neediness, spared Jav the angst of worrying 24/7 about Rina – and apparently spared Rina any obligation to come home before the wee hours.

Unfortunately, Charlie operated on Universal Idiot Time.

"I've got the swatches with me," the prat was saying. "We must finalise table settings for the engagement party."

Jav pinched the bridge of his nose. "Rina isn't at home right now. And you can hire people for this sort of thing."

"I want your opinion, since you've recently planned a wedding," Charlie interrupted, aggressively jovial. "Let me up, there's a good chap."

What an idiot. Even a blind man could see Rina was patently not interested. Despite his best efforts at ignorance, Jav knew that Rina was stringing Charlie along. How this insured her against Robert Langley's inevitable wrath was anybody's guess.

Privately, Jav suspected that Rina simply enjoyed making fools of others, and the whole charade had more to do with Charlie's ego than CM15. Whatever her motives, enough was enough – the man had proposed, for heaven's sake.

"Alright," Jav conceded. "Gimme a second."

"Goodo!" said Charlie and hung up.

Setting his book aside, Jav walked over to the nearest intercom. "Charles Langley is here," he enunciated, standing still for the biometrics. "Let him in." Jav left his suppressors off. With any luck, he could make Charlie so uncomfortable that this would be a very short visit. The intercom flashed an unhappy colour: *visitor is not on permitted guest list, override authorisation required.* Typical Rina. "Just this once is fine."

The intercom chirped in assent.

All too soon, the lift chimed, and Charles strode into the penthouse. Jav didn't know how one person could make so much noise doing something so simple.

"Javvers!" Charlie's smugness felt coarser than Peter's baseline, but they both stank out a room.

"Afternoon." Jav eyed the swatch-book under Charlie's left arm and a thick leather case in the other. "Shoes off, please."

"Ha! Rina will never know. Let's chat."

"I do have somewhere to be..."

Charlie was already halfway to the living room, shoes on. "You have no idea how difficult it's been, trying to plan this engagement." He dropped the leather case on a coffee table. "Are all your sisters secretly ghosts, or just the hot ones?"

Jav narrowed his eyes but didn't take the bait.

"We barely spoke at my uncle's birthday." Charlie collapsed onto a couch, knees spread, manners absent.

"It was a busy event," Jav deflected. Perhaps a frank one-on-one *was* sorely needed. God knows Rina wasn't going to let Charlie down gently. "Tea? Coffee?"

"Scotch, cheers."

"At three in the afternoon?" Jav resigned himself to the wet bar. "What are you having?"

"Gin and tonic," lied Jav, pouring himself sparkling water. "Don't you think Rina should be here for your swatches?"

"Rubbish." Charlie paused to accept his drink and threw it back. "Rina listens to you, which can't be said for the rest of us."

Jav snorted. "You'd be surprised."

"The lads have been hounding me for a date. Need to finalise numbers. It's time sensitive."

"I'll ask when I next see her."

"I'm happy to wait until she gets home."

No bloody way. "That mightn't be tonight."

"What's she so busy with that *isn't* our engagement?"

"The mind boggles."

"You can't blame a man for thinking he's been given the run-around." Charlie dipped into tangible irritation beneath his nonchalant smile.

Jav sat on an adjacent chaise. He stretched out his legs, putting one ankle over the other. "Far be it for me to comment on your relationship..."

"No, please, comment away. Women. Can never tell what's going on between their ears."

"Look." Jav slid a coaster beneath Charlie's empty glass, stalling. "Rina's not great at expressing her feelings."

"How so?"

Jav resisted the urge to drag a hand down his face. "You'll have to pardon my bluntness, but Rina doesn't respond well to surprises. And from what I've heard, you sprung that proposal on her."

"So you two *have* discussed it."

The vivid memory of Rina smashing vases. "Sort of." Jav projected a sense of contentment, not liking the way Charlie's emotions were ratcheting up so quickly. "If you want my advice, I'd say call off the engagement for now."

Something spiked beneath Charlie's static expression.

Jav wrinkled his nose and summoned his most recent memory of Ethan drooling onto his shoulder. *Be happy about this,* he pushed towards Charlie, *no one wants you here!*

"Rina told you she wanted to break off our engagement?" asked Charlie.

"Not in so many words. I'm sure she doesn't want to hurt your feelings."

"My feelings, ha!" Charlie's lip curled. "Your family does like trotting you out whenever there's an optics issue."

"What?" Jav realised he was holding his breath, an instinctive (and useless) response to unpleasant emotions. "Look, you're the one who came here with swatches. I don't want things to escalate more than they already have."

As soon as the words left his mouth, Jav realised he had stepped on a landmine – Charlie's anger flared like an oil fire. It rippled his expression for an ugly, revealing moment. His smile returned, but the fury stuck like tar to Jav's throat.

"She did say 'yes', you know. Made me a few promises, even."

Jav rolled his eyes. "I'm not sure what you were expecting, proposing in public before discussing things with her first."

"This has been years in the works."

"Rina saved you from public humiliation."

"As opposed to going back on her word when things are already in motion?"

"That's a conversation you need to have with her." Jav couldn't resist adding, "You should never back anyone into a corner. Not with this kind of commitment."

"How unfortunate." Charlie paused. "My uncle will be so disappointed."

"Postpone it then?"

"How? The election is almost upon us."

Good lord, the priorities on this man. Jav's patience was running thin. "You made things tricky for yourself with all those photos at the restaurant. But the press has a short memory. It'll blow over."

Charles squinted. Silence stretched, viscous. "...Are you talking about the actual engagement?"

Jav glanced at the swatches. "What else would we be talking about?"

For a minute, Charlie seemed lost for words. Then he started guffawing, slapping a hand on his knee. Perhaps Jav needed to try another emotion to persuade Charlie to leave. It was like tugging on a stray thread: one could never be sure whether it would unravel or snap.

"Alright," said Charlie. "If that's how you want to play it."

Jav stood. "I'll let Rina know you dropped by then."

Charlie didn't move. "I think you should call her. We're both here. Why wait?"

"I'm meeting someone for dinner. Have a few errands to handle. I'll walk you out."

"No, you won't," drawled Charlie. "Sit down."

"I beg your pardon?"

"Call your sister."

"You're free to call Rina yourself." Jav didn't need to be an empath to know that Charlie was teetering. He let his own impatience seep into the air, hoping to nudge Charlie into leaving.

"Like I said: Rina's been avoiding me." Charlie nodded at Jav's phone, laying on the sofa. "This won't take long."

Jav had had enough. "And as *I* mentioned, Rina does as she likes."

"It's just a phone-call."

"I have places to be." Jav took Charlie's unmasked irritation and reflected it back. "As do you, I'm sure."

"I'm so sorry, where are my manners?" Charlie reached for his leather case.

For a split second, Jav thought Charlie was finally leaving. Then something curled through his oesophagus, furious, invasively foreign.

Charlie pulled out a gun. "Call Rina," he said, resting the weapon against one knee. "Please and thank you."

Jav couldn't move, disbelief seizing his lungs. "What the hell do you think you're doing?"

"Persuading."

"You're not going to shoot me."

Charlie laughed. "You sound mighty confident."

Easy now. Easy. Maybe Jav could put Charlie to sleep. He thought desperately of Ethan's steady warmth, but the sensation slipped through his fingers, vision narrowed to the gun on the table. Jav breathed in slowly through his nose. He needed skin contact to make this work.

"There are records of you coming into the building," Jav tried. "It'd be obvious, if I'm dead."

"Nobody's dying. Don't be melodramatic."

"*Melodramatic*? You're the one threatening me with a gun because Rina doesn't want to marry you!"

"Marriage will be the least of your problems if you don't get Rina on the phone right now."

"And you think I'm more inclined to do so with a gun to my head? Put Rina in danger?" Jav cast out his senses in vain, trying to feel for Peter's familiar presence. *Where was the stupid ghost when you needed him?* "How do you expect to walk out of here?"

"With functioning kneecaps, unlike you." Charlie sneered.

"Though you are holding up better than I expected. Thought you'd have pissed yourself by now."

"And I thought *you'd* have left by now, yet here we are." Anger overpowered feared, apparently. *Stall for time until Peter gets here.* "Shall I call the healer, before you shoot me?"

"I suppose you and Rina did pop out of the same test tube." Charlie grinned. "Speaking of healers: yours should be in that ride I sent for him soon."

Jav's heart stopped. He opened his mouth, but no sound came out.

"Oh-ho. *Now* he listens." Charlie's breathing sped up to match the tempo of Jav's leaking panic.

"You're bluffing." Jav's voice cracked on the last syllable. "Ethan's shift—"

"Ends in about two hours. Enough time for Rina to come home. After we've had a nice chat, I'll call the lads off. How's that for persuasion?"

"Ethan's one of only three healers at St Ophie's. His father's at the SIA." Jav dug his nails into his palm, but his hands still shook. Static roared in his ears. "People will notice if something happens to him."

Charlie's mock-frown contrasted nauseatingly with a gleeful thirst. "What's there to notice? Dr Faulkner gets into a different sports car every night."

Jav was clammy with fear, and he knew Charlie could feel it too. Could he pretend to call Rina and message Ethan a warning? But if Charlie realised, the repercussions didn't bear thinking about. *The safe room. Contact Ethan and Peter from there.* First, Jav had to get past the gun.

Charlie was still talking. "The last thing I'd want to do is harm a healer. Imagine the bad luck." He chuckled. "Then again, I'm not a superstitious man."

Jav bolted for the stairs. He almost made it.

"I don't *think* so!" Charlie shouted, a second before something split the wood at Jav's feet.

Jav threw himself forwards. Another *thwuck* of air; burn of heat.

An arm hooked around his neck. "You—!"

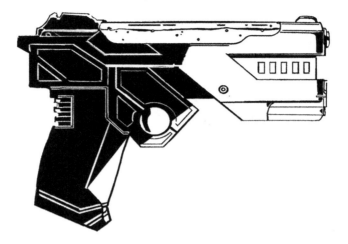

Jav swung his elbow back – it connected with Charlie's sternum, making him stumble. It had been years since Rina forced Peter to teach Jav 'a few moves', but Jav always had good balance. He swept Charlie's feet out with a kick. The man went down like a tonne of bricks, genuine surprise breaking through his violent exhilaration.

"Fuck!"

Jav turned, heart in his mouth. He made it past the landing before Charlie tackled him bodily to the floor. Jav's chin clipped the hardwood step on the way down, blood filling his mouth. He coughed, blinking away the starburst of pain.

Charlie flipped him onto his back, pinning both of Jav's wrists with one meaty hand and crushing the air from Jav's lungs with a knee to diaphragm. They were both heaving, hearts tripping in tandem as fear and excitement looped and refracted larger and larger. Jav's empathic echo reduced them both to a racing cocktail of noradrenaline and adrenaline; impossible to tell where the fear began and where the vicious giddiness ended.

He stared down at Jav, eyes wild.

"Listen—" Jav's head snapped to one side as Charlie punched him hard across the face.

"I didn't come here to make a mess," said Charlie, out of breath, "but God, it feels good to wipe that smug look off your face."

Jav coughed wetly. "I—"

Charlie hit him again. And again. He quickly settled into the rhythm of things. "Rina thinks she's so bloody clever. Thinks she's got me eating out of the palm of her hand. It takes it out of you, pretending to be a simpering idiot for so long." He wiped his bloody knuckles on Jav's shirt collar. "After everything my uncle has done for your family, Rina thinks she can go behind our backs? Cut us out with Sainte-Ophies? No." He yanked Jav's head up by the hair. "*Well?*"

Blood trickled over Jav's chin. He tried to blink the blurriness from his vision. "I d-don't know what you're talking about."

"And I suppose Marc Sainte-Ophie just happens to be here on holiday?"

"Stephen's wedding," Jav managed. Consonants hurt. "We invited—"

Charlie backhanded Jav hard enough to stun. "Don't *lie*. No wonder Arden Pharma has been so brazen about fusive investments. You've thrown your lot in with the Mansfields – and no doubt Sainte-Ophies have agreed not to rock the boat. Tell me, what were their terms? Not to encroach on territory? Price fixing? They've been stonewalling me, so I assume you must have offered something good."

The aquarium light rippled across Charlie's dark eyes. Jav could feel the rachet of bile and marrow-thick anger.

"I told him this would happen," Charlie continued, voice low. "I fucking told him: can't trust any of you snakes. Beatrice Arden isn't running the show anymore. But Uncle Bobby's getting old. Short-sighted." Without warning, Charlie relinquished Jav's hair in favour of his left hand. "That's the dangerous thing about living too long: you think you'll live forever, you stop caring. We all need an expiry date."

Charlie pressed against the base of Jav's thumb – and casually dislocated it.

A gasping *pop* of pain, scarlet bright. Jav screamed.

"I suspected that Rina had always planned to squeeze us dry," Charlie said, matter of fact. He bent Jav's thumb backwards, dragging the scream into a choking sob. "I did try to warn her first, you know. Make the point that it'd be best to maintain our current relationship."

"No, *no*, s-stop—" *How was Charlie not feeling this? God, it hurts.*

Jav couldn't breathe through his nose or his throat, tacky with blood. He choked.

"Maybe I should have gone for a more direct approach from the get-go," Charlie continued, his slick-hot satisfaction filling Jav's lungs. "Instead of letting Nathaniel bumble around. I mean, what a time for Rina to develop a sense of self-control! I delivered a perfect scapegoat on a silver platter, and she never capitalised on it." He massaged Jav's dislocated joint, attention sharpening in pleasure at every flinch and spasm.

Jav's heels caught uselessly on the lip of the staircase. *Scapegoat? Oh god, Nathaniel and the shooter.* He gulped desperately for air.

"Fucking useless, the lot of you." Charlie buzzed with something close to lust but twice as visceral. He shifted, knee in Jav's stomach.

It hurt to think, words rattling against Jav's skull like loose teeth in a jar. Peter was right – just about the wrong Langley. Charlie was behind this the whole time.

"The funniest thing is that Uncle Bobby didn't think my plan would work either." Charlie leaned in, nose to nose. "But I'm not letting him flush my inheritance down the sewer."

Jav wrenched his good hand free, clawing blindly at Charlie's face, palm to cheek, a thumb against his eye socket. Knocking Charlie unconscious was out of the question; Jav was in too much pain to try. He thrust all the heart-tripping fear outwards, projecting, deafened by the internal shriek of *go, leave now, you're scared, get off me, just leave, run, LEAVE!*

There was an answering jolt – a heart flipping over.

Charlie let go of Jav with a full-bodied flinch, eyes growing wide. "What the fuck was that?" he shouted.

Jav scrambled backwards, hitting the wall. For a suspended moment they stared at each other, Jav's palm outstretched, placating. He went cold at the realisation dawning in Charlie's eyes.

"Holy shit," Charlie said, syllables like molasses. "*You.*" He started to laugh, high and manic. "Oh, this makes so much sense. You're an empath. You've—!"

Jav threw himself sideways as Charlie lunged forwards, but instead of a fist, Charlie wrapped both hands around Jav's throat. Jav choked, kicking but contacting air. He projected revulsion to try and trigger a reflexive recoil.

"Don't even think about it," Charlie snarled. "You're not gonna be able to manipulate me now that I know what you are."

Careless of his dislocated thumb, Jav clawed at the unyielding fingers around his trachea, vision narrowing, hyper-focused. *Oh god, he knows. He knows.* The vicious hammer of spite, fear, and desperation threatened to snap his ribs. *He can't know, he can't be allowed to know, he can't—*

Jav wrapped his hands around Charlie's wrists. He could feel Charlie's pulse trip and race as he pressed harder on Jav's throat, the empathic loop sewing them together. They were both choking now.

Summoning his last thread of control, Jav projected a shrieking panic that finally, *finally,* forced Charlie relinquish his grip. But Jav didn't let go. He let the undiluted terror balloon into Charlie's lungs in a sobbing, gasping mess.

Charlie jerked like a marionette, lips blue, eyes bulging, wheezing as if he were the one pinned by the throat. Jav kicked blindly. His heel met Charlie's right knee.

Charlie stumbled backwards – and crashed bodily down the stairs. He did not get back up.

For a long minute, Jav knelt, frozen on the landing. "...Charlie?" he croaked.

No response.

Hand on the bannister, Jav stumbled downstairs, heart slowing to match the steady drip of dread. He dropped to his knees, taking in the whites of Charlie's eyes and blue of his lips. Jav's hands shook so badly that he couldn't find a pulse. He checked beneath Charlie's nose and above his open mouth. Nothing.

Oh god, thought Jav, nerves numb. *What have I done?*

He staggered towards the sofa, fumbling for his phone with his non-dominant hand. *Rina would know what to do. Rina.* Jav hesitated over her name, long enough for drops of blood to hit the glass. He wiped it away and hit call.

The phone rang and rang.

A few feet away, Charlie stared sightlessly up at Rina's multicoloured fish.

The phone kept ringing. It was hard to focus on the text, too bright. Jav counted the dial tones but had to keep starting over. Eventually, he couldn't wait anymore.

Jav pressed Ethan's profile, leaving Rina's line ringing in the background. *Please be okay. Please pick up, please pick up...*

Ethan answered on the third ring. "Good timing. Just came out of surgery."

The familiar voice splintered the frame of Jav's shock, rending a sob from his throat, phone slipping onto the coffee table with a clatter of glass and metal.

"Jav?" said Ethan, clearly alarmed. "What's wrong?"

It took several coughs for Jav to find words. "Where are you?"

"I'm at work, what's going on?"

"Don't leave the hospital," Jav pleaded. "The cameras...stay with someone. Somewhere public. Don't move. Is Vegas...?"

"Breathe," Ethan raised his voice above Jav's hiccupping gasps. "Vegas is two floors down. What's happened?"

Jav coughed, trying to inhale past the blood clogging his nose and glass in his throat. He could hear movement, other voices in the background: Ethan was walking.

"No!" Jav shouted. "Don't go outside!"

"I'm inside, calm down. You're okay. Breathe."

Every sense was blurred by horror and water. Charlie's face, and the rictus of his last moments, were the only things in focus.

"Tell me what's happened." Ethan's voice cut through. "Jav?"

Jav pressed a fist to his mouth. "*Ethan,*" he sobbed, "Ethan, I think I've killed someone."

TWENTY-THREE
—— PART II ——

The Sentinel Studios, Upper Bloomsbury, Level 13.
Tuesday, 11 April —— 4.10 pm.

With the election barely three weeks away, the entire newsroom was over-caffeinated and under-slept. There was wall-to-wall coverage of the CM15 versus fusive debate. Everyone and their pets had an opinion.

Florence kept muttering, "If I hear the word 'infrastructure' one more time..."

Any nuance had long since been whittled to an argument about long-term gains and short-term pain (read: terms in office). And when those with the shortest life expectancy were expected to bear the cost of transition...it was neither constructive or interesting.

The phone rang, interrupting Ollie's procrastination. Vegas. *Odd.* She rarely called mid-shift.

Ollie swiped the screen. "To what do I owe the pleasure?"

A voice that was decidedly not Vegas said, "This is an emergency, don't hang up."

Ollie sighed. "How many times do I have to say it: stop using Vegas's account—"

"There's no time, shut up," said Ethan. "I can't get a hold of dad. Where are you right now?"

"The studios. Why? Did something happen to Ian?"

"Dad's fine. I assume. But he's not answering me so I need you to go down to the precinct. Tell him to call me back and...actually, no tell him to meet me on Level 22. I'll give you the address. Do *not* talk to anyone else before dad."

Well that's not ominous. "Ian's still pissed at me, what makes you think I'll have better luck? Are you okay?"

"No time for an interview," Ethan snapped. "Please, for once in your life, help me without the twenty questions."

Ethan, for all his faults, was much like Vegas in several respects. Chiefly, neither were prone to fluster. This panic was real.

Unease stirred in Ollie's stomach. "Sneeze if you're not okay."

"What?" Ethan was clearly distracted. "Look, I can't stay on. Have to call Ja— get dad. I wouldn't ask if I wasn't desperate."

"Javier's involved?" Ollie demanded, instead of screaming 'I told you he was bad news!' at the top of his lungs. He swiped his satchel, checked his phone, and sprinted towards the lifts. "Are you safe or not?"

"I'm fine," Ethan said, inflectionless. "There's been an incident. Jav didn't sound right on the phone. I don't think he's alone right now. Police bursting into his flat might make things worse."

"Why? Wait, you've called an ambulance, right?"

"Don't call *anyone* else until I figure out—"

"If it's an emergency, then it's a situation for emergency serv—"

"I *am* the emergency services!" Ethan shouted.

"You're..." Ollie hammered the lift button. "Ethan, are you *not* at St Ophie's?"

"...I'm en route to Jav's place."

"If you think it's not safe—!"

"Hang on." A horn blared; the sound of wind screaming close to the mic. "Fuck, I need to talk to dad. Jav said Charlie had people waiting for me outside—"

"What?!" Ollie hollered.

"—can't see anyone following me though. Maybe I gave them the slip. I left via the Level 10 A&E bay, but Vegas is still at the hospital."

"Back up, back up. Charlie. As in Charles Langley?"

"Corinna's fiancé, yeah."

"And you're running over to do *what* exactly?" howled Ollie, thankful for the empty lift.

"Dispense medical care."

"No! Stay put! Stay where you are!" The lift arrived at street level and Ollie tore through the lobby, attracting curious glances. He tried calling Vegas from his watch to no avail. "Have you called Nick? He'll get a hold of Ian faster."

"Nick blocked me."

"Shit," Ollie muttered. The *one* time Nick took his advice. "Is Vegas okay?"

"She can't take calls, her shift doesn't end for a couple hours. I need to go, Jav isn't replying." Clang of glass and metal. "Everything should be on emergency mode when dad gets here."

"Wait—!" Ollie shouted, but the line went dead. "*Fuck.*"

The cold evening air leaked, grime and all, from lungs to bone. It was fastest to take the pedestrian lift to Level 10, but Ian might not even be there. Ollie pulled up Nick's personal number. After ten rings, he swapped to Nick's work number. When that also went unanswered, he resorted to texting.

> 16:13 · OLIVER — Emergency. Need to talk to Ian. Is he at L10?

> 16:13 · OLIVER — This isn't about a story or Hersch. Actual emergency.

> 16:13 · OLIVER — NICK.

> 16:13 · OLIVER — Ethan's in trouble.

As Ollie joined the long queue for the Level lifts, his phone rang. "Well, look who it is," he said, tabbing his recording app.

"Cut the crap," said Nick. "What's going on? I'm out."

Ollie knew he had less than ten words before Nick hung up. "Ethan's running away from Langley's people."

"*What?*"

"He called me, en route to Javier's place. Said Charles Langley had people waiting outside St Ophie's, so Ethan 'gave them the slip', quote unquote, and flew—"

"By himself?" Nick demanded. "He doesn't know how!"

"He couldn't get Ian on the phone and I'm having no luck. Said he called you—"

"I'll try Ian now. How did Ethan get on Langley's radar?"

"Via Javier, obviously. For Ethan to run off mid-shift...I mean, the hospital's gonna know almost immediately that a healer's MIA, right? Why wouldn't Javier or Ethan call nine-nine-nine?"

"I'll find out," Nick replied. "Give me the address."

"Aren't you emotionally compromised—"

"If something happens to Ethan while we're chit-chatting, I'll kill you."

Ollie chewed his lip. "Fine, they're on Level 22." He took the stairs two at a time, battling against the tide of early commuters. "Forwarding you the location now. Upper Chelsea."

"Good, I'm not far." the ride down was tortuously slow. When the call reconnected, all he could hear was wind and strained breathing. A sudden hush, isolated by a helmet.

"You there?" asked Nick.

Ollie sprinted across the street before the lights changed. "What about Ian—"

"Claudia says he's in a meeting. She's gone to get him. Ian wasn't answering so I messaged the pod. Figured someone would be at the precinct."

"That was fast. You never text me back that quickly."

"If you ever give me a good reason to, I will. You at the precinct yet?"

"Two blocks away." Ollie weaved past a school of pedestrians. "What did you tell Clauds?"

"That it was a family emergency." Nick's breathing through the mic was strained, metronomic in a way that suggested he was calmly freaking out. "How long ago did Ethan call you?"

"I dialled you right after we hung up, so..." Ollie checked his phone log. "4.13 pm."

"And you said he tried calling me before that."

"Yeah." Ollie paused outside the precinct's double doors for the security scanner. "Alright, I'm here!" He pushed past the small line at the reception desk. "Sorry, I have Agent Holt on the phone. Ian Garner is expecting me. It's about his son."

The receptionist raised her eyebrows. "And you are...?"

"Oliver Roskopf. Nick, I assume you told Clauds that I was on my way?"

The receptionist tapped something on their console.

Nick didn't seem to be following the conversation. "He's not picking up. Fuck. I shouldn't have blocked him. A lot can happen in fifteen minutes. All for some petty, stupid—"

"Hey! Snap out of it." Ollie eyed the door leading to the non-public areas of the station.

Another leaden pause.

"I'm here," Nick announced. "There's a solo-flier. EMS bike. Can't see Ethan. One sec." The acoustics shifted as he discarded his helmet. "Hate breathing in that thing."

"Ethan mentioned the place should be on emergency mode."

"Why?" Nick asked sharply.

"No clue. Ethan hung up on me, I think he's already upstairs."

Nick's breathing rasped, shallow with impatience above the faint noises of the street. "Fuck it. I'm going in."

"Oi, I'm just as worried about him as you are, but you need to *stop* and think about—"

"I'm not sitting around for twenty, thirty minutes while—"

"We don't know what kind of—!"

"Ethan rang me and you about being followed. Whatever's going on, a healer is not qualified to handle it. He's not responding. I've got my stunner, I'll be fine."

"Christ, I — stay on the line then," said Ollie.

"Right," said Nick. A brief silence. "I'm in the lobby."

"Oliver!" It was Ian in the doorway, Claudia hot on his heels. "What the hell is going on? Where's Ethan?"

"Thank god, finally." To Nick, Ollie said, "I've got Ian. Putting you on speaker."

"Is that Ethan?" asked Ian, mouth thin with worry.

"No, it's Nick." Ollie followed Ian and Claudia through the double security doors and into the nearest free interview room. He set his phone on the desk.

"Where are you?" asked Ian.

"One Madeleine Avenue, Chelsea, Level 22." Nick recited. "Ollie will brief you. Entering the private lift now."

"Ethan's at Javier's place. He got a call from Javier about Charles Langley having him watched or followed at St Ophie's," Ollie recounted rapidly. "Said that Javier wasn't 'safe'. Asked for you specifically; adamant that we didn't call triple-nine." Ollie was conscious of the ticking time and Claudia's presence. "Any idea what he's talking about?"

Ian's hands were white knuckled. "No. His text was bare bones. When was the last mes—"

A tinny *ding* rang through the phone, followed almost immediately by a distinctive *crack*.

"Ethan!" Nick shouted.

"Nick, I—" Ethan's voice cut off.

The blood drained from Ian's face. "Ethan? Holt? What's going on?" No response. "Report!"

A sudden peal of laughter sliced through Nick's harsh breathing. The call cut out.

For a cold, awful moment, no one moved.

"Did Nick hang up?" Ollie frowned, redialling.

It rang, and rang, and rang.

Claudia was wide-eyed. "That sounded like..."

"MMLA handgun. Not a firearm." Ian took a step towards the door and swayed slightly on his feet. "God." His voice broke. "*Ethan.*"

Ollie and Claudia shared a concerned look.

"Sir..." she began.

Something shuttered over the grief-lines of Ian's face. "Alert med dispatch. We also need a team to go to St Ophie's. I'll handle it." He pinned Ollie with a glare. "Wait here for me."

And before Ollie could protest, they both swept out of the room. Later, Ollie would blame the shock for his inertia – because a whole minute passed before he realised that Ian had taken Ollie's phone with him.

1 Madeleine Avenue, Upper Chelsea, Level 22.
—— 5.15 pm.

LUCKILY FOR OLIVER, he still had his Sentinel employee-card, which allowed him to hail a cab. Less luckily, rush-hour had started.

Ollie arrived at a scene of controlled chaos.

Police cruisers blocked the intersection. Two ambulances, three solo-fliers, and a few black cars with tinted windows clustered around a private entrance at street level. Curious passers-by hovered, patrons gathering outside shop fronts to gawk.

Ollie sprinted down the main road (the autocab refused to stop any closer) and spared a wondering glance up at the tall trees lining the pavement. Beyond the foliage was an unobstructed view of the *sky*.

An officer flung out an arm as Ollie tried to shoulder past. "Street's closed," she said.

"Is Ethan okay? Garner's expecting me — hey, Claudia!" Ollie waved madly, craning his neck around the parked vehicles.

For a second, Claudia clearly considered ignoring him. Then she walked over. "Garner's aware," she explained. To Ollie, she crossed her arms. "No recordings."

"Where's Nick? Ethan?"

"They're fine, but — oi!"

Ollie swerved around the nearest ambulance. And there was Ethan, wrapped in a foil blanket, alive and well enough to be arguing with his dad. Ollie exhaled in a rush.

"You didn't see the state of him!" Ethan was shouting. "I'm the only healer here, so let—"

Ian shook Ethan by the shoulders. "If you think you're going anywhere near an Arden ever again, you have another think coming!" he roared.

"Sir, you can't heal anybody right now," the paramedic tried. "Your VM—"

"Fuck my VM," spat Ethan, squirming in Ian's arm-lock. "It's amber because you lot are pissing me off." His eyes widened at the sight of Ollie, frozen next to the ambulance.

Ian followed Ethan's gaze "For the love of...Roskopf, this is not the time or place."

"You took my phone," Ollie blurted. To Ethan, he said, "Glad to see you're alive. Where's Nick?"

"Let go. *Dad.*"

"I thought either you or Nick got shot," said Ollie. "What happened?"

Ethan opened his mouth.

"No," said Ian sharply.

Before Ollie could persist, Nick emerged from the building, flanked by two officers – no visible injuries.

"Oh, thank fuck, *Nick*," called Ollie, relief flooding his lungs. "Nick!"

Nick looked over. His gaze slid from Ollie to Ethan as he drew level with them, expression crumpling, thin as paper but twice as sharp.

One of the officers stepped towards Ethan. "Sir, I'm afraid you'll need to come back to the station with us."

"Can't this wait?" asked Ian. "He's in shock."

They all looked at Ethan's annoyed, dour expression.

The officer nodded towards the paramedic. "If Dr Faulkner's been cleared, I have instructions to question all witnesses." His tone grew sheepish under the weight of Ian's disapproval. "Without delay."

Nick held up a hand. "I already said I shot him."

Ollie stared, dumbstruck.

"There's no need to keep Ethan here," Nick continued, "I'm sure St Ophie's is desperate to get their healer back."

"Sorry, you shot *who*?" asked Ollie.

"Stay out of this." Nick raised his voice as he was ushered towards a police cruiser. "I mean it. Ollie!"

Ollie tried to follow – then froze. A pair of medical personnel had emerged from the building, stretcher afloat between them. Blurred by the translucent cryo-seal over the stretcher was the silhouette of a body.

Ollie spun on his heels, mind careening. But Nick was nowhere to be seen.

TWENTY-THREE
—— PART III ——

St Ophie's Hospital, Lower Lambeth, Level 9.
A few hours earlier ↺ —— 3.41 pm.

E than became hyper-aware of every single person around him. In
his ear, Jav was an incomprehensible mess of sobbing hiccups.
"Jav, listen to me. Slow breaths." His chest ached in sympathy
with Jav's wet coughs. "That's it. Are you alone? Are you safe?"

"Yes."

"Yes, you're alone, or yes, you're safe?"

"Um, both. Charlie's here, but..."

Ethan frowned. "Douchebag Charlie?"

"I only wanted to scare him, so he'd get off me," Jav slurred. "I
overdid it. Oh *God*, Ethan, I—"

"Deep breaths." Ethan cut him off before Jav could say anything else over an open phone line. He pitched his voice low and unhurried. "Can you do that for me? Three in, three out."

"O-okay. I'm sorry."

"Don't be sorry, it's alright. Are you hurt? You sound different."

A pause. "Blocked nose. Punched. Can't move my thumb."

Ethan's universe narrowed to Jav's voice, drowning out his surroundings with painful static. "Stay on the line, I'm calling emergency—"

"No! Don't! Charlie's dead, and if they find out about my—" Jav dissolved into sobs again.

"Okay, okay, what if *I* head over—"

Jav shrieked, the sound raising every hair on Ethan's arms. "You can't leave the hospital! Charlie said there's people waiting for you outside, where I usually pick you up, he said he's been watching you, please stay inside where everyone can see."

At this rate, Jav was gonna have a panic attack and pass out. "Javier, listen to me!"

Jav hiccupped into silence.

"I'm perfectly safe. My VM tracks my every move, remember?" Ethan strode down the hall, taking a shortcut to the goods-lift. "Hun? You still there?"

"Yes, but..."

"Are you at home?"

A wet cough. "Yes."

"I'll be there as soon as I can." With luck, Ethan could slip out the A&E bay on Level 10, avoiding any unpleasant encounters on Level 9. He entered the goods lift. "I'll take an EMS flier. Fifteen, twenty minutes, tops."

"But Charlie said..."

"Emergency vehicles automatically reroute other vehicles. Anyone weaving around will look very suspicious." The lift chimed to a stop. "I need a favour though."

"Okay."

At least Jav had calmed down. "Make sure your flat's security is set to emergency mode," said Ethan. "Sometimes called 'first responder mode'. Can you do that for me?"

"I think so." Footsteps. Muffled words.

Ethan increased the volume in his earpiece just in time for someone's ringtone to drill a hole through his brain. "Shit!" he hissed.

An answering *thump*. "Sorry!" cried Jav. "It's Rina, she didn't pick up before. She'll know what to do. Hang on."

"Wait—!" The hold-tone cut him off.

Cursing, Ethan slammed through two sets of doors and into the emergency dispatch bay. A few ambulances and solo fliers were parked in their charging stations.

A paramedic looked up as Ethan walked in – recognition flashing across his face at the glowing VM on Ethan's temple. He leapt to his feet. "Sir, what do you need?"

"I've been called out to an incident on Level 22," Ethan lied. *I'm so fucked after this. The disciplinary panel will have a field day.*

"Ambulance three is charged, I'll—"

"No need." Ethan undocked the helmet from the nearest EMS bike. "I'll take this one."

"Really?" The paramedic cleared his throat. "I mean, surely you'll need a team to assist. Sir."

The man's hesitance was understandable: on the rare occasions that healers were set out, they never went unaccompanied, let alone fly themselves. This paramedic looked around Ethan's age, which was to say, younger. Inexperienced. Probably wouldn't push back too much.

Ethan swung a leg over the seat and tried to hide the wobble. He slapped his pass to the dashboard, wrapping his hands around the handlebars for verification. The built-in sensor glowed between his fingers, the loading animation idling as it scanned. After a pause, the flier hummed to life, a green light whipping up and down the length of its tailfin: authorisation cleared.

Phew. "I'll be fine, thanks—" Ethan glanced at the man's name tag "—Hamish."

Stabilisers extended beneath Ethan's feet. He pressed his ankles against the body of the flier. Safety bands clicked snug around his ankles and calves. Pulling on the helmet, he slotted his phone into the mount and tapped Jav's address. Jav's contact photo smiled up from the console. The hold-tone beeped like an empty IV drip.

Ethan minimised the picture, selecting the flier's driverless option with a twist-push of the right handle. "Alright phone. Call dad's personal number."

He prayed that flying in real life was going to be as easy as in VR.

▶━━◀ ▶━◀ ▶━◀

Somewhere on the express flight path near Level 14, the City of London —— 4 pm.

THE LAST TIME Ethan flew solo was two years ago on a closed course, under Nick's watchful eye.

This was different.

As the route cleared itself for him, the flier ratchetted faster until Ethan's torso almost detached from his hips. St Ophie's emergency designation allowed him to switch rapidly between roads, express-ways, and other airspace with dizzying speed.

Ethan flattened himself against the dashboard when the flier began its curving ascent, bypassing Level 13 via a light-rail route. His kidneys were still on Level 11. Ten minutes had passed since he left St Ophie's: his dad wasn't picking up and Jav still had him on hold. After this, Ethan never wanted to hear a dial tone again.

"Alright, phone: call Nick."

The call disconnected before it could ring through. For a moment, Ethan couldn't figure out what happened. He tried Nick's work number: straight to voicemail. In a fit of desperation, he switched to Vegas's account. Both calls were rejected. *Blocked.*

It never occurred to Ethan that Nick might cut him off so cleanly. It hurt, in the way I-told-you-sos often did. A voice (Ollie's) piped up: *karma.*

Ethan shook his head. There would be time for emotions later. He dictated a message into the helmet. "Sorry to randomly text. I can't get a hold of dad. It's an emergency. Is he with you? If not, do you know where? Please get him to call me ASAP."

An instantaneous response: message could not be delivered.

"Fuck." There was no telling what kind of conversation Jav was having with Rina right now. And if Jav really was home with a corpse...

'Ethan, I think I've killed someone.'

The flier banked left as all the lights switched green ahead. Ethan ground his teeth against the swooping gravity. Was it even *possible* to kill someone via empathic projection? Perhaps Jav had simply overdosed Charlie on noradrenaline and adrenaline. Respiratory failure was plausible. But anything sustained enough to trigger cardiac arrest would surely loop back on the empath themselves. If Charlie was dead, Jav wouldn't be lucid enough to make a phone call.

Whatever the facts, a healthy wealthy thirty-something did not casually drop dead for no reason. With Jav sobbing a confession...Ethan wondered to what lengths Rina would go, to keep the bodies buried.

He tried texting his dad again. Several minutes passed, elongated like the blur of passing city lights. Ethan's lips would have been chewed raw if his skin could sustain such memories.

Defeated, Ethan switched his number and rang the one person who never failed to answer when Vegas called.

1 Madeleine Avenue, Upper Chelsea, Level 22.
—— 4.13 pm.

BY THE TIME Ethan arrived at Jav's building, he couldn't feel anything below the waist. He stumbled off the flier, hissing expletives, and almost faceplanted thanks to pins-and-needles. He wrenched off the flight helmet, gulping in the crisp early-evening air as he depressed a latch to pull out the heavy EMS kit.

Ethan staggered through the gate, the private lobby, and into the lift. The intercoms were blinking red: first-responder mode. His knuckles were stiff enough to break skin as he clutched the bag.

Ethan took one step into the flat and the giant vase to his right promptly exploded. "Bloody hell!" Shards of china sliced through his sleeve, one scoring across his cheek.

"Oh," said Rina. "It's you."

"What the fuck do you think you're—" Ethan dropped the kit. "Shit, *Jav*."

Across the living room, Jav sat hunched, Rina standing over him, one hand in his hair, the other palm-up towards Ethan and flickering blue. Smoke settled fast, weighed by kneecapping relief.

Rina squinted at Ethan. "How did you get in?"

"The lift." Ethan couldn't look away from Jav's face.

Jav stared back. He might have been wide-eyed if they weren't swelling shut. The left side of his face was blotchy, a ring of bruises forming around his throat. Blood stained his hairline and mouth.

"*Ethan*," said Jav, hoarse. "Thank god, you're okay."

"I'm—? You're the one who—" The last time Ethan felt so blindsided, Jav had been unconscious on the floor. This time, anger thawed the paralysis. Ethan found himself kneeling by Jav's chair with no memory of moving. "You told me someone punched you, not *beat you to a pulp*!" His gaze fell to Jav's swollen hand. "This won't take a minute."

"Wait." Rina grabbed Ethan by the shoulder. "Not yet."

Ethan prayed for patience. "What do you mean, 'not yet'?"

"I haven't figured out what to do with Charlie. That's evidence."

Calm down. The last thing Jav needed was Ethan's anger making things worse. He turned Jav's injured hand over carefully, making no effort to reign in his instincts. Jav's bruises flashed dark in a colourful timelapse as they healed. *No splinters in the bone.* Ethan laid Jav's hand flat on his palm. "I'm going to set your thumb, okay? It'll only hurt for a sec."

Jav nodded. The split in his lip knitted itself closed.

"On the count of three," said Ethan. "*One.*" Jav made an awful sound as Ethan pressed the joint back into place. "Shh, almost. We'll scan your hand then get you to the hospital. Keep still." *No internal bleeding.* Jav's pulse tripped against skin contact – perhaps due to secondary healing or stress – but gradually, laboriously, it began to slow.

Ethan waited a second longer before getting up. He palmed Jav's cheek, chasing the last of the swelling. It did nothing to clear the rage filling his throat.

Jav twitched but didn't pull away.

Rina tutted. "*Now* who's gonna believe that Charlie attacked Jav?"

"If it's the police you're worried about, they'll take my word for it," said Ethan. "No reason for Jav to be in pain while I'm here."

Disdain lined every angle of Rina's pretty face. She turned to her brother. "Have you invited anybody else that I should know about?"

"N-no."

"Why? Need a new vase to shrapnel them with?" Ethan thumbed the bridge of Jav's nose, double checking for residual swelling. Blood flaked onto his nail. *No fractures. Good.* "Let's get you cleaned up," he said gently.

"But Charlie—" Jav started.

"Is dead, and can wait," said Ethan.

"He's not dead," said Rina.

"I'm sorry?" Ethan looked from one twin to the other. "Jav said..."

"Charlie still has a pulse. Or he did, when I checked ten minutes ago." Rina stepped aside to reveal a body at the foot of the stairs.

"Good Lord." Ethan strode across the room and crouched down. He braced himself and pressed two fingers to Charlie's wrist. Sure enough: a weak pulse. *At least Jav isn't on the hook for homicide – yet.* The knuckles of Charlie's right fist were bloodied and bruised.

Ethan lifted his hand before any injuries could heal. "How long has he been out?"

"Forty minutes," said Jav.

"Can you wake him up?" asked Rina. "I've got questions."

"We need an ambulance." Ethan pulled out his phone.

Rina slapped it out of his hand. "Charlie's not going anywhere until I'm finished."

"Good luck asking questions if he can't wake up!"

"Rina's right," said Jav. "Charlie can't leave. He knows about me." The temperature wavered with each word. "He knows I'm an empath."

Ethan froze. "What? *How?*"

Rina rolled her eyes. "Jav was too heavy handed. Weren't you, Jav?"

"I wanted to scare him off!"

Jav's guilt hit the back of Ethan's throat like bile and he caught Jav's wrist before he could start wringing his hands.

"Keep still." Ethan thought calm thoughts as forcefully as possible. Judging by Jav's pale face, it wasn't working. "It'll be alright—"

Jav shook his head, movement jerky. "I tried to be careful. But Charlie got more and more worked up. Excited. Angry. I didn't mean to—"

"You just panicked." Rina sounded both fond and derisive. "No pain tolerance."

"I couldn't block it out, he—! Skin contact!" Jav mimed bending his thumb backwards. "I can't control my reaction and Charlie realised the spike wasn't his. Maybe if I had been wearing suppressors, my projections wouldn't have been so—"

"Are you sure Charlie thought it was *empathic*?" asked Ethan, conscious of the seconds slipping by.

"He said so, b-before I...before..." Jav trailed off, eyes drifting to Charlie's prone form.

"Gave him a panic attack until he passed out," Rina finished.

Jav covered his face with both hands and moaned.

Ethan glared at Rina. "More likely that the fall knocked him out, rather than any empathic influence."

"That doesn't make it better," cried Jav.

"Exactly," said Rina. "*I* can push someone down the stairs. Inducing a panic attack is much more impressive. If only it didn't send *you* into a spiral of angst."

Ethan raised his eyebrows. "You seem far less concerned about your violent fiancé knowing about Jav's aptitude than you were about me."

"Why should I be concerned? It's not like Charlie's gonna be able to talk, once I'm done with him."

And I'm sure I wouldn't be able to talk if you had it your way. Ethan shoved the doubt aside, fighting Jav's hair-raising anxiety.

On the floor, his phone rang – and Ethan lunged for it: two missed calls from Nick, the third call having just bypassed silent mode. He muted the volume with a flick of his thumb. "Work," he lied, shoving the phone into his pocket. "Someone's noticed my absence."

Rina smiled, eyes shrewd. "You should answer that. People might be dying."

"They tend to do that in a hospital." Ollie must have got through to

Nick, but no one's reached dad yet, otherwise he would have called by now. At least fifteen minutes must have passed since Ethan arrived. "We should do something about—" Ethan nodded at Charlie "—now."

Rina leaned over her fiancé. "Do you think he sustained brain damage? Can you check with your...?" She wiggled her fingers.

"I didn't feel any fractures, but that's no prerequisite for a brain injury," said Ethan. "Especially with the empathic variable thrown in. There's no guarantee that Charlie will – or won't – wake up lucid."

"He'll tell Robert," Jav whispered, face pale. "The police—"

"Nah," dismissed Rina. "This is perfect leverage. Charlie will blackmail us, given the opportunity."

"Opportunity we won't give him," said Ethan. "Right?"

Jav's nail-on-chalk fear was sanding all the enamel from Ethan's teeth. He coughed, trying to dislodge the bitter film, disturbed once more by Rina's unaffected demeanour.

"Why are you looking at me like that?" she asked. "I told you, Peter and I need some answers. He's less than half an hour away."

"We don't have that kind of time," snapped Ethan.

Jav was still mumbling, glassy-eyed, "—suppressors all the time, or in isolation, so I can't project accidentally, can't hurt anyone else. What if they give me sedatives? Everyone feels dead with those, Rina, I can't, if they find out, you said—"

Ethan cupped Jav's face in both hands. "No one will make you take anything. I promise. *Hey*, look at me." *Feel how calm I am? Calm thoughts. Steady, steady.* He glanced at Rina. "Are you gonna deal with your fiancé, or must I?"

"Peter's better at interrogation. I'm too impatient, apparently."

Ethan wished he'd never called Ollie. His nerves had failed him in the face of Jav sobbing on the phone. But whatever he had anticipated, a choice between Jav's secret and Charlie's life was not it.

"The extent of Charlie's injuries is unclear," Ethan said, jaw tight with the effort of remaining civil. "We can't risk him waking up in a hospital, knowing what he knows."

Rina sighed. "I'm not in the habit of repeating myself. We'll take care of Charlie once I've got the information I want."

"Not if the police arrive first," said Ethan.

"What," said Rina, very quietly.

"Or the ambulance," said Ethan. "Either way, no time."

Something ugly flashed across Rina's features. "You called them on your way over, I presume. What did you say?"

"They know Charlie's here," said Ethan.

"Well. That severely limits our options, doesn't it?"

Ethan cast about the room, taking in the shattered vase, the blood stains on the landing, the walls of water and silver-eyed fish.

A handgun, left on the rug.

Ethan pressed a kiss to Jav's temple, to gather his conviction. "Don't look," he said, reaching past Jav to take the gun.

Jav turned to follow. "Wait, I—"

"Close your eyes and you'll be able to say you don't know what happened."

"What the fuck are you doing?" asked Rina. For the first time since Ethan arrived, she sounded uncertain. She stepped forwards – but stopped when Ethan raised the gun. She grinned. "You're not gonna shoot me."

"Correct," said Ethan, palming Jav's neck to ease his spike of panic. He walked over to Charlie, keeping the furniture between himself and Rina.

The gun's palm-sensor glowed green. Unregistered unit; unlocked to any biometrics. Made sense. Ethan was surprised at how familiar it felt to the ones Nick gave him at the shooting range.

"Well. At least you've got guts," Rina scoffed. "I don't want to upset Jav, but I *will* explode that gun in your face if you don't drop it now."

"Rina—" said Jav.

"Your fiancé wasn't stupid enough to bring a firearm to a firestarter," said Ethan. All those hours playing VR first-person shooters was finally paying off. "And I'd prefer you do the honours if I wasn't worried that you'd shoot me afterwards."

Rina circled around as Ethan stepped over Charlie; two vipers considering a corpse. "I can stall whoever's coming. You wake him up."

"That's not how healing works." *Being alive was very different to being cognizant.* "And your lift's on first responder mode. How do you think I got in?" He planted a foot on either side of Charlie's torso, staring down at the man's face. *Well, this is a familiar view.*

Rina rounded on Jav. "Why would you open the fucking doors after what happened?" she snarled, striding towards the nearest intercom. "I should have never let you switch off voice control. Can't believe I didn't notice. Fuck."

Jav stuttered with indecision.

Ethan aimed carefully between Charlie's eyes. *Straight through the head. Steady does it.* Many suffered worse on the operating table without death being called. Murder would not recognise a state so brief, an intent to forget and not to kill. They could revive the body, even if the mind was gone. And as long as the mind was gone, everything would be okay. No murder, no leverage, nothing. Ethan wouldn't even feel things this time. Nevertheless, his heart lurched, reflexive: it knew what to expect.

Everything was going to be okay.

The lift *dinged.*

He pulled the trigger.

A familiar voice shouted, "Ethan!"

Ethan turned, dread rising fast like bile. "Nick, I—"

Nick made a slicing motion across his throat, hand flying to his earpiece. Everyone stared at each other for a single, stunned moment.

Then Rina started to laugh. "See, Jav?" She gestured between Nick and Ethan. "I told you so. *I told you.*"

Before Ethan could react, Nick crossed the lobby and pulled him into a rib-crushing embrace.

"Jesus Christ," said Nick, a hand fisted between Ethan's shoulder blades. "I thought that was — that you'd been—!"

"I'm okay. Nick, I'm fine." He wasn't lying. Everything felt too much of nothing. Paralysed by second-hand horror, Ethan was too scared to look at Jav, to see his expression.

Nick pulled back. Belatedly, Ethan realised his hands were empty: Nick had taken the gun.

Rina was examining Charlie's head wound. "I gotta give it to you, Ethan: good aim. Very neat."

Nick shoved Ethan behind himself. "Hands where I can see them."

"Me?" Rina pouted. "*I* haven't shot anyone."

"Nick, I can explain—" Ethan started.

"I'd rather you didn't." Nick took stock of the room, eyes darting, muscle ticking in his jaw.

"It was in self-defence," said Ethan.

"Self-defence." Nick glanced from the neat hole between Charlie's eyes to Rina's smile. "Is that something we all agree on?"

"Yes," said Jav, just as Rina drawled, "Dunno."

Ethan's heart sank.

"What?" Rina fluttered her eyelashes. "It all happened so fast. Pretty sure I saw Ethan shoot my fiancé in the head."

"He was beating Jav's face in!"

"Jav looks fine to me."

"Rina, what are you doing?" Jav's knuckles were white around his recently injured hand, wrapped tight in lieu of suppressors.

"Cleaning up your mess," said Rina. "Ethan's been waiting for an opportunity like this for months. To shove one or both of us under the bus. I'm sure your father's so proud."

Ethan threw up his hands. "What are you talking about?"

"We don't have time for this," said Nick.

Rina held Ethan's gaze like a moth to flame. "You thought Jav had killed Charlie. So you went straight to Holt and, no doubt, Garner."

"I had no way of knowing whether Jav was safe or not," Ethan retorted. "Of course I called the professionals, listen to yourself!"

"You set us up," said Rina, eyes like a pair of old coins, stolen from the ferryman.

"I was protecting Jav." *Intention is cheap. You wanted insurance, didn't you? To prove that I'm loyal?* "We're on. The same. Page."

"Ethan," said Nick through gritted teeth, "stop talking."

Rina jerked her chin towards Nick. "Does he know?"

"Know what?" Nick demanded.

"Of course not," said Ethan.

"Even if I believed that, what's stopping you from pinning Charlie's death on me?" Rina eyed Nick up and down, lip curled in derision. "No doubt you'll say whatever Ethan tells you to."

Ethan's inner voice, one that sounded remarkably like Ollie, chimed in: *you don't think Jav will choose you over his sister, not when it comes down to it.* He realised abruptly that the inverse was true; Rina genuinely had no faith whatsoever in Ethan's promises to Jav — not in the face of family. Whether this doubt was a reflection of Rina's own priorities...

Out loud, Ethan said, "I shot Charlie in self-defence. End of story."

"This is my fault," said Jav. "I pushed him down the stairs."

"Then he shot himself in the face?" said Rina.

It was getting harder to tune out Jav's anxiety. "I'll be fine," said Ethan. "Self-defence is—"

"I can't let you take the blame when this is all my fault!" cried Jav.

"Listen," said Nick, "I just got off the line with Ian. We have maybe ten minutes before the cavalry arrives." He clapped a hand over Ethan's mouth when Ethan tried to interrupt. "Nope, no more from you."

"Hey!" said Jav, stepping forwards.

Nick ignored him. "We don't have time to play prisoners' dilemma. *You* don't trust Ethan—"

"It'd be our word against yours," said Rina.

"Quite. And I wouldn't be too confident about your brother holding up under questioning if Ethan might go to jail."

Ethan licked vengefully at Nick's hand over his mouth until Nick relented with an exasperated huff. The moment jarred them loose from the tense stand-off. Nick's grip on Ethan's shoulder faltered.

"They won't put a healer in jail," Ethan tried. "Probably."

"The evidentiary burden is not lower merely because you're a healer!" snapped Nick. "But it might be if it's *me* defending *you*."

Ethan's brain took a moment to catch up. "No. Don't be stupid."

"I imagine neither of you have any moral quandaries about my neck being on the line, which should help with keeping our story straight," Nick said. "You think you can manage, Mr Arden?"

"This isn't your problem to fix—" said Ethan.

"Yes, it is," Nick said quietly.

"Let's go with my original plan," Ethan persisted. "That I shot Charlie because he attacked Jav—"

"I'm not letting you go to jail!" said Jav.

"Jav, I swear to god—"

Nick sighed loudly. "See?"

"I'm fine with Holt going to jail," said Rina. "If we're putting it to a vote."

"Thanks," Nick said dryly.

"Nobody is going to jail!" Ethan shouted.

Nick spun Ethan around by the arm, pulling him in so they were nose to nose. "You're more sensible than this," he said, voice frayed with impatience. "If you insist on doing things your way, that idiot is gonna confess, his sister will pin it on you because she thinks you'll pin it on her, this will all drag out in court, and you're not the one with a net-worth of — no, look at me. Ethan, *look at me.*" Nick palmed the side of Ethan's jaw to turn his face. It was like staring directly into a theatre light. "Robert Langley isn't a man to be messed with. There'll be repercussions—"

"That's exactly what I'm—!"

"Repercussions that I can deal with better than you. Plus, my defence is stronger if they decide to prosecute. Stronger than yours."

Guilt tasted worse than fear. "Nick..."

"I can't stand by and watch you destroy your life for this man. I *can't.*"

"And what kind of person would I be if I let you do the same for me?"

Nick snorted, and his smile cut Ethan to the bone. "You're a healer at a public hospital, consulting with emergency and trauma. If that doesn't tip the court's algorithm in my favour, nothing will."

"Did anyone set a timer for ten minutes?" asked Rina.

Nick's expression shuttered. "No. We should all take a moment to recollect our memories." He wet his lips. "When I arrived, Mr Langley was threatening Ethan with a gun. I attempted to disarm him, but he became violent. I shot him in the ensuing altercation." Nick looked around the room. "If anyone recalls differently, speak now or forever hold your fucking peace."

TWENTY-FOUR

7 Kensington Palace Gardens, Level 16.
Wednesday, 12 April —— 11 am.

The officer nodded at all the right places. Jav wished she wouldn't: the dissonance between her sympathetic expression and scepticism sanded his eyes dry.

"I'd like to clarify a few points, if I may?" she asked. Jav glanced at Arthur, who nodded. "You mentioned that you changed the security protocols. When did this occur?"

"After Ethan told me to. I don't remember the exact time."

"Was your sister home at that stage?"

"No."

Jav wished Rina was here to keep his heart steady. The police had insisted on interviewing them separately. He should have worn his suppressors: Jav could barely control his own emotions right now, let alone project with any finesse.

"You said that Mr Langley argued with your sister when she arrived. Did he wake before she got home, or after?"

"Afterwards."

"When did Mr Langley reclaim his gun?"

Jav swallowed. "Not sure. Rina and I were busy with the first-aid kit."

"Can you describe Mr Langley's interaction with your sister?"

Finally, back on script. "Charlie was upset about their engagement. Rina isn't the type to mince words, especially if you shout. Things escalated."

"And what happened next?"

"Ethan arrived. I don't think Charlie expected that; he said he had people watching the hospital." Jav took a deep breath. "Ethan tried to grab the gun and it went off – singed the floor. That's when Holt arrived."

"And Mr Langley still had the gun?"

In his minds' eye, Jav could see Nick efficiently wiping down the pistol. "Yes," he said.

"What happened?"

"Charlie threatened to shoot Ethan unless Nick dropped his weapon, so Nick did – then he tackled Charlie to the ground, trying to grab his gun. I heard it go off."

"Did you see Agent Holt shoot Mr Langley?"

To hell with all of us. "Yes," said Jav.

"And then what happened?"

We laid out the correct version of events. "Ethan set my thumb. Healed my face. Then everyone else arrived."

A pause, oozing discomfort like a blister.

Jav struggled to project a counteracting ease. It was like trying to hold onto a shadow. "Is there anything else I can help with?"

"Not at the moment. Thank you for your time, Mr Arden." She held out a hand. Jav shook it, wincing internally at her prickly impatience. "I'm just a phonecall away. We'll be in touch soon."

5 Turing Court, Upper Chelsea, Level 20.
A few hours later.

SINCE RINA and Jav's flat was now a crime scene, they had to stay elsewhere. Thomas Arden wanted all his children under his one roof, where he (and the extra security detail) could keep an eye on them.

Giulia disagreed. "The last thing you need is more time with Rina," she said, as Pascal brought in Jav's suitcases.

"This wasn't her fault," said Jav.

"No," Giulia snorted. "It never is."

Jav rarely visited his oldest sister at her townhouse. They spent more time together in an office, or on opposite ends of a dining table. The fact filled him with regret now, Giulia's guilt trickling past his suppressors, an itching burn of irritation and love.

The townhouse hadn't changed much: a new waxy-green monstera, orchids near the piano. Giulia was a bastion of consistency, and the old-fashioned bookcases and no-nonsense décor reflected her better than any mirror.

Two pairs of oxfords sat by the door. Neither Giulia's size. Milky sunlight streamed through the window of the guest bedroom.

Pascal lined the suitcases neatly at the end of the bed and dropped a phone atop the duvet. "If you need to contact anyone outside immediate family: firstly, don't. Secondly, use this."

"Thanks," said Jav.

"You're welcome," said Pascal, and left.

Jav took in the eggshell-blue sheets and pillows. He could hear Pascal and Giulia in the kitchen, a low murmur filling the afternoon lull.

Minutes later, Giulia appeared in the doorway. "Here." She held out a glass bottle: guava and pear juice.

Jav rubbed his eyes with the heel of his hand. "Thanks. That's my favourite."

"I know. There's Greek yoghurt in the fridge if you want something before dinner. Manuka honey's in the pull-out pantry." A long pause when Jav didn't move. "Do you need me to open that for you as well?" she asked, tone dry.

Jav burst into tears.

Giulia sighed and held out her arms.

"How do you know about my yoghurt?" cried Jav, burying his face in her shoulder. He couldn't remember the last time they hugged. Going by the stiff angle of Giulia's arms and the ginger patting on his back, she hadn't gained any extra practice.

"I know everything." Giulia sounded so much like Rina that Jav sobbed harder. The patting tempo increased. "Okay, okay. Let's sit down."

Reluctantly, Jav pulled back, wiping his face with a sleeve. They both sat on the edge of the bed – Giulia waiting as Jav tried to reset his crying by holding his breath. A familiar unease hung between them, their hands almost touching. The edges of Giulia's stress felt blunted by distraction.

"Maybe we should talk over the phone." Jav sniffed. "Different rooms. I don't want you to feel uncomfortable."

Giulia sighed again. "There's bigger fish to fry right now."

"But—"

"At least you *know* I'm uncomfortable. No one's pretending." She cleared her throat. "I'm always honest with you. I can't turn my emotions off."

"Of course," Jav agreed hastily. "That's why we—"

"And this isn't something you can turn off either."

Jav blinked.

"Look," said Giulia, then stopped. Hesitation did not suit her. "I know I've said things that...I haven't been the best. With your aptitude. I've clearly made you feel as if you can't talk to me. And I'm sorry." Giulia rested her hand on the blanket so that the side of her wrist touched the back of Jav's hand. "If I feel angry right now, it's not at you. You could have *died*. You should have called me right away. You should have felt like you could."

Jav fiddled with his watch, unable to meet her gaze.

"I'll be in the study, so you can turn that off. Take a bath or something." She stood, brushing off invisible lint. "Dinner's at seven."

"Giulia, about what happened…"

She paused in the doorway, eyebrows raised. Giulia had yet to ask Jav about what 'really' happened. Perhaps she already knew.

"Ethan did the sensible thing," she said at last. "And lucky timing, Holt appearing when he did."

Jav swallowed. "Is Charlie — did they manage to—?"

"It's too early to be certain, but the doctors don't think he'll be waking up anytime soon." Giulia's lips thinned. "Either way, not your problem."

"Oh." Jav's lungs caught on his ribs, splintered with guilt. "I love you."

"Yes. Good chat."

JAV KNEW Ethan's number by heart.

> 22:10 · JAVIER — Are you alright?

> 22:11 · JAVIER — Sorry, this is Javier. Temporary number.

> 22:53 · JAVIER — If I don't reply, it's only because I fell asleep.

He lay awake, trying not to stare at his phone. There were many explanations for Ethan's silence. Perhaps he was already asleep, or needed space, or…

Jav turned onto his side, pulling the blankets over his head.

7 Kensington Palace Gardens, Level 16.
The next evening, Thursday, 13 April.

AFTER EVERYTHING, Jav was too scared to mute Rina. But he needn't have worried: Rina never called or messaged, not even after the witness interview. Far more unsettling was Peter's radio silence. Combined with Ethan's absence, it created the perfect cocktail of insomnia.

Giulia's car rotated, lowering them into the secure garage beneath their parents' house. "Grandma and grandpa are here already," she said.

Jav considered all the extra hugs. He smiled. "Can't wait."

As it turned out, he should have waited.

"Sweetheart!" exclaimed Beatrice Arden. She pulled him into a hug and tweaked his nose. "My poor boy. You're a bit pale."

Because Robert Langley is standing behind you! Out loud, Jav said, "I'm okay, gran. Evening, Mr Langley."

Robert Langley was a hundred-and-fifty-year-old man who looked barely half that. He had hawk eyes, a square chin, and a metal-smooth temperament. Jav dared not focus too hard, for fear that his own anxiety would leak through his suppressors. He glanced at Rina, slouching near the Medusa statue, eyebrows raised. *Thanks for the warning...*

"I'm glad to see you're up and about," said Langley. "No long-term damage, I hope?"

Jav managed a nod.

"Rob and I had a spot of tea, just now. It's been too long." Grandma Bea patted Jav's arm. "Pity the circumstances."

"An unfortunate mess." Langley felt mild, unyielding in a way that suggested forced composure rather than genuine calm.

Jav cleared his throat. Easing his stress into something more grief-like, he said, "I'm very sorry about Charlie."

"So am I," said Langley. "Difficult to imagine what was going through that boy's head."

Beatrice tutted. "Young love."

Langley pinned Jav to his own shadow with an unfaltering stare. "He was never very patient. A shame." His attention shifted back to Jav's grandmother. "Speaking of patience, I wonder what Marion thinks of the kids'...activities."

Beatrice shot Jav's sisters a pointed look. "Giulia, go sit your brother down before he falls down." She thumbed Jav's cheek as if he was still a toddler. To Langley, she said, "Marion's been petulant ever since Marie married my Thomas."

"Mémé Marion wants Jav and I to visit for Christmas," Rina offered. "Maybe we could pass on a message?"

Grandma Beatrice snorted. "I think you've done quite enough for now, my dear."

With a spike of exasperation, Giulia swept her siblings out of the lobby.

THE ENCOUNTER with Robert Langley left Jav shell-shocked all through dinner. He excused himself early, escaping to the family library. He was halfway through making a cup of tea when Rina appeared.

This was the first time they had been alone in a room together since Ethan shot Charlie in the head.

Jav watched Rina slap a slim, grey disk onto the door frame. "...You know that dad doesn't like locked doors in the house. What's that?"

"Eavesdropper repellent," said Rina.

"I'm not in the mood for a lecture."

"We're worried about you."

Jav made to sit – and promptly leapt away from something disturbingly warm and lap-shaped. "God!"

"Just 'Peter' is fine," said Peter, crossing one knee over the other.

"No!" Jav shouted, saucer on the ground and tea all over his trousers. "No, fuck you, fuck!"

"Maybe there *has* been some kind of damage," Peter said to Rina. "He doesn't usually take this long to notice me."

Rina snorted.

"Get out," snapped Jav.

"Trauma impacts empaths differently," Peter continued. "I once knew an empath who—"

"Get out!"

"Calm down," said Rina.

"I will not. I will *not* calm down." Then, unable to handle the smug look on Peter's face, Jav threw his empty teacup at him.

The ghost caught it one handed. "Really, Barbie?"

"You don't get to crack jokes," Jav hissed. "Where the hell have you been?"

"I'm not the one who let Charlie in, unsupervised."

Jav frowned. "I was with him the whole time."

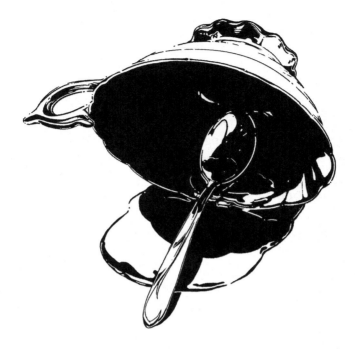

"*You* were unsupervised. There's a reason he wasn't on the white-list."

"If Charlie had shot Rina, that wouldn't even be the first time she's been shot this financial year, you useless excuse of securi—"

"Yes, about that." Peter leaned forwards, elbows on knees. "Rina said—"

"Though you did leave her to bleed out in a gutter, so who knows," Jav continued. "Perhaps just as well that you were off frolicking."

Peter's amusement evaporated. "I was handling urgent export issues. I won't burden your delicate constitution, but there's only one of me and we've yet to discover teleportation."

Rina threw herself onto the sofa. "Now that you're less hysterical, tell Peter what you told me." When Jav remained in stony silence, Rina patted the space next to her.

Jav shot her an incredulous look before striding away to make the world's slowest cup of tea.

Remorse wasn't easy to fake. Guilt, which often sat sharper on the tongue, came reflexively and was harder to suppress. Right now, Rina actually felt of both – but Jav knew it would soon evaporate like water in the heat of unrelenting obsession.

"I'm *sorry*. Is that what you want to hear?" Her annoyance grew with his silence. "I'll make sure Charlie pays."

Jav sighed. "With what? He's dead."

"A vegetable," Rina corrected. "Bobby's still around."

"Have you considered doing nothing?"

"And let him think his scare tactics worked?" A flash of real emotion, peeled back from bone. "Over my dead body."

"Over someone else's dead body, I'm sure." Jav sipped his tea. "Gran wouldn't let you anyway."

"Enough," said Peter. "What did Charlie say about Nath?"

I don't want to be responsible for another death. Jav couldn't recall precisely what he told Rina in those nail-torn moments when she first saw Charlie lying at the foot of the stairs. But if Nath had some mysterious 'accident'...Jav wouldn't be able to lie to Stephen. He couldn't stomach another secret.

Rina sighed, abandoning the sofa for Jav – who took a matching step backwards. "Jav, come on." She held out both hands. When he simply stared at her, Rina backed him up against the side-table and wrapped both hands around his wrists.

And despite the irritation, despite the annoyance, despite everything – he exhaled all at once.

"I think Charlie set Nath up." The admission cut Jav's lip on the way out.

"Explain," said Peter.

"Charlie was furious about Marc being in town. Thought we were making deals with Sainte-Ophie behind his back, reneging on whatever Rina had promised him. Charlie said he should have taken a more 'direct approach', instead of letting Nath try."

"Try," echoed Peter, expression blank. "Then Nath is complicit at best."

"Charlie mentioned arranging a scapegoat for Rina," said Jav. "That must have been the shooter, right?"

"What makes you think that?" asked Peter.

"You said the shooter had Sixty-Fourther connections or

something." *Why am I so nonchalant?* Maybe Rina had spiked his tea again, somehow. "You said it would be great media fodder. Why didn't we tell people about that, by the way?"

Peter cocked his head. "Because we needed to keep pressure on Nath, and the story was too neat. And now we know why." He turned to Rina. "This doesn't absolve Mansfield, but if Robert had a hand in this, we have bigger problems."

"In what universe does Nath and Charlie have the same bottom line?" asked Rina, pride twisting so tight that it cut the blood-flow to Jav's fingers. "It's obvious why Nath wants me out of the picture, but if Bobby thinks offing me will somehow endear him to gran—"

"I don't think they cared whether you died or not," said Peter. "The point was to create leverage over Ascenda. Robert set us up, he knew what Charlie was doing."

"You've got it backwards," said Jav – then winced. Rina and Peter's impatience was the empathic equivalent of a bullhorn. "Charlie said he disagreed with his uncle on how to handle Project Earthflown. Something about his inheritance."

"*And?*" Rina demanded.

"I don't remember—"

"What do you mean, you *don't remember?*"

Jav stared at her. "He didn't go into specifics, and I was getting my face bashed in."

Rina was disappointed. The knot in Jav's stomach tightened. Disappointed that he didn't get enough information. Disappointed that Charlie isn't alive to interrogate. Dissatisfied. The realisation felt anticlimactic for something that hurt so much. It was like searching in a mirror after a long absence – and finding something unrecognisable, staring back.

In his mind's eye, Jav could see Charlie's smirk, face flushed with the thrill of being honest. '*...takes it out of you, pretending to be a simpering idiot for so long.*'

"I think Charlie has played you," said Jav.

Rina's irritation sparked. Insulted.

"And you never picked up any signs?" asked Peter.

"Lies are not emotions." Jav ignored the searing chill radiating off

Rina. "Charlie's always been a smug insufferable ass, I made that clear from day one. You always said that you were using him to keep Robert in check. Have you considered that it may have been the other way around?"

The serrated edge of Peter's attention caught Jav's skin and sleeve, threatening seam and sinew.

"Bobby thinks *I* shot Charlie," said Rina.

Peter snorted. "Your *grandmother* thinks you shot Charlie. I'm sure Robert suspects things aren't as neat as Holt's confession made it sound."

"But he's going along with the jilted-lover theory, for now," said Rina. "We can't trust him."

Jav could barely swallow his guilt. "Will Nick be alright?"

Rina raised both eyebrows. "Why, is Ethan asking?"

"No," said Jav. *'I can't let you throw your life away for this man'.* "But Nick didn't kill anyone."

A spark-hiss of amusement, water splashing on flames. "Who are you performing for right now?" asked Rina. "I was impressed with how you panicked Nick into falling on his own sword. Should have known you were panicking for real."

"I didn't — I *wasn't*—"

"Jealous and wanted to get rid of him?"

"Holt's a loose end that'll need to be tied, sooner or later." Peter shrugged at Jav's horrified expression. "Not right *now*. Too much attention."

"We could always tell Bobby the truth," said Rina. "That Ethan shot Charlie." Jav wondered if she was saying these things just to punish him. "But that would raise unnecessary questions right now. I don't want *you* doing anything stupid. More stupid. Like running to the police."

"I won't. Rina, please."

"Even if they find out that Ethan shot Charlie?"

"Everyone who knows is in this room," Jav said sharply.

"And Holt," said Peter.

"Nick loves Ethan, he wouldn't say anything." Those seven words were so painful that Jav ran his tongue over his teeth, half expecting to find a chipped molar.

Peter snorted. "Many have second thoughts when in court."

Rina collapsed back onto the chesterfield. "Stop *fretting*. You're giving me a headache. Sit down." She waited until Jav obeyed. "Look. No one wants a hoo-hah over Charlie's death. Too many skeletons in everybody's closets. Plus, scrutiny and press speculation three weeks out from an election? Why do you think I was avoiding Charlie this whole time? *Trying* to be good." She scooted closer. "If it all goes to plan, Holt might get a rap on the knuckles but that's it."

Jav stared at the rug.

"I'm only telling you this so you can stop stressing," Rina continued. "If you have any panicky urges, let's get them out now."

Lies aren't emotions. But Jav very much wanted to hold her hand and believe otherwise.

Rina waved a hand in front of his face. "Hello?"

"Sounds like things are under control," said Jav.

"They will be, if you stick to the story," said Peter.

"No accidents," Jav insisted.

Rina yawned. "I never said that."

"Promise me that Ethan will be okay," Jav said quietly.

"Ethan knows you're an empath," said Rina.

"The good doctor shot a man to keep them quiet," said Peter. "That's reassuring, empathic influence or not."

"There's still a chance he was trying to frame one of us," said Rina. "In any case, Vegas and Oliver might know. They're all so close."

"The former is obvious leverage for the latter," said Peter. "Roskopf must be aware of the risks."

"Wait," Jav choked. Rina's eyes snapped up at his anxiety. "Vegas is Ethan's best friend, you can't—"

"You reassured us that Oliver and Vegas were none the wiser," Peter cut in. "Has something changed?"

"No, of course not!" Jav had never told Rina or Peter about his missing cufflink, nor the confrontation with Oliver. And now...Jav didn't want to be responsible for anything happening to Vegas. Ethan would never forgive him.

Peter's expression remained mild. "Then they've got nothing to worry about."

"Ethan can't control what Oliver writes," Jav blurted out. "And Vegas has nothing to do with this." He looked at his sister. "You *like* Vegas."

"True," Rina agreed. "Last resort, then."

"Rina!"

"What? I'm *protecting you*."

Jav buried his face in his hands, pressing the heel of his palms against his eyes until he saw stars. "If my empathy became public knowledge, would that fix things? Nath will lose his leverage. You and Peter won't have to worry about Ethan, Vegas, or Oliver..."

Rina's eyes narrowed. "Let's not spend time on pointless hypotheticals."

Belatedly, Jav realised that Rina still had not promised to leave Ethan alone. Why was it so important to hear her say something she would never mean? Perhaps it was the comfort of knowing that she still cared enough to lie.

Peter's chin was tilted; a magpie surveying something shiny.

"Oliver's inconveniently connected," said Rina. "Peter and I will keep the lid on any scandals. You think I *like* playing nice with Marc et al? Mum's family is the *worst*. But I had to show Bobby who was holding the leash. Project Earthflown—"

"Then don't pretend you're doing this for me!" snapped Jav.

Rina scowled. "Just because I'm killing two birds with one stone doesn't mean I'm not doing this for y—"

"Your pride?" Jav stood up.

Rina followed suit. "Outing you *would* be a scandal that the Sixty-Fourthers can only dream of." She prodded Jav hard in the chest. "*I'm* the reason no one knows for all these years. Look at you, blabbing your heart out at the first opportunity. If I hadn't taken care of Lucas, your life would have been over years ago."

That hurt, more than Charlie's fists had done. Jav bit the inside of his mouth until he tasted blood.

"Stop thinking about risks we'll never take." No doubt sensing Jav's recoil, Rina wrapped both arms around him. "Why scare yourself?"

Jav returned the hug, thankful that he had his back to Peter so that the ghost couldn't see his tears. Shame goose-pimpled his arms. "Okay.

You're right." This was easier than trying to articulate the resignation blooming in his throat, its roots having taken hold in his lungs long ago. *You won't change her mind. You've never changed her mind.*

Rina propped her chin on his shoulder. "I just want you to be happy."

"Ethan makes me happy."

"For *now*. You're not gonna be happy being outed, I can promise you. Forget going back to the Royal Ballet, ever."

Jav pressed his cheek to her hair. "Promise me you'll let the chips fall where they may. The tender or the subsidies be damned, Rina."

"Mmhm." A long pause. "Tell us if Ethan mentions anything about anything. His father, his friends, Holt." Rina tapped him on the nose. "More warning, more options. Harmless options, like injunctions."

"Okay." A lie, for both of them. Jav wanted nothing more than to be alone. "I might turn in. Have an early night."

Rina smiled. "Good call. Stay here with me."

"No, I think I'll go back to Giulia's." Jav pried himself from Rina's arms – but not before doubt passed between them like an electric current.

His twin cocked her head. "What's she been saying?"

"Nothing."

"Giulia gives you migraines."

"I need some space, that's all." Jav ignored the weight of Rina and Peter's gaze on the back of his neck and made towards the door.

Rina's ire flickered back to life. "I *said* I was sorry."

Jav stopped. He stared at the door frame for a moment before turning around. "I know. I'm just tired." He managed a smile. "Door, please."

Neither Peter nor Rina moved.

When Jav tried the handle, he found it unlocked.

5 Turing Court, Upper Chelsea, Level 20.
The next day, Friday, 14 April.

"I THOUGHT THOSE GAVE YOU A HEADACHE," said Giulia from across the breakfast island.

Jav glanced at his suppressors – bracelets today – and shrugged. "Thanks for coming back to have lunch with me." Their father probably instructed Giulia to babysit.

"Tell me what's wrong."

"Nothing," Jav stuffed his mouth with food to buy a few extra moments. His sister waited, eyebrows raised. "...Ethan's not returning my calls. Do you know when I'll get my old phone number back?"

"Send an email." This close, Giulia's sympathy was sandpaper rough through his suppressors. She sighed at whatever expression Jav made. "I'll ask about your phone. I'm meeting with Arthur in an hour anyway."

"Oh. Thanks."

Giulia disappeared into the bathroom, returning with lipstick a little darker, hair knotted a little higher. "Be good," she said, gathering her tablet and sympathies.

The townhouse was too quiet once she left. Jav put the leftovers away and retreated to his room. He took another shower and drew the curtains, so the world would look gentler, blurred by shadows. He must have fallen asleep at some point – because the next moment, the bedroom was dark and the intercom was bleeping.

"We're home," Pascal announced through the speakers. "Dinner's here."

Jav sat up. "Okay, m'coming." Swiping his suppressors from the bedside table, the vanity mirror glowed to life as he passed: 7 pm.

Reliable Pascal, wired in five-minute increments.

Making his way to the kitchen, a familiar warmth hit Jav like a barrelling embrace. He froze in the hallway, one suppressor on, the other still in his hand.

"Hi," said Ethan.

"Oh, and you have a visitor," said Pascal, unloading two bags of Italian food onto the kitchen counter.

Jav gaped. "I...*Ethan?*"

"Surprise?" Ethan waved.

"I thought it'd be more efficient to fetch him for dinner, given your communication issues." Giulia pilfered an Arancini ball as Pascal transferred pasta onto dinnerware. "We'll be in the dining room. You two can have the kitchen."

Pascal followed her out, laden with cutlery and a bottle of red wine.

A moment of stunned silence.

"So..." Ethan began, features obscured by his blinding affection and knee-buckling relief. "I didn't see your messa— *oof!*"

Jav yanked him into a tight hug, hands fisted in the back of Ethan's coat. He buried his face in Ethan's hair, breathing in the too-strong soap scent, eyes stinging, chest so full he might have burst.

Ethan looped an arm around Jav's waist. "I missed you too," he said, voice muffled against Jav's throat.

"I've been so worried, I didn't expect..." Jav pulled back, just enough to see Ethan's face whilst remaining in the hug. *You're so happy to see me,* he thought, helium light, *I was scared that something might have changed. Unless this is a feedback loop...*Jav shoved the doubt aside by kissing Ethan, hard.

Ethan made an approving noise, pulling Jav down by the neck. He kissed with awkward clicks of teeth, socked feet slipping on the floorboard. "I was worried too. Forgot to write your number down. Couldn't get a hold of you, and I kept thinking...well." Ethan thumbed Jav's dimple, eyes darting, uncertain. "You okay?"

"Yeah," Jav exhaled. He kissed Ethan again, cupping the side of his face. After a long moment, he stepped back. "Sorry, you can probably feel all my — everything."

"Sort of." Ethan caught Jav's hand before they broke skin contact. He pried Jav's fingers open to reveal the suppressor bracelet and a clean red line across Jav's palm. "Giulia said you didn't know I was coming."

Jav nodded. Gaze locked, Ethan pocketed the suppressor and unclasped the other bracelet too, pausing to give Jav a chance to move away.

"Didn't want anyone to get a headache," said Jav.

Ethan spun the bracelet around his index finger. "Maybe *I* should wear these if you're not feeling—"

"*No*, no, I've missed you."

It had only been three nights, but perhaps the three worst possible nights to be alone.

"Okay." Ethan ran his fingers through Jav's hair. "So fluffy. Did we interrupt your nap?"

Jav cast about for his reflection. "God, is it terrible?"

"Sticking up on one side. No, leave it alone, I like it." Ethan's gaze wandered towards the kitchen. "You hungry?"

They ate in companionable silence for ten minutes, tucked close at one corner of the breakfast bar. The air was heavy with unspoken questions, but Jav loathed to break the peace, for, aside from the more-frequent-than-usual stares, Ethan felt like he usually did: fond, calm, a little tired.

Then Ethan's phone rang, accompanied by a flip-switch of cortisol. Ethan kept chewing. The phone persisted.

After a few long seconds, Ethan dropped his fork. "Sorry, one sec." He shot Jav an apologetic look before picking up. "Hi dad. Yes. Dinnering at home...fine. So what if I am?"

Jav stayed quiet. He could hear Ian Garner's unhappy voice climbing in volume on the other end of the line.

Tension crept up Ethan's shoulders. "I know what the police said, but — dad. I'm *trying*, but you keep interrupting." He pinched the bridge of his nose, shovelling the last forkful of pasta. "Okay, well on my head be it."

Jav topped up Ethan's water glass with exaggerated care.

"I'm perfectly able — that was *not* his fault. I'm not giving you the address. No. Because I'm staying the night." Ethan shot Jav an uncertain look.

Jav nodded rapidly.

"*Yes*, okay. I'm sorry, I'll text. Fine." Ethan stabbed the off button and drained his glass. "Sorry about that. It'd be worse if I didn't answer."

He projected no irritation or resentment, let alone anger. There was guilt, but Jav couldn't tell to whom it belonged.

"He didn't sound happy," said Jav.

"A problem for tomorrow-Ethan. Are we okay?" Ethan asked abruptly.

Jav set down his fork. "Of course."

Ethan felt a lot calmer than their steamed-egg-almost-break-up conversation. But his unwavering gaze stripped Jav of confidence.

"You're..." Ethan cleared his throat. "There's nothing you want to say or — after everything?"

Anxiety prickled Jav's palms. "Not if you don't want to talk about it. We can just..."

"Pretend nothing's happened?" Silence stretched across the kitchen. Ethan sighed. "We should probably talk about it. After dessert. And a shower."

IN THE END, they had sorbets in the bath.

"You know," Ethan said, hair speckled with foam, lashes drowsy with steam, "I was working on a list of things to say, for when I saw you. And now we're here..." He snapped his fingers. "Amnesia."

Jav thought of Charlie, surviving on machines. "It'll come to you tomorrow."

Ethan shook his head. "I haven't slept for days. Let's get this over with. Unless—"

"If you're going to leave me, please just say it," Jav blurted. "I can't — I can't do this."

For a moment, Ethan simply looked at him, heart metronomic, a balm of exhausted affection. He ran a hand from Jav's ankle up to his knee. "Jav. I shot someone. For you. And your first question is whether I'll leave?"

Jav swallowed hard. "Yes. For putting you in that position. For making you—"

"You didn't make me do anything," said Ethan sharply.

"I panicked. I turned off my suppressors before Charlie came up, so I could...manage him. I knew he wouldn't take rejection well." It was a testament to Ethan's inexorable calm that Jav could speak at all. "I didn't expect him to get violent. I tried to scare him off, but it backfired. *I* gave him a panic attack. You were scared because I was scared. If I wasn't projecting so loudly, if I hadn't lost control, you wouldn't have — wouldn't have shot him. You—"

"Don't know that," said Ethan.

Jav blinked. "What?"

"Counterfactuals. I felt *you* panicking, but I wasn't scared, per se." He traced the edge of Jav's kneecap with a finger. "I was pissed off. Seeing you hurt like that."

"But..."

"Maybe there was empathic influence, maybe not. Doesn't matter. Given the variables, I'd do it again."

"You can't know that."

"I *can*. It was the only way to guarantee that Charlie won't blab." Ethan's gaze lost focus. "I've felt people die before, sometimes for a while, sometimes permanently. Almost no difference. And that's presuming you recognise it in the first place, which is trickier than people think. Being arms length is really something though, isn't it? Or nothing, rather."

"Ethan..."

"I digress. You didn't make anyone do anything. *I* wasn't willing to gamble, like Rina was. We didn't have time. Plus, Charlie had just strangled you half to death."

Ethan's eyes were pale in the soft light, like one of Rina's many fish. It took a minute for Jav realise the source of his déjà vu: Ethan's clinical recitation, the unaffected mannerisms. He resembled Rina, casually speaking of death whilst feeling of love.

Jav's hesitation was not lost on Ethan, whose gaze fell away.

"I'm being honest because I don't want you to feel responsible. Even if it means you see me differently."

"Ethan, you're a good person—"

"I'm not. I just love you. And god knows anyone could."

A thousand questions threatened to dissolve Jav's teeth. He wanted to ask, 'How are you so sure it wasn't my fear that made you do it?' and 'I felt how much you hurt, when someone passed away' and 'what if this is all me?'. Instead, Jav said, "I love you too."

An answering relief seared across his palm.

"That's...that's good." Ethan's smile creased his eyes.

Their skin had started to prune, and Jav laced their fingers together. Neither moved to leave the tub.

"This conversation's not what I expected," said Ethan.

"What do you mean?"

"You're always...you're the sweetest person I know." Ethan scooped a handful of dying bubbles. Then, as if confessing a secret: "You felt the same, when I walked through the door."

Jav's heart contracted two sizes.

"Is it because you blame yourself for what happened?" asked Ethan.

"...I don't think it's *your* fault." Jav could still taste Ethan's surprise when the gun went off. Perhaps it had been reflexive – except Ethan was not the jumpy sort, and he certainly did not have twitchy hands. Empathic panic was the only explanation. Ethan was trying to rationalise Jav away from guilt.

You say you don't feel anything, and yet... "You feel regretful," Jav said gently. "That's not nothing."

"I shouldn't have let Nick take the blame. He only did it because—"

Because he loves you. Nick might as well have been projecting, with how loud he had been, emotions nerve-pinchingly bright. Though Nick and Ethan had been standing so close together...it wasn't always easy, pinpointing to whom an emotion belonged. It hurt to wonder, but Jav was too scared to find out for certain.

Ethan appeared to be waiting for the unspoken question, the dread tight around their throats. They were still holding hands.

Jav's courage failed him. "Is Nick alright?"

Ethan exhaled. "He's on admin leave, like me. Dad says that's standard procedure, but it all comes down to the review. There'll be a hearing."

"*You're* on administrative leave?"

"Yes...? I left everyone at St Ophie's in a lurch, took an EMS bike, flew it without a licence. I'll probably get suspended. Fired. I hope it won't affect the lease." Ethan shrugged, movement sinew tight. "Not as bad as what Nick's going through. Maybe I should come clean. Tell dad what happened."

"*No,*" said Jav, aghast. It came out louder than he intended and

Ethan felt taken aback. Jav thought fast. "Nick's already given his statement. We'd all get done for lying if we changed the story now."

"I'd tell them that I shot Charlie," said Ethan. "Nothing more."

"That's not the point." Jav didn't like the way Ethan was looking at him, eyes dark and brows knitted. No healer could ever wipe away the bruises upon Jav's conscience, but he had years of practice, turning blind eyes. Rationalisation came easy as breathing. "Nick said he had the stronger case, remember? Defending a healer."

"But he might have to go to court," Ethan insisted, the pressure of his guilt like finger-points digging into Jav's bare skin. "Dad said it comes down to political pressure. You're not a nobody. *Charlie*—"

"They won't prosecute."

Ethan paused. "You sound very sure. Why?"

Jav opened his mouth, but nothing came out.

"Did Rina say something?" Ethan's expression softened. "I can see why she would tell you that."

"She—" Jav aborted the lie. "Robert Langley stopped by to see my grandparents. They're still in town, from the wedding. No one wants a fuss. It'd open a whole can of worms about Charlie, what he did to me, why he...everyone's keen to lay this to rest."

"Right," said Ethan. "A stalemate, then. For how long?"

"I don't want to lose you," Jav whispered. "Ethan, *please.*"

"If Nick — if things escalate, I'm telling dad. Nick wouldn't be here if not for me."

"No, this is my fault. I shouldn't have dragged you into this mess, should never have asked you to dinner, but I had to—" Jav broke himself off, but it was too late.

Ethan looked and felt as if Jav had struck him. "You had to what?"

"I — no, I didn't—" Panic hit Jav; a kaleidoscope of intimate moments summoned only by the knowledge of imminent loss and the death of a secret.

The silence dragged on.

"It's okay," said Ethan, eventually.

"I just meant that I should have left you alone," said Jav, words tumbling. "If I was a better person, knowing what I knew about the—"

"It's fine. Rina told me."

"What?" Jav croaked. "What did she say?"

Ethan took a deep breath and held it for so long that Jav thought he might not answer.

"That taking me out was her idea." Ethan's voice tremored, at odds with his steady hands. "That you felt indebted."

"*Of course* I was grateful, but that's not—" Jav could feel Ethan slipping through his fingers. "We were worried about what you might say. About me flying Rina out to Highgate. I wanted to see you regardless. To apologise for the things I said, how I behaved."

Ethan's mouth pressed into a tight line. He was close to tears, Jav realised with a shock. There had been no emotional shift, no discernible ache or squeeze of air. Only lung-shredding dread, the ends of Jav's nerves unspooled in the bathwater. It was impossible to tell where they ended, and Ethan's began.

"Please say something," Jav pleaded.

"Did you know that my dad was working on Rina's case?"

All the blood drained from Jav's face. A swift, answering recoil from Ethan.

"No! I didn't know!" Jav exclaimed. "Not until Ian saw us together. I didn't make the connection – you had different surnames. I confronted Rina about it afterwards. She already knew, but she never mentioned it before."

Ethan's eyes darted all over Jav's features, searching.

"I swear I didn't know." It took every ounce of Jav's self-control to not project something to dispel this awful silence. When Ethan still didn't respond, Jav grew desperate. "Maybe we should have this conversation out of the bath. Use the phone, sit in different rooms. I'll wear suppressors—"

"Stop."

Jav froze.

"I shouldn't have asked," said Ethan. "I believe you."

"Oh. But you don't feel...um."

"What?"

Jav swallowed the lump in his throat. "Like you believe me."

"And what does that feel like?"

"The opposite of doubt."

Ethan's gaze shuttered. "I didn't want to ask. Asking means I don't trust you."

"You shouldn't need to ask. I'm sorry." *Secrets have a habit of festering.*

"It's not on you to tell me everything." Ethan squeezed Jav's hand so hard that his fingers went numb. "But I feel like you'd never have told me, on your own. And I...I can't say if I'd have lasted — if I could trust—"

"I love you so much. Please. *Please*, Ethan." *Please don't leave.* Jav threw caution to the wind. "I'm glad Rina pushed me to see you, even if it was for the wrong reasons."

That seemed to be what Ethan wanted to hear. His shoulders lost some tension. "I suppose it doesn't matter how we got here."

He reached forwards...and promptly slipped on his tailbone, vanishing beneath the surface of the water with a yelp and a tremendous splash. Ethan's left foot shot past Jav's ear, almost clocking him under the chin. A wave sloshed over the edge of the tub.

Ethan re-emerged with a comical gasp that shattered any residual solemnity. "Your fancy bath bubbles taste rancid," he spluttered, once he had stopped coughing, hair plastered to his forehead, eyes huge with indignance.

Jav wiped water from his eyes. "Are you okay? Did you hit your head?"

Ethan sneezed.

"I know about concussions now." Jav tried repositioning Ethan more comfortably in the tub and got an elbow in the stomach for his trouble. Ethan sneezed again. "Aww, water up your nose?"

"*No.*" Ethan scrubbed his face with a nearby towel. He tried to kiss Jav – and was aborted by a third sneeze. "Ugh!"

"Let's continue this in bed, before we turn into prunes."

Ethan cough-laughed. "You and your vanity." Ethan buried his nose in Jav's neck. "Tell me again that you love me."

Jav cupped the back of Ethan's head. "I love you."

A stutter-burst of fondness.

"Not like that," said Ethan, muffled. "Empathically."

If anyone cared to open Jav's chest, they would have found space instead of a heart. The uncertainty of tomorrow frayed the edges of that vacuum – waiting to rush in and fill him with doubt. Jav buried his face in Ethan's wet hair, eyes stinging. Love was an incredible high, and they both went loose from the sheer force of it all.

"Good," Ethan mumbled. "Just checking."

Just checking, as if their omissions never mattered. *Good*, as if love demanded no further proof than this.

In the end, Rina was wrong – there did exist a soul willing to forgive his secrets. And Jav would pay any price to be loved so blindly.

TWENTY-FIVE

Bergenia Residences, Lower Lambeth, Level 9.
One day earlier ↺ Thursday, 13 April.

I f ever there was a sign of the end times, it was a quiet Vegas. Ethan had spent the previous night at Ian's and returned in a foul mood. "First day of admin leave, huh," said Ollie, loading the dishcleaner. "Any idea how long it'll last?"

"No," said Ethan.

They last saw each other on Tuesday, sandwiched between police cruisers and ambulances. A lifetime ago. "Is the med council gonna get involved?" Ollie glanced at Vegas. "Will he get fired?"

Vegas rubbed her eyes. "Dunno. Hijacking an EMS bike is...not ideal."

Ethan stomped out of the kitchen.

Ollie followed. "Maybe they'll be lenient if you tell them what actually happened."

"We're not doing this," said Ethan.

"This?"

"Where you bait me for more info."

"We're owed more info. Your boyfriend dragged us into this mess."

"There's no 'us'. This is none of your business."

Ollie raised his eyebrows. "You made this my business when you called me. You made this Vegas's business when you used her number."

"Vegas is sitting right there," said Ethan.

"And she would like to know what happened too," said Vegas.

"I told you the Ardens were bad news," Ollie interjected. "I've been saying it for months, but *no*, Ollie's paranoid. Never mind all the circumstantial evidence, dead bodies, the suppressors. It was a miracle we didn't have to scrape you off the side of a building!"

"Are you done?" asked Ethan.

"Just warming up, actually—"

"Be quiet," snapped Vegas. She pointed at Ethan. "Explain."

Ollie waited.

Ethan seemed to realise that no deflections were coming to rescue him. He scowled. "Fine. Rina's shitty fiancé wanted to talk to her, but only Jav was home. Caught the brunt of it. Charlie had a gun, and when Jav tried to run upstairs—" Ethan gestured vaguely "—Charlie slipped on the stairs. Knocked himself out. That's when Jav called me. He had a panic attack on the phone. Given what he said about Charlie having 'friends' at the hospital, I took an EMS flier. Figured that'd be fastest."

Clinical impatience clipped Ethan's sentences, the rhythm smoothing his brow as he recounted. Rehearsed.

"So Javier *is* involved with the glass trafficking," said Ollie. "That'd certainly explain him teleporting to St Ophie's the night his sister was shot."

"What?" Ethan shook his head. "Charlie was angry about Rina calling off their engagement. He took that out on Jav."

Ollie drummed his fingers on the back of the couch, ticking the names off in his head. "Then who did Nick put in the body bag?" He cursed at Ethan's silent stare. "For heaven's sake..."

"Charlie."

"Nick killed *Robert Langley's* nephew?"

"Nick walked in on Charlie waving a gun in my face. Things escalated."

"Oh, I'll bet they escalated, with an empath around!"

"We've been through this. Jav is not an empath."

Ollie laughed, mirthless. "Come on. You're stubborn, but not this obtuse."

"You can't assume that everyone who wears dampeners is secretly a—"

"They were custom empathic suppressors, not dampeners. If someone was paranoid enough to get custom anti-empath wearables, don't you think they'd ensure said wearables had the effective range—"

"Short-range disruption versus long-range dampening is based on firestarters and telekinetics—"

"The cufflinks were empathic suppressors. *Suppressors.*" Ollie wanted to smack Ethan's apathy right off his face. "Putting that aside, you've been acting out of sorts, and it's clearly getting worse. I mean, stealing an EMS bike? What could have possessed you? Oh wait!"

Ethan snorted. "Empathic projection works over the phone now, does it?"

"You've been spending so much time with Javier, who knows what it's done to your brain. You've never been this impulsive—"

"Jav said there were people waiting outside the hospital. Forgive me if I made a snap decision."

"Instead of alerting security? You went from neurotic risk aversion to abandoning patients, flying without a permit – again, you could have died!"

Ethan didn't seem to know how to arrange his features. He settled on disgust. "Well, I hope Vegas never has to call *you* in an emergency."

Vegas buried her face in her hands. Ollie could relate. Caring about someone like Ethan was exhausting, the way that loving family often was.

"Can you drop your contrarian shtick for one second?" said Ollie. "When has Nick ever been trigger-happy? Never. And now he's shot someone? How did Charles Langley bleed to death with you there anyway?"

It took a beat for Ethan to answer. "Nobody said anything about blood loss. Head wounds are tricky."

Vegas jerked upright. "Nick shot someone in the—?! Is he okay? Have either of you talked to him since Tuesday?"

Ethan shook his head, eyes on the floor.

"Not for the lack of trying," said Ollie

They lapsed into silence.

"I know that *you* know who Robert Langley is," Ollie tried, at last. "What do you think will happen to Nick when Langley finds out who killed his nephew?"

Ethan's jaw tightened. "Hindsight's twenty-twenty. I shouldn't have called either of you. I panicked."

"What you should have done is stopped seeing Javier months ago, when I told you to."

"Has Jav contacted you since Tuesday?" asked Vegas.

"No," said Ethan. "Dad has my phone."

"Maybe you should play it safe, until the dust settles," said Vegas quietly. "Reassess things."

"What's that supposed to mean?" snapped Ethan.

"Now that we have security detail..." Vegas glanced at Ollie. "Ian said they didn't find anyone suspicious at the hospital after Ethan's warning, but they're being cautious."

"You want me to break up with Jav," said Ethan flatly.

"No, just. Time. If you're going to Edinburgh anyway. Maybe Ollie has a point."

Ollie frowned. "Since when were you leaving for Edinburgh?"

"Dad wants me to go stay with grandma for a bit," said Ethan. "I'm not going. And I'm not breaking up with Jav."

"Ethan—"

"You should have seen how bad he looked." Ethan crossed his arms, hugging himself. "Black and blue. Just the other month, Corinna drugged him *for convenience*. He needs me."

"But the point is that Jav is caught up in *something*," said Vegas. "If Nick hadn't shown up, who knows what could have happened?"

"Javier might not be directly culpable, but he's complicit," said Ollie. "His hands aren't clean."

"You can't prove that," said Ethan.

Interesting response. Ollie tilted his head. "You should reconsider Edinburgh. Some space to clear your head—"

Ethan stood. "Don't fucking patronise me. My head's plenty clear."

"I'd rather you be angry and alive than happy and dead," Ollie shot back. "If love is blind, then being with an empath must—"

"For the last time, Jav is not an empath! And even if he was, who cares?"

"None of us would be here if it wasn't for that!" Ollie shouted. "Nick shooting Langley, Ian in hot water. I'm not trying to find an exciting story angle or say 'I told you so'." He pinched the bridge of his nose, at a loss. "Ethan, I've practically lived with you on and off for, what, eight years? That's a long time to know somebody. Listen when I say that I've never seen you like this before. You must at least entertain the *possibility* that you've been influenced."

The impasse yawned between them.

Ethan looked to Vegas – perhaps for support, perhaps for some solidarity in scepticism. Whatever it was, he didn't seem to find it. "I'm going for a walk," he said, inflectionless.

Vegas leapt up. "Dad said we shouldn't. What about our security?"

"Yes, don't be stupid," said Ollie.

For a second, Ethan looked like he might leave, regardless. His knuckles were white around his sleeve, a tremor at the corner of his mouth. "Fine," he snapped, veering ninety-degrees towards the bathroom.

The door slammed shut.

Vegas rounded on Ollie. "I told you it was too soon!" she hissed. "You know how Ethan gets when he's backed into a corner. Was this supposed to be constructive?"

Ollie collapsed onto the sofa. "There's something he's not telling us. We can't wait around to see who else gets offed. Nick's head is already on the chopping block."

In the bathroom, the shower switched on with a wall-vibrating hum.

"You should stay here tonight." Vegas sat next to him. "Safer."

Ollie pulled her close. She curved to meet him until they were a pair of speech marks, bookending an unfinished plea.

"How sure are you that Jav's an empath?" asked Vegas.

"Pretty sure."

"Not enough to confront Ian about it," she added, as sharp as ever.

"Situation's changed though."

"Is there any point trying to talk you out of it?" Vegas pulled back. Looked him in the eyes. "If you can publish without accusing Jav of being an empath, that would be the kinder thing to do."

And there was the matter of Arden retaliation. Ollie was grateful she hadn't asked for a promise – he had none to give. "I should talk to Nick first anyway."

OLLIE SCROLLED THROUGH HIS DRAFT, the cursor blinking in time with his migraine.

> For those familiar with Thomas Arden's life-long friendship with Harold Mansfield, it is easy to follow the money. Both attended St Paul's College at Oxford and both were best men at the other's wedding. Together, they maintain controlling interest in Ascenda – the construction firm to which London owes its post-flood foundations.
>
> The events of October 3rd should be examined beyond whether Parliament lowers or maintains the CM15 subsidy by one or two percentage points, beyond Corinna Arden's would-be assassination, and beyond Tim and Martin Hersch's deaths. If Ascenda wins the Earthflown tender, the Ardens will be tasked with architecting CM15's not-so-obsolescence to the tune of billions in public funding.
>
> With these stakes, it is perhaps unsurprising the lengths one might go to silence any suggestion of scandal.

The next evening, Friday, 14 April.

NICK GREETED OLLIE with no enthusiasm, despite the food offering. They inhaled the noodles in silence. Nick's bloodshot eyes suggested insomnia or tears, his shoulders tight with the spectre of recent events.

For a healer, Ethan was remarkably bad for Nick's health.

"How're you holding up?" asked Ollie

"Fine."

"...I'm worried about you."

"Thanks."

If Nick was feeling monosyllabic, tonight was going to be like pulling teeth.

Ollie waited until Nick finished eating so he could assess his friend's expression in full. "They've booked you in with a therapist, right?"

"For?"

"Shooting someone in the face."

Nick poured himself a glass of water, unhurried. "I see you've spoken to Ethan."

"He told me you shot Charles Langley." Ollie paused, disarmed by Nick's non-reaction. "I'm not convinced."

"Maybe you should believe him."

"Maybe you should tell me why you hung up so fast when the gun went off." The inconsistencies had kept Ollie up all night. After all, the liar's in the details.

"Reflex," said Nick.

"You stepped out of the lift, shot Langley with a gun you don't carry, then hung up. Reflexively." Outside, the wind pounded on the window, promising rain. When it became evident that Nick was quite happy to let the silence go on, Ollie groaned. "What if I guess what happened and you nod or shake your head. Multiple-choice quiz."

"You don't trust me?"

"Usually, yes. But you make bad decisions where Ethan's involved." Ollie swore internally. *I'm too late.* Nick and Ethan were already on the same page. "I think you ended the call because you didn't want us to hear what happened next."

Nick rested his head on the back of the couch, throat bared, hands loose in his lap. The picture of easy honesty. "Why on earth would I hang up on purpose when you're on the other end? I know how you get."

Ollie chewed his lip, unable to deny the logic.

"The gunshot you heard was from Langley," Nick continued. "Not sure if it had been a warning or just twitchy fingers. I thought he had shot Ethan, at first."

"But why hang up? You gave Ian a heart attack."

"Accident."

"Really."

"User error adjusting the earpiece. Langley threatened to shoot Ethan if I didn't drop my stunner. I planned to stall until backup arrived, but Ethan tried to distract Langley? To disarm him? Who knows. Ethan fell over."

"...That's the most believable thing about this story so far. Please go on."

"Not much more to it. Langley and I scuffled for the gun, and I shot him. Didn't exactly have a buffet of options, or the leisure to consider them. I thought Ethan—" Nick broke off, staring into space.

Causality was elusive at the best of times. Here, Ollie didn't know what could be attributed to the empath, Nick's blind spot for Ethan, and Ollie's own confirmation bias.

"The only reason I'm telling you all this is because I'd rather you have the facts, and *not* publish something we'll all regret later," said Nick.

"Regret how?"

"People getting hurt."

"Hm. They assigned Vegas and Ethan with security detail," said Ollie. "Where's yours?"

"I'm not the one that Langley threatened."

"Vegas said the police didn't find anybody at the hospital."

Nick snorted. "You and I both know that doesn't mean much."

"*You're* the one I'm worried about, Mr I-have-no-family-connections."

"Then don't publish anything."

"On the contrary, an exposé is probably your best insurance right now." Ollie threw caution to the wind. "Robert Langley will find out who shot his nephew, if he doesn't know already. You don't think he'll want retribution?"

"I'm not sure he'd want anyone looking too closely into why that nephew was holding a healer at gunpoint."

"Oh, so you won't even make it to court: you'll get thrown off a motorway. Hooray."

"We can't do much about that now," said Nick.

"Wrong. Someone could tell Robert Langley about the empath that Charles was with when he died." Ollie raised an eyebrow meaningfully. "And why stop at Robert?"

"Ollie..."

"The mere presence of an empath will throw the whole incident in a new light, regardless of whether Javier was traumatised or putting it on. You'd be off the hook. There'd be a media circus if you got prosecuted—"

"Enough with this empath obsession!" Nick shouted. "We don't have *proof*."

Time to put all his cards on the table. "I have the suppressor," said Ollie. "I kept one of Javier's cufflinks."

Nick let out a wordless gust of exasperation. "You told me you had returned them."

"...I lied."

"No shit. Do *you* want to get thrown off a motorway?" Nick scrubbed his face with the heel of his hand. "The chain of custody for the cufflinks is muddied. You'd have a hard time proving ownership."

"All I need is to satisfy the balance of probabilities. I have enough to ground a reasonable belief—"

"That Javier's an empath?"

"—interfered with due process, or the carriage of justice."

"How nice, you've spoken to a lawyer."

"Like I said: I've been worried about you."

Before Nick could answer, his phone buzzed on the table. A split second later, Ollie's flashed an identical message:

19:20 · IAN — Is Ethan with you?

Nick's entire body tensed. *I bet he's with Javier,* thought Ollie, watching Nick type out a response in the negative. Ollie followed suit before Ian could call. Nick tossed his phone back on the table with a wince-worthy clatter and buried his face in both hands.

"Hey..." Ollie slouched closer. "You want tea or something?" No response. "Vodka?"

Nick remained bent in half, suspiciously silent.

Ollie cleared his throat. "Are you crying?"

A muffled cough. "No."

Ollie yanked Nick sideways by the elbow, locking him into a hug. A difficult manoeuvre since Nick was slightly taller, but Ollie had years of practice. "Stop *struggling.*" He winced as Nick kicked Ollie not-so-accidentally in the shins.

Nick sniffed, loudly. Ollie pretended not to notice the damp patch growing on his shoulder. Neither of them spoke for a long while.

Eventually, Nick said, "I'm just tired."

Ollie wondered if Nick was aware of all the mannerisms he had borrowed from Ethan, and how long these things took to return.

"I know I haven't been a very good friend lately," said Ollie. "But I'm here for you. I'm gonna put my money where my mouth is."

"You're putting your life where your mouth is, going after an Arden."

"I plan to be so public that it'll be too suspicious for me to have an 'accident'."

"You overestimate who would care," Nick sighed. "Do you really think Javier Arden is an empath? Or just that other people might believe that he's an empath?"

Ollie bit back a smile. *You always had the most unerring moral compass.* "I think that given the facts and circumstances in front of us, a reasonable person might believe that Javier is an empath. I'm a reasonable person."

Nick didn't respond.

"If it helps, this isn't just about Tuesday," Ollie continued. "Hopefully it'll be sufficient grounds to reopen the Herschs' cases."

"Ah. So that's how you're rationalising it."

"Are you gonna ask me not to publish?"

"You already promised not to," said Nick.

Ollie's stomach knotted with guilt. "I promised to hold off if it affected ongoing investigations. The Hersch cases are closed."

Nick barked out a laugh. "Well, aren't you clever."

"You said yourself—" Ollie started.

"Yes, yes. Fool me once, et cetera." Nick drained his glass. "I'm surrounded by such clever, clever friends."

Ollie's hands went cold. "I didn't mean it like that. Fuck the story, okay? You deserve better than this. I don't understand why you'd — I just don't want to see you get thrown under a bus."

They stared at each other for a quiet, rain-filled minute.

"I've got an early start tomorrow," Nick said at last.

He's not going to help you, Ollie realised. There were few things more dangerous than love gone wilfully blind. Ollie stood. Gathered the dirty cartons. Grabbed his satchel.

Nick hesitated. "Are you taking the pedestrian route upstairs?"

So you are *worried.* "I'll text you when I'm there." Ollie mustered a smile. "You get some rest, and I'll get going." He had an article to finish, and a best friend to save.

AN EXTRACT FROM DRAFT VERSION EIGHT.

Two days later, Mr Arden attended his sister's witness interview, where he met Ian Garner of the Special Investigations Agency (SIA). Although Garner is a familiar presence in many glass trafficking prosecutions, he is less well-known as the father of one Dr Ethan Faulkner.

In the weeks that followed, Mr Arden relentlessly pursued a romantic relationship with Dr Faulkner. As the investigations continued, and the general election drew closer, the venues of Mr Arden's overtures would become more conspicuous: the Level 10 SIA precinct, the annual Charlotte Hall Gala, the Mansfield-Zhang wedding.

Mr Arden appears to favour a personal approach to risk

mitigation – perhaps for the same reason he so easily persuaded St Ophie's staff to act against a healer's orders, the same reason he attended his twin's police interview, and the same reason he wears custom, short-range empathic suppressors: Javier Arden is an empath.

Forty hours later, Sunday, 16 April.

FLORENCE SET Ollie's tablet aside. "There's a lot of first-person in here. I thought we weren't supposed to become our stories."

Ollie grunted. He was lying, resigned, across her chesterfield.

"You're begging for a defamation suit," she continued. "Or an injunction if you've already spoken to Ethan. How do we know he hasn't tipped the Ardens off?"

"Another reason to publish ASAP. But Ethan's had months: either he still doesn't believe me, or he doesn't want to confront Javier. Ethan's a man of least resistance when it comes to relationships."

Florence considered him, cheek in hand, elbow propped on one knee. "Do you want me to talk you off the ledge or pat you on the back?"

By now, the draft had etched itself into Ollie's eyelids in caffeine and migraines. "Tell me what to do," he whined.

"Go to Ian directly about Javier's cufflinks," said Florence. "If your goal is to reopen the Herschs' cases, then—"

"It'll just get buried. Precedent—"

"You haven't told Ian about the suppressor, though."

"Ian isn't top of the food chain." Ollie sat up. "The election is in two weeks; prime time to drop this bomb. It'll be politically untenable to sweep under the rug."

"You realise Damien won't have your back on this."

"Duh. I have a plan."

"A plan deeper than the Ardens' pockets?" said Florence. "You accuse Javier Arden of being an empath, imply he's interfered with criminal proceedings. The cartel allegations alone..."

"When I publish, things'll pan out in one of two ways. If the Ardens sue for defamation, the onus is on me to show that the imputations – him being an empath and interfering with shit – are substantially true."

"All you have is circumstantial evidence. The public interest defence has a high bar, but shouldn't *that* be your Plan A?"

Ollie shook his head. "I want a court-ordered aptitude test. They're granted if there's reasonable grounds to believe that empathic influence has or is likely to have induced a miscarriage of justice, interfered with due process et cetera. Super broad."

Florence raised an eyebrow. "Do you even have standing?"

"When an aptitude test is the only way a defendant can establish a fact..."

"Wow. That reverses the onus completely. Just for empaths?"

"Pretty much. A legal relic from World War Two. Disappeared for a while, but it came back when we left the EU."

"Speaking on principle, this is fucked."

Nick was all about principles, and look where that got him. "Your mum said there's a good chance the court will grant the order." Florence's mum had been kind enough to provide Ollie with pro bono legal advice.

"So you're banking on that test," said Florence. "What if the court seals the results?"

"Here's the thing: the Ardens won't sue me if Javier *is* an empath. Why risk the court ordering an aptitude test in the first place? Even if the results are sealed, the outcome will be obvious if I win. But if they *don't* sue me, people wonder why. They'll ask questions."

"So, if you do get sued, we can be assured that (a) Javier Arden isn't an empath, and (b) you're royally fucked. How jolly."

"I can fall back on the public interest defence."

"Then I'd tone down these unequivocal accusations."

Ollie groaned. "I'll tweak them. Thanks for the Ascenda notes, by the way. I owe you." Florence's bottom lip extended as she continued scrolling his draft. "What else? Spit it out."

"Seems to me that you don't have a plan. *Seems to me*, you're gambling."

"If empathy was easy to prove, the tabloids would have done it by now."

"And if Javier's *not* an empath? The Ardens will sue you past Level 1 and straight to hell."

"Then we'll know that Ethan's just a selfish idiot."

Florence nudged Ollie's knee with one stockinged foot. "What're you actually trying to accomplish here?"

"Justice. Due process. The rug is twenty Levels high with the amount of shit that's been swept underneath it. They're not even hiding it anymore, are they? The blatant self-dealing. It's exhausting."

Florence considered him for a moment, winding a strand of hair between her knuckles. "How long have we been friends?"

"Ages."

"Ages. And as your friend, I'm telling you: this is a bad idea. Even if you're not sued into oblivion, even if Herschs' cases get reopened, we might get procedural lip service. The media attention moves on; pressure's gone."

Ollie tongued the ulcer on the inside of his right cheek. He had worn on a hole with his chewing. "It's worth a try," he said eventually.

"Yeah? What's it worth, exactly?"

She wasn't backing down, and Ollie knew if he stared into the chasm of doubt for much longer, he would lose his nerve.

"There have been two lucrative – or at least convenient – murders that Javier helped cover up," he said. "The man might as well have been blackmailing me and Ian for the past few months, sticking to Ethan like glue. Oh, and guess who left the Royal Ballet a year ago to spend more time with the family business?"

Florence sighed. "When Project Earthflown was first floated."

"And when there was speculation that Sainte-Ophie Biotech was entering the CM15 market here? Cold-chain-logistics-Langley gets a dead nephew in the mail. And who was that nephew hanging out with? *Javier bloody Arden.* Now, I can't prove that has anything to do with shutting out Arden competition, but if they lose the CM15 subsidy, I assume they'll have to lean on Langley to price Sainte-Ophie imports out via logistics costs, especially if the French won't budge on the tariffs—"

"Hang on. You said *Nick* was the one who shot Charles Langley."

"No. I said Nick lost his fucking mind and is hiding something."

"Then he's unlikely to corroborate your story." Florence sat next to him. "It's just me," she said, after a minute. "There's no need to put on a performance."

"Don't you think this is the right thing to do?" Ollie stared at the ceiling. "Truth, the pursuit thereof?"

"It's not about doing the right thing. It's about doing the smart thing at the right time."

To be so clear-eyed. "But the election—"

"Is in two weeks. I'd take that cufflink, those recordings, and go to Ian."

"And get all my evidence and leverage confiscated?"

They pondered, knees and wrists touching. On the coffee table, the tablet winked into sleep mode, minimising the projection of Ollie's article.

"If someone *is* suppressing this from the top, then nothing short of an aptitude test *and* a positive result will trigger anything for Tim and Martin," said Florence. "Even then, what will a re-investigation prove? That the Ardens or the Langleys had a direct hand in things?"

"Okay, but—"

"These are risky odds to stake your career – let alone safety – on. Not just *your* safety either." Florence shoved Ollie until he looked at her. "But it makes more sense if you're trying to muddy the waters for Nick. If you were confident about Javier being an empath, you'd have published this exposé weeks ago."

To that, Ollie had no answer. Somewhere in the building, a door slammed.

She lay a hand over his. "No one can give you permission. You've got to be honest about why you're doing this. Rationalisation begets regret."

"I dunno how fast things are moving on Nicks' side." Ollie's resolve felt like water between his fingers. "I'm worried they'll make an example out of him. Robert Langley isn't exactly a man you want to cross. Charlie's threats make a good cover but—"

"You want to protect Nick."

Ollie's heart turned over. "Ethan's already given his statement, and so it'll come down to proportionality. The presumption always falls against the empath. And in the court of public opinion—"

"*I know*," said Florence gently. "Ollie, I know."

He squeezed her hand in lieu of eye contact, skin worn thin by doubt or conviction. Like guilt and vindication, the two tasted much the same.

Reasons were reasons were reasons. In the end, it was a matter of pulling the trigger while he still had the gun.

ARTICLE EXTRACT, FIRST PUBLISHED ON MONDAY, 17 APRIL.
INTRODUCTION:

The call that changed Martin Hersch's life came one crisp October morning: his son was dead. Glass overdose, they said.

At first blush, the details appear familiar. The glass and water business are ends of the same vial and Tim Hersch is not the first Sixty-Fourther accused of using charity banks as a front for glass trafficking, nor will he be the last to deal CM15 'for a good cause'.

Such narratives often end where they begin – with an unfortunate accident and a sobering statistic. Glass is notoriously tricky to dose, and associated deaths have doubled over the decade. But these incidents are rarely preceded by shooting an Arden heiress or followed by a vote to renew the most generous water subsidy in Europe.

They also do not typically involve empaths.

"This isn't one of those stories," Martin had insisted. If the police were not willing to listen, a journalist must suffice. "Someone's getting away with murder. I'm going to find out who it is, if it's the last thing I do."

One week later, the police found Martin dead in his flat.

Eight weeks after proposing to Corinna Arden, they found a bullet in Charles Langley's head.

This is that story.

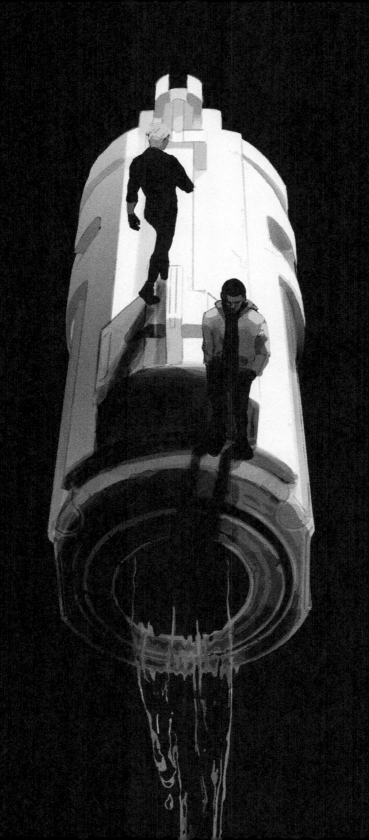

END*

Thank you for making it all the way here! If you enjoyed *Earthflown*, please consider leaving a review on amazon, your favourite store, or share with a friend! It really makes a big impact for indie creators. You can find more illustrations + bonus content on earthflown.com.

* There is an in-universe sequel coming!

Earthflown was written as a standalone (in that the lingering questions are deliberate) — but we will hear more from the cast + see some of the fall-out in Book II.

Book II will focus on Nick's perspective, and we will meet new gremlins! Reading Earthflown is not required for this sequel, though there will be significant easter eggs.

Don't miss out on the sequel + other bonus content: subscribe.earthflown.com

INDEBTED TO:

Dr Bekius   for 9 months of emergency-room consults;

Mies   for years of inane, life-saving shitposts;

Jackie   who thought this novel would be out by 2021
and still stuck around to edit the mess;

Tilly   who read every draft of the manuscript and
hated Ethan in every single one;

JWB   the most generous man in the world;

Erica   for endless kindness with my sleep-deprivation;

+ Shoga   for the midnight operas & zoomies.

ABOUT

FRANCES is a kiwi author, based in Australia. They lawyer during rent-paying hours and paint during sleeping hours. They left big-law for NFP med research. They illustrate book covers sometimes at FRANCESWREN.COM *Earthflown* is their debut novel.

LITARNES is a self-taught, US-based illustrator with a background in bio-med. Growing up as a transient child, they spend much of the year in airports, en route to art conventions. They are inspired by liminal spaces and nature. Portfolio at LITARNES.COM

Printed in Great Britain
by Amazon